When I Died for the First Time

When I Died
for the First Time

A novel

TIM BOOTH

CONSTABLE

CONSTABLE

First published in Great Britain in 2024 by Constable

1 3 5 7 9 10 8 6 4 2

A CIP catalogue record for this book
is available from the British Library.

ISBN: 978-1-40871-888-9

Typeset in Garamond Premier Pro by Hewer Text UK Ltd, Edinburgh
Printed and bound in Great Britain by Clays Ltd, Elcograf S.p.A.

Papers used by Constable are from well-managed forests and other responsible sources.

Constable
An imprint of
Little, Brown Book Group
Carmelite House
50 Victoria Embankment
London EC4Y 0DZ

An Hachette UK Company
www.hachette.co.uk

www.littlebrown.co.uk

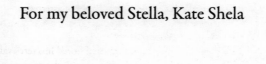

For my beloved Stella, Kate Shela

Foreword

By Tim Booth

I hate forewords. I always think, What's this? Just get on with the book. Forewords and prologues. Both. Prologues usually look like some part of the story the author wasn't able to weave into the narrative. Hate them. I suspect most of you won't be reading this, but I feel some explanation is called for.

I became the mid-wife for this manuscript as Seth Brakes's attorney had instructions to pass this directly on to me if anything happened to Seth. And unless you've been hiding under a rock, you will know that something has happened to Seth Brakes. If I were in his shoes, I would have left this document in the hands of my manager, but he clearly doesn't have a great a relationship with his. Indeed, Jon Brunt tried to take out an injunction against this book's release, as The Lucky Fuckers manager wanted 25 per cent, but after some costly legal to-ing and fro-ing, he backed down.

Did Seth send it to me because a psychic told him to? He had said complimentary things about James in past interviews, which suggests he admired us, but still, I was greatly surprised to be used as his conduit. I've worked with his producer Rupert Stokes on my solo projects, so maybe Rupert had some nice things to say about me. Or perhaps Seth related to the fact that I am generally a sober singer, and sobriety is rare in our profession. To my knowledge I only met the guy two times. Once at a party (no, not that one! I don't get invited to those kind of parties), and once at Eno's house where he dropped in on one of Brian's acapella nights. That night he was not in a great condition. He found it hard to sing gospel and folk songs he was unfamiliar with. I guess like most indie singers, singing was not his forte.

The note with the manuscript was concise:

Dear Tim, I'm sending you my writings of the last year and some demos for safekeeping. If anything happens to me I would like you to get these out to the public. Someone in your position hopefully has the clout. I trust you and trust is not something of great abundance in my life at present.

I tooled around with the songs as they needed fleshing out. I re-sung the vocals, not to get songwriting credit, as some trolls have suggested, but because they were unusable.

I read the manuscript and was hooked. Raw, meandering maybe, but a good read. Better than most of his lyrics. Is it a diary, confession, fiction . . . who knows? Little, Brown snapped it up. We did some editing, but here, more or less as the author intended, is Seth's account of his last year with The Lucky Fuckers.

Prologue

When I died, for the first time I experienced peace. Real peace. The kind of peace you only read about or see on some Indian guru's face in a framed photograph by the bed of a friend who's become lost to a cult. The peace of the dead, I guess.

I was at Pitbull's, moaning about his recent wraps of coke, they'd been cut more than usual. I was following him round his dingy flat from kitchen to bedroom, coked up, yap yapping on his shoulder about the relationship between consumer and producer and how, if he became a relative island of integrity in his profession, it would enhance his business, and that the customer is always right, or some such bullshit. He escaped my monologue to the bathroom. I crouched down, peering in through splintered holes in the locked plywood door.

'Oww.' My finger's pricked by a splinter, a drop of blood oozes out, I suck it. The door's been kicked in and fixed, kicked in and fixed so many times that I watch him squat on the bog, head in his hands, lid down, just avoiding me and my whining.

'I know you're not shitting,' I say through the hole.

And I guess, I guess he felt, Fuck it, time to shut this fucker up.

1

He thunders out of the bathroom, grabs me by the throat, lifts me off the floor, pins me up against the hallway wall with one hand and shakes a wrap, of what I presumed was coke, between the finger and thumb of his free hand, growling at me in his Tom Waits gravelly don't-fuck-with-me-motherfucker dealer voice.

'Fucking try this then if the coke don't do it for you, you ponce.'

His piggy eyes drill into me, his breath would make roses wilt, and I'm wondering if you can catch AIDS from spittle. He's left the bathroom light on, cord swinging. On the bathroom wall a beard of mould hangs down from the groaning extractor fan, a whole ecosystem of dark grey and browns that matches the one rising up the plastic shower curtain. I marvel at the speed and strength of him.

Fuck, there's nothing I can do to get down from here, and this, this must be what putting your head in the mouth of a tiger feels like. The wrap of white powder is balled up in the cling film, sperm shaped. He holds the twisted tail and shakes it.

I shiver with that magic feeling when you know – you just know – something special is about to come your way. From the living room, a duck quacks.

I laugh.

'What you fucking laughing at?' He tightens his chokehold and leans his granite chest into me, rag-dolling me deeper into the wall, fusing the quantum particles of wall and chest with those of your not so humble narrator, Seth Brakes, lead singer of The Lucky Fuckers.

'Your ringtone . . . duck,' I gasp.

'It's for my kid,' he snarls.

'It's . . . a bit inconsistent . . . with your brand.'

'Ugh?' he says.

'I'd suggest . . . a dog barking. You know . . . Pitbull?'

A steely look clouds over him then breaks. His face lights up like a child and he laughs, laughs through his nose, snorts, like a warthog. The laughter turns off like a tap. He puts me down.

'So. You want it or not, then?' He turns and swaggers off into the kitchen.

I'm a sucker for a hard sell. When you're famous, freebies are a perk of the trade. Be it Nikes or crack cocaine, I never say no to a freebie.

If anthropologists want to know how Neanderthals walked, they should watch Pitbull. His gibbon arms swing so wide they catch last night's tin-foil curry containers, piled up on the sideboard, scattering them and their contents of chicken tikka masala across the lumpy linoleum floor. The lurid orange sauce joins mouldy chunks of debris from kebab houses, Burger Kings, fish and chip shops.

'The melting pot of racial integration. I guess dealers don't trust cleaners.'

'What?' he growls, as he rummages in a kitchen drawer.

'Nothing.'

There's no way dealers let clients try the merch *in* house, but fame gives me kudos and bragging rights for Pitbull, so he lets me hang out in his shitty council flat, where we see each other as 'friends' rather than dealer and client.

He finds his crack pipe. Coke's my weapon of choice but hey, I'm in the middle of a three-day bender, no sleep, smoked heroin yesterday, I'm game for whatever. Need to forget. Forget we just buried Alex.

He's unwinding the wrap and easing it into this glass pipe. The stained bulb at the end has dark brown spirals radiating up from the bottom. He points to my favourite armchair. A 1950s stuffed square piece, as big as a throne, worn dark green with age.

I sit and the troll squats in front of me, pipe and lighter in hand. He's gone all serious like.

That fella from *Breaking Bad* stares at me from the lurid sleeve inked on Pitbull's brawny arm. Walter White – that's his name – winks at me. His face is framed against a turquoise background, a honeycomb of chemical compounds. My foot has the tremors. My breathing's shallow. I clear my throat. I hold the pipe to my lips; it smells of stale breath. His. I take the pipe from my mouth.

'It's crack?' I ask.

He smiles. 'Not quite. A mongrel.' His eyes dare me.

Oh fuck, Pitbull likes to play chemist. Likes to try out unruly combinations. A childlike voice inside of me is pleading – *Don't do this* – but I haven't listened to this kid in years, not going to start now and I *never* back down from a dare.

Sometimes it's exhausting being Seth Brakes.

Pitbull clicks the lighter and holds the flame above the compound.

I put the pipe back in my mouth, lean forward and suck.

There's a sound, like rushing waves clawing through a pebble beach. Smells acrid, chemical, plastic, ugly – wrong.

BOOM.

Within seconds, the rush envelops me. There's a ringing in my ears and I slump back into the chair in a full body spasm. A tsunami of power blasts through me, devouring every thought, feeling, memory, pain. All that is Seth Brakes is scrambling for cover.

Old footage of a nuclear blast when palm trees and buildings disintegrate into nothing. It's that within every cell, never ending, simultaneous.

It blasts me out of my body.

I'm instantaneously above, looking down at me in the chair, at Pitbull, kneeling before me like a supplicant.

I watch the two men in the scene beneath me. I've never seen me from above before. Pitbull pulls back, frowning, studying me, the me down there.

I'm up here, I shout, but the sound goes nowhere. He's fixed on the waxworks. I'm an astronaut floating in zero gravity. I'm the guy in *Mary Poppins* who can't stop laughing on the ceiling. I'm just bobbing here like debris from a shipwreck.

This is fucking rad.

Pitbull's shitty room throbs with magic. Everything's lit up from within. There's a hazy glowing light coming from inside everything, everything's illuminated, radiant, alive.

I'm on the ceiling next to the light fixture. The light fixture's an upside-down Japanese pink crêpe parasol cupping three bulbs. In its wooden spokes, there's a plastic green toy marine, a machine gun held at its hip. I had the same one as a kid. But this one's alive. Pulsing light, glowing. Not the character but the plastic.

Plastic! Even plastic's alive.

By the marine there's a rainbow eraser on its side. Its colours swirl, mutate. If I focus on one colour, it fractals into colours I've never seen before; impossible colours, colours with no name.

Pitbull reaches forward and gently slaps my face.

I – the I on the ceiling – laugh.

'Come on, you fucker.' He slaps me harder. 'Fuck.'

His frown lines match Walter's on his sleeve.

He's up on his feet, it's like stop motion, there's gaps between movements. His Doc Martens skid on curry. He tries to pull open a drawer. It only opens a crack. He squeezes two fingers in and prises out pencils, pipes, Scotch tape, batteries, condoms, chucks them behind him.

He grabs the sides of the draw and with a roar he wrenches it off its sliders, throwing sheaths of papers into the air. They cascade down in slo-mo like white birds. He slams the splintered draw on to the counter; the sound reverberates through the room.

He reaches in and plucks out a sealed plastic bag. Pitbull runs, bag in hand, to the me in the chair. Ripping open the bag he pulls out a capped syringe. He pulls off the stopper, lifts up my sleeve, jabs the needle in and pushes down the plunger.

Huh, thought this would be a Pulp Fiction *stabbing through the sternum jobby.*

We wait for something to happen. Nothing does.

He shakes the husk of Seth Brakes. He stares at me. Waiting.

He lifts an eyelid, then lets it go. Holding clenched fists up to his forehead, the knucklehead roars, 'Fuck.'

And I realise that . . . I'm dead.

And I realise that . . . I'm OK with that.

More than OK.

It's a fucking relief.

Nothing's triggering me, nothing's weighing me down. Nothing. The absence of all my baggage, my history, my bullshit; it's gone.

I'm free. Free of the weight of everything that made me who I am.

I'm detached. It's someone else down there.

No heat, no fear, no responsibility.

No shame, that's the biggest one.

I didn't realise the density of shame. Its absence is massive.

That's why I'm so light.

I'm free of Mum and Dad and even Lizzie. Even Alex.

As I bring them to mind nothing rises in me.

Nothing.

I feel good about them. I even feel good about Mum.

I turn my attention to the band.

Nothing there either. No expectations, no connection, no guilt. I'm free. Free of everybody who's invested in me. Everybody who wants a piece.

Who wants peace?

I do.

I want peace. This is peace and it feels . . . so simple. Like it was there all the time, waiting for me.

Pitbull scrambles for another syringe from the bag on the floor. Injects it in my arm. Pounds on my chest.

It's OK, man, I'm good.

'Come on, you fucker,' he shouts.

He pulls back and studies my face with the hunger of a lover. He drags me by my ankles on to the floor, reaching a tender paw to catch my head from thumping the rug.

He climbs on top of me, pinches my nose between finger and thumb and kisses a lengthy breath through my open lips. He inflates me then rhythmically pushes down on my chest, counts.

'One, two, three, four.'

Like he's starting a slow Ramones song.

He's done this before, he's good. His gentleness moves me. Like Kong with the blonde. I watch as he kisses breath back into me then pumps the air back out with two hands on my chest.

'One, two, three, four.'

I lose interest as something weirder is happening to astronaut me on the ceiling.

My back arches, arms rise up. Like when members of a black gospel choir lose it, filled with the Holy Spirit. My hands go through the ceiling like it's not there. Clean through. Two hands hold mine on the other side. Can't see them but *feel* them, gently, with the sensitivity of an elephant's trunk. They're familiar. They fit. My hands feel small, tiny. The contact makes me cry.

'One, two, three, four,' grunts Pitbull below.

8

He's fucking relentless!

I'm between worlds. The hands above me.

Joey Ramone below.

I laugh and feel a sharp tug in the pit of my stomach. It's followed by a violent suck in my gut. I try to hold on to my father's hands but they're slipping.

No. Please.

Another lurch and they're gone.

My hands pulled back down and the ceiling above solidifies.

'*Come on*,' I hear from below as Bull breathes fresh life into me.

'One, two, three, four.'

No! Stop!

I reach out to the hanging light flex to grab hold. My hands pass through the cord but the parasol lightshade swings and strobes the room in its pink glow.

'What?' Pitbull looks up and pulls a sour face.

We both watch, hypnotised. The pull in my gut subsides.

I swat out at the swinging shade to give it more momentum. He ignores it and turns back to my body.

Philistine. I'm sure I'd be more interested in psychic phenomena.

I want to feel the hands again. I want to feel my dad's hands. I'm crying hard now. Raining tears. A tear lands on Pitbull's shaved head. He looks up again, like he's looking for rain, but it doesn't stall him. He doesn't stop.

Kissing then pumping, kissing and pumping.

No, no!

'One, two, three, four.' And I'm being sucked down again,

away from the ceiling,

away from the light, swinging like a pendulum,

down the plughole, back into the corpse on the floor, like a genie back into the bottle,

and just as unwelcome.

I enter with a jolt, through the crown of my skull, sit up with a gasp and crack heads with Bull as he reaches in for a last kiss.

I'm crying. He's laughing. Laughing with relief.

I'm crying with grief.

'You Lucky Fucker.' His hands to his face, holding a bloody nose.

'You Lucky, Lucky Fucker.'

I'm panting and crying. Panting and crying. All my gravity, my density's returned, instantaneously. Every cell is Seth Brakes again. I can feel the stories, the memories in my muscles, in my bones, the anger in my jaw, the grey fug of my heart.

A spasm ripples up my spine. I retch. A cup of milky liquid lands on my crotch.

In my head, over and over again, I hear the Devil's mantra: *Again, let's do it again. Let's do it again.*

Chapter 1

Five hundred and twenty days later, September 2012.

'Happy birthday to you . . .' sings Kareem. 'Happy birthday to you.'

'Oh fuck.' Lee jumps up and joins in, me too. It's Pavlovian. I don't know who it's for.

'Happy birthday dear . . . Daaaan. Happy birthday to you.'

Our keyboard player Dan has been ambushed by Kareem holding this Hulk-green cake with piano-key icing and three candlesticks. Dan blushes at the attention.

He's thirty!

No one in this band is in their twenties any more. Stanley's forty!

'Make a wish,' says Lee.

Dan removes his John Lennon glasses and closes his eyes. On cue, a shaft of sunlight frames his willowy figure against the window. With his lambswool hair he reminds me of a pre-Raphaelite painting of an angel.

'Cream made the cake,' whispers Lee to me.

Cream, Cream, Cream cake. I'm bound to forget. Used to be Kareem. Now he's 'between genders'. I look for a mnemonic – *Cream's between.* Cream's name-change and transformation is taking some getting used to. Until a year ago he was a bearded, devout Muslim praying five times a day. Now, he's wearing blue eyeshadow, leather pants and a mohair polo neck. Looks cool and cute and years younger than Kareem did. Who is this man? Woman? Person.

Kareem has left the band a dozen times. His Islam didn't gel with my behaviour. Lee always talked him back. They'd been mates since primary school, share an Iranian-English heritage and have a bond I've been known to envy. Kareem plays great sexy dirty basslines that seem much more suited to this Cream than the Muslim one.

He brings me a piece of cake on a plastic plate.

'The icing was a bitch.' She smiles.

The band are back together again!

Fuck, it's really happening.

Two weeks ago, we had our first tentative rehearsal. To see if we still had it, to see if they'd forgiven me and for them to see if I could hack it. They tested me out. Stanley, my former drug buddy, gave a little speech 'on behalf of the group'. He wanted to know how long I'd been clean. Told *me* I'd have to stay sober for them to give it another go. He fucking isn't! Cunt. Came to visit me *once* in rehab, in his cape and aviator sunglasses, brought coke with him!

I could see the band's embarrassment at his oratory but also the truth; they'll need some convincing and more apologies. Fair enough, really; I need convincing.

Think positive Seth.

Lee sits back down next to me and continues to work up a sketch on his iPad. His focus is total, deeply charismatic and simultaneously geeky. His crooked nose protrudes through his black hair curtain. His nose was broken in a fight. He never bothered to fix it even though he'd be massively handsome if he did. He looks a bit like George Clooney. George Clooney with Iranian-English heritage and a broken nose. Amazing guitarist, proper artist, love him.

Lee's my best mate, came to see me weekly in rehab, daily when I was high risk. Came so often Dr Paul mistook him for a patient. Lee's why I'm here. Here in this band meeting and *here* on this planet, if I'm honest. Even with my money issues, I wouldn't be trying this again if it wasn't for him. We are a *great* fucking band, but Lee's special. He's Keith Richards to my Mick Jagger, Marr to my Morrissey.

'Stop fucking staring at me, cunt,' he says, without altering his focus.

It's 9.30 a.m. but looks like dusk, grey skies, no sun, wind and rain. England doing England. This is our first band meeting since I crashed. The rehearsals didn't worry me so much, I knew the music would still be on tap, but now we get to find out what the record company and manager think of our 'restart'.

We're sitting in a glass box, a Universe Record company meeting room, fifth floor, overlooking the muddy green River Thames. On three sides of our box the smoky grey glass is opaque. Shadows pass in the corridors. It's unsettling, private yet not private.

'Take a seat, gentlemen.'

Jon Brunt makes an entrance, followed by his latest P.A., Monica something or other. A man's man with a rich voice to match. His black suit and matching polar neck doesn't hide his ballooning weight – he looks like Brando from *Apocalypse Now*. As our manager, he straddled our world of the (piss)artist with the demands of business, navigating us through two albums, hit singles and – the holy grail for English bands – growing interest from America. We rang him a week ago, after the rehearsals went well, to see if he's up for another round.

'Good to see you, good to see you.' He works the room greeting us individually.

'How's Moira and the triplets, Olly? You look like you haven't slept for a year.'

He comes to me last. 'Come here.' He takes me into an embrace, 'prodigal son returns, huh.' He pulls back holding my shoulders and says quietly, 'Remember, I was in rehab in the eighties. I know where you've been and I know how hard this is.' I clear my throat.

Bastard, he's good.

'Take a seat everyone.'

We settle down. He waits for our attention. 'May as well jump right in. Good news. We still have a record contract with Universe Records. They've picked up the option.'

'Yes!' Olly stands and shakes a fist in the air. He's echoed by fist pumps from the band.

'Which means they need an album. Recorded before December.'

Further cheers from the band.

Holy shit.

'Jon, that's impossible, that's under three months.' I try to keep the panic out my voice.

'Tax write-off, Seth. They need it for their accounts before the end of the tax year. You told me you had the songs written. We can do it.'

My armpits have flooded with sweat.

He leans in. 'I've got to tell you the truth, gentlemen. The record company had just about written you off. Hip hop's *it*. Pop's *it*. indie music . . . ? Nah. You've been on a major for five years. That's a lifetime in this industry. They've moved on to the next young thing.' He scrutinises our wan faces to see if we're taking him seriously. 'So yeah, you're on probation. You've *got* your fan base, but the most we can expect is dwindling returns. Unless – you – get – an – it. A real "it" this time, one that crosses over. Crosses the Atlantic.'

'We always need an "it", Jon. You always say that.' I try to diffuse the situation with a laugh, but no one's buying it.

He takes a sip of coffee, winces, adds some sugar, stirs, looks mournfully at a slice of cake. 'Right now, Radio 1 won't play you. *Gone*, our main outlet in this country. Their demographic is teens to twenty-nine-year-olds.'

I'm past it at thirty-two.

'Your music's too edgy for Radio 2. And after Seth's meltdown . . . That doesn't leave you much, gentlemen. Radio 6, Absolute and Virgin. They still care about music more than age, but you need a breakout song, a viral video, something different—'

Hang on, I know this routine. The bad news, a depressing build-up and then the punchline.

'You need a collaboration.'

Stay cool.

'Collaborations are big right now. Everybody's guesting. That's how you do it.'

Laughter from the office next door breaks the silence.

Brunt slides a paw across his clean-shaven skull.

'How is the writing coming along, Seth? Do you have anything we can take to Faith?'

'You what now?! Who?' My voice is high pitched.

'Didn't the guys tell you? Faith's up for a collaboration.' I look at the band, no one meets my eyes.

'Who the fuck is Faith?'

'Your genius manager has set you up for a collaboration that should get you back on Radio 1. Should get you on fucking Letterman – a once in a lifetime worldwide "it".' He reaches out and scoops a finger of cream cake into his mouth. 'Faith? A pixie with the mouth of a docker. Crazy image. She's everywhere at the moment, can't believe you haven't heard of her – and she's a massive fan. *Massive*. Her manager reached out to *me*. It's a perfect storm. A gift horse. A collaboration with Faith would change *everything*. Once she's bolted on, Universe will go from seeing you as a tax write off, to a cash cow.' He looks around the table. 'The boys should 'ave told you.'

Yeah, they fucking should.

I'm flushed at the betrayal.

And then I remember an article about some young Gaga wannabe and a string of photos where you wouldn't realise it's the same person.

'Isn't she that kid ... who won *The X Factor* a few years back?'

The X Factor! Fuck!

The death of music. It made pleasing a panel of celebrity arse-holes and the pursuit of fame the endgame for a generation of singers.

'I've slagged off *The X Factor* in every interview I've ever given!' My words trail upwards in panic. 'I'll look like a dick.'

Silence.

I can't work with a kid reared at the tit of Simon Cowell.

'Jon, this isn't us, we can't do this.'

It isn't. Our whole ethos has been about making a racket *without* compromise.

Silence.

I look around for support. Olly's straining to wipe baby puke off his lapel. Stanley's trying not to smirk. The other three are working on their thousand-yard stares.

'I've never written to order like this . . .'

I feel a panic about to break over me. I'm a busted flush. No support here. They're not knackered at an a.m. meeting, they're evasive, they planned this.

They want this!

Lee!

Fuck you.

I feel trapped. My heart's kicking in like a double bass drum. A fierce longing overtakes me. I want to storm off, out of here to Pitbull's to score . . . something. Something to take me out of this. There's a hunger in my body to blank all this out. This is what I'd have done in the past, this is what would help me deal . . . to not feel. Eventually they'd come and find me; 'cause I'm the singer-songwriter. They need me.

ODing on crack, or whatever that shit Pitbull had put together was, should have turned me off. It turned me on. I figured the problem hadn't been the crack but the shit it was cut with. So all I had to do was make sure the crack was pure. Non-GMO crack. Organic crack. Wholefoods crack. Wholefoods crack crashed me in weeks. That and the smack, but I think it was the crack.

That . . . and what happened to Alex. According to AA, you only get sober when you hit bottom. There are false bottoms and then there's bottom bottoms. After Alex, my true AA, I hit bottom bottom. My time at Pitbull's was an attempt to hide from the fact.

In the adjacent room a shadow approaches the opaque glass wall. The lighting must be weird, because as it gets closer to the glass the figure grows giant, grotesque. Yet surely it should get smaller? The figure pauses at the glass, then presses its face up against it. Its breath spreads on the glass, fades and blooms, fades and blooms.

I jump as my phone lights up, pulses like a wasp. It's Lizzie, my sister. I turn the ringer off. As if I need reminding she and the twins need money. I need money! Blew the last of my money on three rehabs. *Three!*

My anger evaporates to guilt.

I blew it. Just me. My fault. My behaviour's fucked up everything. For all of us. I've got to make it up to them. I have to find a new way to make this work. I can't let this be my defining story. I can't.

I close my eyes and go into what Dr Paul taught me. I focus in on my galloping heart and take slow deep breaths.

One two three four

Slowing it down. Relaxing the muscle. Repeat.

My life revolves around these numbers.

One two three four

I see the old Seth Brakes walk out the room to Pitbull's. The new one stays put.

'I'm . . . not averse to a collaboration,' I say in a tight, unfamiliar voice. 'I may have written a song someone else could sing on.' Everybody in the room takes a breath.

'How are the songs coming along, Seth?' Brunt leans in.

'Fine,' I mutter.

'Care to enlarge?' He makes a magnanimous gesture with his hands.

'Not really. Look, you know . . . It's a process.'

'Have you worked on any of them with the band yet?'

'No. No. Two rehearsals. We've been getting . . . up to speed. Two! Rehearsing old songs for the warm-up gig you booked *next* Wednesday.'

'How many have you got?'

'I've got lots . . . lots of . . . sketches, not finished, but going well.' I hear the words ring naked in their dishonesty. 'You know . . .' I rub crust out the side of my eye, 'they're coming along . . .'

'They sound great, Jon,' Lee lies. 'He's played them to me – they'll be fine.'

Relief floods my body. Cavalry.

'Monica, make a note of that.' Brunt's in a staring match with Lee. 'Lee's heard the tracks and they sound "great".'

His young P.A. Monica types away on her Mac. She's lovely. She's new. They never last.

'Festival offers are slowly coming through. Indie tents on the big ones, main stages on the small. What you'd expect really. But when you've done this Faith thing, they'll upgrade you to main stages everywhere. *Everywhere.*' Brunt reaches for a plate of cake, he takes a bite, cream oozes out the middle.

'All you guys have known is the acceleration of success. You had momentum. Now it's against you. *Now* you have to prove yourselves. Now you're working *against* your reputation.' He licks cream off chubby fingertips. He looks at me. 'I've got faith in you – but you have to compromise – it's not on your terms any more – you have to play the game. Are you ready for this?'

I hadn't thought this through. I'm dazed. When we started this band, it was an adventure. You don't name a band The Lucky Fuckers and expect success. The not-giving-a-shit was part of our attraction. We were as shocked as anyone when the first single took off. It was all on *our* terms, no one touched the music. It was inevitable, unstoppable, and we rode it, took it for granted.

Success fucks you up. Does anyone get through success successfully? Cracks in the psyche, cracks in the band became fissures. No sleep, and an all-you-can-eat buffet of the clichés of rock and roll. Fame separates a singer from his band mates. They got resentful that I was getting all the attention, all the press, all the girls and I got resentful that I was doing more of the work, carrying the pressure. None of this was spoken, acknowledged. So, I drank more, took more drugs, whatever was going, it was all free, encouraged even. The gear made me wilder and the wilder I got, the more publicity we got. The more publicity, the more successful: a feedback loop.

The *role* gave me licence, licence to become a fucking cliché.

'Chili Peppers came back from rehab bigger than before. It can be done. Just doesn't happen often.' Brunt tries to read the future in my face. 'All right.' He claps his hands. 'Dick is booking you a tour to go with the album release, around June, Monica will get back to you when the dates are in.' He goes stern. 'And listen up. No one mention the Faith thing, until it's locked in. You got that? We have to play our cards right on this one. It's a trump card, but it's not a done deal.' He gets our agreement, shuffles his papers together and says in a lighter voice, 'All this activity will enable us to put you all back on retainers, so you three,' he points at Cream, Oliver and Stanley, 'will be able to give up your day jobs if you're OK with that wage cut we discussed?' A tsunami of relief spreads over their faces. Cream closes his eyes in prayer. Ol looks like he's just had a stay of execution.

I feel beat up, there's a ringing in my ears.

'Good luck with the writing, Seth.'

He stands. 'OK.'

He raises his mug.

On cue we all stand and raise ours. Five years ago, in one of these faceless rooms, it was champagne, now it's cold coffee and tea.

We clink mugs.

'LUCKY FUCKERS' we say in unison.

Chapter 2

'What you doing in there?' shouts Lee under the cubicle door.

'Coke.'

That's his fear. Haven't done a gig without coke since . . . Haven't done a gig without coke.

First gig in three years. London. I'm scared shitless. That's no turn of phrase, this is my third trip to the bog in the thirty-minute countdown to showtime. Lee's head attempts to squeeze under the cubicle door.

'I'm calling my sponsor.' I was. Jada King, a Jamaican mother of four grown-up kids.

'It's yer fifth kid, again,' I hear Rufus, her husband, shout through the house.

She's always there for me, regardless of the hour. I met Jada at AA. She'd been a one-hit wonder in the 1980s so had an understanding of my world. They frown upon opposite-sex mentors in AA, but fuck 'em, I do better with women.

'They love ya Brakes. They waiting for yer. Take yer mind off yourself and go do that which God placed you here for.' Though I'm a card-carrying atheist, somehow in her mouth the word 'God' doesn't trigger me.

'Jada, you could convert the Devil.'

'Don't you forget it.' A gut chuckle rumbles down the line. 'Now get yer arse out there. God's got a gig for you.'

'Yeah, Brakes, get your arse out here. God's got a gig for you,' says Lee.

Unfortunately God was a no-show on the guest list.

When you play a great gig, it's the best high in the world – well, nearly.

You feel lit up, connected to an invisible power source.

A bad gig is equally amped – in the opposite direction.

A bad gig seems to take

F O R E V E R

Tonight's shit.

I can't get in it. Stand back, criticising everything. Two years ago, tanked up on coke and alcohol, this kind of gig would have been a blur of ease, a pharmaceutical wash of confident spontaneity.

I can't stop comparing.

Tonight, I'm an awkward spotty teenager. Every movement feels premeditated, self-conscious. My boots are full of concrete. *I've lost my dance!* There's no fucking way I can dance. Spotlights are searchlights, band mates jailers, the audience a firing squad.

I keep trying to say something appreciative to them but all I manage is, 'Thanks,' or, 'It's great to be here,' or 'This song's called "Fucked Up".' I think about stage-diving, always an icebreaker, but the distance between me and the crowd

S T R E T C H E S

It's a fucking moat.

23

Fake, fake, fake, loops the chant in my head.

Tonight, we are the Rusty Fuckers. Our last gig was over two years ago. From fear we've over-rehearsed this set to death, to *death*. Killed all opportunity for magic.

We played our four hits like a covers band; karaoke imposters.

The audience loved us. They welcomed us back with tears and extended applause. They bounced to the hits in that awkward indie way. Wore our merch (the black Luc£y Fuc£ers T-shirt outsold everything) and by the encore bouquets of flowers were placed onstage.

Should have been a wreath. To blow our first gig back, in London, before press and record company . . . not cool.

We retreated to our dressing rooms, where management knew best to keep out.

I sat alone in a foul mood, bracing myself for the 'celebratory' after-show bullshit.

Shit, is this what doing gigs straight is going to be like?

The backstage after-show is the usual soulless affair. Guests are packed into a nondescript holding room with the strip-light ambiance of a hospital. There's an overflow of VIPs hanging out in the busy hallway, trying to look cool and relaxed.

Monica has me by the arm, she's navigating me to post-gig obligations. She directs me to the two record company minions, our new radio plugger and a minor celeb from a reality TV show. Monica's cool, she whispers their names in my ear before we meet them and if we're ambushed by strangers, she drops their name into the conversation. They tell me how good the gig was while scanning for clues to my state of mind.

Brunt is talking conspiratorially with two Yanks.

'The man, the man!' Our American promoter, Dick Connors, flashes his superior dentistry, hugs me to his gym body and expects me to know the latest high-five routine. 'Great gig, Seth, well done.'

'Bit rusty, mate' I say.

'Yeah, well. Only way is up.' He pats my shoulder. 'Crowd didn't notice. Did you see those flowers?'

Ah, they were from him, not Brunt.

'Geoff not here?' I say to Jon.

'He couldn't make it, he flies to Germany tomorrow,' says Geoff's stand-in, a younger version of Geoff, the new head of marketing, Roger something.

'What time?' I say.

'What?' He blushes and adjusts his glasses.

'What time's he flying to Germany?'

'I . . . I've no idea.' He clears his throat.

If the boss doesn't come to your gig, it's never a good sign.

Brunt couldn't have told him about the possibility of recording with Faith yet or he'd be here.

'Monica,' says Brunt, 'the *NME* need a few words. The journalist's waiting in the band dressing room.'

She stands there, mouth open like a fish, wondering why she doesn't know this, then gets the hint.

'Yeah, come on, Seth; can't keep the *NME* waiting.' She tugs on my arm. I'm tempted to have another dig but let myself be led.

We slide past a group of people who stare, then look away.

'You're free now, Seth.' She uncouples herself and turns to leave, then, 'The gig wasn't *that* bad.'

My duties done, I look around for old friends to talk to, to not feel so exposed.

I don't see any. My old addict friends weren't invited, or are dead. I invited a few people from AA. Two declined as gigs are an 'unsafe' environment, the other two aren't here, so I latch on to our boffin producer Rupert. He talks tech to me, of reverbs and EQs, when I notice Stanley on the prowl, cruising the hallway in his fucking cape and top hat, on a mission. He *thinks* he looks like Slash. He looks like a shit magician.

Beers in hand, he's heading towards two girls. One has her back to me, she's wearing thick black leggings, red skirt and a red and black horizontal-striped 'Dennis the Menace' mohair sweater. I used to have that jumper in my teens.

I've got a weird déjà vu just looking at it.

Dennis the Menace is with a model friend. A blonde ghost of a teen in a white dress.

Stanley hands the blonde his spare Corona, clinks bottles, takes a swig. She follows his lead, wide eyed, spaced out by the flattery of his attention.

'So the upshot is,' Rupert continues, 'he's sending me a Binson Echorec from Belgium but I can't tell from the photos if it has valves or not!'

26

'Come with me a minute.' I take his arm and we make our way upriver to eavesdrop on the girls.

I position Rupert with his back to them.

Dennis the Menace isn't drinking. She's watching Stanley work on her friend.

'. . . glad we got it over with. Our singer's a bit fucking fragile. Anyway, here's to you, Tilly. Congratulations on your modelling contract, may you find the freedom and adventure you're looking for.' He and Tilly clink and swig. 'So, where are you from?' Dennis doesn't exist to him. She does to me. Shoulder-length brown hair. Black trench coat draped over one arm. A presence to her stance.

'Let's get out of here,' says Stanley. He puts his arm around Tilly's shoulder. 'I know this great little watering hole. Does the best cocktails in London.'

'How old are you?' interjects Dennis. As a singer, voices are my thing. A clairvoyant reads palms, I read voices, and this one this one ain't buying his bullshit. It's direct, cleanly powerful with a sexy rasp.

'Age is irrelevant.' Stanley's face pulls into a tight smile. 'It's how young you feel that counts.'

'Well,' says Dennis, 'I can see you'd like to *feel* this young.' She links her arm in Tilly's and shows me her profile. Attractive face, pretty, but looks like she doesn't know it. There's a gamine delicacy to her; she shines from the inside. Maybe twenty-five? '*This* young, by the way, is my seventeen-year-old cousin. And a man in his – what, his forties? – should know better.'

Stanley's one-way train lurches to a halt.

'Stella! You're not my mother.' Tilly blushes, shakes her peroxide bob and takes a huffy swig of Corona. She has gaunt, dark circles under her eyes. Haven't met a model who doesn't starve herself for the camera.

'Don't mother her. She's old enough to make up her own mind.' Stanley takes off his hat and wipes his brow with the back of his hand. There's a white indentation line on his forehead. He tightens his grip around Tilly's bony shoulders.

'Age is irrelevant.' He beams his badger-like nicotine-stained teeth at Stella. 'There are *old* seventeen-year-olds and *young* seventeen-year-olds. And Tilly here is an old, old soul.'

'There are *old* parasites and *young* parasites.' Stella unhooks his hand. 'And you are an old, old, parasite.'

Stanley gawps and goes into shutdown. As the oldest band member, he's touchy about his age. His curly hair masks a receding hairline. His piggy brown eyes look up into his pre-frontal cortex, flailing for a comeback. I know this look. I know if he doesn't find an effective put-down, full-on rage will be close at hand.

I brought Stanley into the Fuckers. Nice guy full of new-age jargon and a bottomless bag of weed. His descent from dope to coke transformed him. Can't stand it when he blows. And it tends to be at women.

Stella drags Tilly back, sensing an eruption.

'Hey, Stella,' I call out, breaking from Rupert. She turns in surprise. 'There you are, girl. I've been looking for you everywhere. Thank God you made it.' I wink at her just before I hug her. I pull back with my hands on her shoulders as if to take in a long-lost friend. She gets the game and is so convincing that I question whether I do know her. She *feels* familiar. Stanley glowers. This is taboo, to pick up girls marked by fellow band members. But hey, I'm after Stella. Tilly's collateral.

'Is this Tilly?' I ask.

'Yes,' Stella replies coolly, 'my cousin.'

'Nice to meet you, Tilly. Stella told me all about you,' I say.

'She did?' Tilly draws pink fingernails through bleached white hair. 'Stella, why didn't—'

'She did.' I nod. 'You've met Stan? Great gig tonight, Stan. You were *amazing*.' I turn back to the girls. 'Ready to go? Come on. I'll get my shit from the dressing room. It's this way. See you later, Stan.'

I lead, the girls follow. I scrawl a couple of autographs as we weave through the throng.

'Stella, you didn't tell me you knew Seth?' says Tilly in a whisper.

'Yeah,' she says, smiling, 'we go *way* back.'

'Many lifetimes,' I say over my shoulder and keep walking.

Monica blocks my path.

'JustJoe's here to see you.' I'm nonplussed. 'The DJ – you've got to say hi.'

'Lee can do it,' I say.

'Brunt wants you,' she insists.

'I'm done.'

She weighs me up, looks at the two girls in tow.

'Yeah, looks like it.' She leaves.

We swing through a set of saloon-style fire doors. I nod at the seated security guard.

'I think my dressing room's down here?' I say.

The corridor comes to a T-junction.

'Turn left,' says Stella.

'How do you know?' I turn back for an excuse to take her in.

'I can read,' she says.

My eyes follow her gaze to a Sharpie-written A4 that says 'SETH'S DRESSING ROOM', with an arrow pointing left. Alongside is a sign saying 'BAND DRESSING ROOM', with an arrow pointing right.

I lead the way.

'So, the band gets one room while you get your own?' remarks Stella.

'What can I say? Perk of being the singer.'

'Five of them sharing one room, while *you* get your own.'

'Ow.' I turn to defend myself. 'I have a different job to do. I need to sleep before a gig and they like to drink. A lot. I don't drink.' She blanks me. 'I should have left you with the shark.'

'That would presume,' she tilts her head back, 'that you aren't one.' Her tone and delivery are as measured as a stand-up's.

'You're trouble.'

'I hope so,' she beams. 'Is he always like that?'

'Stanley? Like clockwork. He was just gearing up into something less pleasant. You wouldn't want to be on the end of that.'

'Oh, so you're our knight in shining armour,' she says in a little-girl voice.

'*My* knight in shining armour.' Tilly interjects. Stella gives her a look. 'Well, Stanley *was* after me.' She clip-clops ahead of us with a swagger. I give Stella a look, she chuckles.

We come to the door with my name on it. I realise at this point that we are following momentum and I haven't thought this through. I push the door open. It's a harshly lit narrow box that last saw a coat of paint twenty years ago. A small rider of nuts, hummus and fruit, guarded by bottles of Evian, sit forlorn on a table top.

The place is a dump, won't impress anyone, especially this sharp-tongued assassin. The jaws of my suitcase lie open, revealing a mess of clothes, gadgets and toiletries spewing out onto the sticky carpet. A cluster of vitamin pills and Chinese herb bottles crowd the ledge below the make-up mirror. My day clothes are chucked over the only available soft chair, an old brown leather affair with stuffing erupting from a hole on the arm. Someone has drawn the lips of a vagina in forensic detail around the hole.

'This is palatial,' says Stella. Tilly laughs.

I bend to pick up the dry-cleaning plastic wrapping from the floor, crush the metal coat hangers and cram them in the bin. I reach for my clothes and chuck them into the gullet of my case.

'God,' Stella says, shaking her head. 'Straight men.' She bends down, picks up my T-shirt and folds it neatly. She looks into the chaotic bag, gives me a sorry look.

'I have a system,' I say.

She laughs and starts to unpack my clothes from the bag.

'Stella!' says Tilly. 'She's anal, does this to my bedroom. And thanks, I will have another beer.' She puts the empty down.

'I don't . . . have any, beer. I don't drink.' She looks shocked.

'Evian?' I say.

She pulls a face, helps herself, then hops on to the ledge. I bet she looks better on camera. Stella continues to fold clothes on her knees. Her hands are delicate and precise. Lips pursed in concentration. Dark hair hangs over pale skin. I remember what's in my bag and come out of my trance.

'Err, you don't need to do that.'

'No, but you do. Mummy doesn't come on tour, I guess.'

'Stella!' says Tilly.

'Yeah, Stella!' I echo. 'Jesus.' I feel a buzz of anger rising.

'Sorry,' she says unconvincingly. 'I can't help it. I'm a stylist; packing's half my job and I hate seeing clothes disrespected.' She holds up a denim shirt with paisley sleeves. 'Pretty hard to disrespect *this* monstrosity.' She pulls a vomit face. 'When I see something like this – what's this?' She holds up a bottle. 'Rogaine?'

She proceeds to read the label.

'Prevents hair loss—'

'Hey!' I shout. I move forward and snatch it from her.

'Thank you.'

This fucking woman. I save her from Stanley, bring her to my dressing room, and she humiliates me.

'And this!' She holds up a loose condom. 'Rock stars,' she scoffs.

'Get out of my fucking bag.' She ignores me and continues to root around, like a pig in shit.

No mas.

'Get . . . out . . . of . . . my . . . fucking . . . BAG!' This time she hears me and rises, smiling at my anger.

'You can go now,' I say in a cold voice.

'Come on, it's only—'

'Now!' I bark.

'Wow . . . OK.' She steps back, squinting.

'You, you . . . you come in here, snoop through my fucking bag . . . That's not – th-that's not OK . . .'

'I know, I know, I'm sorry. I'm really . . . inappropriate,' she says.

And on that note, she farts. It's a perfect raspberry, a parody of itself, a cartoon fart ending on an upward note.

Stella holds her breath and pulls a face as if the walls are about to come down. I burst out laughing, both girls join in.

'Well, that was an icebreaker,' I say.

She holds out her hand.

We shake. Her hand is warm.

'Stella Freidman.'

I'm sat with them in an intimate corner of Wells, the cocktail bar Stanley had alluded to. An act of bravado for which I'm now suffering. It's only when you give up booze that you realise it's the engine of the culture. But where else would we go?

Stella drinks Vodka Martinis, Tilly Burning Mandarins. I feel panicky at the smell of alcohol but I focus on Stella, and I'm OK. Stella, hasn't a clue about our band, came to the gig to chaperone Tilly. She asks poignant questions and listens, listens in a way that draws out an honesty that usually only surfaces in AA meetings. I talk about my sobriety but Tilly just wants to hear about Seth Brakes's outrageous past and incite me in the present. She's like most of the girls I used to date – attracted to the wild, the taboo, hoping for some crazy adventure to tell her friends about. So I'm a huge let-down, boring. I play nice and give her a few wild stories, censoring some as I read how they land with Stella.

We leave at 2 a.m. It's a mild evening. I don't want it to end, so we start walking to Hampstead Heath.

Tilly calls it quits, unhappy to be backing singer to Stella's lead. We put her in a black cab.

'The park can be dangerous at night.' I lock arms with Stella as we enter.

'Bullshit,' she says and unwinds from me.

She's staying with her parents in Watford. She's over from Paris, where she's an assistant to a big-deal stylist I've never heard of.

We go sit on a bench.

'It's a supermoon,' she tells me.

'It is pretty – pretty super.'

'No, they're called "supermoons"; they're closer to the Earth than usual.'

'A good omen, then.' I give her a meaningful glance.

'Not in Mesopotamia.'

'Good thing we're in Hampstead. Where is Mesopotamia?'

'You've never been?'

'Wouldn't remember if I had.'

'You were that messed up?'

Don't scare her off.

'No, not just that . . . you lose track of everything on tour,' I say. 'Sometimes you wouldn't know what month it was or what city you were in.'

I put my arm around her. She leans forward and looks back at me.

'Uh-uh. I don't date rock singers.'

'You date by profession? Who else is excluded?'

'Journalists. Politicians. Accountants. American footballers. Models. Film stars—'

'So long as I'm in good company.'

'Men who drive Porsches,' she barrels on. 'Anyone who reads the *Mail* or works for Rupert Murdoch. Anyone with a PlayStation or an Xbox.'

'Your pool of potential suitors is a puddle.'

'Soldiers, traders and Jews,' she completes the litany with a smug sigh of finality.

'Jews!'

'I am one.' She shrugs. 'It's a running joke in my family that I've never dated a Jew.'

'Vive la difference.'

'That's why I'm in Paris, darling.'

'Well, I'm different.' She rolls her eyes. 'Just have to find a new profession.'

'You're not the kind of different I'm looking for.'

'I'm surprised anyone is – with that list.'

'I don't date players.'

'I'm not a player.'

She arches a caterpillar eyebrow. It's almost a monobrow.

'I'm a monk. A sober monk. Almost celibate.'

'So how many women have you slept with?'

'You can't . . . Don't ask that. That's a ridiculous question on a first date.'

'This is not a date, Seth. I don't date singers.'

I want to kiss her.

'Oh, come on. It's a date. There's the moon, supermoon, there's the stars, and here we are. It's a date.'

She gives an enigmatic smile. Underneath that sharp tongue, I sense warmth. 'I really like you.'

'And tomorrow night – you'll really like someone else.' She stretches her legs.

'That's not true. I don't meet people like you. Girls that fart, tell me I'm useless – have an in-depth knowledge of Mesopotamian folklore.'

Her laugh is contagious.

'The gig wasn't great tonight, by the way,' she says.

'It wasn't! It sucked! I'm so happy you said that. Look, I have a day off tomorrow, please, please, spend the day with me. I want to get to know you.' She gives me a look. 'Damn.' I point at her face. 'You can do the Roger Moore eyebrow!'

She takes a moment, shakes her head.

'Fine. We can meet up, but it's not a date.'

'Not a date.'

We lie on our backs on our macs. Planes draw white lines in the blue sky. It's a freak sunny day for November, so we came back to the park, safe, neutral ground. She wouldn't come to my place and I can't go to her parents', who wouldn't be happy to see their one and only daughter with a non-Jew ex-addict.

Daylight makes us awkward on this not-a-date. The romance and momentum of the evening, the gloss of the moon, is replaced by the reality that we don't know each other.

My critic's out –

Don't trust love, it's another drug, more lethal than crack.

I've been infatuated before, it won't last.

Simultaneously, I'm like a puppy dog romantic desperate for some encouragement, a crowd of contradictions jostling each other.

She's taking the Eurostar back to Paris tomorrow for an advertising shoot. I want to leave some kind of mark, so she'll comes back for more.

'How do you get time off work?' A green-brown leaf parachutes down to my side. 'And when will you be back?'

'It's random, depends on work. If Lynn books an advert, a video or shoot, I'm there doing all the grunt work.'

'You don't get to choose any of the clothes?' I roll the leaf stem between my fingers.

'Mostly I do the returns, appointments, organisational shit – sometimes she lets me choose – or at least make suggestions.' When I look unimpressed she shrugs. 'Anyone in fashion at my age would give their right eye for this job.'

'You'd look sexy in an eyepatch.' She pulls a face. The banter worked last night, but her guard's up today and I don't seem to be able to stop.

'I work with some of the most beautiful, sexy women in the world. When you're around that all day, every day, you look in the mirror and see Shrek staring back at you.'

'I've a great fondness for Shrek. And anyway, you'd be Mrs Shrek, the woman he kisses, and turns into a princess.'

'I know exactly what you'd turn into if I kissed you.'

'A frog?' I get no laugh. 'A sane, dependable human being?'

On the far side of the duck pond a heron stabs a minnow.

A toddler stumbles down the hill and crashes into us.

'Woah!' I catch him, laughing. He stares at me, on the cusp of being afraid. I make an exaggerated smiley face and clown roll over backwards. He smiles but looks around for backup. Twenty yards away his mother – nanny? – is lost to her phone. He's between that point of excitement and fear. I don't want him to cry.

'There was a man lived in the moon.

In the moon. In the moon.

There was a man lived in the moon.

And his name was Aiken Drum,' I sing. This song comes to me from deep childhood. He smiles.

'His hair was made of spaghetti, spaghetti, spaghetti.'

I point to his hair, he touches his curly locks.

'His hair was made of spaghetti

And his name was Aiken Drum.

His eyes were made of . . . fried eggs . . .'

The boy giggles. I glance at Stella for support and she joins me.

'Fried eggs, fried eggs.

His eyes were made of fried eggs,

And his name was Aiken Drum.'

I'm choked up suddenly by a memory of Dad singing this to me, in a park somewhere. I take Stella's hand and the boy's.

'And he played upon a ladle, a ladle, a ladle.'

We start to dance in a circle.

'He played upon a ladle and his name was Aiken Drum . . .'

'I told you not to run away like that.' The woman's harsh tone cuts through our joy.

39

'Sorry,' I say. 'We were just singing . . .'

'Yeah, well, thanks.' She scowls at me, snatches up the boy, who bursts into tears. She stomps up the hill with him wedged under her arm, legs kicking, arms reaching back for us.

I turn away from Stella to gather myself.

'Do you want kids, Seth Brakes?'

There's an intimate formality to the way she says my name. I lie back down on my mac, brush mud off my knees.

'Can't say I've really thought about it, Stella Freidman. Don't think I've met the right woman.' Her eyes frisk me.

'I guess kids don't fit into the rock 'n' roll lifestyle.'

'I don't fit into the rock 'n' roll lifestyle.'

'Ah, I don't know, you seem to have made a good fist of it. Google has very interesting things to say about you – and some wonderful pictures.'

I groan and turn around.

She's gazing into the distance, arms strapped around her knees.

'I'm past all that.'

'Are you?'

Three hundred and twenty-three days past it.

Chapter 3

'How was it with sexy face then? I know you've been dying to tell me.' Lee doesn't look up from the canvas.

'Don't know who you mean.' I keep my pose intact. He continues to paint me.

'Not cool, taking her from Stanley.' He changes focus between the canvas and my face.

'He was after the other one – Fizzy – they came as a pair. And anyway, he was about to have one of his . . . conniption fits.'

'Not cool,' he bites his bottom lip with concentration, 'nicking band members' birds – especially as the singer.'

'Birds! When were you born? The sixties. Nicking! And what, it would be OK if you'd "nicked" her?'

'Hmm.' He pauses. 'Lead guitarist ranks above rhythm guitarist – so no.'

'Oh, I always wondered how that worked. So, if you rank above another band member, it's unfair to use that advantage?'

'Yeah.' He sits back on his stool. 'Dead right, singer gets all the attention.'

'In this hypothetical ranking—' I use the respite to bend down and take a sip of coffee; it's cold and so am I, even though

Lee's got the heating cranked to the max; 'Who's higher in the pecking order – drummer or bass player?'

'Drummer and bass player,' he muses, 'are twins. Equal.'

'Keyboard player or . . . lead guitarist?'

'Depends on the band. Generally, guitarist.'

'You're biased.'

'Course.' He glugs some wine. 'No – definitely guitarist. Because they can move around, strike poses and impress the girls – guitarist has a distinct advantage.' He illustrates the point by playing air guitar and pulling rock guitarist faces.

'Don't do that.'

'What? This?' He takes it further by sticking out his tongue à la Kiss and imitating a trebly guitar solo. 'Bedobedobedidede.'

'Your tongue's all furry; that would not impress the ladies. Anyway. Rick Wakeman.'

'What about him?'

'Can't even remember the guitarist in his band – so he ranks higher.'

Lee gives me a sorry look.

'If you think dressing up as Gandalf gives you a sexual advantage, then good luck to you. Anyway, back in position please. And don't change the subject. How was sexy face?'

'Good,' I say, trying to remember my pose.

'Uncross your legs. Yeah, that's it.'

'Nothing happened. She doesn't "date rock stars".'

'Well, that's OK for you. You're a "has-been rock star".'

'I never thought of that – "has-been rock stars" weren't on her list. Which, by the way, makes you a "has-been guitarist".'

He winces. 'Not much more redundant than a has-been rock star.' He goes back to painting. 'She has brains and beauty.'

'Thanks, I knew my best friend would be supportive.'

'Seth,' he puts down the brush. 'In the name of truth, I need you to know. I may be *your* best friend, but that doesn't mean you're mine.'

'Fucking bastard. So where am I on your best friend list?'

He adjusts his jacket collar and plucks a wilting rose petal from his pocket.

'Top ten.'

'You fucker.'

I swear he used to come to rehab just to take the piss out of me. He takes a sip of wine. The acrid smell tweaks my background chatter.

'Play your cards right and you might make top five.'

'Steady on.'

'So . . . are you keen on her?'

I draw her to mind. My body lights up.

'Yeah, I'm really keen on her.' He waits. 'But I don't really trust myself. I've been there before, you know, I'm all keen on somebody and then once I have them – pfffttt. The attraction just evaporates.'

'Well, hopefully it's going you give you good material for lyrics. Always has in the past. How many songs have you written?'

Canvases lean up against the bare brick walls of his apartment, stacked like a giant's playing cards. The washing-up's piled high, peering above the sink top.

'How many?' He puts his brush down again.

'I like your octopus.' I point to a painting of a lurid purple cephalopod, a paintbrush held in one of its tentacles.

'Octopi, don't change the subject. How many songs have you written?'

I can't look at him.

'None? You've written none?' He stands up. 'None!' He walks to the side. 'We're rehearsing them in a week, recording in three! Fuck, man, I vouched for you to Brunt, he'll kill me.' he raises his voice. 'What happened? Have you tried?'

'Of course I fucking tried! Just . . . nothing comes.' I stand up. 'Nothing. It used to be easy, when I was drunk or coked. I wouldn't think about it. Songs would arrive, like a gift from the tooth fairy. Especially after sleep, I'd wake and there'd be these lyrics written down on fag packets, napkins – lyrics I had no memory of writing. *Now* . . . I don't know where to start. Now nothing comes easy. *Now* I hear all these doubts, and, choices – there's so many choices – and – I freeze before them all. I'm, I'm standing back listening to all these thoughts inside my head. These endless repeating useless thoughts. I can't – I can't get *into* my life, the flow of it. I'm just . . . lost in this numb bullshit and it's driving me fucking crazy!'

'All right, mate, all right.'

'Feels like I've had a personality transplant. I used to be all . . . impulse. Now I'm bricking every move.'

'Mate, you've got to open the songwriting up to the band.'

44

'Fuck off!' He knows this subject's taboo. 'I write the songs. I've always written the songs. It's my fucking band! That's *not* gonna happen!'

My fists are clenched. He goes quiet – knows it's a stalemate.

The light's changed. We've lost the magic hour.

'It's getting cold now, Lee – can I put my clothes back on?'

'Sure, mate. Sit down a moment, though, let me finish your dick.' He returns to his easel, picks up his brush. 'Won't take a minute.'

Chapter 4

'Mum's had a fall,' my sister says over the phone.

'Well, of course she has,' I say. 'Just one?'

'No, it's serious, Seth. They admitted her into the infirmary last night.'

'How serious is serious? It's not just one of her ploys to get more attention, is it?'

'It's the real thing this time.' She exhales. 'They found her passed out on the bathroom floor. She whacked her head on the sink and cracked her knee. They doped her up on morphine again, so she was all over the shop.'

Mum's a *Daily Mail* reader who considers her state-sanctioned drugs and alcoholism superior in every way to anyone on 'drugs'.

'How was she on morphine? Was it like last time?'

Last time she told us that the staff of her Presbyterian home had made all the inmates take showers together. How well endowed some of the men were. Told us she was playing Ophelia in *Hamlet* and Hamlet was a dish. Everything was sexual, fun almost. Not like Mum. There's a silence on the line. Lizzie's not playing.

'You think she's dying?'

46

She doesn't answer.

'I can't come up to Scotland right now, I've got all these writing deadlines and I'm completely blocked.' Which is true and not true. Stella's a distraction and when I try to write lyrics to some set of clichéd chords, I end up getting sucked in online, following a paper trail of conspiracy theories; apparently, the Mayan calendar ends this year.

'You could write up here. The twins are at school in the day, I'm at the hospital. You'd have the house to yourself.'

'I can't stay! I'm just getting my shit together with the band.'

'Why are you doing that again? It's crazy. You're just asking for trouble.'

'Liz, you're not my mum.'

'I fucking hope not. Look, we haven't seen you in years. If you're going to come all this way . . . The twins would *really* love to see their uncle . . .'

There's a desperation in her voice I'm unused to.

She didn't come see me in rehab.

'If mum dies . . .'

'If mum dies? Really?'

I spy a baby-blue plectrum by the skirting board. I go pick it up, sit back down and use it to remove dirt under my fingernails.

'I'm not driving all the way to Scotland. I know it will be bullshit.'

Three days later I'm on the M80, south of Stirling. Mum's off the critical list, back in the home, but I've been guilted into seeing her.

Crisp packets litter the passenger seat, empty Starbucks cups litter the floor. I've been driving eight hours, the last hour in torrential rain. A piercing FaceTime chirp jolts me out of my focus. It's Stella; we've been FaceTiming daily. Brilliant invention. She's on a styling gig with a bunch of surfers, in Paris, for a cigarette advert. It's going well. The job and our communication; for two people not in a relationship we talk a hell of a lot. We're easy on the phone together – I *think* she's starting to come round. The car speakers amplify the sound, interrupting the delicate beauty of 'Should Have Known Better'. I've got one hand on the wheel, and one navigating the iPhone. I press the green answer button and rest the phone on my lap.

'Hi,' Stella says. 'I can't see you.'

'Hang on a minute.' I lift the phone carefully behind the steering wheel and find a place to lodge it on the dashboard in front of the speedometer.

'I'm driving,' I say.

'Really.'

'Fuck off.'

'Shall I call back?'

'No, this is as good as it gets. How are you?'

'I'm good. You?'

'All the better for seeing you. Nearly at my mother's.'

'I want to talk to you about something.'

My skin prickles. You know, when someone says, 'I want to talk to you about something,' you just know it's not going to be good. I indicate and pull into the slow lane behind a bus.

'Maybe now isn't the right time?' she says.

'Well shit, you started now. Hang on.' A car cuts into my lane. 'Fuckers. OK, do I need to pull over?' Emotionally, I'm braced in the crash position.

'Maybe that's a good idea.'

Beef crisps repeat in my throat. I peer through the sleepy drone of the wipers, looking for service signs.

The rain's unrelenting.

If she's about to finish with me . . . before we've started. I look down to see if cigarettes are within reach. The packet's on the floor.

'OK,' I clear my throat, 'it doesn't look like there's anywhere for me to pull over. You'd better say what you have to say.'

'Well . . . I'm feeling bad.' She takes a breath then dives in. 'On the shoot . . . I met someone. A surfer, a Jewish surfer. And, you know, Jews don't surf. And I've never really gone out with a Jew before; I think I told you that. Anyway, I had to check it out. The attraction. My parents have always wanted me to date a Jew—'

The screen goes blank.

Trying to connect, the screen says. *Trying to connect.*

I'm glad she's not there watching me now. I feel like a child that's fallen down a well, all the wind knocked out of me. Everything looks far away and separate.

Then she's back.

'. . . too, because I've made it clear I'm not going out with you, but I felt guilty. Like I was being unfaithful or something. And when I was with him, I couldn't stop . . . inking of you. Which kind of . . . off. You know, I liked him and all that. He was cute. But I really didn't fancy him.'

Trying to connect. Trying to connect.

'Fuck off!' I thump the wheel.

Headlights dazzle on the water-filmed windscreen. Stella's image returns.

'Oh, you're back,' she says. 'How much of that did you get?'

'You fucked a Jewish surfer.'

She winces, and the phone freezes her like she's just sniffed Camembert.

'Ahhhhh!' I scream.

The car hits a large pool of water, the vehicle drags as jets rise up from beneath the right wheels. The motorway lights hang like scaffolds. There's a whooshing sound at regular intervals as I pass them. One, two, three and then the fourth one skips a beat. You could get hypnotised by that shit and just turn the wheel, turn the wheel into the barriers. It would be so easy.

'Yes. I did, I slept with him,' she says in a cartoon voice as the video speeds up to compensate for the freeze. She raises her jaw and comes back into real time. 'But that's not what I'm trying to tell you. I'm ringing to tell you. I want to be with you. Well, I can't be with you. You're in England, I'm in France. But I'm more attracted to you than I realised. And I want to see what happens with that.'

She wants to be with me? I shake my head.

'Well, that was a romantic way to ask me out.' I get a laugh. 'I take it he was shit in bed.'

I get a throaty laugh. It's a good sound. It makes me smile, though inside I feel sick. On the outskirts of my awareness, I hear a voice saying, *You can't trust her – she'll hurt you.*

'Fucking men,' Stella says.

'Sounds like you have been.'

I push open the door to my mother's room. I step back around her wheelchair, catching my shin on the metal footrests. I stifle a cry, grit my teeth, letting the pain fan out from the point of impact. I catch the hint of a smile on her thin lips. Apart from an ostentatious head bandage that would honour a war victim, Mum's fine. She's not high on opioids either. This is no fun.

I wheel her into her room and stamp down on the brakes.

'Do you want to be in bed, Mum?' I say.

She won't talk to me. I lift her foot off the footrest and place it on the ground. Her black shoes are flecked with mud. I undo the shoelace, take hold of her heel and ease her foot out of her shoe. She's wearing transparent holed stockings.

Nothing gives away Mum's age as much as her feet. Her toes are gnarly oak twigs, the little toe crushed in and under from years of wearing cheap shoes. She tries to stretch them and they move as one. I take off her other shoe.

'Where are your slippers, Mum?'

No response.

Gin fumes radiate off her like gasoline from an old truck in a hot sun.

'Just a small G and T on the rocks,' she kept repeating to the waitress. This ended up translating as at least four, and probably a fifth she snuck in when I was in the toilet. She got meaner and meaner as her eyes glazed over. Prattling on about the home and the sins of her fellow inmates. I bit my tongue until she turned her vitriol on Lizzie.

'She only comes to see me once a week. And those poor kids, the way she treats—'

'Mum, don't fucking start on Lizzie with your unsolicited parenting advice – you're lucky she ever comes.'

After that it was this sulky silence, silent prayers and the constant fingering of the crucifix round her neck.

Back in her room I unfold the wonky concertina doors of her wardrobe, reach inside, and pull out her blue slippers. I ease them on to her feet.

'Come on, then, let's get you out the chair.'

She doesn't move. I reach under her armpits to lift her.

'Stop that, I'm not an invalid.' She smooths down her Brillo-pad hair. 'Get me a glass of water.'

I wait for a 'please', give up and trudge to the bathroom.

I pull the light cord. The room is over-illuminated and soundtracked by the extractor fan. The room stinks of air freshener failing to mask the smell of shit. A brown-stained nappy hangs across the mouth of a white-lipped bin. I shut the door behind me.

I open the bin lid and lift up the nappy. The bin's full of nappies and toilet paper, draped around an empty gin bottle. With prim fingers I rearrange the contents until the lid mouth shuts with a clunk.

To the side of the bin is a cheap pine cabinet, with a silver key in the lock. I turn the key quietly and open the stiff door. Inside, two full bottles of gin stand proudly flanked by a carton of tonics. On the little shelf above the bottles sit a row of pills. All the same. White-labelled prescription bottles, fifteen of them. I pick one up, Zolpidem. Not morphine but sleeping pills. How'd she get so many? The name of the patient is typed. *Mrs Emerson* printed on four of them. Not her, then, and neither is Mrs Cartwright, printed on two more. She's stolen these or bribed a nurse? I pocket two bottles. Behind them is a silver flask. It's empty, no smell even. Guess she doesn't need the subterfuge. On the side's an inscription.

For my darling Rebecca. For ever. Alan

There's a heaviness in my chest.

'"For ever" was a fairly relative term there, Dad.'

I don't have anything of his. *She doesn't need it.* I pocket the flask.

I close the cabinet door and go to the sink.

I cup water on to my face and towel down.

I wipe down Mum's toothpaste glass and fill it with water.

'Cheers.' I knock it back and fill one up for her.

So Stella had to sleep with someone else to realise she wants to go out with me? Guess I deserve it. Done worse to others. I write in my lyric notebook.

Consequences, ricochet, amor.

I pull the bathroom light cord and stand in the near dark listening as the fan grinds to a halt. It reminds me of Dad's lawn-mower. I step back into Mum's room.

Click, click, click.

I shudder. She's propped up in bed, knitting.

As kids, knitting was a sign that she'd kick off. Either with beatings, blows that a teacher wouldn't see, or she'd go on a bender. And there'd be blows at the end of that, too.

She looks up. 'What kept you? Was the well dry?'

She makes no move to take the water, so I use the glass to budge photo frames out of the way on her bedside table.

Click, click, click.

The sound spooks me, and I knock over a photo. It's an old one – of Lizzie, me and Mum – that survived her purges of the past.

Click, click, click.

'Can we talk?'

She continues to knit, ignoring me. I wheel her chair to the door.

'I'm just going to put your wheelchair away.'

I wheel it down the hallway, across the ancient yellow-green carpet, past the dining area, smelling of overcooked cabbage and beef, past the TV room, blaring out a celebrity dance contest. I dock her chair with the others by the exit and keep walking, out into the bitter night, in search of a drink.

Click, click, click.

I'm driving fast down winding country roads. There's a half-moon in a clear sky. I turn off my headlights and drive by it. I used to love playing chicken drunk, never played it sober.

A couple of mistimed corners gets my adrenalin flowing.

I'm approaching some crossroads.

If there are any other cars coming, I'll see their headlights and put mine on. Unless, of course, I meet another one like me.

Another idiot.

I put my foot down.

I accelerate through the crossroads.

I'm buzzing.

There's a straight bit of road ahead. I wonder if I could close my eyes and drive it.

I'm about to do so when I see a pub on the left, hit the brakes, turn the lights back on and pull into the parking lot with a screech of tyres. I turn the engine off and sit in the quiet of the car feeling the hot pulse of my heart, listening to the engine tick down.

The pub glows warm and inviting.

I could call someone.

Jada?

Someone who understands.

Don't want to.

Haven't been to a meeting in weeks.

I bang my head against the steering wheel.

Fuck Stella.

Bang.

Fuck Mum.

Bang.

Fuck 'em all.

I close my eyes on the steering wheel.

Mum stares out the window, fingering her crucifix, fag in hand. Behind her Lizzie and I exchange looks. Danger, level 6. She's wearing her pink kimono dressing gown hanging loose, revealing her green shift showing too much bosom. 'Bosom,' I say under my breath. Lizzie smiles. Mum's shift is wrinkled in all the wrong places, sagged up, under her armpits, around her belly. Lizzie points with her eyes to look up at the top of Mum's head. Her bird's nest hair's all over the place, mad. We mime laughter, too afraid to release the real thing. She had a man back last night. We could hear them.

'Shit,' says Mum as she lurches for the frying pan and hoicks it into the air to rescue the fish fingers. One burnt fish finger escapes the edge of the pan and flies beneath our table. I push my stool back and hop down, eager to reach it before Lizzie does. I duck under the tabletop.

Mum's cooking supper for us. A rare event. After school it's usually sandwiches at best. It's a make up meal for yesterday. In the morning as usual she paraded us in church in our Sunday bests, then in the evening she locked us up under the stairs so she could go out drinking. It's not so bad when I'm with Lizzie. We cuddle up on the mattress. She left us there till the man left in the morning. I was bursting for the loo.

Fish fingers, chips and peas. Yum. I retrieve the stray fish finger but drop it, as the fat encrusted breadcrumbs burn my tender seven-year-old skin. Lizzie lets out a snigger. Her head is dipped under the table watching me. I smile. There's a loud clang of a pot getting tossed into the sink and Lizzie's head disappears up top. I carefully pick up the fish finger, juggling it till I manage to bring it back up top, where I flip it onto my plate. Lizzie stares enviously at my winnings. I break off an end and blow on it.

'Don't eat that.' The edge in Mum's voice is final. She's not looking at me, she's fussing with the food. I put it back on the plate.

'Don't put it on the plate. Put it in the bin.' How does she do that without looking?

I take my plate to the bin, lift off the cracked white plastic lid and slide the broken fishfinger into its smelly mouth.

'Bring your plates over then,' Mum says.

We jump down from our stools and race to stand behind her. Lizzie's first. Mum portions out her plate with chips, peas and four fish fingers, dark brown but still a treat.

Lizzie says, 'You know Seth won best essay in his class this week?'

'You did!' says Mum, turning to me with a smile. 'Well done love.' She hugs my head to her belly. I don't know what to do with the hug, but it feels good.

'Extra chips for you.' She plucks a few off Lizzie's plate, puts them on mine. Neither of us react.

'What do you say?'

'Thanks Mum.'

She fills up my plate. I bring it back to the table and climb up onto the high stool.

'Sorry,' I mouth to Lizzie.

She shakes her head.

I whack the bottom of the glass tomato ketchup bottle two or three times before a glob splatters out onto my plate. I tuck in, heading straight for the fingers. Crunchy on the outside and soft on the in.

'Mmmm.' I'm starving. I hear the sound of a match being struck. Mum lights up another fag then wipes up the cooking mess. I guzzle down the food.

'Don't bolt your food. Chew it properly and sit up straight while you're at it.' She's still not looking at me.

'Eyes in the back of my head,' she says, answering my thoughts. She's scary is Mum, a mind reader.

Lizzie's hunched over her plate. She's carefully slipping her knife under the breadcrumb coating, sliding it the full length, then twists her wrist to remove the crispy skin. It joins a small pile she's already made, separated from the grey-white fish lying naked on her plate. Her concentration is total, like a safe cracker.

'What you doing?' I ask quietly.

'It's the best bit. The coating. I'm saving it for last.'

I look down at my plate. All my fish fingers are gone and I'm left with a few stray peas and chips. I feel sad. It had never crossed my mind to save the best for last. Don't think I could do it.

'What are you doing?' Mum is at the table.

Lizzie looks up, startled. Mom is staring daggers at her plate.

'I'm skinning them. The best bit's the coating, so I'm going to save it till last,' she looks up at Mum all innocent, puppy dog eyes. 'It's delicious, Mum. Thanks.'

Mum is still. Dangerously still, like a heron. I'm holding my breath. Lizzie acts like it's fine and holds her happy face. A car horn blares. I'm not raising my head from my plate, not getting in the firing line, just staring at the blood red ketchup smeared on skinny chips.

Mum's hand grabs the pile of skins off Lizzie's plate, and lifts them onto mine, leaving only scraps behind.

'Well, if you're not going to eat them – Seth can.' I stare down at them.

'Mum!' says Lizzie.

'Go on Seth. Eat up.'

I'm frozen. I can't do this to her.

'Mum!' Lizzie rises from her stool. I hear a sharp slap. A flush has broken out across Lizzie's cheek.

'Sit down and shut up.' I watch Lizzie control her face. Push her jaw forward then sit, trying not to cry.

'Now eat them up, Seth.'

I feel the pulse of blood in my face. I look at Lizzie, she's not looking. I shovel a few skins from the pile onto my fork and raise it to my *lips. I pause, too long. Mum jerks me back off my stool by my jumper and I hit the door frame with my shoulder.*

'Right, off to your rooms, both of you,' she says, then shouts: 'Now!'

We leave the kitchen.

'Fuckin' kids.'

I lift my head from the wheel and touch my forehead. In the darkness, blood looks grey.

I wind the window down. The chill cuts.

I light a cigarette and watch clouds play now you see me, now you don't with the moon. A shooting star rifles the sky.

I wish.

I wish.

I wish she were dead.

I sit quietly in the emptiness of the moment.

The pub door opens, releasing the murmur inside, and three men come out into the night, breath visible on the crisp air.

I smoke the cigarette to the stub, flick it through the window, get out my phone. Google Maps. Great invention, hope it works up here.

Only ten minutes away from my sister's place. I turn the engine on and pull back on to the road.

One day at a time.

One day at a time.

Chapter 5

I'm in the belly of an airplane. It's cold in the hold and I'm only wearing a swimsuit.

I'm me, but I'm a younger me, thirteen, pimply, skinny and freezing.

I'm with all the luggage. There are cages stacked up around me, covered with grey blankets, thin sheets. Cages full of animals. I know they're animals because they're making a racket as the airplane shakes with turbulence. I keep nearly falling but catch myself.

Among the shaking and vibrating of the plane there's a faint scrabbling sound. It's calling me. I'm looking for its source.

The plane lurches. I reach out to steady myself and pull a blanket off a cage. A Rottweiler attacks the bars, barking furiously. I jump backwards and knock into a stack of cages. The sheets drop like curtains. Small monkeys, frozen, terrified, clinging to each other. With each shake of the plane they whimper.

In a cage standing alone to the side is a bobcat. Alert yet calm, unaffected by the chaos. It stares at me like it sees right through me.

The scrabbling sound becomes a knocking. The bobcat turns its head to the side. The sound makes me feel sick. A continuous repetitive knocking. I move towards the source.

It's a large battered twin-tub washing machine, one of those old stand-up ones. The beige paint has cracked, bubbled and peeled like sunburn. I'm sweating with fear.

Bang.   Bang.   Bang.

The tub moves with the strikes. There's something inside, trying to get out. I shiver. The knocking intensifies, becoming random. The closer I get, the more it shakes. I'm going to open it. The lid on the top is rattling, threatening to burst upwards. I gather my courage, reach out and fling the lid open.

Birds stream out. An impossible number of brightly coloured birds streams out into the hold. The hold opens up into sky. I fall backwards on to the floor. A swirl of colours arches above me. The birds are singing, singing so loud. It's an ecstatic, joyful sound like in documentaries where millions of birds meet at African watering holes.

'We are free, we are free,' they sing.

Hundreds, thousands of them whirling above my head. Flashes of turquoise, purple, pink, grass green, scarlet, arching over me like a rainbow. My heart is leaping with them. It's breathless, dizzying, ecstatic. I'm on the floor of the plane looking up in wonder.

The birds move as one, like a shoal, creating shapes. They're spelling out a geometrical language that I nearly understand. I've known this language before – forgotten it.

'We are one.'

I catch that. The rest's a blur, too fast to take in. They form fractals, spirals, double helixes, kinetic geometrical shapes, gone as fast as they appear.

I know it's important.

I'm trying to work it out, but I don't understand and it fills me with grief.

62

Bang. Bang. Bang.

That sound again.

Slow now, different.

It's not of this plane.

It's from somewhere else.

What does this mean?

It's in my room. I'm dreaming. It's a dream.

I'm back here. There's a pain of grief in my throat.

It's freezing. I'm fully clothed from last night and I'd layered my trench coat on top of the Harry Potter duvet in an attempt to keep warm. I open my eyes a slither to the dim dusk light. Rice-paper-thin curtains ripple in the draughty room. It's my niece's room. She's sharing with her twin Joe. I'm at my sister's.

Creak. Creak.

I lift my head and peer across the room to see Holly, on her rocking chair, knees tucked up inside a large *Lucky Fuckers* T-shirt. It's at times like this that I wish we'd named the band something else. Her eyes are locked on me.

'Finally,' she says.

'Morning, Holly.'

Her lips pout in disapproval. I shake off the dream and prop myself up out the covers to glance at my phone: 6 a.m. *Damn.*

'You couldn't sleep?' I ask.

'You could.'

'Aren't you cold? Shorts and a T-shirt, Holly . . .' She picks her toes. I curl my head round on the pillow, pulling the duvet tight around my neck.

'Have you been in a fight?' She picks her toes.

I reach to my bruised forehead.

'No. I . . . had an . . . I fell over.'

She looks puzzled, then says, 'What does . . . *I fell upon the crack and there's no coming back from that* mean?'

'It's a lyric . . .' I rack my brains for an alternative to its true meaning. It was about a week when I was holed up at Pitbull's, on crack.

'Well, I know it's a lyric, stupid. Is it sex?' she says.

'No!' I say. 'Why d'you . . . why d'you ask?' She doesn't answer. 'It's about falling between the cracks – you know?'

She stares at me, doll faced, no smile where you'd expect one.

'Why didn't you sing *cracks*? You sung *crack*.'

'It's a typo.'

'You sing *crack*.'

'It's just an error.'

She clenches her jaw and goes back to fiddling with her toes.

'How does that *remind us who we are again*?' she asks, referencing a later lyric.

What is this? An interview from hell?

'I don't know . . . It's difficult.'

'Unless you know about sex?' She searches my face. 'I do know about sex.'

'You're twelve, Holly. You might know about sex – but you don't – I don't want to have this conversation – it's not about sex.'

'I know about sex.'

'You can't really. At twelve.'

'I'm nearly thirteen and I've seen *Game of Thrones* and other things.' Her voice trails off on 'other things'.

Oh God.

Behind her are photos of animals, mainly horses.

'Are you into horses?' I say.

She pulls her goosebumped arms in through the T-shirt armholes.

'Why don't you put your dressing gown on?'

'Did you see Granny?'

'Yeah. Last night.'

'We waited up for you. I made you this.' She looks downwards. At her feet is a baby-blue mug.

'Oh, thank you. Can I see it?'

'It's yours.'

I swing out the duvet. The cold snaps at my ankles. I reach for my hoodie and pull it on. I bring the mug back to bed.

It's glazed powder blue, with white lettering. In an uneven child's hand it reads *Lucky Fuckers,* written in musical staves and clefs. It walks the line between being really well crafted and yet rough and ready that only a child could achieve.

'That's . . . I love it. Brilliant. Did you make it?'

'On a wheel. At school.'

Bet they loved that at school.

'It's really great. Thank you. Do you love pottery, then?'

'I like making things.' She hides a shy smile of pleasure. 'It's for your tea – not alcohol.'

'I don't drink any more.'

'Mum said. Have you got *me* a present?'

'There's one coming.'

She looks confused.

'When?'

'In a bit.'

'Why don't you have it with you?'

'It's a surprise. You . . . just wait.' I'll get her some chocolate when she's at school.

'I don't believe you.' Then, nodding at the duvet cover, 'I hate that duvet. Harry Potter. Granny gave it me after Joe burnt my other one. Did you like it?'

'The film? Didn't see it. What films do you like?'

'*Game of Thrones*, but I know it's not a film. I like Arya and Daenerys and the big sexy man. And the dragons.'

'Mum lets you watch that?'

'She can't stop me! I watch it when she's asleep. She knows. Doesn't want Joe to watch it, though. Don't tell him. Promise?'

'I promise.'

She investigates a bruise on her leg.

'How d'you get that?'

'Football. Fell over.' She suddenly looks awkward, young and vulnerable. 'I'm cold.'

I hold open the duvet for her. She shimmies into bed with her back to me. She's freezing. I put my arms around her and draw her in for a snuggle. She's like a little frog, all limbs. She puts cold feet on mine. I squeal. She laughs.

'Are you staying?' Her body tenses with the weight of the question. I can feel her need, hope – expected disappointment. A car drones past the window. Somewhere in the house I hear movement and low voices.

'Maybe just a few days.'

Her body softens. She snuggles into me for warmth.

I help Lizzie get the twins off to school. In daylight, every scuff and dent stands out on the walls and cabinets. It's depressing in this house. Her poverty's depressing. I feel guilty for not helping her out more, but between her and Mum's home I'm skint. You can tell she's one fridge/oven malfunction away from financial ruin.

She looks ten years older; twins as a single parent on a nurse's pay packet will do that for you.

Holly tries to feign illness to stay home but Lizzie's not having it. She shepherds them towards the child factories.

'I hate school,' Joe mutters to me. 'The teachers just want you to do what they want you to do.'

'Have you done your homework?' Lizzie asks Holly.

'Most of it.' Holly puts on her coat. 'It's not for today.'

'Where's your coat, Joe? For God's sake, it's minus two.'

'I'm not cold,' says Joe.

'It's called central heating. Get yer coat on.' Then she shouts at them. 'Why do I have to go through this every fucking day!' The kids are silenced into obedience. We're all shocked.

The minute the Fiat's out of sight I go upstairs and chuck my gear into my bag. I've got maybe thirty minutes before Lizzie's back from the school run. In the kitchen, bag in hand, my phone pings. It's a Stella text.

Really sorry. Hope you'll forgive me ♡ ♡ ♡

Will Lizzie forgive me?

Always.

She patched me up when I came in last night, like she did when we were kids. We never argue but there was an uneasy stand-off between why I hadn't visited in two years and why she hadn't come to rehab. Was Mum really hurt or was it a ruse to get me up here?

Numbness is my background state. It's how I function. Feelings are like a swarm of bees threatening an attack. There's so much emotion here. So much expectation of me. I can't deal with it. Kids, family. We never had it. Well, we did. Our own fucked-up version – Lizzie and me against Mum, against the world. No one saw the daily terror we lived in, no one bothered, or if they did they didn't want to take it on. Lizzie was my mum. My real mum.

Since she's had real kids, it's not the same.

Chapter 6

I'm high as a spy
Are you who you say you are?
Who should I be?
Best be what you see in me
To protect your projection
I can be your self-deception

Bollocks. Way too heady. I put away my notebook as a blue BMW pulls up outside St John's Wood station. Stella unfolds from the passenger door on to the kerb and bends back down to say goodbye to her dad. The car pulls away. She's wearing a super-cool black woollen coat and black beanie. Straps from a small knapsack partition her chest. She's home for Hanukkah. Hasn't told her parents she's seeing an addict has-been rock star. I wonder why.

She catches my eye, gives me the tiniest of nods, then walks away from the car into the station. I watch the car pull away driven by a stocky well-dressed man in his fifties.

Stella is standing in the entrance of the station. Her gaze follows her dad. She crosses the road and walks towards me. She's looking down at her feet with a smile that tells me she knows I'm watching.

Moment of truth. It's the first time I've seen her since she fucked the surfer. *Is this real or one of love's apparitions?*

70

We hug but she holds back her hips and offers me her cheek. Damn, despite our frequent FaceTiming this is far from a done deal.

'Hi.' I lift up her collar against the cold. 'Nice coat.'

'Isn't it! Got given it after the shoot. Vivienne Westwood!' She gives me a twirl and it fans out at the waist like a dervish's robe.

'The surfing shoot?' I ask.

'No!' She slaps me on the chest. 'Is that going to be a thing?'

It's already been relegated to a 'thing'!

Embers of hurt suggest it might.

'Listen.' She steps in closer, grabbing my lapel. 'You're a rock star, who, if Google is to be believed, has slept with many, many beautiful women, in many permutations. You're going to have to get over this one. I'm a relative virgin. It took me sleeping with him to get how much . . . how much I like you.' Her eyes twinkle with pixie mischief. 'So maybe you should be thanking him, rather than sulking about it.'

'Wow! Not quite the apology I was expecting.'

'I've got nothing to apologise for. We were not dating. We still aren't – we're checking it out.'

'You've got balls.'

'No. A vag. Much more powerful than balls.'

She steps back. Whips off her beanie.

'Da-daah!'

Her hair's dyed white, shaved off round the sides. She fluffs her mini Mohawk into place. I'm shocked. Her face is so exposed. Not sure I like it.

'Wow!' I say. 'Wow. Who are you? That's fantastic.'

'You don't like it.'

'No, I do, I do. It's wild. It's rad.'

She looks sceptical.

'Eh. It was time for a makeover. David Mallett was on the shoot and he gave me this. I fuckin' love it. Feels like freedom. I feel like a new me.'

'You look like one.'

She laughs and puts the beanie back on. 'I can read you like a book, motherfucker. Not feminine enough for you?' she says.

Busted.

'Give me a moment, will you? I was just getting to know the first Stella.'

'Mm. OK.' She threads her arm through mine. 'Now, where are we going to eat?'

I take her to my favourite dim sum. Badly lit, unpretentious, family style.

'Mum and Dad think I'm staying with my best friend, Peter.' She punctuates her words with chopsticks. 'Peter's a girl. Just in case . . . I haven't told them about you . . . and I'm not going to until I see how it pans out. No need to put them through hell,' she says, stabbing a dumpling. She gulps it down without chewing.

'Hell? Really?'

'Really. You don't know my parents.' She chews and talks at the same time, then washes it down with a glug of Merlot. 'You don't know my brother!' She's a skinny thing but she wolfs her food down.

'Are you going to eat all that?' she says, pointing at my spring rolls with a chopstick. I *hate* sharing my food, but it's our first date.

'My brother would have a heart attack if he knew I was seeing you. A rock singer! And a goy!' She laughs with glee, her face expressing the enormity of his potential reaction. 'He *freaked* at my haircut. Hair's a big deal to Jews.'

'Are you sure you're not Amish?' She grabs one my spring rolls, even though her own plate is half full.

'Oi! Enough of my food.'

'Sorry.' She replaces a stub of a roll on my plate.

'Your parents are religious?' I ask.

'God no! They hardly ever go to synagogue. Only on high holidays. My brother is. Very orthodox, and he has a . . . an undue influence on our family.' She raises her glass in a toast. 'To bad Jews!' she says, a little too loudly for the table next to us. 'You don't know *any* Jews, do you?'

'Course I do.' I've no idea if that's true.

'Do you like my hair yet?' She turns it sideways.

'It's growing on me. Brings out your—'

'Inner lesbian.' She laughs. 'More women have hit on me in the last three days . . .' She runs her fingers through her hair. 'With my lack of tits I look pretty androgynous.'

'You don't lack tits.'

73

'Compared to your Google girls . . .'

'Fuck . . .'

'And compared to all the beautiful girls I get to work with on set.' She shakes her head. 'Do you prefer tits or bums?'

'In a shop window? Hanging on a . . . butcher's hook?'

'Come on, tits or bums?'

'Eyes!' *Damn, she's challenging.* 'Cock or balls?' I say.

She snorts wine over her food. She's drinking a lot, it's bumming me out.

'Do you think anyone – anyone – *really* finds balls attractive? They are the *weirdest*-looking things. You men slag off women for the minutest imperfection but do we bring up balls? Hmm.' She takes another slug.

'Please don't drink any more. I want to sleep with you sober,' I say.

'Too late for that.' She gives a guilty laugh. 'The daft thing is I hardly ever drink. I feel completely pissed on two glasses.'

There's a pause as she considers whether to carry on.

'I haven't slept with many people. So I was drinking to . . .' She looks down.

'I mean, I've had good sex,' she says, 'just . . . not really. Didn't get many opportunities when I lived in London. My family vetted all applicants.'

I take a sip of water.

'I want to sleep with you tonight and I want you to remember it in the morning. I've been into you from the moment I met you. Don't know why, could have been that Dennis the menace sweater – or how you took down Stanley – or your farts. I love your honesty, rudeness . . . inner lesbian, I don't give a fuck. And I want the experience to be real . . .'

Colour rises to her cheeks.

Got a bit carried away there. Have I blown it?

She looks down at her empty plate and my full one, and says, 'Better eat up, then.'

I close the door to my flat, turn round, and she kisses me.

It's all in the kiss, isn't it? It's the moment you know, after all those calls, texts, dreams, it's the moment you know if it's going to be all right, if there's going to be a physical connection. There's so much invested in that first kiss.

We're hardly moving, hardly breathing, yet there's so much going on in the sensation of the kiss. Don't know how long it goes on for.

Time kicks back in. We come up for air.

I grab her hand and pull her through the living room into my bedroom. I undo her jacket and slide my hand inside beneath her shirt to feel the warmth of her skin. Her lower back. She bites my lip. She pulls back and starts to undo my sheepskin. She struggles with the bulbous buttons.

'Oh, fuck it.' She stands back and laughs. 'You do it, I need to go pee.'

I point to the bathroom. She rushes in and shuts the door.

'Don't listen!' she shouts through the door.

I feel goofy, then my mind kicks into action. I throw our clothes on the chair, go to the thermostat and turn up the heat. I pull my jumper over my head and get tangled up. *Where are the condoms? Shit, shit. They're in the bathroom.* I remake the bed, pulling the sheet tightly over the corners, lifting and floating the duvet down into a neater position. I draw the curtains and turn on a bedside light. It's too harsh. I turn it off. I turn on the table light in the living room, then open the bedroom door a crack until I get the right amount of light spilling in. I hear the toilet flushing, the tap running, and Stella emerges from the bathroom at a run. She knocks me off my feet and we both fall backwards on to the bed.

My mind's chatter dissolves in her mouth.

All the world's a kiss.

Stella's asleep in the foetal position half-covered by the duvet. She's bellow breathing, face flattened on the pillow, her breasts framed by the covers. Slats of sunlight inch across her body. A beautiful girl boy.

I can have this amount of pleasure sober?

Her hunger for me, for my body. *She owned me!*

I had to slow her down or it would've been over before it

began. I pinned her wrists above her head, pulled out and teased her, the tip of me rubbing, nudging, shallow thrusts followed by deep ones. I pulled out again near a peak and went down on her – building her charge, controlling mine. At one point we hit some crazy rhythmic breathing – sounded like we were in a boat race – we cracked up laughing and had to start all over again.

There was no performance. Which for a singer . . .

It felt like my hands, my lips, my body *knew* her, knew where to go.

Inside her felt like home.

When the time came . . . when the came time, her body arched and shook around me . . . the sounds she made took me over the edge.

'I've dribbled all over the pillow.' She sits up and wipes her mouth.

'That's nothing; you fart even more in your sleep.' She looks horrified. 'Cleared the room.'

She punches me on the arm, then pulls my body into hers. She smells of cardamom and sweet corn. There's a fire between her legs.

'Really, really?'

'We've only just begun,' she says, rolling on top of me and holding my wrists down.

The smell of fry-up pervades my flat.

'Shit! You don't eat bacon!'

'Wrong Jew,' she says, without looking up from the massive book of Schiele paintings opened up on the glass table. 'You know half of these paintings would be banned today and Schiele locked up. I don't know what to think about them. They're brilliant and . . .'

'He *was* locked up. His crimes absolved by time and genius.' I turn over a rasher with metal tongs. She gives me a look. 'I didn't make the rules, just stating it as fact.' I shrug. 'Most artists are arseholes – doesn't change the art.'

She turns back to her book. 'So sexy and yet so wrong!'

'That's sex for you. Sex and morality – good luck with that one.'

'Said the rock star.'

'I haven't had sex for at least a year – unlike some.' The toast pops up. 'Could you butter that?'

Her chair scrapes back on the floor. She comes over and gets busy. She's wearing my baby-blue T-shirt that reaches her thighs.

I haven't cooked for anyone in ages.

This flat hasn't seen any social activity in ages. I look at the white walls, the bare wood floors, the 52-inch screen. The place is Scandinavian bleak, beige. A fake Zen emptiness masquerading as style.

'Where have you gone?' Stella studies me.

'I'm wondering what you make of this place?'

She looks around. Wish I hadn't drawn her attention to it.

'Very male. Neutral. Playing it safe. Doesn't give anything away. Don't really see *you* in here . . .'

'Me neither. Will you help me add some colour?'

She smiles. 'Sure. My speciality. Lots of potential. Do you own it?'

'So long as I can pay the mortgage.'

'Haven't I just fucked a rich rock star?'

I laugh.

The money that went up my nose, the cost of rehabs.

I crack another egg, it sizzles and spits, the yolk edging out into the bacon. I use a teaspoon to ladle hot fat on to the egg yolks so they develop a whitish glaze, but my peripheral attention is with her, sensing her, this warm beautiful alive creature in my kitchen.

I jump at an unfamiliar ringtone.

'Mine.' She walks across the open space out of the kitchen into the living room. I catch flashes of her white cotton knickers as the shirt hikes up.

I'm overcooking the eggs. I flip them on to toast.

'It's Dad.' Stella calls from the other room. 'I won't pick up.'

I bring the plated food to the table where she sits, attention on her phone. The phone pings.

'He's left a message. Do you want to hear what my dad sounds like?'

I nod yes, but I don't. I don't want *that* reality in here, here in our magic bubble. Her scent, her warmth, her juices all over me. I haven't felt this . . .

I haven't felt this good for so long.

I hear Lou Reed's 'Perfect Day' playing in my head.

She plays the message back on speakerphone.

'Stella,' growls a deep voice with the hint of a lisp. 'We know you're not with Peter. In fact, we know you're with this rock singer, this . . . Seth Brakes.' He says it like he's reading my name. Stella freezes. She looks at me.

'Your mother and I are very disappointed,' he says. '*Very* disappointed.'

'And me!' Another male voice in the background.

'And Aaron. We are all very disappointed in you, to lie to us like this. I want you to come home now. Right now.' The light in Stella's eyes has dimmed. A film of bacon fat reflects rainbows of grease that swell across her plate. I watch a tear drop from Stella's eye, roll down the side of her nose and land on egg yolk. The line goes dead.

'I don't get it,' I say.

She's showered and ready to go. She's pulled away from me.

'I have to go home,' she says.

'Why?'

'You heard them.' She checks herself in the bathroom mirror, applying concealer under her eyes.

'*Tradition*,' she sings.

'But you're twenty-six,' I say. 'You live in Paris. You have a queer haircut!'

She gives a cynical laugh.

'Your parents disapprove . . . So you just go?' I sigh. 'I mean, I don't get that.'

She gives me a sympathetic look and touches my hand.

'No, you don't, love. It's called family,' she says.

No line of argument there. I'm looking for the right words to keep her here. The magic of the last twelve hours has gone, evaporated. Just like that.

'Do they really have a say in who you date?'

'That's not how I would put it,' she says. 'Don't worry, I'll be back.'

'How would you put it?'

'Do you have any Q-tips?'

'In the drawer.'

She opens it, looks down and freezes. Her head drops with a sigh. The draw is *full* of condoms. A mountain of pink ones, blue ones, thick ones, thin ones, ribbed ones, strawberry ones, all shapes and sizes. She reaches down with finger and thumb and plucks a Q-tip daintily from the box at the front.

'Well, at least I needn't worry about an STD.' She turns back to the mirror and uses the Q-tip to apply the concealer.

'Hang on. What? Yes, I have condoms,' I say.

She reaches a hand into the drawer and picks up a fistful, lets them drop.

'You don't just *have* condoms. You bought the fucking factory.'

'I won them!'

'You what?'

'It's a long story.' *And not for now.* 'Stella, don't do this. Yes, I have condoms, but I haven't used them in ages. Don't you have condoms?'

She laughs.

'No.'

'What about the Jewish surfer?'

She gives me a full-on Medusa stare.

'No, but I mean you can't go crazy at me for owning condoms when you clearly . . . you clearly . . .' I try to catch my foot before it disappears into my mouth. 'You know.' She lets me run out of steam then stuffs her make-up into her purse.

'What was I thinking? A fucking rock star. I'm an idiot, of course.' She tries to push past me. I take her by the arm.

'Please!' I say. She just looks down at where I'm holding her by the elbow, then looks back up at me. Her eyes are steely. I let go of her. She pushes past me out of the bathroom. I follow behind. She puts her coat on, picks up her bag and heads to the door.

'Stella, please. Don't leave like this. We just had the most amazing night! Amazing. The condoms were given to me . . . It's in the past . . . I can explain this . . .' I can. These condoms were an award from *Loaded* magazine in the year of my crash, for racking up three kiss-and-tells in one year.

'Oh, this should be fun.' She drops the bag, folds her arms and waits.

The *Loaded* explanation sounds better in my head than it will in daylight. I try to think of ways to make it palatable. Nope. My past's caught up with me. *I deserve this. I don't deserve her, she's too good for me. I'll never hold a woman like this. Once she gets to know me it'll all be over anyway.* I wilt but try one last reach.

'This is really important to me. You are really important to me. I've never met anyone like you before. Please. Please?'

She must feel like an idiot to have opened to me, a loser, an addict. She can't trust me. She bends down to pick up her bag, gives me a sad, sad smile, and leaves.

Chapter 7

Clack boom.
Clack clack boom.
Clack boom. Clack clack boom.

I'm slouched behind the drum kit hitting rim shots and a kick drum. I'm first to our rehearsal rooms at the Vaults, waiting for the rest of the band.

I've got no fucking songs
I've got no fucking songs.
Clack boom.
Clack clack boom.
Clack boom. Clack clack boom.

I smash the sticks down hard, a tip flies off.

No word from Stella for four days, despite increasingly desperate begging texts and voicemails from me. No songs, and a band turning up to rehearse songs in ten minutes.

I'm a fake who's gonna break

Lee catches the tail of that as he barges through the sound-proofed doors, a guitar case in each hand.

'Wotcha, fucker. New song?' He takes me in. Little sleep, a train wreck. He spots his amps all set up and strides over to them, stripping off his chunky coat. 'Elves not here, then?'

'Crew's getting lunch.' I get up from the kit and replace the broken stick with a fresh one from the sheath.

'Cuppa tea?' he asks.

'Sure.'

He goes to the kitchen area and fills the kettle.

'She's not got back to you?'

'No.'

'Ah, mate, I'm sorry.' He turns. 'We've been there before.'

'No we haven't. This is different.' I go to one of the double-glazed windows, slide open the first layer and try to lift the second. It's been painted shut. 'Fuck.'

'What's different?' he says.

'I'm in love with her.'

He winces. 'Ah mate, you're not, one night—'

'I was in love with her the minute I saw her.'

'Aw mate, come on.'

'I'm not a romantic! Have I ever said that before?'

I join him in the kitchen area, find a small serrated knife, take it back to the window and dig around the painted-over frame.

'No, you haven't. But it's too quick, mate. It doesn't happen like that.'

'No, it doesn't happen like that,' I turn to him, *until it does happen like that.*'

'Gotta let go of her, mate. If she's meant for you she'll—'

'Don't!' I slam the knife down on the sill. 'Don't. That's a bigger cliché than love at first sight.' I turn back to work on the window. Four floors down teenagers are playing in a concrete playground surrounded by a fifteen-foot-high chain-link fence.

'Seth, that's the addict in you.' He comes over to watch my efforts. 'Booze, drugs, sex – you always want what you cannot have. Like right now, you're desperate for fresh air. These windows don't open. Most people would give up – you can't. You can't have her, so now you're in love with her.'

'I was before she left.' I keep my back to him. I'm welling up. 'She made me feel alive again . . .'

'Like the booze.'

'Fuck off. So you're saying anything that makes me feel more than flatlined . . .'

His phone pings, he reads the text. 'Can't anyone in this band read emails?' He pecks at his phone. 'They can't find their way through the complex.'

I try lifting the window. 'Fuck!'

'Listen, they'll be here soon. How many songs you got?'

I need air. I move to another window. It's worse, I can only slide the inner pane a crack, can't even get at the window proper.

I turn around. 'None.'

It sinks in – but I think he expected it.

'We've got to open the songwriting to the band.'

'No!'

'Got no choice, mate. Got any other ideas?'

'The two of us,' I say. 'Writing together.'

'We're a group . . . six years. It's fairer.'

'It'll be chaos.'

'They're all skint. They've got kids! You've got all the royalties! Record company's got all the album sales. Come on, man, it's not all about you.'

I'm stung.

'Stanley having input!! Come on. We'd last a week. At best.' That point lands.

He softens. 'Step back into the band, Seth. It's always been a bottleneck with you doing the songwriting. The decisions, the interviews. It's too much pressure and I don't want to watch you crash again.'

'I'm in the programme. I'm OK.'

'You're in the programme and you're not OK.'

I turn back to the window. Caught in-between the layers of glass is a fat bluebottle zigzagging frantically up and down the pane looking for a way out. It hasn't spotted that I've opened up a crack. It's looking at the outside. Up and down it weaves. I can hear its faint pneumatic drone as it goes crazy with frustration and fear.

'You'll write the lyrics still. It won't be equal splits.'

The fly can see freedom, smell it, but can't reach it. See a world that looks so inviting. See a world where it can fly. Fly, for fuck's sake, open up those wings and feel the buzz, feel alive.

Imagine that rush! And yet here it is. Stuck here. Banging its head over and over on the glass. I tap the glass. *Look down, motherfucker.*

'Seth, I'm not going to watch my best friend crash and burn again.'

Below the fly, on the sill, looking like remnants from a tank battle, is an insect graveyard. Upended husks in varying degrees of decay. Beetles on their backs that never made it to their feet, daddy-long-legs limbs strewn like hair, dull grey carcasses of wild invention, decaying back to dust.

'Actually, forget that,' says Lee.

I turn to him, confused.

'I don't want to watch my *seventh* best friend crash and burn.'

'You fucker.' I laugh. 'Seventh? You mean I dropped below Matt! Cunt.'

The soundproofed door slams open and Stanley enters, laden with guitar and amp, followed closely by Kareem. Cream!

'I'm going to try it out,' Stanley says. 'Might be shit.' He sees us and forces a smile.

'Evening, gentlemen,' he says. His nose twitches at the tension in the room. 'All good?'

'All good,' says Lee.

The rehearsal was a washout. I told them I had a sore throat and so we'd just focus on the music without singing. I bluffed a few old chord patterns that had come to nothing three years earlier. They came to nothing. The band tried to chug along but it sounded old and tired. They looked to me to lead, I couldn't. I hope they chalk it up to flakiness. Bet Stanley thinks I'm using again. Lee sulked but didn't say anything.

I left early, citing man-flu symptoms.

Dear Stella,

I'm writing this because you aren't answering my calls. Where have you gone? Please talk to me.

The condom thing's ridiculous. They were actually a gift from a men's mag after they ran some kiss-and-tells on me two years ago, at the height of my decline. They delivered a bulk order of condoms to my apartment as a cynical follow-up.

I realise this story might not exactly help my position, but better you know than imagine something worse.

Sorry, I'm a singer with a dickhead's past.

I haven't met anyone like you. I haven't felt this way, I don't think ever. And I think you were feeling something similar.

Look, I don't want to use the word 'love'. My mother used it every day, especially after she'd beaten us. So it's not a word I use. But I think that's what this is. And if it is, please don't walk away from it, because it's so rare and precious and it might not happen again. I'm 34, I've never felt this before.

Stella, please call me.

I don't know what to say about your dad's call. It's 2012, you're twenty-six years old. I don't understand that someone so independent can be affected like that. I'm sorry if I'm insensitive to it, it's just so far outside my experience that I don't get it.

All I know is that I feel awful, lost without you.

Seth

Chapter 8

Ella Bhagati keeps making these high-pitched whimpers. I can tell she's holding back. It's hard to fuck in an apartment when you know people might hear you. Dev Bhagati's not holding back, sounds like a water buffalo. His grunts are on the offbeat to the thud of the bedhead hitting the wall.

I prowl around my apartment. Streetlights hit the white bars on the window, casting shadow on the walls. I wish there was an email recall button. I've got another rehearsal tomorrow and nothing to take in; but I'm way too upset to write.

I wonder if the other neighbours are entranced. I imagine them frozen in their boxy rooms, ears pricked, turned on and jealous. I doubt it; I have a singer's hearing. They won't hear it over the noise of the telly, the computer, their headphones.

Ella's moans walk the line between pleasure and pain. It's like she can't let go of something, some grief that's holding her back.

They must be close to a climax by now. It's been at least thirty minutes. I read the average man comes after five minutes, the average woman twenty. That's fucked up.

Maybe he knows some Indian tantra techniques? Is that a racist assumption?

Oh my God.

Ella's second orgasm, I think it's her second, goes on a looong time. They're locked in now, digging deeper, faster. I'm turned on. They're a sweet couple, late twenties, very straight, shy, married two years. He's a banker. She's a teacher.

Jesus, it just keeps going.

I'm transfixed.

The doorbell rings. I jump like a frog.

I can't open the door with a hard-on.

'Just a minute,' I shout. 'In the bathroom.'

I run to the bathroom. Is it Stella? I splash some water on my face; that's not going to put the fire out. The buzzer rings again.

'Hang on!'

Stella, it's got to be Stella. My hard-on melts enough for me to adjust the angle downwards. God, I feel like a perv. I am a perv. I open the door.

It's Lee. His trench coat drips rain on to the floor.

We stare at each other.

'This a bad time?'

'No.'

'Come in?' he cues me.

'Yeah . . . Sorry.'

He peels off his coat to produce a bunch of orange tulips that were sheltering inside. He presents them with a magician's flourish.

'I never knew you cared. How sweet.'

He tosses them into the air. I catch. He saunters into the living room. After a few steps, he stops and raises a finger to the ceiling, ear cocked to one side like a pointer spying a partridge. Together, we listen to the Bhagatis.

Ba-boom, ba-boom, ba-boom, ba-boomba.

After twenty seconds, Lee pulls an impressed face.

'Hmmm,' he says. 'Beats Sky.'

Ba-boom, ba-boom.

'How long?'

'Half an hour,' I say.

'Fuck,' he says. 'Bastard.'

'I know!'

I take the flowers to the kitchen and improvise a vase from a plastic water bottle.

'Tea?' I ask.

'Well, I'm not expecting a Martini.'

The engine of the kettle temporarily competes with the Bhagatis. It stops and they seem to go up another gear.

Ba-boom ba ba, ba-boom, ba-boom ba ba, ba-boom.

Does this happen every night?' Lee walks over to the epicentre and looks up, searching for a portal.

'*No*, thank God!' I say. 'Stop drooling.'

'Can we take notes?' he says in a tiny voice.

I bring in the tea and we sit in the open-plan living room, he on my white sofa, me opposite on a chair.

After another minute of *ba-booms*, he stands up.

'Let's put some music on, shall we?'

'Absolutely.'

I get up and stream Sufjan Stevens at low volume.

'Well, you know why I'm here.' He blows on his tea. 'You don't want another day like that, do you?' he says.

'Can you and I try first?'

He looks beyond me, foot jiggling with thought, wondering if it's worth going back to the impasse of trying to get me to write with the whole band.

'OK.' He sighs. 'Sure.'

'You play guitar, I'll just sing.' I turn off the music. 'Maybe I'll get a better vocal pattern if I'm not worrying about playing along with you.'

I go get my acoustic from the other room.

'Now let's be clear,' I say, 'you're not getting fifty per cent for a bunch of chords.'

He shakes his head and starts to play. I turn on the recorder app on my iPhone and place it on the glass table between us.

He starts with C, E major and G minor over and over again. *Boring*. I wait till I hear a melody. I mutter/sing it under my breath, till it's clearer.

Fa-yum a hey sha-moya, heyy-ya, here in this place, you gonna wooo-ba dis place . . .

Not a good read – you had to be there.

Feels awkward stumbling around with Lee. Easier on my own.

Fuck it, we're desperate. Just go for it.

An off-kilter melody starts to evolve from the first banal one.

I use half-words and phonetic noises when no words come. We go round and round the same pattern while I reach for lyrics and phrasing.

> *It's my birthday*
> *It's the worst day*
> *I don't remember*
> *Nor will you*

Where did that come from? I can't bring it into focus. A few snippets make sense among the nonsense. I can weed them out later when I listen back with my editing hat.

> *Raising a smile takes a crew.*

Some songs take a while to work out. One song took a year to get all the parts together and present to the band. But the best songs come quickly. Feel like downloads. Downloads from the unconscious. That's the magic we're looking for. Not done this with anyone else before. The uncertainty, combined with a trust in each other, brings out a vulnerable edge in my voice.

> *I'm the same age as my father*
> *When my father disappeared*

That hurt.

Was it any good?

And what's it to do with the birthday bit? The words pass by too quickly to judge, but I think I could use that.

Lee's fingers shift to a new chord.

'No,' he mutters. He tries another, then shifts back to the original to see how it flows.

'Too Oasis.' He winces, hunched over the guitar, black fringe half-mooning his face, chin near resting on the body.

He tries another, smiles, finds a second and third to go with it, ending on a mournful note, offsetting the chords that came before. He weaves around them till I join in – not on the first chord of the progression – where you'd expect it if I was accompanying myself – it's hard to sing a different pattern to what my hands are playing – but I land on the second chord, putting me nicely out of alignment with the chord sequence. I surf his progression.

We rise entwined a figure eight
Our past as future realigned.

Prog rock lyric! Can't see myself using that, but the relationship between my melody and Lee's chords works. It's hypnotic. We loop round the two patterns in variations, sucked in to the rush of it, building and building, turned on by the dance, the weave.

He plays a new chord midway through my pattern. It should have thrown me, but I instantly adjust with a strange note that leads to another. I feel him shift to accommodate me and this beautiful, truly original melody comes out of nowhere, out of the space between us, an accident, plaintive and desperate, a baroque pattern we'd never consciously choose, soaring higher and higher. My voice is close to breaking, a beautiful strain that swells with emotion. I'm speaking in tongues again, but I hear potential words in there.

Lee digs in with the rhythm behind the chords to give me the platform to fly. We ride and rise together by instinct, no time to think, to judge.

Then Lee hits a dissonant chord that undercuts my pattern and takes the floor from beneath my feet. It seems like he's breaking the connection, but then he re-emerges with the next chord, sounding even more beautiful in contrast to the dissonance. Every two cycles of the pattern, he sticks that fucker in, brings us crashing down to earth, only to lift us higher and higher. Coherent words are coming through. I don't judge them.

> *You've got to do it on your own*
> *you're not alone.*

It's a chorus! my songwriting brain shouts. I thought we had one earlier, but this is it.

> *You've got to do it on your own*
> *But you're not alone.*

I can hear how this will sound with the band playing behind us. I think we both can. We race on breathless, terrified of stopping and losing our way.

> *You've got to do it on your own*
> *But you're never alone.*
> *When two stand together*
> *We can face the big whatever.*
> *Never alone.*

The door buzzer rings. Lee and I jump like we've been caught fucking. We get the thought at the same time, and belly-laugh.

It rings again, more insistent. *The neighbours?* I go open it.

It's Stella.

She lunges to embrace me and holds me, sobbing. Soaked from the rain, she's covered up from head to toe in a coat, scarf, hat and sunglasses. I hold her tight. She's *really* sobbing.

'Hey, it's OK, it's OK.'

Didn't think my email was that good.

I shut the door, take off her hat, and move to unwind her scarf, but she holds up her hands, backs off.

'You have to promise to keep calm,' she says.

'What?'

'Calm,' she repeats. 'You can't do anything crazy.' Fear adrenalizes me.

'You're getting me worried now. What's going on?'

'Promise. You have to promise.'

'OK.' My mind's racing.

She takes off her glasses, puts them in her pocket. Her left eye has bloomed into a purple and yellow flower, whose angry petals curl around the socket. Her eyeball is bloodshot with lightning capillaries defined against white. I take a step back. It's grotesque and beautiful. I don't understand what's happened.

And then I do.

Tears come to my eyes. Tears of anger. There's a ringing in my ears.

'Who did this?'

'You promised.'

'Who – the fuck – did this?'

A cold fury comes over me.

'You promised.'

Where do they live? I clear my throat, squeeze my hands together, close and open fists. Stella's watching me, waiting. *I have to hold this for her.* I take some long deep breaths.

one two three four

And let the third one out slowly. I settle then step back into her and hold her. She softens into me.

'Are you OK?' I say.

She nods.

'Are you hurt anywhere else?' I ask.

She pulls away from me and unwraps her scarf. On her throat are angry red fingerprints, clearly outlined, like the leaf prints on Holly's wall.

one two three four

'Is that it?' I say.

She nods again. I hear a noise behind me, shock shows in her eyes.

'Lee's here,' I say.

She wipes away tears. Replaces her glasses and scarf.

I call over my shoulder. 'Lee.'

'Hi, Stella,' he comes forward and I swear he nearly offers to shake her hand. 'Nice to . . . You OK?'

She nods.

'Come, come on in,' I say to her.

I guide her into the living room.

'She's had a rough time,' I say to Lee. 'Put the kettle on, will you, mate?'

I wrap her up in a blanket on the sofa. Lee brings tea.

'Anyway,' he clears his throat, 'I think I should be . . .'

'Yeah, absolutely. See you tomorrow.'

He leaves.

'Can I take a look?' I reach to unwind her scarf.

'No, please. Can we just sit here?'

My mind's whirling.

I want to go round now with a baseball bat.

And another voice says, *She's mine now.*

And yet another, buried under the jubilation, freaks out at the responsibility. My ears are still ringing. It's not tinnitus. It's alive and potent, an alarm bell. She puts her hand on top of mine. It stills me and we drop down into the quiet of our sadness, listening to the sounds of the night in the dark room.

Later she says, 'My brother lost it, went crazy.' Her body goes tight at the memory. 'Even my parents were shocked. My father pulled him off . . . they were shouting and screaming . . .' She trails off, wiping her nose on the back of her hand.

'They'd grounded me and taken my phone. Aaron had hacked into my Gmail before, that's how they knew your name.'

Family violence, I'm used to. Grounding and hacking some-one's phone, not so much. This is some controlling shit.

'He caught me trying to text you. He attacked me . . . thank God my father was there.' My anger swells into a wave. I shudder it off. This could have been worse.

'They didn't stop me leaving after that,' she says. 'They were ashamed.'

I make a mental note to move the baseball bat from my closet to the front door.

Chapter 9

Don't tell me it's my birthday
Another birthday
Another cake, another life review.

Where are these words coming from?

Lee's leading the band through the song we wrote last night, using my iPhone recording as a reference. My mind's with Stella at my place. She insisted I come in, and with our schedule I have no choice. Her response to my sixth text of the day read,

I'm OK motherfucker. Stop bothering me. Get on with your work.

The band drift into the new song, adding layers, creating their own parts, and the song evolves.

Lee gives Olly an instruction to try a funkier, more rhythmic groove.

'No cymbals,' he says.

I think Olly's going to tell him to fuck off but instead he tries it. It snaps into Cream's bass line and the whole song shifts subtly as if a lock has been turned. It's a good moment. Everyone's spirit lifts.

The song keeps spiralling upwards in search of something else, some escape. As usual I can't hear a note Dan is playing. He's as shy a musician as he is in person. His birdlike features are intently focused on his computer screen, where he switches and modulates sounds, while his right hand plays whatever the fuck he's playing. I never worry about him as he's never played a note I haven't loved, but at some point curiosity gets the better of me.

'I'm turning you up, Dan,' I shout. He says nothing.

I turn him up and there it is – the transcendence the song is looking for, a spiralling Middle Eastern keyboard line that weaves in and out of the chorus. Sealing the deal.

You've got to do it on your own
But you're never alone.
When two stand together
We can face the big whatever.
Never alone.

And I'm not, not alone. The whole band is here making a piece of magic that is of us – yet separate from us. Are we playing it or riding something that pre-exists? It's glorious. We all feel it. Lee's shaking his head and laughing. Cream's beaming. We're on a communal high.

In a break Cream and I sit alone on the well-worn sofa.

'That must have taken balls, coming out to your family,' I say.

'Balls, coming out . . . that's next bro.'

'Holy fuck.' I redden.

She laughs. 'If we make enough money . . .'

'How did you . . . get here?' I ask.

She sits back, looking for a place to start.

'You sparked some of it.'

'*What*?'

'Your wildness. Not giving a fuck what others think. Selfishness.' She laughs as she gets out paper and tobacco. 'I knew this was in me, hadn't felt right for a long time. Used to wear my sisters' dresses as a kid, you know, the girls would make me up, put on fashion shows, when my parents were out . . . and then, then my dad found out, and threw me to the mullahs. "Rigorous Islamic instruction will make a man of you." It did that. Ugh.' She shudders. 'That and their extracurricular touch-ups really fucked me up.' She rolls a ciggy like a pro, another new habit.

'I hated you, you know,' she laughs.

'I know.'

'Well, you were doing things – things I didn't dare. You were so . . . out there, while I was so . . . hidden.'

'Can I have one?'

She hands me her rolly and starts on another.

'Your family?'

'Uncle Ali talks about an honour killing.'

'Fuck! Is that . . .? Could he do that?'

'Don't know. Anything's possible with my family.'

Anything's possible with family. Could Aaron do that?

'I walked away from everything.' Her voice thins. 'That's been the hardest thing, really . . .'

We sit and listen to the rain.

'Your faith? Do you still believe?' I ask.

'Nah. I mean, I'm sure Muhammad, Jesus, Buddha, all of 'em, were amazing men, but once they died the magic died with 'em and . . . I think they'd be horrified if they could see what the little men have done in their name. The blood spilt . . . carnage, over differing ideas about the nature of some God that no one really knows anything about.' She finishes rolling and lights us both up, looks me in the eye.

'I'm sorry.'

'What for?'

'Judging you so hard and being a righteous arse.'

'Fuck me, I was a cunt. I'm sorry.'

We take a drag and exhale together.

Later that afternoon Brunt rolls up.

'I was in the neighbourhood, lads, thought I'd 'ave a listen,' he lies.

We play it through for him. He shifts awkwardly from foot to foot. I can't read him, he seems pent up. Does he like it? At the end of the song, he bursts into applause.

'Fucking brilliant, I knew you guys would do it. Well done lads, good work, really strong. How many of those you got?'

'Five or six,' Lee mumbles, pretending to be busy with his foot pedals.

'Wonderful, that's,' Brunt speaks over his clapping, 'I mean,

It's my birthday

It's the worst day

it's not exactly a bestselling happy birthday song but . . . work in progress. We're going to book some more rehearsal time for you to get them together.' He turns to me. 'Well done, Seth.'

'I'm . . . I'm writing with Lee now,' I say.

'Well, great – it's working.' I feel his scrutiny. He knows I've resisted this. 'As it's all set up, we'll keep this room on for the week – so you can work on the other songs.'

'What? No!'

'Let's regroup; do it next week,' Lee backs me up.

'No, that's crazy,' says Brunt. 'You're all set up. Everyone's free. To regroup would cost us—'

'We need a bit more time,' I say. 'They're not as ready as this one.'

He folds his arms.

'Well you'd better get them ready. We need these *now*. I have to have something to show by next week.'

'You *what*?' I say.

'OK.' He clears his throat. 'Listen up. They had a cull of acts at Universe last week and we were on the list. I persuaded Geoff, as a personal favour, for a stay of execution, until he hears these demos.' He takes in our shock.

'I thought we were a tax write off,' I say.

'Yeah, well, it's hard times for record companies. But look, it's fine. If they're as good as what I just heard,' he claps his hands and smiles, 'it's a no-brainer.'

'You told him about Faith yet?' I ask.

'I hinted something was coming down the pipe. Need to have a song for her first though, before I play that card.'

Back at the apartment Stella's still wearing my black dressing gown.

'Are you OK?'

Foolish question.

'Thanks for the texts.' She takes a jagged breath. 'I've written, I've written them a letter.' She hands me a few handwritten sheets of paper.

Chapter 10

Dear Mum and Dad,

I don't know how to write this letter. I've thrown so many rough drafts away. Angry letters wanting to hurt back, hurt letters, victim letters. I hope this letter is different, but I'm so in shock, I'm unsure of my ground.

You have always shown me such love and support throughout my life, always encouraged me to be free-thinking. You sent me to the Lycée, a school of such mixed culture where many of my best friends were Lebanese. You brought me up in the faith, yet never its most bigoted aspects.

We lost so, so many of our ancestors. To you, they were uncles and aunts and whole families. You never taught me the hate and fear that comes from the murder of families. You never taught me to hate gentiles like Bubba Sadie does. You taught me to judge people by who they are, how kind they are, and how they behave under pressure.

You taught me as a woman to stand up for myself and speak my truth, never to assume that my voice has less import than a man's. And now here I am at twenty-six, making my own decisions based on the movements of my heart. But it goes against your desire, your fear of being judged by the clan, and thousands of years of tradition that you never wholeheartedly embraced.

You say I can't be with a gentile and I hear it as racism. To you, he's just a rock-singer goy with a past of addiction.

Well, this is the man I choose. I have no idea where this will end, it's true. Now you have to make a choice. A choice about whether you condone the actions of Aaron, his violent threats, his fists and his hands around my throat. Who is the Nazi here, and who the Jew? Should my man wear a cross to mark him out as racially unclean?

This story has been repeated time and time again. There can only be one choice if I am to trust myself and my heart. If that means I lose you as my parents – so be it. I love you and I believe you love me, but in becoming the woman you've helped me to become, I may have to let you go. If so, that will be your choice, not mine. I'm staying at Seth's. Digest this letter for a few days and then, if you want to talk to me, my phone will be on.

Your loving daughter,
Stella

I'm choked up, can't talk.

I put down the printout. *She's leaving her family for me!* I'm beginning to get what this means to her. *Jesus.* I'm relieved and terrified. Terrified of fucking up. The responsibility.

'Let me see your eye.' It's like an LA sunset. I kiss her.

'Love you.' It's the first time that I've said those words. I remember what Lee said. Fuck him, he's wrong, I do.

'Love you too,' she says.

We sit in silence, feeling the hum of our bodies.

'I'm really sorry, but Lee's going to have to come over tonight – and maybe each night – to write new songs with me that we can take into the band. I'm sure you'd rather not see anyone . . .'

'It's OK,' she says.

'Our schedule's crazy condensed . . .'

'It's OK.'

'Everything's such a fucking pressure.'

'It's OK!'

When Lee arrives Stella puts on dark glasses and retires to the bedroom to watch a crap romcom.

'Right then,' says Lee. 'Pressure's on.'

I start by setting a cheesy disco beat on an app. I'm hoping its insistent childlike energy will give us something to bounce off.

Within half an hour we have the outline of a possible second song recorded.

'This is fucking nuts! Can't believe how easy it is. I caught some good lyrics in there.'

I was born to shatter
It's no laughing matter
Scatter my thoughts
Scatter my ashes
Teach me to roll when I get battered.

We nail the outlines of two more. Don't think they're as good as the first but we figure the band might elevate them.

Chapter 11

Stella lies on her back naked, looking up at the ceiling. The linen curtains sway behind her. I could look at her all day.

'I want to marry you.' I'm shocked at what I said. It just came out of me. *Never thought of marriage. Ever.*

'What?' She sits upright, looks at me. 'No you don't. That's the sex talking.'

'It wasn't *that* good.'

She punches me.

'Violence runs in your family,' I say, rubbing my shoulder.

'You shouldn't play with things like that.'

'What, saying the sex wasn't great?'

She hits me again.

'I'm beginning to understand why your brother strangled you.'

She pulls a face. 'You shouldn't say things like . . . "I want to marry you".'

'Well, I've never said it before – and I guess,' I laugh, 'that's how I feel.'

She looks at me, waiting for a trap.

'You've never said "I want to marry you" to anyone else?'

I think for a moment.

'Nikki Ramsbottom.'

'Nikki Ramsbottom?'

'Aged six. We were pledged to be married for at least two weeks before I realised I'd made a terrible mistake.'

'Couldn't handle the commitment?'

'She told me – in graphic detail – how she put a toy car up her bottom. That kind of thing . . . you can't unsee . . . as a six-year-old. Traumatising.'

'There's too many "bottoms" in that story for it to be true . . . What kind of car?'

'I don't see how the make of car is relevant to this conversation. I'm beginning to regret sharing with you.' I shift my weight off my elbows. 'Do you . . .? Did that statement . . .?'

'The car or proposal? I'm not taking it seriously. Ask me when we haven't had great sex.'

'Will you marry me?'

She punches me again. I punch her back.

'Ow,' she says, rubbing her arm.

'I'm not your punchbag. This is how it's going to be after we're married isn't it?'

Later she asks, 'Tell me . . . about the time you nearly died?'

'Which one?'

'Oh shit,' she laughs, 'which one! Glad my dad's not here.'

'So am I!'

'Come on, fool, the first time.'

I pull the sheet round me. My open-window policy's a bit nuts when it's this cold.

'I ODed at Pitbull's.'

'And did anything woo-woo happen?'

'Thanks. Reduce my most meaningful experiences to "woo-woo". I lean over and write

ODed at Pitbull's

On my lyric pad by the bed; maybe there's something to mine in there. 'Don't want to fucking tell you now.'

'Oh, don't do that. I was only joking.' She reaches out a hand to my jaw and turns my face to look at her. 'Come back.'

'I guess it was pretty woo-woo.'

She rolls in towards me, wraps a leg around my hip. 'Come on, tell me, tell me, tell me.'

'I had an out-of-body-experience thing. Up on the ceiling, looking down, down on everything. You know.'

'You did! What did you see?' She puts her head on my chest and looks up at me excitedly.

'It was just a hallucination.'

'Come on.' She elbows me in the ribs.

'Well, apart from Pitbull giving me the kiss of life, which was pretty fucking weird . . . everything was alive. Vividly alive. In the lampshade there was . . . a rainbow eraser and a toy soldier and they were glowing with light, stronger than the bulb, glowing from within . . . And I was able to make the lampshade swing! Even though I was out of my body.'

'You were able to make the lampshade swing?'

I nod.

'And in the lampshade was a rainbow rubber and a toy soldier?'

I nod again. She's picturing this.

'So you were looking down and you watched yourself being brought back to life?'

'Yeah . . . but I don't trust that—'

'And you saw those things in the lampshade,' she interrupts.

'Yeah,' I say, mildly irritated.

'Were they there in the morning?' She sees my confusion. 'You checked in the morning to see if they were real?'

'No.'

She gives me a face, then sits up. 'So this is the guy who has difficulty with AA because he doesn't believe in a higher power, yet . . . has these supernatural experiences . . . that people would die for.'

'Very good. *Die for.* See what you did there,' I laugh. 'I don't trust "supernatural experiences". They're not proof of a higher power. They're just . . . things we don't understand yet. "Higher power". What AA means by higher power is God. Fucking God. And I've seen and experienced enough abuse in the name of God not to fall for that one.'

I'm not going to tell her I held my dad's hand through the ceiling.

'Calm down, Seth,' she says, 'I'm not talking about God, or any religion, we all know what you think about religions. I'm just asking why didn't you check the lampshade afterwards? If there was a rubber and a toy soldier in there that would be verifiable . . . of – I don't know what word to use now – a higher power.'

'Higher powers don't bother with rainbow rubbers and toy—'

'The objects aren't the point. You should have checked the lampshade. Your biggest problem is you don't have faith . . .'

'My biggest problem . . .?'

'Well, you know.' She appears to be backing down, then doubles down instead. 'Well, you don't.'

'Whereas you come from a family of *real* fucking faith.'

'Well, I did actually *have* a family . . .'

And suddenly we're off, like a pair of dogs snapping at each other. Our first row. We know we're lashing out yet we can't stop ourselves, grabbing words like crockery in a kitchen fight. It's a relief actually, to let fly like this, a relief.

There's no truce and we try to sleep in this wound-up state, holding our positions, back to back, but it's hopeless, and within an hour we've had make-up sex. The heightened orgasm blasts us into the sleep of the dead.

And on the sixth day God made a miracle. Which in our world means a single. And by a single I mean something that is personal and yet universal. A song that crosses boundaries.

I had set FunkBox at 124 bpm, which any record company exec will tell you approximates the tempo of a human heartbeat. Lee gave me G, E and D on the amped-up semi-acoustic he'd brought home from the studio and I thought, *Not these chords, we'll get fuck-all from this.*

It was effortless.

The song felt so familiar I was convinced I'd heard it before, that we were ripping someone off.

I thought you were past, not future tense.

Then a chorus. A proper chorus:

Don't remember your name
The smell of your scent
The sound when you came
You came and you went.

Lee shifts chords to a halfway house. Later, I'll realise it's the bridge. I get a rap/chant:

It doesn't happen like that
Until it happens like that.
It doesn't happen like that
Until it happens like that.

We go round the same pattern and I get,

That look's as hard as a fence

It stakes my heart.

And on the third pass,

We gamble love will last,
The bookies laugh.

I want to laugh but I'm frightened we'll fall off this song. We have to hang on. I reorder the lines.

We gamble love will last
The bookies laugh.
That look's as hard as a fence
It stakes my heart.

Lee's face is locked in concentration; he opens the chords up into a big release.

I'll do the time
Gods get away with murder
If love's a crime
Ending it is murder.
If love's a crime
Betraying it is murder.
Love's a shrine
Murder. Murder. Murder.

I'm saying the words before I get their meaning. They were there before I got there, waiting to be sung. They have this feeling of rightness and that feeling is everything.

At the end of the song Lee and I sit there breathless, in silence, in awe, humbled.

Chapter 12

The control room of Swan Song studios looks like a Manhattan skyline in miniature. Stacks of early 1970s reverb units, EQs and other jerry-rigged amps and effects totter on top of each other like skyscrapers. They fan out around and alongside the starship *Enterprise* hi-tech mixing desk. Rupert's vintage gear takes up nearly all the space, leaving The Lucky Fuckers to cram on to the ubiquitous leather sofa. We're listening to the first live take of 'She Came and She Went' – our working title for the big song Lee and I are banking on as the single. Well, Universe Records are doing the banking bit. They loved the demos and so here we are making an album. Yeah! But of course, it's not that simple. Brunt dropped in last week to tell us.

'Your genius manager has lined up a short support tour of Germany with The Addickts in two weeks' time. Fuzz dropped out the tour and we are dropping in.'

Two weeks' time! Welcome to my world. Always some last minute extra fucking hurdle. I was going to visit Stell in Paris.

'Not The Addickts, Jon; they've completely ripped us off,' was my response.

'They love you, say nice things about you in the press and our audience crossover's good. It's a forty-five minute set, fourteen gigs. We . . . us, the record company, feel it's the perfect way to ease you back into performing. And . . .' He paused.

'If you're so much better than them, now's your chance to prove it.'

He's right. I can handle a forty-five-minute set and it's just long enough to blow the fucking Addickts off stage but Germany! Germany was the scene of my last disastrous gigs before I crashed. Lot of ghosts in Germany. On the plus side it gives me more time to catch up on lyrics before our second batch of recording.

Rupert reaches forward and rides the faders down on some splashy cymbals in the middle eight.

'Best bit, that,' heckles Oliver.

'I think we should drop the cymbals completely,' says Lee, sitting at the desk next to Rupert, who mutes them.

'We'll have to re-record the drums then. Too much spill.' Rupert wipes his glasses with his handkerchief.

'Fuck off,' says Olly. 'Not again.'

'They take up too much space, mate,' says Lee, swivelling his chair round. Olly, who knows he won't win, mutters, 'Fuck.'

I'm trusting the music to Lee's ears so I can focus on lyrics. Previously my attention would be split over the whole song, micro-managing each instrument, pissing off the band, adding to my isolation. Now I get to hear them bitch about Lee taking that role.

He's particularly good at adding some original musical hiccups where once lived clichés. On 'She Came and She Went', we slow the beat down a tad into the chorus; a trick nicked from Motown.

When the song finishes Rupert calls over to Joe 90, King of

all Nerds, Rupert's engineer, to string some orange cables round the back of the sofa into a vintage tube amp. 'It'll give the guitars more body,' he says.

'OK,' says Lee, 'what's wrong with that song?' He turns to the group.

'Rhythm guitar's not loud enough,' says Stanley.

We groan in unison. Stanley always thinks his guitar's not loud enough.

Rupert spins his chair around to face us.

'I'm not interested in the mix right now. What do you think of the arrangement?' he says in his posh-boy voice.

'The middle eight sounds . . . like a middle eight,' says Lee. 'I'd rather not have one that just sounds like we put it there to give us a break from the rest of it. Are you attached to the lyrics?'

I find them on my new iPad:

Is the bed still shaking?
I'm up here in the mirror on the ceiling
My dreams are laced with double meaning.

'They're OK . . .' I say.

'Clever . . . but they're not up to the rest . . .' He sees me acquiesce. 'Kill your babies. Let's scrap it and that will take it down to . . . How long?'

'Under,' Rupert squints at the screen, 'three minutes.'

'Two minutes fifty.' Lee applauds. 'Great.'

Lee and I have an affection for brevity in a song. Wire's first album has a great song under a minute that we aspire to. We prefer either concise songs or looong journey songs, songs under three minutes or over five. Stay away from the overused 3.30 made-to-measure-single zone; a dead giveaway of financial considerations coming before artistic ones.

'I think it needs to be two bpms faster,' I say.

'I'd like to hear it ten bpms faster,' interrupts Dan. We feign shock at his presence.

'That's a mighty fine jump you're calling for there, Chief,' says Lee.

We've taken to calling him 'Chief' after the silent Indian in *One Flew Over the Cuckoo's Nest*.

'Hmm,' says Dan.

'That will sound comical,' says Stanley.

'Well, there's only one way to find out, and better we try it out than discuss it,' says Lee. 'Do you have the technology, Rupert?'

'I do indeed. Give me a moment.'

Ten minutes later 'She Came and She Went' does indeed sound comical at the new tempo. It sounds cartoonish, until we rid ourselves of the memory of the previous version – so, half-way through, it starts to sound pretty good to me, and to Lee. The old version now feels ponderous.

'Ahh, relativity, Einstein was on to something,' I say.

'Two minutes thirty! Now we're talking,' says Lee, looking at the track length.

'It's outside heartbeat range,' says Rupert.

'Not after a shag,' says Stanley.

'Does it sound good?' Lee says to Rupert, who nods. 'Then fuck the algorithm.'

'Fuck the algorithm,' chorus me and Cream, clinking our mugs of tea.

'Should be the album title,' Cream says.

Joe 90 goes to the large whiteboard on the wall behind us where fifteen potential new songs are written in vertical columns in black marker. On the line for the song 'She Came and She Went', he writes the new bpm in royal purple.

'She's turning purple,' says Oliver.

'Well, I think so,' says Rupert, scanning the board. Purple indicates the song's foundation is there. Joe 90 writes in another column, alongside the other potential album titles, 'Fuck the algorithm'.

'*Lucky Fuckers fuck the algorithm.*' Cream's wearing fake lashes and turquoise eyeliner today.

'Management want to send early versions of this and "Horseman" to Faith.' I say.

'"Horseman" needs some work from you two then, maybe tonight?' Rupert looks at me and Lee.

'Horseman' is on the board in red, which indicates its vital signs are fading; I'm fearful it could fall off the list into a coma. 'Horseman' is the most personal lyric on the album, about the death of my friend Al. The lyric wrote itself – always a good sign. The chorus isn't working yet and the end coda sucks.

She will ascend to your descent

A pearl to wake the orient.

'What's that about, mate?' asks Lee.

'It's Al's daughter. I was trying to – you know – give her an uplift at the end of the song. She's called Pearl.'

' "To wake the orient"?' He gives me a look.

'It's a pun – orient means the lustre of a pearl.' I shrug.

'Oh yeah, everyone gets that one. There's my nerdy English lit scholar boy.' He laughs. 'Shame, though, cos the music's good in that section.'

'And it's shit in the rest of the song.' I finish his thought off.

'Fuck off,' growls Stanley. 'It's good.'

'No, it is shit,' says Lee.

So we're deep in Week Two, Phase One, of recording the provisionally titled *We're Not Dead Yet*. Or maybe *Fuc£ the Algorithm* – the £ sign will match the one we always use in Luc£y Fuc£ers promotion. We have to be out of here in five days so the intensity's high.

The rehearsal-room transition from jams to demos to here has flowed, and – I'm scared to say it – was fun! Making an album can be a bitch. The crazy short deadline has helped us get our shit together.

For the month leading up to these recording sessions Stella has been Eurostarring between Paris and London every six or seven days. I love the balance between having the time for myself, to focus on the lyrics, and being totally wrapped up in her. She's effortlessly entwined in my life in a way I've never experienced before.

I have a new insecurity – there's someone in my life I couldn't bear to lose.

She's at home now, painting the living-room walls burnt orange.

It's part of her master plan to 'colour' my life and find the new me. It's kind of working but she can go too far. She's tidied my drawers, folded clothes. She dumped some in our local Oxfam last week – without telling me! After a row, I repurchased some mutually acceptable pieces. The condom collection in the bathroom has been culled.

She's heading back to Paris in a few days for a shoot for a French DJ. Martin Solveig? Apparently, he's a big cheese.

Our new songs are on a constant loop in my head. I regularly wake at 5 a.m. with some lines that seem to have seeped in from a dream. They don't always make sense but they sound great – better than the ones I sweat over. It's a such a relief to be in the zone again and this time I'm getting the downloads clean. Stella puts it down to her and the intoxication of love. Luckily she's a great sleeper so I peck the words down by the light of my iPad.

Last night I got a lyric as we were having sex.

I was robbed
By the canal.
Gave everything away.
No loss.
The ropes had all begun to fray.

'Can you remember that?' I said to her as she was reaching a climax.

'What! *I was robbed by the canal* . . . What?' She looks at me, incredulous.

'*No loss. The ropes had all but frayed.*'

'Fuck off.'

'AHHHHH.'

Two weeks later four songs on the whiteboard are written in purple. Four! By the time we leave we'll be halfway to an album. We're booked to finish the remaining five immediately after The Addickts tour, which starts next week. Rupert will work on them while we're away and Dropbox me and Lee the revisions. We've four days left in the studio to overdub, and tidy things up. Bang on schedule. A fucking miracle.

'Are you ready to sing "Birthday", Seth?' asks Rupert.

'No, lyrics aren't finished.'

'Blimey, it's not *War and Peace,*' says Lee. 'Bit behind with the lyrics, mate.'

'I'm just waiting for the right experiences to come along.'

This is the best bit for us. The songs are ours. Once the album's delivered to management, to the record company, to the public – it's someone else's.

The Lucky Fuckers get pissed tonight, as they have done for the last two nights. The four songs are on repeat playing blazingly loud in the live room. There's a joint going round which Stanley is hogging. Lee and Cream are headbanging to a guitar solo. Oliver's moulded into the upholstery of a comfy chair, eyes glazed, dumb smile on his face. Dan's gone home to his newly pregnant girlfriend. I'm part of this in a way I wasn't before. I didn't realise it was wrong until it got right.

Didn't realise it was wrong until it got right.

It feels like they're . . . they're ready to risk being my friends again, risk that I won't fall. They're risking their financial livelihoods on another roll of the wheel with Seth Brakes. Fuck.

Stanley's joint smells good. There's something amazing about hearing your own songs stoned. It's a litmus test. You are placed three-dimensionally *in* the music. Once I experienced synaesthesia, seeing the music as colours. It's a trip. All musicians use weed. In the ashtray is a stubbed-out roach. There's still some mileage in it. On impulse I pocket it. I don't crave it, like I do booze or coke, so it shouldn't be a problem, though AA would say otherwise, I'm just curious to hear the songs stoned – see if they hold up, if my lyrics work.

I leave the room and walk down the studio corridor to the kitchen. I glance up at the security camera perched on the ceiling. I've committed a crime just having it in my pocket, for which I will be punished. In the kitchen, I find a lighter in a drawer, open the back door and sit on the stone steps. It's freezing. I straighten out the stubbed end of the roach and listen; no one's around.

Am I gonna do this?

I light the end and take a long drag, hold it deep. Skunk. I take another drag and repeat. I stub it out on the stone step and chuck it in the bushes. A dog barks, men drunk, shouting from the street.

My phone buzzes in my jacket pocket and I jump up, then laugh. Stella's name flashes on screen. I check myself.

Yeah, I can talk to her.

'Stella.' It's strange how the quality of a silence can convey itself down a telephone line more eloquently than words. There's a weight of sadness coming down the line, a tangible weight of emotion. I wait and listen. I crack first.

'Hey, darling, are you OK?'

The texture of the silence at the other end deepens.

Had another row with her parents? No. She's blocked them now.

Is she angry with me?

'Stella. Stella, can you hear me?'

Nothing.

Nothing. It's not a line fault, I can hear and feel someone at the other end.

'I'll be back soon. Has . . . has something happened?'

Nothing.

Is she crying? I can't get a bead on her. It's unnerving. I strain with singer's ears to read her but my superpower fails me. Why's she not responding?

'You're starting to freak me out, Stella – what's wrong?' The live-room door opens and 'Give It All a Name' blasts out. Sounds pretty good; more to do on it though. I want to go in and hear it with my new ears. I get up – open and close the back door with my free hand, wafting the scent of skunk out the kitchen.

'Stella. Listen, I can't hear you. I'll be home soon. I hope you're OK. I've got to finish off a . . .'

There's this swirly ambient wind sound. Are there words in that swirl or am I imagining things? Faint words repeated against the background noise. Two syllables in D or E. I close my eyes to let my focus fall fully into it.

It's a raspy old voice, not Stella's. I must be imagining it. *It's the skunk.*

It sounds like a . . . a nursery rhyme I recognise from childhood . . . being whispered in such an insubstantial way . . . I'm not sure what I'm hearing.

'Liar.'

'Liar, liar,' says the voice. The room's going weird now. I can smell – cheap perfume.

'Pants on fire. Liar, liar, pants on fire.'

The smell, it's my mother's heady mixture of alcohol and Elnett hairspray.

'Liar, liar, pants on fire.' I'm jamming the phone to my ear. It's coming down the line, *her* voice. I'm in a flop sweat.

'Liar, liar, pants on fire.'

The line goes dead, switches to the dial tone. Instinctively I throw the phone on to the floor. I'm panting, freaked out.

I retrieve the phone. The glass is cracked. *Fuck. That was weird. Skunk? Spice? Calm down.* I take a few more deep breaths, nodding to myself. *Weird. Sounded like my mum, smelt like my mum.* I laugh and then laugh some more at the sound of me laughing. *I'll ring Stella later when the drug's worn off.*

I stumble out the kitchen. I'm off my tits. The corridor elongates and warps into a void. The framed gold and silver discs lining the walls sparkle like stars.

'She Came and She Went' plays muffled in the live room. It's an anchor. I stand and listen, sounds great out here.

I get to the door. I'm going in. I brush lint off my sweater, which makes me giggle. *Oh fuck. They mustn't fucking know. Lee will go ape. It'll be fine, they're all wrecked, they won't notice.* I push open the door. The music blares to meet me, rolling through all my cells with physical impact. I can hear each instrument separately; each sound produces distinct colours that pass through me. I stand in the open doorway, eyes closed. I hear the instruments' relationship to each other, as a whole, as an interwoven whole. A high bass note pops out and does a handoff to a guitar line. It's mathematical yet arrived at by group intuition. Cream didn't think about that bassline, he just responded to Lee's guitar and framed it by some unconscious storytelling awareness in him that sounded right. This song is now a separate thing to that which Lee and I jammed. And Faith's going to sing on this? This is our golden ticket? Feels like a sell-out. We made this – it's a third thing, comprised of our histories, our biology, both conscious and unconscious. Where will she fit in? How does a collection of notes, rhythms, sounds produce such a visceral effect on our bodies? Music is magic, right, the universal language.

And then the vocal kicks in.

Don't remember your name
The smell of your scent
The sound when you came
You came and you went.

My voice, it sounds so small, like a child, a damaged child. I can hear my history in the tone of my voice. I can hear what my voice *wants* to do, how it *wants* to appear, how I usually hear it – cool and together, a bit sardonic, a bit Britpop – but I also hear the fear and desperation behind it, and I'm gutted. Gutted to be so exposed in the rawness of my lostness. The fatherless boy, the son of an alcoholic mother, it's all there like a signature, a tattoo. I'd no idea it sounded so revealing. The voice doesn't fit with what I heard before. Isn't part of the transcendent magic. It brings me down to earth with a thump, my fucked-upness, my desperate need to impress. It's devastating, a fucking sham.

Do they hear this? Do the band hear this?

It's the skunk.

I open my eyes. Lee's staring at me, phone in hand. He's in shock, like he's just worked it out too. He looks as devastated as I feel. He's gone white, which considering his half-Iranian parentage is some achievement. I'm about to make that quip when he says, 'Turn it off, Ol.' Then louder. 'Turn it off!'

Olly reaches down to his feet and hits the space bar. The music shuts off like a curtain dropping.

'Mate,' Lee says, 'I'm so sorry. Lizzie just called. Your mum's just died.'

Chapter 13

Ten a.m. I'm backstage, early at Mum's cremation, staring up at the inscription above the door to the antechamber.

O Lord, make me know my end and what is the measure of my days; let me know how fleeting I am! Psalm 39:4

Nice. It's freezing down here despite the layers of clothes under my trench coat.

Margaret something or other, the head honcho of the crematorium, steps forward and lifts the heavy lead latch with a clunk. She swings open the door and ushers me in. She stinks of perfume, I'm guessing it's so she doesn't bring the smell of work home. *Homework.* I stifle a giggle.

Inside, Mum awaits me. In the windowless room on a metal support frame sits a cheap Manila cardboard coffin (£220 plus VAT). The lid is off the casket! Fuck, I'm not ready for that. I'm unprepared for such a reveal. There she is, cosy, tucked up in her cardboard bed, lit by large fake candles on tall stands. I freeze in the doorway entrance till I hear Margaret's polite cough behind me. I turn to her.

'Would you mind if I have a moment with her alone?'

'Of course.' She steps back out through the door and closes it behind her.

I stand with my back to Mum, eyes adjusting to the flickering light.

One two three four

I turn to her.

She looks peaceful, an expression I'm unused to. I step closer. She's wearing a lilac shirt petalled around the collar and a long dark-brown pleated skirt down to her too-tight shoes. No coat, she must be freezing. Don't know what I was expecting. Can't bury her naked, I guess, but I didn't think of clothes. I move closer. It *is* a body, there is no life in it, no animation. This is just a shell.

'Where have they put you? Where are you?' My voice echoes in the stone room. I look up at the arched ceiling to see if she's hovering there.

'Got yer phone call, hypocrite. Don't frighten me. Got anything to say to me?' The words echo off the stone.

One two three four

I swallow hard and step closer.

'See you've got your Sunday bests on. Keeping up appearances. Bit chilly for a Scottish winter.' I sniff around her. She smells faintly chemical with a hint of an unknown perfume. 'And you smell good. Best clothes, smelling good. Good work.'

I peer in. Her eyes seem to be stuck shut, her cheeks tinted, she isn't breathing. That's what's wrong, she's not breathing. A wax model. I keep expecting her to move, to wake up, to sit up, to tell me off. I'm coiled with the tension of violence. This tension in me, what will become of it now? Will it recede because the source has gone? The sauce! Oh yes, the sauce. I pull out her old silver flask from the breast pocket of my coat and unscrew the top.

'Here's to you, Mother,' I say, and take a sip of vodka. Some occasions deserve a drink.

Started the night she died. No one knows. I've kept away from Lee, forbidden him to come to the funeral. I'll stop. Afterwards. I will. Just need a drink to get through this. God knows what Lizzie's lined up for the service . . . and a fucking party after, sounds like a right circus. It's 'for the twins'. They liked her! Fuck me, she brought them up wrong.

Lizzie's moved into a shared house. She tried to persuade me that it was 'by choice', to 'move in with friends'. I know it's because she's broke.

One two three four

'Here, Mum. You need some of this. Dutch courage for your journey.' I nozzle some vodka from the flask onto her lips, but they're clammed shut and the alcohol spills down the side of her cheeks.

'Oh Mum, you're lacking spirit.' I try to part her lips open with gloved fingers. A wisp of cotton wool protrudes from the bottom lip. I jump back.

'Shit, they've stuffed you.' I take a glove off and tease the wool back under the lips. Under her jaw is a metal tack. *They've nailed her jaw shut!*

'Fuck. Well, that'll shut you up. Should have done that years ago.' I stand back from her body and sprinkle a bit of the vodka over her shirt. It splatters in patches.

'*In nomine Patris*, blah blah blah blah,' I intone. I lean over her and sniff. 'Yeah, that's better, that's my mother. Could pick you out in a linefold, blind, blindfolded, line-up.' I giggle.

For a moment I'm tempted to slip the flask into her cask.

Slip the flask into her cask.

I take a swig and slip it in my breast pocket.

'Naww. I'm going to need this more than you.'

Chapter 14

The now closed casket sits on a claret carpeted stage.

Alliteration! Tongue twister!

The coffin sits on rollers at waist height behind open red curtains. I'm waiting for the magician to start his performance – 'Ladies and gentlemen, the death and resurrection show!'

The magician in question is Victoria Finch, 'Christian humanist celebrant', whatever the fuck that is. Lizzie's hired her to run the memorial as Mum's usual priest, vicar, whatever, is on his way to meet his maker. Victoria is mid-forties, middle-class English – mid-everything, really. Stell sits next to me, holding my hand. The twins next to her. Lizzie's bookending them. Lizzie's off with me. Stell's being sweet but her sympathy's misplaced as she's mistaking me for someone who gives a shit.

Victoria Finch has clearly never met my Mum and so is dishing out a whole load of bullshit that is winding the fuck out of me. This 'Rebecca Brakes' sounds like quite a woman, but there's scant relationship between her and the vicious old crone dead in the coffin. The more she talks of this 'single mother struggling to raise two fine young children' the angrier I get.

'Rebecca had a strong faith.' I snort. Stell squeezes my hand. I turn it into a cough. 'She was one of those kinds of women who would do anything for others. With Alan gone' – *'Alan gone' – amazing how reductive a statement can be, bearing no relationship to its fucking content* – 'she held down a job as a nurse, mainly working with those with a terminal illness, and yet was always there for her children.' I clench my jaw as the pressure builds on me to say something.

'Rebecca was a speak-from-the-hip realist. You don't survive twenty years on a terminal ward without being so. Those that are close to death can smell platitudes and dishonesty a mile away.' *So can fucking singers!* I'm burning up with a bait-ball of emotions.

'I know that quite a few of you who have gathered here, who are not family, are either families who lost a loved one and were administered to by Rebecca or fellow nurses who worked on the same ward. You witnessed the caring woman beneath the sometimes rough tongue. The fact you took time from your busy lives to come and pay your respects speaks volumes.' *Where were these busy people when she was alive?* I crane my head to look behind me. There's the Campbell family, Joe and Holly's best friends are sandwiched between their parents, but apart from them everyone's over seventy. Must be weird watching this shit when you know you're close to death yourself. They look solemnly ahead to Victoria Finch reading from the dais. *My mother looked after some of these people? She looked after others well enough for them to turn up here – but didn't look after us?* I lean forward to look across the pew at Lizzie. She glances at me sideways, rolls her eyes then puts a protective arm around a teary-eyed Holly. Seeing Holly cry makes me feel really weird. I cough it down. This is torture.

'. . . Don't cry because her life is over. Smile because it happened.'

You didn't fucking know her!

She took everything out on us.

The beatings . . .

All her fury, out on us!

'And now Holly and Joe, supported by their best friends Karen and Tracey, are going to sing a song for their beloved Granny.'

This brings me up short. Lizzie didn't warn me about this. The twins are squeezing past her. Karen and Tracey, I can never remember which is which, are carrying an acoustic guitar and a recorder. They shuffle onstage alongside a smiling Victoria. I look over at Lizzie who refuses eye contact. Stella's looking worriedly at me.

'Are you OK?' she whispers while the guitar is being tuned.

'No, I'm not fucking OK. Am I meant to be? It's my mother's funeral,' I whisper.

'I am aware of that fact,' she hisses, then catches herself. 'But you're . . . OK? I just want to . . . help, that's all.'

The recorder starts up.

'Then shoot the kid.'

I hate recorders. The instrument that all kids are forced to start on when what they really want to play is guitar or drums.

The recorder starts the melody of 'Abide with Me' but strikes some quite fabulous bum notes.

Abide with me; fast falls the eventide . . .

The kids start singing along with the guitar. Unfortunately Karen/Tracey's no better at playing chords on the guitar than her sister is on recorder. She keeps pausing to make chord changes while Holly and Joe plough on. I giggle. Stella squeezes my hand. I giggle some more. Lizzie leans forward to glare at me. I bite my tongue hard.

Swift to its close ebbs out life's little day;
Earth's joys grow dim, its glories pass away;
Change and decay in all around I see –
O Thou who changest not, abide with me.

I'm rocking with suppressed laughter. There's one chord in the cycle that demands large hands. The poor girl cranes her neck forward to watch it coming, and every time it comes around the whole song hiccups them further out of sync with each other. The more I try to hold it in, the worse it gets. I can't get up and leave. The twins will see me and be devastated. Stell digs nails into my palms, I grunt, she lets go and leans away from me. I put my hands over my eyes and try to make the laughter look like grief. Through my fingers I see Holly struggling not to cry. It makes her voice quiver with emotion.

The tempter's power

Now there's a line for an alcoholic. I'm managing to turn my laughter convincingly into sobs now. I congratulate myself on the subterfuge then realise I can't stop. *I can't stop.* I'm sobbing with tears and laughter, and I have no idea how to control any of it any more. Any of it.

The good thing about not drinking for a year is that when you do, a little goes a long way. At my peak I could down a bottle of Stoli and pass sober, while now, three, four flasks and I feel it. I have to focus to walk straight, to act straight.

I totter out of the service once 'Abide with Me' has abated. Round the back of the crematorium, I fortify myself with a few shots more.

Back here, there are these massive smokestacks, but no smell. Guess it would disturb the neighbours. Big carbon footprint. I light a fag to calm my nerves. Crows perched on a giant oak heckle me. I throw a stone at them and they scatter.

I top up my flask from where I'd stashed the refill, finish my fag and walk round the front. There's a group of people in finery milling around the entrance. They're a diverse bunch, younger than ours and cool-looking. Next service, I'm guessing. I tug on the arm of a man in his thirties, dark-blue suit, Afro crammed under a homburg.

'Who you burning, man?' I crack up, then check myself. 'Sorry, sorry, Burning Man, the festival . . .'

He stares at me open-mouthed.

'My nephew,' he answers.

I re-enter the service. They are singing, droning 'What a Friend We Have in Jesus', to a pre-recorded backing track. I'm with Nietzsche's 'You'll have to play better songs if you want me to join your religion'.

Or something to that effect. I slide into one of the back pews so as not to make a commotion. Three old crones dressed in black across the aisle give me a look of earnest sympathy, one puts her hand on her heart. I cast my eyes down and nod my head. I pick up the battered blue hymn book lying open like a dead bird, find the page and drone along.

The curtains around Mum's coffin start to close with an electronic whirr.

Shit, this is it! She's going. I'm panicked. This woman has been the backdrop to my entire life. Awful, yes, awful, but the backdrop nevertheless – now what? *She can't just leave. She hasn't . . . hasn't apologised. She hasn't APOLOGISED. Never owned up to any of it. She can't just GO! You're the reason . . . I'm so . . . fucked up. You're the reason . . . What happens now? This is the . . . I . . . don't feel . . . I'm not ready for this.* I think I'm saying some of this out loud. I'm standing up, shaking, moaning. I grip the pew in front of me, close my eyes. Someone's shouting, 'Stop!'

Shouting.

It's me!

Shouting.

'STOP!'

Twenty minutes later I'm in Margaret's office.

'I want to be present at the cremation itself. I'm . . . I'm not finished.' My eyes are locked on her sensible shoes. Lizzie stands beside me, arms folded, oozing pissed-offness. She tried to persuade me out of it but backed off when she saw I'd make another scene. My outburst apparently scandalised the congregation. Personally, I think the show needed a lift. Stella's taken the kids to the gathering. Victoria Finch gave me this idea, after she'd calmed me down. Told me the actual cremation was taking place later and that, in some cases, relatives could *watch the burning*. She agreed to come with me to ask Margaret. She's kind beneath the kant.

'We do allow relatives to be present,' says Margaret, fiddling with her wedding ring, 'but we need advance warning. We're not set up for it.'

'I don't mind if it's . . . It doesn't have to look perfect. I understand – I just would like some . . . some more . . . closure.' Then I burst out to Lizzie, 'You've been here the whole time, I've just got here.' She glowers at me, saying nothing.

'I'm happy to sit with Mr Brakes for a witness cremation, Margaret. I've explained that it's not set up for show,' says Victoria, breaking the tension. 'I thought maybe the new cremator would be appropriate.'

Go Victoria!

She gave me the word '*closure*' too – seems to have magical powers in her world.

'I really advise you to think again, Mr Brakes. This is not something that most people want to see,' says Margaret.

'I'm not most people.' My resolution echoes in the silence.

'You'll need to sign a waiver . . .' says Margaret. 'OK, Vicky, you can take him down.' She looks at her watch. 'I'll send word to Jack to prepare everything down his end.'

Victoria Finch smells of jasmine. Her white bob of hair precedes me as we make our way through the upstairs offices of the crematorium, down into the areas that have the smell and feel of

141

a hospital and then down a further set of stairs into the belly of the building, a huge dusty industrial warehouse space. There we pass two blackened brick ovens, hard at work, the source of the dust, as big as trucks, blasting heat and the smell of cooking. I try to hold my breath, don't want to breathe in dead people.

We walk fast through the space and I nearly run into the back of her when she stops before a large door. She pulls open the door and we step in to an enclosed room, maybe twenty foot by thirty, newly painted, immaculately clean. No windows.

At the far end of the room is a pristine aluminium oven with a glass front and a control panel to the side. Waist height, on a trolley, is mother. An older man in overalls is bending over her, his back to us, hands deep inside the box, rummaging around.

'Hey!' I shout.

He straightens up and turns around, raising his yellow rubber gloves in the air like a doctor scrubbing up. He pulls off one of the gloves with a snap and lowers his surgical face mask. He's missing two fingers on one hand.

'Hello, Victoria, Mr Brakes. Sorry. I wasn't quite ready for ya,' he says.

Victoria steps forward. 'Jack would be checking Rebecca for any metallic objects or rings that shouldn't go in the cremator.'

'That's it.' He looks like a mid-1950s pirate. White beard, grey beanie. 'I've just got a bit more to do.'

'There's nothing on her.' I'm relieved I didn't gift her the flask.

'I've still got to check, it's protocol.' He pulls back on his glove. 'If you'd like to turn around.'

'No need,' I say. 'You carry on.'

He looks to Victoria, who nods. He goes back to frisking Mum.

More action than she's had in years.

When he's done he puts the cardboard lid back on the box. Victoria beckons me over to two green leather armchairs on the other side of the room facing the cremator. We sit.

'Got any popcorn?' I ask.

She blanches. On the table between us are some fake white orchids. On the wall hangs a painting of Jesus, walking up a giant staircase, into a technicolour heaven. Jack presses some controls and the fire picks up. The glass is clear, unlike in the two previous ovens, which were smoky with use.

'How many times has this oven been used?' I ask.

'Cremator,' Jack says, 'we call them cremators. This is our second week. I'm still getting used to it, to be honest. Instructions in bloody German.' Out of the slit of a side pocket he clumsily pulls out a folded piece of paper, opens it up and lays it down on the table. 'I just want to check something . . .' He reads for a moment, moves back to look at the dials on the wall, then looks down at the paper again.

'It's going to be a wee while.'

'She's not going anywhere.'

I'm happy to be down here, missing the gathering. I swig from my flask. Victoria gives me a look.

'Care for a tipple?'

'No, I don't, thank you.'

'Ever?'

'Oh, I used to – too much. In my rebellious days.'

'What were you rebelling against?'

'My dad was a vicar.' She takes a moment to decide whether to share more. 'And an alcoholic. And you?'

'Her.' I wave the flask in Mother's direction. 'Cheers.'

'Not much of a rebellion if we become those we rail against.'

I turn to her.

'So you do have teeth.'

'Sorry.'

'Don't say sorry – that's the first true thing you've said today.' I chuckle. She gets up and goes to the water urn.

'You're not meant to drink in here,' growls Jack.

'Jealous?'

'Alcohol's flammable.' He returns to his dials.

'She'll put me out.'

Victoria returns with two cups of water.

'Why did you want to come down here?' she asks.

'To make sure you don't miss something.'

She reddens and plays with the crucifix around her neck. I turn to the picture of Jesus.

'Do you believe in that shit?' I ask.

'I do.'

'Even with an alcoholic vicar for a dad?'

She nods.

'What's your secret, Victoria?'

'I thought you were in AA?'

'You've looked me up!'

'I always research my clients.' She's blushing again. 'In AA you believe in a higher power?'

'Ahh, you see, that's where me and AA differ . . . I don't . . . but if I did – a higher power is different to believing in a two-thousand-year-old religion based on a father who sacrifices his son. Shit parenting, if you ask me.' I raise the flask. 'Here's to shitty parents!'

'The main message of Christ was forgiveness.'

'The main *acts* of Christianity have been bloodshed, crusades, imperialism, slavery, decimating Indigenous peoples, murdering women as witches, antisemitism . . . have I missed anything?'

'Christ enabled me to forgive my father,' she stammers.

'Your belief did that. Look, I can see you're a good person. Christ's *words* are one thing the church's actions—'

'My belief in Christ enabled me to become a recovering alcoholic—'

'—Congratulations! You swapped one addiction for another.'

'—and forgive my Father.'

'Some people don't deserve to be forgiven.'

She leans towards me. 'Oh no, you've got it wrong. Forgiveness – is for you – it helps them – but do it for you. Otherwise – you can never put them down. Wouldn't you like that, Seth, to be free of her?' She looks at Mum. 'I know you came down here for your own reasons but I agreed to bring you down for mine. This is an opportunity to not live the next part of your life in reaction to her. Forgive your mum for you.'

Could I do that?

'Easier said than done.'

'That's the higher power bit.'

I've reached this point in therapy, more than once, but how do you do it? I can't just forgive her, just like that, even if I know it would be good for me.

'It's not that simple.'

I look up at Jesus, stepping into a psychedelic new world, after all that suffering. *But if there's a God, why so much suffering? Life is suffering. Wasn't that what Buddha said? How can I believe in a God that would make a world like this? That's not a God of love. It's a sadist God. The God of my Mum. Could I forgive?*

There's a roaring sound as the tempered-glass oven doors electronically open.

'Ready now,' Jack says.

We stand and walk to her casket.

Could I?

'Is there anything you'd like to say before she goes?' asks Victoria. I place my hand on the box and close my eyes. I hear the words in my head – *I forgive you, Mum* – and instantly feel this rage. I try again. *I forgive you, Mum.* I feel the belt on me. There's a pain in my throat like a fist. My face is spasming. I'm gonna lose it. I daren't say anything or I'll cry. I shake my head.

Jack slides the coffin into the furnace mouth. Flames intensify to meet the casket. He presses a button for the doors to close. Nothing happens.

'What?' He keeps on pressing a big red button.

The flames now pour onto the box, furious jets stream from above and the sides. Heat explodes into the room. We step back. The fire is blistering the cardboard, which caves in on my mother's body. Smoke wafts into the room. A fire alarm kicks off, forcing my fingers into my ears. The box sears away around her body. Her hair's on fire. Her clothes are burning off. Her skin melts with a hiss. There's an acrid stench. She starts to twitch, to wriggle, to jerk through the collapsed box. A mad spasmodic dance, back arching, legs kicking, arms scrabbling to get out. I back up against the wall and knock Jesus to the floor.

Outside the crematorium I'm on my hands and knees, dry-retching on the grass. I puked alcohol and bile at first, now it's empty spasms that have me bent double, trying to purge something deep at the core of me. I'm panting and sweating from the exertion.

I keep seeing Mum's body writhing and burning, her blistered face . . . Fuck me. A convulsion works its way up my body.

'Ugh.'

The shuffling of feet on gravel tells me Margaret and Victoria are still waiting. The wet grass soaks through my knees.

'I'm so sorry, Mr Brakes . . .'

Without turning I put my hand up in the air to silence her. A plane rumbles overhead. A song can be heard from the chapel. It's that bloody Eric Clapton song. I wipe my hand on the grass, reach in my pocket for a handkerchief, wipe my mouth.

I rise to my feet, turn to face them.

'Now that's –' I belch '– what I call a funeral.'

'Seth . . .' says Victoria.

I shake my head, hack up some gob and spit.

'Can you give me a lift to the pub?'

'Jesus, you look like you've seen a ghost.' Stella holds me with such love that I have to pull away for fear of falling apart.

'Well,' I clear my throat, 'you aren't so far fucking wrong.'

The gathering, thank God, is nearly over; there's only a few stragglers left. On the silent TV hanging beside the bar a couple is ice-skating. A pint of lager is being pulled. Holly slams into me with a hug.

'Did you like our song?' she asks.

'It made me cry,' I say. Joe approaches but stands back. I pull him into the huddle. 'You guys did great.'

'Is that why you got so upset?' says Joe.

'Yes.'

'Mum said you'd been drinking,' says Holly.

'I don't drink,' I say, as much to Stella as to Holly.

'Let's smell your breath.' Holly pulls my head down before I have time to think. 'Yuck, you smell of sick.'

'It's the, uh, crematorium.'

'Liar,' she says. I catch a glance of admiration from Stella.

'Well, it's not drink, is it?' *Little fucker.* 'Is there any food? I'm starving.' I walk away to a table with the remnants of sandwiches. I grab a handful of peanuts from a bowl.

Peanuts, the best camouflage for all aromas.

Should be their advertising pitch.

'How was it, then?' Lizzie's arms are folded, jaws clenched.

'Terrifying. Look, I'm sorry, I just . . . needed a bit more.'

'Bit more of everything, by the look of you,' she says.

'Holly just told me you think I'm drinking . . .'

'*Don't.*' She leans in close, backing me against the wall. 'Save your bullshit for people who don't fucking know you,' she whispers.

'I'm—'

'How long?'

'I . . . I—'

'How long have you been drinking?' she says. I look over her shoulder at Stell. She has one arm around Holly and is talking to the Campbells.

'How long have you been drinking, Seth?'

'Since Mum died.'

'You told Jada?'

'No.'

'You're going to tell her today – and I'm going to be there when you do.'

'Fuck no!'

'Do you want to stop?'

'Of course. Mum's death, you know. It was just to get me through . . .'

'I'm not going through this again, Seth.'

'You didn't the first time. And seeing how insensitive you are, I'm fucking glad.'

'You think Lee will walk you through this again? Stella?'

'Have you talked to them?' My voice cracks.

'Look,' she changes to a softer tone, 'if being in The Lucky Fuckers is too much – *then drop it*. It's not worth a relapse. We can get by without your money and I sure as hell don't want your drinking on my conscience.' She checks to see no one's listening.

'Is it coke *and* alcohol?'

'No.' She holds my gaze. 'No, just vodka!'

'You got drink on you now?'

I hesitate.

'Give it to me.' She puts out her hand.

'I'm in a pub, if I want a drink it's just there.'

'Give it to me!'

I draw out the flask. She takes it, reads the inscription, laughs.

'We're going to your room to ring Jada now.'

'*Fuck off!* Come on, Lizzie. This was just to get me through the funeral.'

'Right now, or we bring Stella into this.'

'*Fucking hell!*' I blink back tears. 'Blackmail is not how you get someone to stop drinking.'

She leans into my face. 'It's worth a fucking try.'

She frogmarches me out the door, up the stairs, hydraulic fire doors hissing in our wake. I'm cornered, trying to think of excuses to get out of this. Some part of me wants to be cornered, is relieved, wanted to be caught . . . but he's a minority shareholder.

My room stinks of cleaning chemicals. I duck under the forlorn TV on the scissor stand.

'Look,' I say, 'I've just come back from the crematorium. Can't we do this later?'

'No.'

'My phone's broken.' She glowers at me. 'It is!' I wave it in her face.

She hands me her Nokia.

'You making me do this is against all the rules.'

'Fuck your rules.'

I ring, praying for Jada to be out.

'Speakerphone,' says Lizzie.

The phone rings into the room. On the fourth tone it picks up.

'Ya . . .'

'Hi, Jada. Seth here. Thanks for picking up. This a good time?'

I can hear Jada sense trouble.

'Yes. What's on your mind, Seth?'

Tears damn my eyes. The shame has me.

'I've . . . broken my sobriety.' A long sob squeezes out of me. There's a silence on the other end of the line. It's so fucking heavy, full to the brim with disappointment.

'How long?'

'Under a week.'

'What with?'

'Vodka.'

'Every day?'

'Yes.'

'This since ya mum died, ya?'

'Yes.'

'Wondered why I hadn't heard from you.' She swallows. 'You *want* to stop?'

I pause.

'Just that, just that pause.' I can see her nodding her head. 'Have you hit bottom?'

'I don't know.'

'Which means you haven't. Why are you ringing me?'

'My sister . . . My sister's here.' I look up at Lizzie sitting rigid on the bed. 'We've just come back from the funeral.'

'Your sister Lizzie's with you now . . . making you call me?' I hear the familiar creak of her chair as she adjusts her weight. 'Lizzie, you listening? I understand your concern, but unless Seth wants to stop . . . you know . . . It won't work unless he wants to stop.'

'I do want to stop; this was to do with the funeral.'

There's a long silence.

'When can you get to a meeting?'

'Tomorrow, when I get to London.'

'Can you hold out till then?'

'I think so, yes.'

'Text me every two hours – call if you need. Pray if you can. Lizzie, this is the most vulnerable time, can you sit with him?'

'I've got the kids, Jada. His girlfriend's here?'

The shame has me.

'Can you go to meetings every day for ninety days?'

'No! I'm not home; I'm going on tour again!' *Ninety fucking days!* 'Will you stay as my sponsor?' I blurt out. That's my fear. If I'm going to do this, I need her.

There's a scrabbling sound on the other end, followed by the flick of a lighter and the suck on a cigarette.

'Brakes, get a new commitment coin. Talk about your relapse publicly at least for . . . the first ten meetings. Find meetings on tour, in each city.' There's a weariness in her voice I'm unused to. 'Both of you, relapse is part of AA. Don't let the shame keep you

153

away, Seth. We all do it. It's a disease. If you do what I ask – I'll still be here for ya.'

I'm cleaned up, showered and shaved. Foetal in bed. Stella's spooning me.

Consequences. I never think of consequences. Never do when I'm in this place. *I can't do this. I can't sober up again.* It took everything in me before. The only way I know to feel better is to keep drinking. *My mum died!* I keep seeing her.

My skin itches, I'm restless to get up. The drink is whispering, singing to me like a mermaid. I hear her song from the bar downstairs, feel it coil around me.

I'll tell Stella I'm going out for a walk, need to be alone. Just a couple of shots. I'm not ready to stop yet. I haven't hit bottom. It's much harder to stop when you haven't hit bottom. Just a few more days, then I'll hit bottom.

'What are you thinking?' she says softly.

'I'm so restless. I need a walk.'

'I'll come with you.'

'I need to be on my own.'

Pub closes in an hour.

'I don't feel sleepy at all.'

She's looking at me with a kindness I don't like. It makes me feel even shittier about myself.

'You know I didn't want you to come to the funeral. I didn't want you to see this.' I start to put some clothes on.

'I wanted to be here for you.' She stays in bed, watching me hunt a lost sock. 'I know where you're going.'

'I'm just going out for a walk.'

'It's minus two degrees, Seth.' She clears her throat. 'You're going for a drink.'

Liz has fucking told her!

'And what if I am? I need a fucking drink!'

She sits up. 'Seth, I can't stop you drinking and I'm not going to try, but I'm here for you. I love you. I only want what's best for you.'

'I want a fucking drink!'

'Have you texted Jada?'

I go to the toilet, shut the door and pee. From nowhere I start to cry. I'm shaking with tears, trying to stifle them, missing the bowl. *What the fuck have you done, you stupid fuck? Three hundred and sixty-one days sober. Three hundred and sixty-one! Four days from your first birthday!* I hated the woman, it's stupid, yet all I hear is, *My mum's dead.* Over and over again. I sit crying on the toilet. I feel so alone. There's an unbearable cold pain in my chest that my breathing slams into.

Stella lets me be, doesn't call out, just waits.

I turn the bathroom light off and come back into bed, fully clothed. She spoons me. After a while I sob again. She holds me. I don't deserve this. What a fucking mess.

'One step at a time,' she says. 'One step at a time.'

Chapter 15

Harry Addickt has a bad breakout of zits on his forehead, volcanic eruptions. I'm trying not to look but he keeps swinging his head around like one of those toy nodding dogs in the back of cars, and the angry bumps keep flashing me through his greasy pudding-bowl haircut.

'Focking great to have you here, Seth. We focking luv you man. All that crazy insane shit. Seen you a shitload of times.' He's standing too close, uncomfortably close. There's a stale odour to his breath.

We've been on the road five days but this is the first time we've met. After every gig he sends an Addickt emissary to invite us to party. The Lucky Fuckers who oblige spend the next day sleeping it off, looking like extras from *The Walking Dead*.

Harry looks a good ten years older than the twenty-five that's down on his Wiki page. He's from Edgbaston, Birmingham; his eight siblings either ended up as gangsters or junkies. Harry's the creative one. A Renaissance man. Rumour has it that five years ago, he and his brother Phil held up a post office wearing Laurel and Hardy masks. In the eyes of the *NME* this rumour gives him massive street cred. Ours must be the only business where being fucked up is a plus. I get it. My ODs gave me cred. Now I'm sober no one's interested.

Me too.

The Addickts have just soundchecked in the cavernous hall. They *do* sound like we used to sound; one of their songs even has the same chord sequence as 'Death Wish'.

Harry's been running at the mouth in my dressing room for ten minutes. It's coke and E, as he keeps doing weird shit with his jaw and is way too affectionate with me.

'Anyway, man, let me know if there's anything you want, you know . . .' He snorts.

'Thanks, but I'm clean now,' I say. I fold my arms.

'Yeah, but you might change your mind. E, acid, whizz, whatever you want.' He puts a hand on my arm. 'I want to party with the great Seth Brakes.'

'Ah, mate, thanks, but he don't live here no more. I can't do that shit, I'm an addict.'

'I *mean*,' he opens his arms wide, 'we're all Addickts.' He cracks up laughing, abruptly stops, puts a hand on my shoulder, and strokes the fake-fur collar.

'Hey, that's boss, la, is it real?'

Thanks to Google I've managed to locate and attend AA meetings in Düsseldorf, Hamburg and today Cologne.

'Hi, I'm Seth.'

'Hi, Seth.' The group chorused back.

'I've been sober for eight days.'

Eight days!

It's devastating to say I'm eight days sober. Haven't told the band. Don't want to spook 'em. Jada's still on board.

Jada's still on board, praise the Lord . . .

It amazes me how many AA meetings are going on, everywhere. Everywhere, every minute of the day. I guess I'm not so unique. I sit through these German ones understanding nothing specifically, but everything emotionally. It strikes me there's an argument to be had that addiction *is* the human condition. Personality? Just a bunch of repeated routines, opinions, passed down beliefs. We're as predictable as a computer program. There are a set of given parameters and then we self-generate into habits – it's just some habits are worse for us than others.

I missed catering to attend the meeting and now it's too close to the gig to eat or my food will repeat. I write in my lyric book.

> *Missed catering for the AA meeting. It's too close to the gig to eat or my food will repeat.*

Fuck, I miss Stell!

We've only managed texts for the last few days as the internet's spotty on tour and she's styling a nappy advert with a cast of fifty-six babies. Hope it doesn't make her broody.

Touring. I'd forgotten what it's like. Tour bus to hotel to venue to tour bus overnight to venue – and it's only been a week.

My devil on tour was always loneliness. Lee's always kept to himself on tour. Each night I get to watch the band polish off the rider and take the leftovers on to the bus for the crew. What business provides free booze at the workplace? Says it all really. Even Cream's drinking now!

Tour buses.

People who haven't been on a tour bus think they're romantic; seriously! In reality ours is a claustrophobic, cramped, swaying barracks full of men. Men who fart, snore, don't wash up, miss the toilet bowl, get drunk, have a good laugh, and generally enjoy a piratical lifestyle. The booze-coke combination's crucial – covers up the emptiness in the *twenty-three hours* you're not playing.

I'm in an epically shit mood tonight.

Olly showed me a review of our first night's gig in Hamburg. We barely got a mention and most of it focused on my past. So much for blowing The Addickts away.

The Addickts are where we were at – before I hit the skids. The thrill of that meteoric rise. From butcher's van to man with a van to tour bus within a year. Audiences doubling each time you return to a city. What a buzz!

Despite my jealousy, I like them. The songs have a groove and there's a few memorable shouty choruses. They've been styled by Celine Bonnard. Slept with her a few years back. On coke. Couldn't get it up. She told everyone. *Bitch*.

The band wear street clothes, with splashes of bright colour – they remind me of Japanese fighting fish.

Playing the same set each night enables them to get wrecked and still hold it together. There's a sense of will – the train-stay-on-the-tracks that's car-crash watchable.

Harry's in control. With that belly on him he gives off this benign street-cred Santa vibe, big fuck-off grin on his face. I wouldn't mess with him. Side stage you get to witness some vicious looks to the band if they fuck up. He punched Phil Addickt before the encore last night. Just whacked him. Phil was so out of it he hardly noticed.

The Lucky Fuckers?

We're playing to half-empty auditoriums that fill up by the end. I'm on a roll racking up shit gigs sober. I stand glued to the mic with a head full of panic. The predominantly male audience wearing *We are all Addickts* T-shirts soon lose interest. The three singles at the end of the set rescue us – just – but I *hate* being reliant on hits at the end, like every band you've ever seen.

Chapter 16

'Hey, boy, how you doing?' Brunt booms through my speakerphone.

'I'm OK. How's you? That bug still bothering you?' Outside my hotel window the drizzle sheets down.

'If it isn't one thing, it's another. My knees today. Rugby, you know.' The hotel is generic bleak.

'Not my sport, mate.' I pull up a chair and sit down at the desk. 'How can I help you?' I know he's not ringing to swap pleasantries.

'So, we got an interview for you. At TRE, good German television slot, tomorrow morning. It means getting up at six but it's a networked breakfast show.'

'What am I promoting? The gigs with The Addickts are sold out, we've got no record—'

'We're selling your apology.' He lets that hang.

'Really? Three years later? Isn't there a statute of limitations?'

'The internet never forgets. The German record company – the new head – thinks it would be a good way to wipe the slate clean. I think they need to see that you're sober and willing to play nice before they invest – reinvest. The Germans aren't easy

to please when it comes to investment – just ask the Greeks . . .'
He laughs.

'I don't fully remember what I did here in Germany?' I don't,
despite Google's valiant attempts to jog my memory.

'It will come back to you. Look, all you have to do is go there,
apologise for the past, talk about rehab, play the game. You
know how it is. The TV show have promised to play nice, take
it easy on you. You know how it is.'

I do know how it is.

The dressing room at TRE is a windowless, airless white rectan-
gle. A large LCD screen hangs from the wall at a precarious
slant, blasting out the show that I'm soon to appear on. I prowl
the room nursing a headache, feeling crappy through lack of
sleep. I was up late talking Stella down. She'd had a blazing row
with her parents; she foolishly answered one of their calls. I
don't get why she won't just cut them.

'It's a family thing,' Stella keeps saying. 'You can't
understand.'

Makes me glad I didn't have a family, kind of.

God I miss her. There was a point around the nine day mark,
where it went past the point of being painful, to where I began
to question if it was real. I suspect it's my way of dealing with the
pain.

On the red couch Kristina, the record company's TV fixer, nurses a black coffee, watching me with an unreadable expression. Lee sits beside her, head in his iPad. He's come to hold my hand; on Brunt's orders, I'm guessing. Lee wouldn't be up at 7 a.m. off his own bat.

I hate these snidey, chirpy early-morning shows. On the screen above me, a dyed blonde in her thirties is in the stocks, medieval wooden stocks. Kristina informs me she's a German soap star whose ratings need a boost after she had an affair with another actor's husband.

Five competition winners are invited to throw platefuls of cream pie at her from the distance of fifteen feet. A clock ticks down two minutes. So far, her black hair is splattered in a creamy yellow custard, but no one's managed to hit her face. She's taking it well, and taking it well is what the public want to see. Being a good sport.

Celebrity. We love them and we're jealous of them. We love watching them rise and we love watching them fall. We *love* their humiliation. If they make it to some level of stasis, well that's boring, it's the ups and downs that are the fun, the drama's the selling point.

This public torture's not improving my mood. Neither is the bottle of wine that stares at me forlornly from the fridge. Who put that there? Don't they know I'm sober?

I've been to make-up, who have powdered over some crow's feet. Crow's feet that weren't there three years ago when I last did a round of TV shows and interviews.

'So, they have promised to go gentle on you.' Kristina interrupts my gaze. 'No mention of the naked goose-stepping.'

'What?' I say. Lee winces.

'You know, the naked goose-stepping.' She lets out a snort.

I'm frozen rigid.

She looks at me in shock.

'You don't remember?' She stares at me wide eyed.

My cream cheese and salmon breakfast bagel repeats.

I have flashes of this. Fragments that I wouldn't call a memory. I have a lot of those. Fragments that I don't want to remember. Lots.

'*Zehn, neun, acht* . . .' goes a shouted countdown from the TV. It's broken by roars of triumphant laughter from the custard pie mob as the actress cops a pie full in the face. It hangs there suspended.

'Do you want to know about it?' says Kristina.

'No!' Lee says too loudly. She flinches. 'No, Kristina, why don't you go get us . . . Why don't you go see when they want Seth?' She gets the message and leaves.

'The naked goose-stepping?' I say.

He gives me a what-can-I-say look.

'What was I on?'

'Everything?'

'*Naked?*'

'It was a . . . it was a crazy night.' He smiles. 'Flea was backstage. He'd told you about the Chili Peppers' cock-sock gigs . . . the good old days . . . you wanted to show him you had the balls . . .' He winces. 'Your cock-sock fell off . . . goose-stepping . . .'

The regurgitated bagel returns with interest.

'Did Flea like it?' I say. Pathetic.

'Laughed his tits off.'

I remember Stanley, amongst others, alluding to this, but I would always cut them off.

'Fucking hell.'

'She said they're not going to mention it,' Lee says, as if talking to a child. 'There's no footage on YouTube. Thank God.'

'It's illegal in Germany.' I dredge this up from some newspaper memory. 'Any Nazi action . . .' I can't fully remember the details. 'There's nothing on YouTube?'

'2010.' He stands up. 'We weren't so addicted to our screens back then.' He comes over to me and puts his hands on my shoulders.

'Three years ago you were a different person. Just talk about rehab, how sorry you are. That's it. That's all you have to say. Just be humble . . . and . . . and . . . Fritz will forgive you.'

'You fucker,' I say with a smile.

'Just don't mention the var,' he says, in a John Cleese *Fawlty Towers* accent. I laugh.

'I vill not mension ze vor,' I say loudly, putting my two fingers beneath my nose.

'Or ze stepping on ze goose.' Lee meets my volume and begins to goose-step.

'Or ze stepping,' I join him with a high kick and my two-fingered Hitler moustache, 'on ze goose.' He cracks up laughing.

'Or d'fucking of the Jews,' he says.

'Or d'fucking of the Jews,' I say.

We parade the length of the dressing room, spin and repeat, spin and repeat, till laughter makes us stop.

There's a knock at the door.

'Time to go, please,' says Kristina.

A young male intern with a clipboard and an earpiece mic leads the way. We come to a studio door with a red recording light on. He turns to us and puts a forefinger to his lips.

Never done one of these sober. We enter the studio down a narrow corridor between wall and heavy black ceiling-hung drapes. Led by our guide, we step silently over wires and make our way through an opening into the harshly lit studio. Ahead of us, the quite-good-looking-but-not-distractingly-so male and female presenters sit behind desks, speaking directly to camera. Behind them is a large TV screen showing footage of the latest *Transformers* movie. The action is fast, furious, metallic, loud, its choreography unintelligible. The intern leads me to a blue sofa opposite the talking heads.

He sits me down and another man comes over to me and squats down silently. He shows me a radio pack and microphone and mimes placing it on my body. I nod my head in assent. He threads the butterfly mic up through the bottom of my shirt and attaches it to my lapel. He hands me the radio pack and I put it in the pocket of my fake-fur coat. My breathing's shallow, my mouth's dry.

The intern holds up two fingers, I'm guessing that means two minutes. Lee gives me the thumbs-up. I close my eyes and try to calm my breathing but give up after thirty seconds as it only makes me more aware of my terror.

I open my eyes to see a woman wheeling in a cage. In it sits a bobcat. The cat's calm, dignified, seems bored by the action going on around it. It meets my gaze in an impassive stare. Its self-contained beauty is mesmeric. The leopard markings, the black-tipped tufts of hair at the top of its ears.

It's the bobcat in my dream. I feel a sense of foreboding. The woman parks the animal behind Lee and bends to lock the wheels. Lee turns to see what I'm staring at. He jumps forward in shock and gives an involuntary 'Shit!' loud enough to snap heads towards him. I stifle a laugh. The talking heads suffer a minuscule stumble, then continue. The cat maintains eye contact with me. It's so alive. Like all cats, it seems to be part of our world while intersecting with others.

The bobcat's trainer stands and blocks my view, the connection is cut. I'm back here on the fake set, with the fake presenters who will ask disinterested questions. I've been here so many times.

God, I hate this part of my job. Our songs are so personal and precious to me, reflect our lives, yet here I'm just another commodity, fighting for real estate.

A man in a purple suit and floral bow tie approaches, finger raised to his lips. He shakes my hand, sits down beside me. His dyed black hair is coiffured up and back in a frozen wave. Large black-framed glasses magnify fishbowl blank eyes. He must be the pop music journalist on this show. A cameraman moves silently into position in front of us, waiting to segue into our slice of the show. It's a military operation. The light on top of the camera goes from red to green, and we're off.

'Hier im Studio ist jetzt Seth Brakes von den Lucky Blank Blanks. Er ist nach einem umstrittenen Auftritt im Kaiserdom nach dreijähriger Abwesenheit wieder zurückgekehrt.' His face remains impassive as he reads from the teleprompter. 'Die Band startet die achttägige Deutschlandtournee von den Addickts heute Abend hier in Düsseldorf.' He turns to me.

'Your fifth gig, I believe,' he says in over-enunciated English, 'since you are sober.'

'Yes.'

'You have been in rehab? How was that for you?'

How am I meant to answer that? How do I condense that experience into a soundbite for breakfast television? Like a spa for fucked-up wealthy white people? I don't say it. There's an awkward pause.

'I believe . . . anyone who has had the experience of . . . a major addiction knows how difficult it is to give it up. It's a . . . constant struggle. You're never clear of its vortex.' *That wasn't too bad.*

'So, you are clean now?'

'Yeah, I've been clean for over a year.'

Careful.

'So, all that bad-boy behaviour, that was driven by the drugs and the alcohol you are taking?' He sounds like a lawyer leading a witness.

'The substances I *was* taking.' *I can do this.* 'Yes. Though in a sense I was self-medicating. To stop me feeling . . .' I feel tears embarrassingly well up. I blink them down. 'To stop me feeling . . . my shit childhood.' *God, am I really going to give a tacky breakfast show the keys to my pain? I've never gone public with this.* I'm shocked by how raw and ready to confess I am. *Well, fuck it, just be honest.* 'My childhood was really—'

'Do you remember what you did at that last concert in Frankfurt?' He leans forward to cut me off.

'I don't really.' I'm knocked back. They weren't going to talk about this.

'Then you are lucky, a lucky "blank blank"' – again the finger quotes – '*now*, everybody would have footage of it and it would be all over YouTube.' He is straining to control the excitement in his voice.

'Yeah. I'm sure it would. If . . . if anyone witnessed my behaviour, I'd like to apologise. I was very . . . ill.' I steer us back to shore. 'I am lucky. With YouTube now, everybody walks a tightrope. But hey, you don't name your band The Lucky Fu— so sorry,' I tease. 'The Lucky,' I make the finger quotes, ' "blanks" if you're going to be politically correct. The name should warn you we are edge walkers.' I'm feeling better about this. I'm doing quite well. There can't be much longer left.

'You know you broke the law in Frankfurt?'

'Did I?'

'It's illegal to do the Nazi salute in Germany,' he says.

'With or without clothes?' I garner a laugh from the floor. He blanks my winning smile. 'If I did that, and I don't remember a thing about that night, then I apologise profusely. Hopefully your authorities are forgiving . . .'

'You can take the alcohol out of the man but does that change the man?' he says.

'I . . . I . . . hope so.' *This guy is on my fucking case.*

He turns away from me to address the camera directly in German. *Great, thank God, this is the end.*

On the screen in front of me appears footage of me goosestepping up and down the dressing room doing a Nazi salute, shouting in my best John Cleese impersonation, 'Ze stepping on the ze goose.' Lee is virtually cropped out of frame.

'Or d' FBLEEPing of d' Jews.'

With that line, there is a vacuum silence of shock throughout the room as everybody inhales simultaneously.

I am on my feet without realising.

'FUCK YOU.' My fists are balled, and I'm standing over him. 'You filmed me in the dressing room! Motherfucker. I was dicking around.'

He gives me a fake smile. Behind him the live feed goes to split screen. There is now the footage of me goose-stepping and the real-time footage of me standing threateningly over him, fists clenched. Everything in me wants to punch him.

'You cunts.' I storm off.

Chapter 17

From the dressing-room window, I count seventeen people protesting the Düsseldorf gig. I'm officially a racist, and fans who didn't see the breakfast show are now being informed about it. A small media crew is filming their reaction to the footage.

I'm gutted and furious.

I'm not a racist! That's one thing I'm not.

I can't stop watching the hits add up on YouTube – up to 60k by lunchtime – with an accompanying shitstorm of comments, mostly in German. The few English ones defending me are the worst!

'Get over it, Fritz, you shouldn't have murdered all those Jews.'

There's even Holocaust deniers on there! Damn! *Real racists, please don't defend me! I don't want you in my corner.*

In our soundcheck the security stood around giving me the eye. The band are bricking it. So am I.

As I walked into the band dressing room I overheard Oliver saying, 'Our Facebook page is being bombed with German abuse . . .'

Everyone went quiet.

I'm not answering Brunt's calls. He texted.

That went well! You really fucked us in Germany and possibly with Faith's people. Let's just hope the forest fire doesn't spread.

I told Stella what happened. I could have handled her anger but it was grief, grief that her parents will find out. She thought she was winning them round. At least she didn't accuse me of antisemitism.

Half an hour to showtime . . .

I'm shitting it. This time for good reason. The auditorium mood is broadcast backstage over the speakers in the dressing rooms – there's even one here in the toilet! People keep shouting out and then others shout back. 'Racist' is the key word. I pull the wires out the back of the speaker.

I'm rehearsing what to say to them when I get out there . . .

Fifteen-minute call . . .

I'm back in the dressing room. Playing the Pixies LOUD through a boom box. I'm screaming along with Frank Black.

I am un chien Andalusia.
I am un chien Andalusia.

Throwing myself around the room venting my fury, my fear – *It's not fucking fair!*

There's a knock at my door. I stop, panting, drenched, grab a towel, turn the music down.

'Come in.'

Josh, our tour manager.

'Come to see the condemned man?' I say.

He looks up at the wall speaker, clocks the disconnected wires.

'It's getting a bit heated out there.' He can hardly look at me.

'You think.'

'You don't actually have to go on.'

'I think you'll find I do.'

'No. I've cleared it with everyone. The venue would rather you didn't. Even The Addickts get it. They've agreed you don't have to play tonight.'

'You didn't check with me first?'

'It's not just about you, Seth. The band—'

I leave the room at a run and burst into the band's dressing room. Everyone stops when I enter. They look terrified.

'Hey, mate,' says Lee.

'You know about this?'

'That they want to cancel the gig?'

I turn to the others.

'You don't want to go on?'

'You've stirred up an ants' nest and *we'll* get bitten,' whines Stanley. 'Our fucking lives are on the line for this band and he,' Stanley points at me, fuming, 'is fucking it up again.'

I turn to them. 'I'm sorry, I did fuck up.'

'Again!' says Stanley. 'You fucked up *again*. I thought all this shit was over.'

'Hey, that's not fair, you weren't there. They set us up,' says Lee.

'And Seth walked into it. Yeah, you said. I'm just fed up with this shit. Why can't you just be a bit more . . . *normal*?' says Stanley.

We all pause at that word, then crack up laughing.

'Look,' I say, 'I get it. I wouldn't like to have to go out there and face something *you'd* stirred up. So I'll go out on my own and talk to them.'

'No, you're fucking not.' Lee stands and checks himself in the mirror. He's dressed like a steamboat gambler.

'I'll deal with it. It's my mess. I'll play "Fuck Up" ' as an acoustic song.'

'I'm coming with you. If I remember rightly I started the whole goose-step thing. Stanley, you owe me a tenner.' He smiles. 'Told you he wouldn't have it.'

'I'm playing.' Dan doesn't look up from filing his nails. 'But may I suggest we play "Give It All a Name". In these circumstances . . .' he says quietly.

I could hug him, but for Dan that would be like Germany invading Poland.

Oops.

'*A new one*,' says Lee. 'We hardly know it.'

'The lyrics are relevant. And it will give us something else to worry about.'

'You're mad. I'm game,' I say. '"Give It All a Name".'

'You think you're going to leave me out?' says Cream.

'Or me, you fucker?' says Oliver.

'All right, all right, but . . . but let the three of us go on first. When it calms,' I look to Oliver and Cream, 'you come on with "Everyone Loves a Loser". Right?'

'No way, I want to be with you.' Cream stands.

'I think Seth's right.' Lee shakes his head. 'We should start low key, vulnerable . . . acoustic and keys. Bass and drums, sorry, guys . . . not right.'

Cream looks unhappy but sits down. 'So long as you know we're with you.'

'Thanks mate.' We fist bump. 'I do.'

I leave the dressing room before I get emotional.

I tell Josh we're playing – I tell him the set change.

'Tell Kevin to keep the houselights up in the auditorium. Bright.'

I go wait side stage behind the mixing desk, out of sight. The hubbub drowns out the pre-gig music. There are shouts of 'Racist', 'Go home' and even 'Fascist'. It's a full house.

Early Man, our drum tech, is gaffering the new set list to our monitors. A coin clatters into the kit. He goes to adjust a bolt under the snare and pockets the coin. He shuffles offstage with the Mancunian swagger that got him his moniker.

'Is it worth it – fucking Krauts?' he says.

Dan and Lee join me.

175

'This should be fun.' Lee puts his hand on my shoulder. Don't know if I'm going to cry or throw up.

Without coke, without booze.

'Stay on the stage,' Josh says. 'Not that you've been going in the audience, but security says stay on the stage.'

I look at Lee and smile.

'Oh Josh, that wasn't a good idea.' Says Lee.

The music stops. Shouts of anticipation. Shouts of anger. Adrenalin fizzes through my body.

'Woah,' says Lee. I shudder and shake out my arms. Dan's still filing his nails. Behind him the rest of the Fuckers have come to watch. Behind them Harry's rubbing his hands, saying something to Phil and Charlie Addickt.

'Just remember you have the mic,' says Lee.

The sheer voltage pouring through me's overwhelming. I'm terrified, but the terror's also a buzz. I guess that's why I'm a singer, *and* an addict.

'Let's go.'

I walk to the mic. The roar intensifies. My smile is bolted on. A few coins clatter around me. Many of the crowd are standing in front of their flip-up seats. There's at least four thousand here, in a venue that holds eight; more than usual for the start of our set. *There's no such thing as bad promotion.* A coin hits my head, shocks me, staggers me back a step, takes me out of time. It's a euro. I pick it up.

'Thanks,' I say into the mic and put it in my pocket. Some people laugh. Then angry shouting resumes as more coins ping into the drum kit and another coin hits my body. They're coming from off to the side. A small group of men start to chant, 'Racist.' Others join in around the room.

Oh fuck.

In the pit, security are waving me offstage. Cameras flash. The video operator on the track below me slides to the side, out of the line of fire. I look to the left side video screen and see myself looking lost.

Lee sidles up to me.

'You're bleeding, mate.'

I raise my hand, my fingers come away with blood. I feel light-headed.

One two three four

I close my eyes for a second and just stand there listening to the chants, the sounds, the screams, feeling it all and letting it pass through me.

The bobcat comes to mind.

One two three four

I get peaceful. The noise drops away.

I open my eyes.

'OK. OK. Hear me out. Come on, hear me out.' Some of the roar subsides.

'Just in case you didn't know it,' I say, 'I fucked up today. For those of you who haven't seen it on YouTube . . . I did the goose-step—'

'Racist!' somebody shouts out.

'Yes, I suppose it is . . . And I said "the fucking of the Jews" and I totally get how that seems racist. I wasn't advocating it! I was dicking around with my friend here . . . It was dumb . . .' There's more angry shouts. 'Don't you do dumb shit like that with your mates . . . when no one's looking? Seriously? I do. Unfortunately . . . I got caught on camera.' A few boos. 'I mean fuck, man. I'm an addict. You know my story . . . I'm an edge walker and I fell over the edge – it's kinda what I'm known for.'

The hail of coins has stopped. 'I fucked up. I'm sorry. I do it all the time, by the way. Fuck up. I mean, come on – you didn't come to see bands called "The Lucky Fuckers" and "The Addickts" to see saints; you came to see edge walkers.'

More shouts. A euro hits my shin and some fly past me. People duck in the front rows, then turn and shout angrily back at the throwers.

'Fucking pack it in – you'll hurt someone down here!' I shout. The audience are hushed. My voice fills the room.

'Listen, I get it. Here in Germany, racism is a big deal, I've been to the Holocaust museum, I'm glad you're so on it. You're one of the *only countries* that face their past. Seriously, one of the only ones. I mean, *I'm English.*' This draws a laugh. I wipe some blood out of my eyes. 'I'm not antisemitic – my *girlfriend's* a Jew. I love her. Her parents don't want me to marry her . . . I don't blame them. I wouldn't want my daughter to marry me either.' Another laugh. 'But they don't want me to marry her *cos I'm not Jewish*. It's great, isn't it, all this – all this tribalism. It's the big disease, the big fucking disease of the human race. So yeah, I'm Seth, and I'm human, and I'm sorry. Hate me if you want.' Another coin hits the stage. It's from twenty rows back to my left.

'Fuck off!' I bellow. 'You going to stone me? What do you want from me?'

One of them screams, 'Go home, you racist.'

'That *wasn't* what . . .'

Without thinking I walk to the lip of the stage and drop down the six feet into the pit and vault the metal barrier into the auditorium. The room crackles in anticipation.

A security guard tries to climb over behind me. 'No!' I say. He backs off.

I walk up the aisle to the angry gang.

'What do you want me to say? I'm sorry. What do you want from me?' The first man on the row is *jacked*. Why are they all so big in this country? He's screaming, snarling. His mates back off him. I approach.

Now what do I do?

Lee strums the opening chords of 'Give It All a Name'.

Yes, genius!

I start singing to the man, softly, with vulnerability, like I'm trying to calm an angry dog.

I'm so happy to meet you.
So glad that you came
There's nothing like a trembling to remind us who we are
    again.
Didn't catch it the first time
Now it's too late to ask your name.
The intimacy's beautiful
But the leaving makes me blaze away.

Everyone holds their breath, waiting to see what he'll do.

He's confused. I'm singing to him; he doesn't know what to do with this. Would you thump an unarmed man singing to you?

179

He takes in the strange scene around him. It's like he's in a movie. A musical! We're up on the big screens. The sight subdues him, his rage is melting. He unclenches.

Kev's put an orange light on us. It softens the cratered skin on his face. His muscles look well earned – hard labour rather than a gym. A chiselled crude face, weathered from the outdoors. It's an honest face, there's no guile or confusion of identity. I imagine he's looked like this all his life. Not like me, you wouldn't recognise me from my childhood photos. Between birth and now – I look like three different people. I like this man. I trust this man. I like that he's pissed at racism. He looks stoned in wonder at the strangeness of the situation. I see myself through his eyes, a skinny singer gently singing to him. He's searching my face. He's looking for . . . he's looking for some deception in me. He's scanning me for why I'm doing this.

My life's mistakes give voice to choice and values
Live my life with.

Dan joins in on piano. I'm locked in eye contact. Blue eyes, as blue as a Greek-island sea. Only lovers look at each other like this.

We give it all a name
We give it all a name
We give it all a name
Our words define our universe

I feel vulnerable yet strong. Time's frozen, it's just me and him. I sing, sing to the deepest place in him. When I wrote the words to this song, I followed my tongue. I didn't know what I was writing about. This here is its moment, its purpose.

Chinatown the west side.
Projects to the east.
Hispanics, Jews, refugees,
Here for gold and here for peace.
The mob from which they're running from's
the mobs to which they came.
May differ in appearances but inside we're all the same.
We give it all a name.
We give it all a name.
Our words define our universe so small.

Afterwards everyone's buzzing on the gig high. Cracking jokes, shouting over the boom box blasting out house tunes. Oliver empties his pockets of euros.

'I got nine,' he crows.

'They tip racists in Germany,' says Lee.

'Careful,' I say. 'Watch out for the hidden camera.'

'That was brilliant,' says Cream. 'You should be racist more often. Try Islam next!' he shouts. 'Actually, no. No.'

Harry Addickt brings in champagne from the promoter.

'Fucking rad, man! I wondered when the real Seth Brakes would turn up.' He gives me a hug. 'Legend, bro!' He sends bottles clattering off the table, unwraps an eight-ball and prepares it into lines. 'Charlie on the house, lads.'

He grabs me by the shoulders and tries to pull me down to the table.

'No, man – I don't do that. I'm clean.' I pull back.

He pulls a face. 'Come on, man, one line—'

'No! I'm straight.'

'You did that straight? *Kudos.*'

'He doesn't.' Stanley indicates me. 'We do.'

And the band dive in.

Two hours later The Addickts' crew are loading equipment into flight cases, rolling them up a battered ramp and crashing them into the truck. The lights are migraine bright, exposing the sterility of the venue, the debris left behind.

I get nods of respect from crew members and security. I dodge the traffic of working men and jump down from the loading bay into the cold, drizzling night. Twenty yards away sits our tour bus, engine idling. I swing my bag round my back and head up the road. As I approach the bus, a small group of fans step out of a nearby doorway where they've been sheltering from the rain. It's the big man from the gig; he moves to intercept my approach.

Oh fuck.

Without breaking stride, I weigh up my options: there's no one around to help me and the bag's too heavy to run with. If he attacks, I'll sling it at him and leg it. I give him a big smile and keep walking.

'How are you doing?' I say.

His eyes search my face as he steps in. He opens his arms and folds me into an embrace that lifts me off the ground.

Chapter 18

I'm in a loud, packed bierkeller on the other side of town. Still buzzing from the gig. I'm with Klaus and his gang, about eight in all, three women, the rest bruisers like him. Had no choice really and now there's the awkward reality that despite that intimate moment in the gig, we don't know each other. As a vaguely famous person they treat me as some exotic animal they feel the need to touch and photograph. This would normally send me into my shell but I'm still high from the gig, so fuck it. They're drinking heavily and trying to get me to join them. It's tempting. I deserve one. I don't.

We're shouting over the tacky Europop. Klaus, who's sitting next to me, keeps slapping me on the back to punctuate points he's making in German. His eyes burn into mine with the need to be seen, to be witnessed. He's being translated by Lotte. She's late twenties, smoky eyed, catlike. Judging by how she's flirting with me she's not with any of the guys here.

'He wants you to know he loves you – even if you are racist,' Lotte shouts.

'Tell him he's a big fat Kraut . . . and I love him too.'

She does, and Klaus spits beer over me laughing.

'We all love you,' she says. 'You mean a lot to us. That's why it hurt. You being racist. Ah fuck, everyone's racist. We Germans

183

know that more than anyone. That's why we are so . . . politically correct. Good gig, by the way.' She toasts my Perrier with beer.

'You've got to make eye contact. Seven years' bad sex if you—'

'Yes, I know. Stupid though.' She looks into her glass for a moment, then looks directly into my eyes.

'Speaking of sex, where are you staying tonight?' she says.

I try to keep my face neutral while I digest this, but my mouth betrays me and drops open.

I haven't *looked* at another woman since Stell. I've felt so . . . full. I'd assumed my desire had gone for good, melted under the heat of true love. But the thought of sleeping with this girl – turns me on – and makes me afraid. Afraid of fucking up the one great thing in my life. This gorgeous girl in front of me. What would it be like?

Lotte turns her gaze to something floating in her glass.

What a lovely offer. The good old days. Why not? Who wouldn't? It would be so simple. If I slept with her, she wouldn't expect a follow-up. She knows what this is. Who would we be hurting? I love Stella, so of course I wouldn't tell her. It wouldn't affect my love for her.

A red tattoo peeks out from her sweater sleeve. My senses strain to feel her. The anticipation's thrilling. She's cute. Underneath those winter clothes is a yoga body. *How would she come?*

'Is that a German thing? That directness?' I ask.

'I believe in asking for what I want,' she says, with no hint of defensiveness. 'Come on. You are a lead singer in a great band . . . this must happen to you all the time.'

'Say the word "great" again,' I say.

She smiles, bites her lip.

Who's this going to hurt? I can't walk away from this.

She sips her beer. I take it from her and inhale. God it smells good. The smell seems to rearrange something in my brain, makes me relax. I close my eyes and take a long slow sip. Internally I feel tectonic plates shift, the whole internal structure of my being, cogs and wheels, shift over a gear to something else. Something familiar. Something less brittle, more in the flow of life. I put the drink down, lean over and kiss her on the lips.

We stumble into Lotte's apartment, kissing.

'Wait, wait.' She pulls away from me and squats in the doorframe.

'Eva, Eva,' she calls into the dark. I hear the faint tinkle of a bell and a ginger cat emerges from the darkness. Lotte talks lovingly to it in German. She rises with it in her arms.

'Seth, this is Eva. Eva, Seth.' I stroke Eva. She thrums with pleasure.

'Ahh, you've won her over. She's usually cagey with men.'

She goes to settle Eva in a side room, stroking and talking to her like a child.

I'm relieved to get in from the cold but it's a reality check being in her apartment – surrounded by the objects that make up this woman's life. It smells of coffee and cat litter.

Lotte returns and seems to sense how starkly her biography is laid bare. She turns on a lamp and plugs in some blue and pink fairy lights framing a bookcase. She turns off the main light.

'That's better. Want a coffee?'

'Don't think so,' I say.

'Well, here we are.'

'We are.'

I know I should step in here and kiss away the awkwardness, but I miss the beat.

'Sorry it's such a mess. If I'd known Seth Brakes was coming . . .'

'It's not a mess,' I say. 'You should see my place.'

I busy myself in her books and CDs.

'You're in there. Look.' She points to our two CDs sandwiched between *Simon and Garfunkel's Greatest Hits* and Take That.

'Take That!'

'Don't say that. I love Take That.'

Take That.

I shouldn't be here.

This room, this getting to know her, it's feeling weird, but I can't just leave, can't back out now.

I turn and she kisses me. Bubblegum and beer. Her breasts

brush against my chest. My hands slide under her sweater to the silky skin of her waist.

Stella!

Am I going to tell Jada I've relapsed? My mind's spinning into panic.

'Actually,' I break off from the kiss, 'I need to use the bathroom . . . and . . . can I have that coffee?'

She looks like I've slapped her.

'Sure. The bathroom's there.'

I close the door.

What am I doing?

A lava lamp gives off a green tinge. My head's in my hands. I feel sick.

Stella.

One two three four

When I come out, she's sitting on the sofa texting someone. She stops like I've caught her doing something she shouldn't.

'Lotte . . .' I stand in front of her. 'I have to go. I'm so sorry. The bus leaves,' I look at my phone, 'very soon and I . . . I can't do this. I'm so sorry.'

She sits back, one leg tucked under the other, foot twitching from side to side like a cat flicking its tail. 'OK.' She blows on her coffee and takes a sip. I shuffle backwards.

'Yeah, I . . .' *What can I say?* 'OK.' I turn around to leave, then back to her. 'It was lovely meeting you and . . . I . . . I just can't do this now, I'm so sorry.'

On the bus Josh's grey blackout curtains are pulled tight across his bunk.

'You fucked up the driver's hours so we're stuck here for the night.' He said on the phone. 'And your girlfriend called. Said she'd been trying to get hold of you.'

Two missed calls.

In the taxi I listen to her message.

Been trying to get hold of you. Where are you, love? Please call me.

Can't ring her now, too late and she'd smell the guilt on me.

I'm too wired to sleep so I go find Lee, who's alone in the upper-deck lounge, standing over a collage laid out on the floor, shifting images around. The room's a mess of shredded magazines. I make him a coffee, move scissors and glue off the couch and sit with him.

'When's the exhibition?'

'Around the album launch.'

'Clever. What's this?' I nod at the collage.

He gives me an irritated look.

'A collage.'

'Yeah, but—'

'It's an imaginary album cover for an imaginary band,' he says without looking up.

'Uh-huh.'

'A German band – Altz Heimer,' he says.

'Alzheimer?'

'You're quick.'

I try to read the haphazard letters he's cut out from the magazines.

'"I'm lost"?'

'Fuck off and go and annoy somebody else will ya.' He blows out his cheeks then turns to me. '*I've Lost My Keys*. It's the album title.'

I laugh.

'This for your exhibition?' I ask.

'No, my peace of mind,' he says.

'This Altz Heimer's first album?'

He nods.

'Second one should be called *Are You My Husband?*'

His eyes flash me. 'Bastard. That's good, I'm nicking that.'

'The third . . . *Who Am I?*'

His laughter falls into sadness.

'Quit while you're ahead.'

We sip coffee in silence.

'How *is* your mum?' I ask. The silence deepens.

'Not my mum any more. Mum's gone and left this . . . ghost.' He stares ahead, cradling his mug. 'She looks like my mum, but she's not my mum. The only time she comes alive is when she hears music. Music from *her* day, Beatles, Stones. She completely lights up and recognises me . . . and Dad. The power of music.'

He leans towards me and sniffs.

'Have you been drinking?'

'Don't be daft!'

'You smell of booze.' He scouts my face for a lie.

'I was with drinkers, not drinking.'

He doesn't believe me so I offer up a hostage.

'I kissed a girl who was drinking.'

'I kissed a girl who was drinking' isn't cutting it either. Need to give him more.

'Actually . . . I nearly slept with her. That's why I'm late. Don't know what I was thinking.' Genuine remorse infuses my lies but he knows me too well, so I prattle on.

'You know that big guy in the gig tonight? The one I sang to? He bushwhacked me on the way to the bus, dragged me off to some bierkeller with his mates for an armistice. I ended up with this, this beauty in some dodgy part of— Stop looking at me like that, will you! I feel shit enough as it is.'

He doesn't flinch. He picks up his collage and props it up on the seats.

'I didn't drink anything!'

He grabs handfuls of scraps from the magazines and chucks them in the bin. He organises the rest into a stack. He goes to his bunk, climbs in and closes the curtains.

By the time I wake, morning is mid-afternoon. Once I'm clear of the sleeping-pill fog, I ring Stella. There's a silence where her phone should go to answer machine, an alive silence that feels like there's someone there. My body prickles, I'm about to hang up.

'Leave me a message please.'

'Hey, darling, I'm so sorry. I just woke up. We had a rough gig last night. I . . . I – we had some real trouble with the fans . . . I left my phone on the bus and it ran out of juice. Please, please call me. I know you've got your hands full of . . . of babies. We're on our way to Schnitzel Burger or somewhere. Love you. Love you. Call me.'

I want to wind back time. What the fuck was I thinking? I wasn't thinking.

As I enter the downstairs kitchen area, I receive a round of applause.

'At least someone's getting laid,' says Early Man.

'I wish!' I say. 'I'm sorry, everyone. Won't happen again.'

Lee won't look at me.

I clean a coffee cup and use it to brush my teeth, chucking the contents down the toilet. I pee standing up, bracing myself on the side walls. The bus hits a pothole. I splash piss on the seat and my bare feet.

Three hours later I'm settled into another bland hotel room. I'm showered and scrubbed in an attempt to clean off last night. Been giving myself pep talks:

Yes, I had half a pint.

Yes, I kissed a girl.

But I stopped myself.

I stopped. I should be celebrating, not beating myself up.

Don't give yourself such a hard time.

I won't do it again.

I did all right.

My phone chimes. I jump.

Damn, I'm scared of a phone now?

Stella's name's written onscreen.

'Stella?'

'Hi,' she says.

'Stella. Oh my God, I'm so sorry, my love.' And I am. I'm sorry for what I've done. Nearly done.

'It's OK, Seth. I get it, you're on tour. The planet of no ripple.'

'What do you mean?'

'I mean you're on tour – what do you think that means?'

'"The planet of no ripple"?' I say.

'No consequences, no karma – I don't know what you get up to.' She sounds weary. 'I'm sorry, forget that. I'm exhausted from the shoot. Let's not be having any babies for a while. Listen – have you heard from Lizzie?'

'No.'

'You haven't heard what's happened?'

More bad news. Oh Fuck. Everything goes thick and heavy as I wait for something that some part of me already knows. Like there's two of me, the one that knows and the one that doesn't.

'Who's died?' I ask.

'No one's died. Holly's missing.'

'Missing?'

'Yeah, they . . . they had a row and Lizzie hasn't seen her for two days.'

'Two days! She's twelve!'

'Thirteen, yeah. Lizzie's been going crazy. But she didn't want me to tell you while you're on tour. The police are looking for her.'

Chapter 19

'Hi, I'm Seth.'

'Hello, Seth.'

'I'm an alcoholic and drug addict – five days sober.' There's around thirty people at this meeting.

'I don't usually talk at these things – I don't ever talk at these things – just sit at the back and pretend to listen.' There's some laughter. 'Well, your meetings are in German, for fuck's sake.' More laughter.

'I'm on tour here, I'm a singer . . . and tour is the last place I want to be – I'm touring with a band called The Addickts! Seriously, God's got a great sense of humour.

'It's not funny. My, my big problem with AA is I don't believe in God, a higher power.

'Sorry, I'm rambling.

'I didn't get up here for this . . . to tell you this.

'My niece is missing, run away from home . . . four days now, and she's just a kid . . .' I take a while to compose myself. 'I want to be with my sister, her mother, be there for her, like she was for me. She's freaking out – but I'm on fucking tour and if we cancel they'll never insure us for touring again – cos of my history. So I'm . . . I'm stuck here.' I wipe tears away and take a moment.

'My mother was an alcoholic. I hear that at so many meetings . . . This, this disease comes in all shapes and sizes, she was a mean one . . . lots of beatings . . . not as bad as some, worse than many. My sister – big sister – was . . . my saviour . . . saved me, was my protector . . . when she could. It was me and her against the world, no one believed us, no one saw us. Which is why, I guess, I'm a singer now . . . everyone sees me.' I have everyone's attention, that's the beauty of AA; people listen.

'So, this is what I'd like to ask: I would like to ask you – you who believe in a higher power – to pray for my niece. She's called Holly and she . . . You'd like her. Could you do that? Could you pray for her?'

'Are you OK?' I'm in the empty backstage catering, phone rammed to my ear. I can hear a muffled train station tannoy in the background at Holly's end.

'Holly girl, come on. Talk to me. You can always talk to me. Are you OK?'

Some Addickts and crew enter the room talking. Charlie Addickt comes up, sees me on the phone, mouths, 'Great gig the other night.' I give him a grim smile, point to the phone and move to a far corner. Down the line I hear a Scottish-accented announcement. *So she's still in Scotland.* Six days, for a thirteen-year-old.

'Don't want to live with Mum any more.'

'What's happened, Hol? Are you OK? We've been fucking terrified.' I'm trying not to ask the obvious clichéd questions or tell her how freaked out Lizzie is, but it's hard. I put the phone on speaker and find Lizzie's contact number. I text her.

On phone to Holly now.

'Holly, tell me you're at least OK? Nothing, nothing bad's happened?'

'What's with you adults and sex? That's all you think about,' says the little fucking mind reader. I reset and text Liz.

She's OK.

'Are you ready to go home, Hol?'

'I haven't got a home.'

Lizzie told me she wasn't settling into the new house. I swallow my guilt that they had to rehouse.

'I want to live with you and Stella.' *Oh shit . . .*

Where is she? flashes up Lizzie's text.

'Holly, Stella and I don't live together. I'm in Germany right now, she's in Paris.'

'I know,' says Holly, 'but when you get back.'

A train station in Scotland, I text.

Get her to come home!!

I've got to give her something. 'Yeah, we could talk about that.'

'Really?' As she speaks, I hear an announcement saying *Waverley Station*.

'We're not "parents" – but we can talk about it.'

'I don't need a parent. I just need . . . somewhere safe and warm.'

Poor fucker must be freezing.

She's in Waverley Station.

I feel a rat texting that. Both me and Lizzie ran away from home countless times. But Lizzie's not like Mum.

'Ring Mum, Hols. She's in a proper state. The police are out looking . . . You've gotta go home.'

'Haven't got a home.'

'What about your brother?' Silence, but a silence that feels like a strike. 'Look, if you really hate the new house, I'm sure we can talk . . .'

'Have you told her we're talking?'

I think about lying but she'll see through it.

'Yeah.'

The line goes dead.

Two hours later Lizzie texts me.

She's home, she's safe.

Last gig of the tour. I'm staring at a wrap sitting next to three shots of a water-like liquid. Under the glass there's a piece of A4 with 'drink me' written on it in a childish scrawl.

I shut the dressing-room door. I can hear my heartbeat. I approach the table, dab a finger in a glass, taste it.

Yeah, it's vodka.

I crinkle open the foil.

Yeah, it's coke.

I sit down and try to stare them away.

Who? Stanley? He's been the most vocal about how shit I've been since the racist gig. Footage of me getting bloodied by coins and going walkabout in the audience went viral. It gave Brunt a hard-on. It gave the band a hard-on. It gave the German record company a hard on. Even made the news here. Everyone forgot about me being racist. 'Brave victim' trumps racist apparently.

More of the same please, texted Brunt.

Ah, but there's the rub, not so easy with straight Seth back at the mic.

Addickts' audiences started to turn up early to watch the daredevil singer. Unfortunately, he's gone missing in action.

My ears prick up at noises in the corridor. Don't want anyone to walk in and catch me with these. Footsteps walk on by. The speakers in my room pick up Lana Del Rey's 'Video Games', five more songs till we're on. My room smells of beef crisps. That was my supper. Someone must have dropped this off while I was at AA.

In soundcheck, we ran through two new songs, including 'Horseman'. It was a mess but we're going to try to play it tonight . . . to adrenalise us . . . to adrenalise me!

'Drink me' – a reference to *Alice in Wonderland*.

I should take it to the band. Take it to their dressing room, *Who the fuck put this in my room?*

I *think* they'll be outraged. Except Stanley.

Feel like I'm in that spaghetti western, *The Good, the Bad and the Ugly* – charlie's bad, vodka's ugly – and the three of us are just staring at each other, waiting for one of us to make a move.

The gigs have been shit.

As the lesser of two evils, vodka wouldn't be *so* bad.

Maybe if I just have the drink. Just the vodka.

That would be some measure of control. Then I can see if it would make a difference. I mean fuck, if we play like this on our own tour we're fucked anyway. Better try it here, in a no-nothing gig.

I hear footsteps in the hall and move without thinking.

I down the shots, they burn my throat, I drop the glasses through the swinging plastic bin lid and pocket the wrap of coke.

A few shots and now a *world* of difference.

Bottled charisma.

I'm fun drunk!

I'm a great performer smashed. I mean I'm not smashed, but just right. If I could just limit myself to this . . .

There's a don't-give-a-shit going on in my body. I ooze a sloppy authority.

I'm even dancing!

Well, moving, swaying, in the instrumental sections. Lost in music.

Sixth song in, I look at my set list.

'Horseman. Improvise!' is written in red. *Oh shit.*

This was Lee's idea to fire us up – put us on edge – we reasoned it worked for 'Give It All a Name'. The recording of 'Horseman' is naff so – we're going to try jam a new version. *Live!* Terrifying.

I start circling the three chords on acoustic.

Where do I start?

Alex.

I close my eyes and allow myself to remember Alex. Dead on the sofa. A junkie cliché, until you've seen it, been in the room with it, been it. I took the first hit, he took the second. I came back. He didn't. He didn't. How does that fucking work? He'd been clean for months, that's how it works. He'd been out of practice.

I shake my head and come back to the gig.

The auditorium hubbub has dropped to a respectable level. Even in this hall they can see I'm wrestling with something. And I know from experience that a man wrestling with his demons onstage is the definition of charisma; it holds your attention.

Except not everyone here is quiet, is respectful. There's this fucking cluster directly in front of me, drunk, yak yakking away. A gang of six, who have clearly come for The Addickts and don't give a fuck about the support. They're shouting to each other

– louder than the guitar I'm strumming. I want to fuckin' kill 'em. I go round the chords a couple more times, staring them down, dropping the volume, hoping they might get the hint. They don't.

'Will you shut the fuck up, please?'

I stop playing. The amplified words cut through everything. They look up at me, shocked. 'Yeah, you. I'm trying to play a song here . . . and some of those around you . . . look like they'd like to hear it – so if you could just shut up for a few minutes. Or – go outside.'

There is a smattering of applause.

'Fuck off,' says this tall boy, close-cropped black hair, rosacea-cheeked, who chests himself forward from the pack. 'I'll take you outside.' Fuck, of course he's English and up for it. My fucking luck. His gang laugh.

'Kevin, can you give us some lights down here?'

I casually pick up a bottle of water, unscrew it, take a sip, screw the cap back on and replace it. After a moment lights come on from behind me down into the auditorium, blinding him, silhouetting me; Kevin giving me tactical advantage. One of the stage cameras swings round to take the boy in. He looks about eighteen. He looks up at the screen over my shoulder and reddens at his image. I lift the mic off the stand, walk forward and squat at the lip of the stage.

'What's your name?'

I'm soft voiced, not giving him any aggression to bounce off.

'What's your name?'

The auditorium leans in to the drama. His pluck is visibly evaporating in the spotlight, on the screen.

'I'm Seth,' I take the lead, 'and I'm trying to sing a song about my . . . my friend Alex, who died of an overdose.' I feel tears. I clear my throat. Look away to gain composure.

Stay focused. Don't break down.

'What's your name?'

'Trevor.' His voice betrays his nerves.

'Have you ever lost anyone, Trevor?' He's confused. 'Death, Trevor. Has anyone close to you died?' The question echoes round the venue. He looks away. His support group back off ever so slightly and he feels it.

'Has anyone close to you died, Trevor?' I put my head down. A tear splashes on my boxer boots. The silence in the room is complete. I wait. He cracks.

'My mother.' He looks tender. The sharing's dissolved him. Him and me. Melted us into one. Mad and yet that simple. Trevor looks like a little boy.

'Thanks,' I say. 'Thank you.'

I stand up and strum the chords, slow.

I look into the darkness. I talk the opening lines:

My twin soul died in utero
Yeah,
A loss
But one I would never know.

The band drift into the song effortlessly.

Warm body now cold
Autopsy

Who knew
you'd be the first to go?
She'll miss you
Watching you get old
Holding her hand
All alone in this hollow world

Lee comes in, not with the line he recorded, but a quivering, fragile slide guitar, a long-held note. A note that soars over the chorus, threatening to derail it – succeeding in adding to its vulnerability.

I feel the sting
You don't feel anything
It should have been me
My fate, my destiny

The slide dips down into a lonely whale song sound on the word *destiny*. I'm unable to sing. Cream hovers on one note, waiting for me. Warm, syrupy, each note takes on a deeper resonance.

Dan creeps in with a shimmering glissando which sounds like a child's glockenspiel.

I'm sleepwalking in a dream of tenderness and grief. The lyric lands, lands for the first time.

Oh Al, I tried the kiss of life, I did. But he didn't come back. His life was a litany of bad choices and missed opportunities. He didn't want to come back.

He had a kid!

He had a fucking kid.

She kissed you even when you're cold
What possessed you
to leave a little girl alone in this world?
I feel the sting
You don't feel anything
Should have been me
My fate, my destiny

Mo, in the pink butterfly wings I bought for her sixth birthday. She wore them at her dad's funeral. I flew her up off the ground to give her dad a goodbye kiss. I ride the crack in my voice.

It could have been me.
He should have been me.

It should've been me and everything is now . . . just . . . ashes. With Al I hit bottom. His death got me sober. His death woke me up. *And now look.*

I feel the sting
You don't feel anything
It should have been me
My fate, my destiny

Last chorus, Oliver drops it down to the bass drum – it's a heartbeat.

Dum-dum. Dum-dum.

It's genius. Fucking Olly who *never* improvises! I want to kiss him. The fast version we recorded with Rupert has a daft uplifting tag on the end – this is real.

I feel the sting
Now I don't feel anything
It should have been me
My fate, responsibility

Everyone drops out but the bass drum.

Dum-dum.

The lights get dimmer,

dum-dum

and dimmer.

Dum-dum

then

STOPS.

Lights go to blackout.

Silence.

Followed by a God-almighty roar from the audience.

A sound that recognises what we have just witnessed. The sound of our collective humanity. An unrepeatable, precious moment of connectedness. The real thing.

In the Fuckers' dressing room the band are getting loaded. A London Grammar track is distorting Dan's Bluetooth speaker.

Oliver lifts me off the ground in a bear hug.

'Fuck me,' he screams.

Lee and Dan on a sofa are sharing a bottle of red. Cream and Stanley on vodka oranges.

'Come here,' says Lee, arms open. I sit next to him. He pulls me in till our sweaty heads touch.

'Fuck me, that was something.' He leans in and whispers in my ear, 'That's what I meant about us writing together. The whole band. Never thought we'd do it in a fucking gig, though.' He shakes me. 'You OK?' Then to the room, 'Can everyone remember the parts they played? That heartbeat beat, Ol, fucking a-ma-zing.'

Oliver roars and swigs his Heineken.

'We're gonna drop the upbeat end section,' Lee says to the room, 'it sucks anyway. You OK with that?' he says to me.

'Yeah.' But I'm not OK, I'm numb and empty.

My phone buzzes. A text from Brunt.

Faith's on board. She signed off on it today. The Düsseldorf footage won her over. 🙏

I feel flat. I don't know what I feel.

On the tour bus, Kevin, our lampie, comes and sits next to me.

'That's why I came out of retirement, to work with you, Seth. No one does that, these moments. Worth their weight in gold.' His kind eyes beam at me. Josh hands him a beer. 'Don't mind if I do.' He takes my hand. 'You did that without booze, Seth. I'd been waiting to see if you could do that. Well done. I'm so proud of you.' He claps me on the back, spilling beer on his trousers.

I lie on my bunk, close the curtains, put on my headphones to drown out the party noises. I take a sleeping pill. The bus pulls out and heads for home, to England. After an hour, when the first pill doesn't work, I take two more.

Chapter 20

'I've got a week to finish the lyrics. If I don't get them right, they'll haunt me for ever. Please, I *have* to work.'

Stella's staying, her best mate's away, she's bored, wants entertaining. She's gone all needy on me, but I can't think about her right now. *Got to finish these songs.*

I work in my bedroom. The desk is pulled out from the wall by four inches; enough depth for me to gaffer a small bottle of vodka behind the right-hand drawer. I'm not taking much; I mark the spirit level with a Sharpie and am keeping myself to a few finger widths a day. It helps in the writing, helps me flow and shuts my critic up. That's just the way it is. I'll deal with it later, when the pressure's off.

Lee's been over and we've written three more seeds of songs, two of them sound stronger than what we've already got. He's a bit distant, or am I being paranoid? I watch my breath around him.

I improvise lyrics by singing to the instrumentals in GarageBand. I sing five or six takes, listen back, and write down the best lines or ones suggested by the sounds that I sang.

I copy and paste them into a Word doc.

It amazes me that even though I'm not looking for coherence between lines, not consciously looking for a narrative, if I choose the best lines, there seems to be an unconscious coherence that makes sense. I can't tell if that's my mind imposing a story where there isn't one, or my unconscious mind creating a story unconsciously.

I'm creating lyrics with an intensity that comes from outside of myself.

I'm thirty-four, I've never felt this before.
Feel I'm awakening
From a dreaming
This here story's taken
Laced with double meaning
I'm the last to admit it
That I'm needing your lips
But I'm scared of your grip
You can touch but don't stick
You can touch but don't stick
It doesn't happen like this –
Until it happens like this.

Chapter 21

This is it. This is why I'm in a band. This is why I'm here, why I came back.

This moment.

We've just nailed 'Horseman' playing it live in the recording room and it's fucking fabulous. I feel like an artist, a real artist. I could die happy now. That's not just a turn of phrase, I actually had that thought as we listened back. We've captured this genuine moment of collective creativity that I know will affect people in a way we haven't done before. It's dark, it's . . . it's real. This is a breakthrough. We haven't done that before. Yeah, our songs always reflect us but this is something new, something mature.

We haven't recorded live since our first single. Usually, every instrument is laid down separately, like puzzle pieces, to enable the producers to manipulate each component without sound spill from the other instruments. We had to bully and boss Rupert to let us play it live. And good on him, he went for it.

He and Joe 90 spent a full day rigging up DIY sound screens around each instrument.

The sense of togetherness, of connectedness, that you hear in all the great tracks from the 1960s and 1970s, here it is.

The simplicity of a band playing live in a room together. Sure, there'll be overdubs, but the trunk of the song is down. The *feel* of magic happening, all at once in time and space, is there. Yes, it doesn't have the sonic perfection like most of the sterile over-produced bullshit that masquerades as music today, but it makes up for that with an invisible sense of spontaneity and connection.

The sense of accomplishment radiates from us as we listen back in the control room. Take number eight nailed it. It flowed, and no one fucked up.

They're all on beers.

We are glowing.

GLOWING.

'Horseman' has turned purple on the whiteboard. The song will be the emotional core of the album. Not a single, but the album's beating heart. *No way Faith's going to sing on this. It's way too dark*. Her management had the pop version.

I'm relieved.

We're four days into our final three weeks, recording our provisionally titled album, *Good Luck As a Ghost*. I'm scoffing my evening cornflakes on the sofa. ' "She Came and She Went" – that's the best title so far,' shouts Lee over playback.

We're in the living room of the cottage attached to the studio proper. It's an extra working space we need to help us complete on time. We record and try out musical ideas and lyrics in here, before taking them to Rupert to work his magic.

I hit the space bar on the Mac and the track halts.

'The rhythm's not right there, the transition from verse to chorus. It's clunky. The songs are not working,' I say. We're reworking 'Give It All a Name' from the last session.

'Let's get Ol and Cream on it tomorrow,' says Lee.

'I'm singing "Sugar Tongue" at one, it's in your hands, bro.'

Lee and I eat and sleep here at the studio in Watford, no time to waste. We have six songs on the whiteboard in purple, two of which need to be sung, three more with lyrics in progress. I'm managing the booze. I'm microdosing booze as we race to completion. Feeling OK about myself, keeping it under control.

'We should play Faith "She Came and She Went". There's no way she's gonna sing the new "Horseman". Her management wouldn't let her.'

'We've gone through this, Seth. Brunt says stick with the plan.' He slides his chair out from the desk to face me. 'Look I agree with you, they won't go for that song, but we've got to play it his way. If we fuck it up – if *you* fuck it up – he'll blame your resistance to the plan. He might bail.'

'Brunt! He wouldn't bail!'

'I dunno. He knew about the Faith offer when he came back on board. I think it's the reason he did. To make some serious money with us.'

Chapter 22

Two disconsolate paparazzi stand outside the studio in the drizzle like wet vultures. I recognise one of them from my wilder days.

'When's Faith coming, Seth?' Lee asks.

'Your guess is as good as mine.'

We're buzzed into the building and duck out of the rain.

'His guess will be better than ours . . .' Lee says. 'Her people will ring ahead. Faith goes nowhere without a fanfare on socials.'

She arrives three hours late, by which time there's a scrum of paparazzi. Her minder, wearing a chauffeur's hat and mask, looking like Bruce Lee playing Kato, shepherds her out of the never-ending limo, shoving paps out of the way. She's wearing a matching mask and gold cloak with massive shoulder pads. Lee and I watch it play out on the CCTV and then scurry back into our studio, giggling like naughty kids. The girl on reception brings Faith to us in studio two, where we're pretending to be busy musicians.

'What a fucking palaver. Be with you in a mo.' She removes her cloak and mask, ignoring us throughout the disrobing. 'Can't see a fucking thing through that one. Keep yours on,' she snaps at Kato. He goes to stand, arms folded, in the corner of the room.

Beneath her robe, she's wearing a stunning copper mohair polo-neck sweater over an orange Japanese dress decorated with silver-embossed pagodas. Her black-gloss hair is origamied upwards into impossible knots, held in place by chopsticks and an 'I Love Kitty' badge. Stella would die of envy.

'Enjoying the view?' She turns to Lee and me, gawking at the process.

'Yeah,' I say, 'quite an entrance.'

We stare each other down while she dabs the rain off Egyptian henna tattoos that frame her eyes. *I'm not going to be intimidated by this marionette.* She's tiny, despite her platforms. Looks much bigger on YouTube.

'What do ya want to record in fucking Watford for?' she says in a gravelly Cockney growl. 'Anyone got a fag?'

'You can't smoke in here,' says Rupert, who suddenly sounds extremely posh.

'Course I can. I'm fucking Faith, aren't I? This crummy studio will kiss my arse to get me to record here. Do whatever the fuck I want. Now give us a fag, tight git.'

He does.

'You still staring?'

'Love your dress,' I say, taking in the geisha punk outfit.

'You ain't getting into it.' She takes a long drag and blows it out in my direction.

'Seth Brakes. How was the loony bin?'

'Rehab,' I say, feeling a flush in my face. 'A riot.'

She turns to Lee. 'And you are?'

'Lee,' he squeaks.

She eyes us up for an awkwardly long time, sucks on the filter like a baby on a tit, then belts out,

Lucky Fuckers
Fuck you all night
Lucky Fuckers
Know how to fuck you up
Up right!

'Used to sing that at the back of the school bus.'

She plonks herself down on the sofa next to me.

'What you got for me, then?'

We accept this gear change with relief.

'Rupert has a rough mix of "Horseman" set up. You – you have heard the track, haven't you?' I wilt mid-question as Faith gives me stink eye.

'I may *look* crazy,' she says, 'but I know what I'm doin'.'

I don't have to look at Lee to know he doesn't believe she's heard the track either.

'Put it through the big speakers, Rupert.' I'm realising this song isn't a done deal; this is its audition. From Faith's media-savvy position, turning down a Lucky Fuckers song is as much of a story as singing on one.

Faith leans forward, puts her head in her hands.

'Look before we play it, it has changed quite a lot from the earlier version.'

Lee gives me stink eye.

'Just play the fucking thing will ya,' Faith turns to me. 'I get y'er nervous playing it to me, but I'll like it or I won't.' She folds forward, elbows on knees, palms on her forehead. '*Play.*'

It starts with Oliver's heartbeat bass drum. We all go quiet, tense. Lee's lonesome slide comes in.

> *Warm body now cold*
> *Autopsy*
> *Who knew*
> *You'd be the first to go?*
> *She'll miss you*
> *Watching you get old*
> *Holding my hand*
> *All alone*

It sounds funereal. Rupert's done a good job, but this is going to go over her head – she's going to want an up-tempo single with a fuck-you attitude. *Damn.*

> *I feel the sting*
> *You don't feel anything*
> *Gone far too young*
> *My faith, my destiny.*

I've switched the word 'fate' to 'faith' just for the occasion but the chorus's not there yet, I'm still tinkering. When you play a new song to someone, you hear it through their ears; it helps you see what's missing. I still love the song, but it's no single.

She kissed you, even when you're cold
What possessed you
To leave a little girl alone in this world?
What do I do?
Follow you?
Don't want to get old

Faith's body is shaking. Is she laughing? She stays bent forward until the shakes subside. I give Lee a what-the-fuck look.

I feel the sting
You don't feel anything
Gone far too young
My faith, my destiny.

Faith sits up, takes my hand, looks ahead taking deep breaths. I know the song's good – but not that good . . . During the final chorus she's crying uncontrollably. The drum heartbeats stop. After a pause Lee hands her a box of tissues. When she's cleaned up we sit in silence. No one moves.

Finally she turns to me and says, 'Thanks, man. That . . . that was real. You wrote that for me?'

'Yeah,' I say.

'Wow. I'm blown away. Been tryin' to write that song all year. I had to identify the body, you know. Got right under my skin, you fucker.' She shakes her head. 'Fucking hell, wasn't expecting that. Management said a pop song. A fucking pop song!' She laughs. 'Where's the toilet?'

She and Kato leave the room.

'Fuck,' I say. The three of us sit in shock. Lee's on his phone, googling it.

'Dad died a year ago . . . committed suicide,' he says.

'Oh fuck!' I say. '*Warm body now cold / Autopsy.*'

'*Gone far too young / My faith, my destiny,*' chimes in Lee.

'Oh fuck, oh fuck, oh fuck.'

We look at each other. 'You'd better tell her,' he says.

'I can't *now*!' I say.

'Why did you lie?'

'I didn't say anything.' I hold up my hands. 'I just said I wrote it for her.'

'Well . . . at least she's moved by it,' says Rupert.

A vulnerable yet composed Faith returns. She sits beside me, clutches my hand.

'Thank you. I'll sing that. What do you think, Del?' She says to Kato.

'That's real, man.'

'That's real. Go get me coffee, Del. Cappuccino. Extra froth.' He leaves.

'He looks hard, yay?' she says to us. 'Proper ninja.' We nod. 'He's my cousin, Delsun. We dressed him up. Couldn't hurt a fly but he looks cool.' Her eyes sparkle and she starts to laugh like a donkey, long and way too loud. It makes us all laugh, and so she laughs more, and we laugh more, in an escalating loop.

'Try . . .' Fuck, how do I put this? Faith's *X Factor* voice is way too polished and mannered for my liking. *Those fucking shows.* 'Try . . . singing it *less*.' I wince on delivery.

218

'What the fuck?' says Faith from the vocal booth, relayed to us through the speakers.

'Sorry,' I say, holding down the talkback button and leaning forward into the mixing desk. 'It's just . . . it's got to be raw. Hang on a minute.' I take my finger off the button and turn to Lee. 'Got any ideas?'

We can hear Faith's mutterings of discontent from the booth out in the dimly lit studio. All the lights are down to help the mood. You can spot her by the glow of her cigarette.

A few times Faith's broken-down in tears singing and we've had to wait for her to get it together. I feel like a shit, but hey, she gets to sing about her dad, I get to sing about Alex – it's a win-win; isn't it? Songs are always open to interpretation. Unfortunately, she thinks the way to convey emotion is the Whitney Houston 'I Will Always Love You' school of singing. Whereas we're Dolly fans.

I've got to stop her from fucking up the song.

'Why don't we ask her to sing in the low range? She's too slick in that range,' says Rupert.

'In my range?' I say.

'Yes,' says Lee. 'Brilliant, Rupe. It would get her out of the histrionics.'

'OK. So what will I sing, if she sings in my range?'

'You can sing falsetto,' says Rupert.

'Really! Really?' I say.

'It'll make her more gravelly and you more vulnerable. It's worth a try?'

Lee stares me down. I consent. Rupert holds down the talkback button. 'Faith, can you try singing in the octave below?'

'The what?'

'We'd like you to try in your deeper voice, Faith,' Lee says. 'We think it will be more moving for this track. Seth's gonna sing his part in falsetto, it'll be a nice turnaround to have the male voice sounding more vulnerable and you sounding raw.'

There's a pause, an odd clicking sound. We peer into the gloom looking for clues as to how this has landed. I want her to tell us to go fuck ourselves.

'OK,' she says. Lee and Rupert breathe a sigh of relief. 'Got it. So what's the note?'

'It's the note that I was singing previously. *Daaaaa*.' I sing the correct pitch.

She repeats the tone back to me.

'That's it. Let's go straight into the track while you remember it. And Faith?'

'Yeah.'

'Keep going, Faith, even if you cry. It'll sound great,' says Lee.

Rupert starts the track and she's in after the instrumental – a little cautious at first, but she soon settles.

We record through to the end of the track. I'm stunned. It sounds great. Better than great. Faith struggling with her grief is really fucking powerful. I'm shocked, she's got quite a voice on her when you strip away the sheen. I press the talkback button. Lee and Rupe applaud.

'Yeah, I like that,' she says. 'Hardly ever sing in that range.'

'I'll come in and sing the falsetto parts so you can hear what we're thinking. Come in and take a break.'

I pull open the heavy soundproofed doors as she enters. She looks bedraggled, vulnerable, raw. I resist the impulse to hug her and give her a high-five.

I go to the vocal booth and pick up the headphones from the floor where she's discarded them. I adjust the mic's height to suit me.

'OK.' I place my mouth a few inches from the mic's pop shield. It has licks of spittle on it melting like snow. It smells of Faith, an appealing creamy coconut scent on a base note of cigarettes. Makes me want one.

'Start the track, Rupe.'

The song kicks in and I lace a tender falsetto on to Faith's rasp. I ride the track to the end with only a few moments of turbulence.

'That's great, really like it. Let's play it back to you,' says Faith.

They do, it sounds fresh, original, the voices blend. Not like anything we've done before. Fuck knows if it's a single, don't give a shit, just know it sounds great. *Wonder how Brunt will react*.

'Let's get one of you singing it straight – so we've got it,' says Lee.

The rest of the afternoon is spent with both of us doing takes. Different versions, slightly different intonations and timings. Rupert makes us work over the same lines multiple times.

Back in the control room there's a line bugging me in a verse.

No pardons or parole.

Neither of us could sing it right, and I take that to be a sign that something's wrong with the line. I'm stressing at it with a pen and paper, looking for other options, when Faith says quietly, '*Out here's another world.*'

I try it:

Where did you go?
Out here's another world.

'Huh, that's great. Much better.'

She smiles coyly, like the sun's come out.

Three hours later we have it down. It sounds amazing, like it was made to be this way. I can't get my head round it. Against all odds it sounds right artistically *and commercially*. We can have both. Thought they were mutually exclusive.

'The original version had a different end section,' says Rupert. 'Let's get Faith on that section. In case it now works better?'

'We dropped that part,' I say. 'That version sucked.'

'I think Rupert's got a point – let Faith sing it, it might work now,' says Lee.

'No, it's crap. Why are you messing with it, this is perfect.'

'Play it me,' says Faith.

'Really?' I give Lee a look. 'I haven't rewritten the lyric cos we were dropping it, it's pants.'

'She'll nail it in seconds,' says Rupert, recalling the mix. 'We'll just get the idea down.' He drops her in on the end section.

She's just a miracle
Forged in a crucible

She's the one you cannot stop
She's gonna make it to the top.

Absolute bollocks. I calm myself with the knowledge that we'll never use it. Faith nails it in two takes.

She's gone from leopard to pussycat in a few hours.

'I love that,' she says, 'and my dad would love that.'

I sweep the guilt into a closet and lock it up – nothing I can do now.

I'm buzzing. A collaboration with Faith will do it *and* it sounds great. Didn't see that coming.

'Do you want to have a go at another one?' I suggest. 'We've got one that sounds more like a single that—'

'Come smoke with me, Seth,' she says. I sense Lee's slighted, but he doesn't show it. 'I need a break.'

We sit smoking on the kitchen steps under the awning, the doors wide open to the pouring rain.

'Which is yours?' she says. 'Bet it's the Porsche.'

'No,' I laugh. 'I haven't driven for a while.' The memory of slamming into the crash barrier and flipping my old Saab spins into view. Thought I'd killed my girlfriend Hannah. Somehow, we both crawled out of the wreck unscathed. Unlike our relationship.

Faith's watching me.

'That looks like a sad story. Part of your wild younger days?'

'Good work. Yeah.' I take a drag and let it go.

'You really sober?'

'Yeah,' I say.

'How long?'

'Not long.'

'Damn, missed all the fun. . . Boring,' says Faith. 'One state of mind all the time.'

She pulls a face then pauses.

'That's a good lyric. *One state of mind all the time.*'

She gets out a notebook, writes it down.

The rain has picked up. It thuds bass-deep on the cars and patters light on the ivy above us. The detail on her bird's nest wig is incredible. She was a peroxide blonde at the Grammys. Google showed me a parade of extreme identities in the two short years since she's broken through. I'm impressed at how some of her looks uglied her up on purpose. Smeared lipstick, dress covered in fake blood. Derivative of Gaga but it takes balls for a woman in our profession. She's not beautiful but she's *Girl with the Dragon Tattoo* sexy.

Feeling the heat of my thoughts, she glances back at me.

'What's up?'

'Your whole . . . image. You've got balls.'

'A cunt, darling. Balls are easy. A cunt's a world of problems.' She smiles, puts her book away. 'Since when did balls become a metaphor for courage? A cunt, that has to birth big-headed babies through it, now *that's* courage.' She examines her bright red nails.

'I'm a drag queen at heart. It's just image. It's all bullshit. I'm going to keep on changing so they haven't got a clue who I am and then – I'm going to fuck off.' In the building opposite a woman in her fifties does the washing-up. 'Become one of them.'

'Eh, don't see you being domesticated,' I say. 'Too wild.'

'I'm not saying now! I'll retire into it. A few big years in America. A great pension.'

'Damn. You're very real under all that.'

'Which is why I play at fancy dress, darling. My dad was an accountant by day, a drag queen by night. He had all these stage characters, and he would choose one for however he was feeling that day and *he'd be her* – until he felt like someone else. Lolly was my favourite. So funny and bitchy, fag in the corner of her mouth, duster tied around her big hair. A lush.' She laughs at the memory, spilling ash on her dress, brushing it off.

'He went out dressed up as Lolly. Cleaned the house from top to toe, lay down on the bed, took an overdose of sleeping pills –'

'Ah, I'm sorry.' She catches my reaction. 'You lost someone like that?'

'Yeah. Yeah.' *Should I tell her about Alex? Come clean about the song?*

She locks my arm in hers and we sit listening to the rain.

If I fuck it up they'll blame me.

She takes a final drag and stubs it out on the stone steps.

'You guys stay here, don't you?' she asks.

225

'Mostly.'

'I'm looking for a studio with accommodation to cut down on paparazzi runs. You know, less distraction if it's all in one building.'

'Yeah, there's rooms here.' I stifle a yawn. 'There's Monty Clifford's bachelor pad next door. This whole studio's financed by his eighties hits. Me and Lee have built a writing studio there, and sleepover. Might be a bit . . . low-fi for you.'

'Can you show me?'

'There aren't many studios that have accommodation any more. All the big London ones have shut down.' I swing open the door to our pad.

Through Faith's eyes the flat must seem pretty scummy. Unwashed plates piled high in a kitchen that spreads out into the living room.

'We set up a second studio in here to try out ideas before we go in the main room.'

Equipment is stacked on a table. Six of Lee's guitars and four amps crowd out the black sofa.

'It's a mess,' I say.

'I love it,' she says. 'It looks like people actually work here and you're a group, a group of friends.'

'You don't have regular musicians you work with? A band for touring?'

'Session women and a few men. I try to stick to women but female drummers are thin on the ground.'

'Must get lonely?'

'Dead fucking right, yeah. I bring my mates on tour. And my dad . . .' She trails off. 'I'm scared without my dad I'll have less control than I do now.'

'You seem pretty formidable. It's *your* music, right?'

She laughs. 'My manager sends me tracks.'

'You don't write your own lyrics?'

'Nah! No one does in my world. Some of 'em "co-write"', she makes finger quotes in the air. 'You know, the powerful ones claim songwriting credit, but from what I'm told for most of 'em it's bullshit.'

'That line you came up with was good, and the one in the studio. You should write your own. You blushing under that make-up?'

'Fuck off', she laughs.

'Your image is really strong.'

'Course. But the real stuff, the music, the words, I mean . . . my managers find words that look like they suit my life, which is good,' she frowns, 'but they're more like an approximation of me. Not me. No one sees *me*.' She touches her hair. 'You did, with that lyric and stuff.' She pauses. 'I'll get there in the end. How long did it take for Beyoncé to get control of 'er business? Can I smoke in here?'

'You're fuckin' Faith, you can do anyfink.' Earns a laugh.

She gets out her fags, lights one and hands it to me.

She lights a second for herself. 'Is this your only vice, like? The wild man of indie rock. Just fags?'

I make a decision, climb on to the kitchen counter and spider my hands at the top of a cupboard till I find the bottle neck. I jump back down with a bottle of Stoli.

'No. I'm drinking again. And this calls for a celebration.'

'You *bad boy*. Me too, please.'

I go to the fridge and mix us strong vodka oranges with ice. I replace the bottle back up top.

'Promise you won't tell,' I say.

'Is this when you turn into Mr Hyde? I've always wan'ed to meet Seth Brakes, you know, the real one.'

I blush.

'What's it like being a singer in a band and not being able to touch the goods? Must be 'ard for a bloke. It's hard for me. You were wi-i-ild, man.' She belches. 'We fucking loved ya at school. Two fingers up to everythink. Didn't give a shit.'

I see *that* Seth Brakes through her eyes.

'That footage of you naked in the Nazi helmet,' she laughs.

'There isn't any,' I say.

'Oh, you think?'

'There isn't any, I've just come back from Germany . . .'

'It's not on YouTube—'

'Da da da da da DA DA,' I say loudly to drown her out. I can hear her bray through my fingers in my ears.

'You've seen it?'

'I 'ave.' She licks her lips. 'Very tasty. I'm gonna go onstage naked one day. You can't get a more real statement than that.'

I put my hand on hers. 'Don't. It's good in the moment but the echo goes on for ever. It's for eternity and every interview I'll ever do will quiz me on it.'

I hear a sound outside the door and swiftly down my vodka. Her eyes widen. 'Na zdorovie.' She raises her glass, chinks mine and knocks it back. The footsteps walk past the window. 'Let's 'ave another one.'

'If the press see you're vulnerable, that you might actually hurt yourself . . .' I bring the bottle down and pour two more.

'Don't be stingy,' she says.

I make them doubles. 'Everyone stops to watch a car crash.' The ice crackles in the vodka. 'Keep it fancy dress, Faith; keep it at arm's length or the wolves will gather, especially round a woman.' I hand her her drink.

'Na zdorovie.' We make eye contact and laugh.

'Bet you get bored answering the same questions again and again,' I say. 'I mean, we were big in a few countries, but you, you're all over the world.'

'Dead fucking right.' She rolls those beautiful brown eyes and knocks it back. 'And I've got nothink to talk about. Don't write the songs, the music. Feel like a fake.'

She looks at me, makes a decision then lifts the elaborate black wig off in one movement.

'Ta-da!'

She's shaved underneath, a number two. For the first time today she looks twenty years old. She holds the wig in front of her and picks off bits of fluff and stray hairs.

'You look rad. You've got the head for it. I could never shave off mine.'

She walks to the fridge, opens it, pulls out a carton of milk and pours some into a saucer. She puts the wig half over the saucer. She strokes it affectionately.

'Good pussy. Nice pussy.'

She scratches her stubble then pours us both another shot

I reach out and put my hand on her head. It's rough to the touch. She raises her glass. 'Here's to . . . wild men and wild pussies,' she brays, showing the gap in her top teeth. I feel like I'm starting to see her for the first time. We down our drinks. I feel the warmth of the booze flood through me.

'Boiling in this.' She peels off the mohair sweater and chucks it on a chair. The orange silk dress beneath is skin-tight, buttoned up to a small collar. I'm witnessing an unveiling, a discarding of her armour. Underneath's a slip of a girl.

'So, which is your room?'

'I've got the master.'

'Course you have,' she says. 'Show me the bedrooms.'

I swing open Lee's bedroom door.

'Lee's room. Pretty straightforward. En suite, etc.,' I say.

Brightly coloured artwork is laid out randomly on the royal-blue carpet, like exotic lily pads, covering most of the floor space.

'He's got an exhibition coming up,' I say.

'Fuck, he's good.' She squats down to scrutinise a nude.

'Now, my room's different. It was Monty Clifford's sex pad and . . . they've left it that way . . . It has history.'

She's up on her feet, I block the entrance.

'Let me in, let me in,' she squeals with excitement.

In the centre of my room is a circular bed, opposite a wood fire. Wall lights are dungeon torches angled at forty-five degrees.

'Dim the lights.' She's hopping from foot to foot like she's going to pee herself.

'Oh, this is amazing, I *dreamt* this room! Seriously, I *dreamt* it!'

She plops herself down on the waterbed and the whole thing ripples outwards.

'*And the waterbed!*' It's as if she's seen a unicorn. 'I dreamt this great idea for a video – this couple are fucking on a water-bed that's full of blood and the more the couple fuck the more they puncture it.' She looks upwards at the mirror.

'Fucking hell! This is it!' She's writhing on the bed, eyes fixed on the mirror as she rubs herself through her dress.

'Uhh, uhh,' she moans. 'Come here. You've got to see this. This would be a rad video. Come here, look.' She beckons me and when I don't respond she reaches forward and yanks me on to the bed. Water ripples out within the rubber mattress, making sloshing sounds.

'Look up,' she says. I roll over. The novelty had worn off for me, but seeing it through Faith's eyes wakes it up.

'*This is my dream!* We could film the whole thing in the mirror,' she says. ''ere, look, get on top of me.'

'No.'

'Don't be a pussy. Help me out 'ere. This would be great for a video.' Her eyes light up. 'Not "Horseman"! We could do the other song! A proper wicked Lucky Fuckers/Faith collaboration. We could write it together. We'd do "Horseman" and then we'd do another, totally rad, filthy track and video. Is the other song sexy?'

'It's called "She Came and She Went".' *I can't believe where this is going.*

' "She *Came* and She Went". Fuck, yeah!'

I hear Brunt's words, *Make her feel good, Seth. Don't sabotage this thing cos you don't want it.*

Two songs with Faith and a sexy video would do it. *Would do it worldwide! Everything we've been working for. This is it.*

'OK. *OK.*'

'Climb on top, I wanna see.'

I straddle her.

'Hold my hands above my head.' She's focused on our reflection in the mirror. I take her wrists and pin them to the bed.

'Give me yer 'ips.' She can tell I'm holding back. *Fuck it, go for it.*

'Put your hand around my throat.' She's wide eyed, staring at her reflection. 'Squeeze. Look, look!' She directs me with her eyes. I look over my shoulder. It looks pretty fucking sexy. She wraps her legs around me and pulls me in. We're nose to nose.

'I'm digging this. My turn.' She slides out from under, flips me over and climbs on top.

'Now that is sexy.' She grinds her hips into mine.

'Put your hands over your head,' she commands.

'Ahhh. Isn't this great?' She gives me the biggest smile. I'm getting turned on. She rubs her groin against mine and opens her mouth in pleasure. My cock twitches and hardens. Placing a hand on my chest she arches back, grinding. She makes these pouting facial gestures which I recognise from her videos. Is she turned on or faking it?

'No, wait.' I grip her arm. She bites her lip and lets out a deeper moan. It sounds false; it's an idea of sexy.

This is not OK. *Stella*.

Faith is lost, rubbing herself harder up against me.

'Hey, stop!' I shout. It shakes her out of it.

'What the fuck? You're turned on, I can feel it.'

'I have a girlfriend,' I blurt out.

'So do I.' She smiles. 'Come on, Seth Brakes, don't tell me you've given up sex along with everything else. You been tamed, bro!' This stings. She gets off me and slides down my body, puts her hands on the outside of my jeans, rubs my groin and starts to undo my belt buckle. There's civil war going on inside of me, my body's in pleasure, my mind's in panic. My body's winning. She unzips me. This is crazy. She slides her hands down my

233

pants and grips me. The blood flows out of my brain into my cock.

She pulls my cock out of my pants, rubs me along her cheek and watches me as she lowers her mouth on to the tip, sucking hard, going down along the shaft. It goes to the core of me. Each movement of her body causes ripples and sloshing in the bed. One hand holds me while her mouth slides up and down. Her other hand reaches beneath her dress to touch herself. I look up at our reflection. I'm lost. It's fantastic. She tugs off my trousers and pants. *I was about to say something. What was it?*

'Hush,' she says and she's on top of me, hoicking up her dress and guiding the tip of me into her. She eases herself down, all the way. My body arches. She leans forward and kisses me sloppy on the mouth. She tastes of cock. She pulls back to watch me, enjoying the control and the effect she's having with each movement of her hips. With the control of a dancer she slides almost out of me and pauses, makes small thrusting movements.

'You want it?' she says. 'You want me now.' Before I can answer she drops down the whole length of me. The energy lifts up my body.

'You want it now,' she nearly pulls out again to the tip, hovers and with just her hips, pulls up and down on the tip of me, up and down, up and down, teasing, enjoying my helplessness, before slamming down the whole way, moaning, for real this time. She repeats the tease. I grab her hips, and thrust hard, slamming into her. She tips forward, planting her hands either side of my head. Her mouth drops open, jaw pushes forward. The rhythm of the waterbed's against us, it waves out of time with my thrusts. I reach round and slip a finger in her ass. She gasps. I change rhythm and drop my hips back on to the bed so we're both undulating together. It's only then that I realise we aren't using contraception. The thought hits me like a fire alarm. Fuck. I can't do this, too late now.

Faith's rhythm's erratic.

'I'm coming, I'm coming.' Her words suck me to the edge. I lock my cock, anus, everything in me clenches while she spasms over me. I push my finger deeper into her.

'Fuck, Fuck, FUCK.' She buckles, slams down on me harder and harder, flailing forward. We come together in waves, clinging to each other in the wreckage. She falls on top of me shaking with the current. Then peace.

I look up at the mirror and put my arms around her.

Spent, tiny, she looks so fragile slumped on top of me, shaved head like a fledgling. Makes me feel protective. I feel awful, I feel brilliant. I feel alive. I catch some movement in the room and see Lee disappearing out the door.

Faith's asleep on top of me. I'm deflated. Ejaculation drops my energy, and now I'm dropping, dropping into the reality of what just happened. What the fuck? This is trouble. She is trouble. I am trouble, in trouble. Conjugate the word *trouble*. *Fuck, fuck, fuck, fuck, fuck.*

'That was fun.' She rolls off me. 'I'd been wanking to that scene since I was fourteen and . . . that was up there with . . .'

'Does that make me a paedo?'

She punches me on the arm.

'Kind of weird, though . . . when a fantasy comes true like that.'

'Just think of how your fans would feel.' I say.

She reaches for her notebook and writes, *Wanking to that scene since I was fourteen.* 'You're my muse.' She gives me that big smile again.

'That was fantastic.' It was. It's not her fault my mind's divided and fucked up.

I'll keep my reservations to myself.

I look for a cigarette.

'Why so hasty, cowboy?' She slides her hand to my cock and squeezes me. *Damn, she owns me.*

'Are you on the pill? I came inside of you.'

'Oh my God no, and I just slept with that whore Seth Brakes, with no protection. What will become of me?' she says in a Southern belle accent.

'Course I am.' She climbs on top of me.

'Much better question is,' she lowers her face close to mine, 'are you clean? Do you have an STD? Do you have herpes?' She grinds her hips into me. 'We both forgot to ask that one, now, didn't we?' She laughs.

Two hours and a few drinks later, I'm standing in the doorway outside the studio apartment on the phone to Stella.

'I'm gonna stay at the studio for a few days. You know, it's the last few days of singing and I have to get this right.' It's late.

'OK,' says Stella. I can tell she's pissed off. 'So come on then, how did it go with Faith?'

'Surprisingly well. She loved the song and it . . . sounded good.' I take a drag of my cigarette. Two women in niqabs glide past.

'What was she like?'

'A character. Big as you can imagine – but quite sweet underneath.'

'Did you fancy her?'

A black cab hits a gutter full of water and sprays the retreating women, who curse in Arabic.

'No! Why'd you say that?'

'Cos you're a man, Seth.' She laughs. 'You don't need to pretend that I'm the only woman in the world you're attracted to. I live in Paris, remember. And her styling's amazing! She looks rad. I can well imagine the old Seth Brakes having the hots for her. Has she gone now?'

'Yes, yes – though she might come back tomorrow and sing on another one.'

'That's brilliant! Two songs! That's amazing. God, Brunt's wet dream.'

'Yeah.'

'Congratulations, then! You don't sound too happy about it? This will break you *everywhere*! That's *fucking* amazing *and* it went well.'

'I am, *I am happy* . . . you know.' I'm sweating with the lie.

'I've always been ambivalent about this . . . I wanted us to do it . . . you know, to do it our way. Not with a helping hand from a popstar.' I take a drag.

'Well . . . the Goddess works in mysterious ways.'

'She certainly does. Can I come in and watch you sing together? I'd love to meet her.'

'No, sorry. Faith won't have anyone here. She wouldn't let the band be there – just Lee and me. You know, the paranoid popstar thing.'

Down the empty street a fox weaves between parked cars.

'So . . . what should I do?' She sighs. 'Maybe I should go back to Paris now you're being a boring artist? I don't want to sit around here waiting for you and I've got to prep for the *Vogue* shoot in three days.'

'Hmm. That sounds like a good idea. I'm gonna be pretty busy while I finish this up – got to land this album.'

'OK.' She's disappointed. She waits for me to change my mind. I feel like a shit. 'I'll pack up, then.' I can hear her walking from one room to another. 'I'll drop round to say goodbye when I know what I'm doing. Love you.'

'Love you.'

She hangs up.

Mechanically I go fix me and Faith some drinks, trying to think straight. I can't think straight.

Faith is sitting up in bed wearing a bra, panties and headphones, bent over a notepad writing lyrics. She bites her lip in concentration, oblivious to me standing in the doorway. The scene is iconic. It could be an album cover – a trashy version of Leonard Cohen's *Songs from a Room* or *The Freewheelin' Bob Dylan* sleeve. Muse girlfriends.

Maybe with Faith I would become *her* muse.

This picture, *Well, it's me, isn't it?* It's more me than a happy-ever-after with Stella. Who am I kidding to want a normal relationship? A firework with a sexy singer's what I'm cut out for. Boost my profile à la Posh and Becks. Way more than Brunt's wet dream.

But I love Stell. Love her. I know this here is just a moment. A moment from a video. Maybe sober Seth could have Stell by day, and crazy Seth Faith by night. Somehow I don't think the women would agree to that deal. Hmm, poly Faith might.

Faith looks up, pushes the headphones off her head.

'This is it, this is it. This is our sexy song. This is the single! I've got some great lyrics for the girl's part.'

She's listening to "She Came and She Went" – there isn't a girl's part.

She reads out her lyrics:

'I'm gonna make you moan, boy
Take you to the edge then leave you alone, boy
I've only just got started and you're halfway out the party
Men have no self-control, boy
Romeo set to explode.
I'm not just some Barbie to get walked on by your army.'

Oh fuck. Where do I begin with that lyric? 'Romeo'! It's just wrong. 'Barbie army'!

'Hey, that's great,' I say, when she's finished. 'We can work on those . . .'

'I'll come back next week and sing the lyrics. I know just the people to make this an 'it. I got this great programmer, he'll make the beat . . . contemporary,' she says diplomatically. 'You know, your drummer is a bit . . . you know.'

I do know, though Olly might not be so understanding.

'I've got the producer and we have to change the bass – make it funky.'

'I like the bass.'

'I hear slap bass!'

'Slap bass is to music what a male porn star slapping his cock on a woman's clitoris is to porn,' is something I once said to Lee. I decline to share it with Faith.

'It's gonna be sick. I know how to 'ave 'its . . . *and* the video, fucking on this waterbed.' She jumps up.

'Come here, sexy boy. How was it with your girlfriend? Was it all cool?'

'Cool? Hmm.'

'You 'ave an exclusive relationship? So old school! All my lovers know each other. I could never be with one person! *'I'm a million different people from one day to the next,'* she sings. 'One person's never gonna meet my needs!'

I put the drinks down on the sheepskin by the bed. She takes my head in her hands and snogs me.

'I want more,' she says.

She shrieks as I pull her legs out from under her. I pull off her knickers. I step back to pull off my jeans and knock the vodka oranges on to the sheepskin.

'Fuck, fuck.'

'Oh, fuck 'em, just fuck me.'

'No, I've got to . . .' I rush into the bathroom, spool toilet roll on to my hand and grab a towel. I get on my knees to mop up. She's lying on the bed watching me.

'Shall we put a pinny on you? Why don't you do the washing-up while you're at it? What a fucking buzzkill. A non-fucking buzzkill.' She reaches for a cigarette. 'I mean, the loss of the vodka, tragic in itself . . .'

I watch tissue paper soak up the stain and chuck the towel on top.

'Something wrong?' she asks. 'You seem a little tense.'

'My girlfriend's coming over.'

She arches an eyebrow. 'Ahh.' She plucks the lighter from the bedside table. 'And you were gonna fuck me. *That's risky behaviour.* Or maybe you want to end the relationship?'

'No, you just looked too good not to fuck.'

She stands up, comes up close.

'When's she coming?'

Heat's coming off her body.

'Soon.'

She drops to her knees, undoes my belt buckle.

'Better get on with it, then.'

Doorbell rings.

I'm scrubbed clean, showered, shaved. A final scan of the bedroom to check Faith hasn't left incriminating evidence. My heart's pounding with the buzz of deception; I feel like an actor, a spy.

I've missed this. Feel so alive. Reckless.

This character's drowning out another voice, another voice that says, *I love Stella. Don't blow this.* I go downstairs chewing a mouthful of peanut butter. Doorbell rings again.

Stella stands there, rain bouncing off her puffa jacket, bag swung over her shoulder. She looks weird, awkward.

'Hey, stranger, I've got a surprise for you.' Holly steps out from behind her. I don't understand. 'Guess who turned up on my doorstep as I was packing?'

'What the fuck?'

Stella glares. 'Can we come in?' When I don't move, she brushes past me, teenager in tow. Holly's grown. She doesn't look at me.

'You OK, hun? Are Mum and Joe here?'

She says nothing.

'They are *not*,' says Stella, looking for Holly to pick up the cue. She ignores us, hangs up her coat, places her rucksack on a chair. She sits down, arms folded.

'She's "left home" again,' says Stella. It takes a while to absorb this. 'She wants to live with us.'

It sinks in.

'You came here on your own?' Holly's got lockjaw. 'Does Lizzie know?' Stella shakes her head. 'Ah, fucking hell, Holly!'

Stella gives me the 'cool it' sign. I sit on the arm of her chair.

'You OK?' I put my hand on her head, she jerks away.

'Seth, I have to go.' Stell looks at me apologetically. 'I'm catching the last Eurostar tonight, booked it before she turned up. *Soo* sorry.'

Motherfucker.

'No. You can't change it? I'm, I'm finishing the record . . .'

'I'm sorry, I've got stuff booked tomorrow – in Paris,' she says too fucking sweetly. 'You said you didn't need me . . . so I made plans.'

I've got to deal with this now!

Holly's on the edge of tears.

'I have to jump in a cab.'

'Wait, wait, hang on . . .'

Stella swishes across the room and gives me a hug. 'We'll talk in the morning. What do you smell of?'

243

She's gone, leaving a thick silence behind her.

Motherfucker.

One two three four

'You want a hot drink?'

Nothing.

We listen to the kettle boil.

I make a coffee, trying to get my shit together.

I place a coke in front of her.

Nothing.

I can't deal with this kid now.

I reset. Go sit next to her.

'What's up, Hols?'

The milk's curdled, chunks whirlpool in my coffee.

'Come sit over here?'

She's turned into a nightmare teenager, no wonder Lizzie can't deal with her.

'You've come a long way to sit here in silence.'

Nope.

'Like your hair, by the way.' It's the same as Stella's, shaved at the sides, Mohawk on top. Oh God.

'Are your clothes wet? We should get you into something dry. Come on.' I walk upstairs and wait outside my door until finally I hear her follow. I put another log on the fire and pull the sheepskin over in front of it. The orange stain glowers accusingly. Holly stands in the doorway.

'Come sit by the fire, Hol.' She does. I turn the lights down. 'Take your hoodie off so I can dry it.' She does. I put it on the back of a chair, pull the duvet off the bed and wrap it around her. I throw a pillow on to the floor. I lie behind her and put my arms around her. After a while she starts to sob.

'She's with you? In London?' Lizzie can't contain herself. 'The little fucker! She said she was staying the night at Karen and Tracey's – fuck!'

I'm on the downstairs sofa in the dark. The backs of Lee's guitars are silhouetted against streetlights shining in through the closed blinds.

'She got the train.' I watch the glow of my cigarette as I inhale.

'Jesus. Let me speak to her.'

'She's asleep. She cried herself to sleep. She was in . . . quite a state.'

'Wake her up; I want to speak to her.'

'No.'

I hear her readjust.

'Did she say why? Why she ran . . .?'

'She said you hit her.'

Red neon numbers flash on the half-open dishwasher door. Drunken shouts echo from across the street. Must be closing

245

time. A steel guitar string hangs uselessly from Lee's Strat. I can hear Lizzie's breathing.

'She says you hit her – a lot.'

'She can be a real teenager, that one . . .'

'She showed me the bruises on her legs.'

'They're from football—'

'Shut up.'

We sit in a silent shared space across hundreds of miles. In the weight of grief. Connected by the memory of our mother's beatings. I recognise the distrust on Holly's face, the suspicion that she won't be believed. That it won't stop. That it will never stop.

Lizzie's crying. I'm crying. Crying for this endless fucking loop, can any of us break out of this? I thought my sister had but it has us all. 'The sins of our fathers.' Mothers? How far does it go back in our family? I'm crying for the little girl upstairs who feels she's betrayed her twin by leaving him behind. Whose hope lies in her fuck-up of an uncle, who can't help himself. Who can't help anyone.

Chapter 23

'Say that again?' I ask.

Three days later, Brunt and I are in a packed Soho restaurant perched on bucket stools. It's amazing how tense a badly designed chair can make you feel. With a slumped posture and wedgie combo it's impossible to get comfortable.

The dance music is just below nightclub volume. 'Flesh', as it's called, used to be a butcher's shop, high ceilinged, marble walled, bare wooden floor. It looks fantastic but like a church has appalling echoey acoustics. It's famous for its ambiance and staff. The waiters mirror old Soho, the only place in London where the freaks and geeks, the she/hes and queers could hang out in the days when it was illegal to be anything other than male or female.

Illegal. Illegal to be a different gender! *What the fuck!* God bless you, Bowie, Lou Reed, Elton and all the other exotic coral-reef fish that willowed in the current of rock and roll.

Our waiter, Nong, is a beautiful ladyboy from Thailand; wearing traditional Mexican peasant clothes that Frida Kahlo would be proud of. Turquoise-blue eyeshadow matches an alpaca shawl. Nong talks in an urgent whisper, as if delivering top-secret information. I can't understand a word they say, but love it when they lean in close, bat those long lashes and talk dirty to me. I *think* I've ordered half a chicken roasted on a spit with chips, but it may have got lost in translation. No wonder Cream was jealous of the date.

Lee's babysitting Holly back at the flat. Brunt's never taken me out for dinner solo. I thought it was to congratulate me on getting Faith to sing the two songs. I'm realigning my expectations.

'You know how it is, Seth. You're a grown up. Well, sometimes.' He takes a sip of champagne. 'Yeah, they talk a good talk. Promise you this, promise you that, but in reality . . . all the artists' gains of the seventies and eighties have been lost. The future's downloads, algorithms; it's iTunes and Spotify.' He chucks bread into his mouth and looks around. 'I'm starving; where's our waiter? Least Spotify's better than Napster. Music for free! Ha. The record companies were so desperate for a model that enabled them to actually *sell* music –' he dabs the red paper napkin over his brow '– that they bit Spotify and iTunes's hands off. Made shit deals – deals that fucked the artists.' He raises a finger to attract Nong's attention, fails, raises his arm, gives up. 'Bands used to get a few pounds each time a single was played on radio. *A few pounds per play!* Now you're lucky to get a few grand for a million plays on Spotify. Fucking robbery.' He knocks back his champagne, and refills the glass.

'Will you get to the point, Jon? What's that got to do with you wanting me to change the title and lyrics for "Horseman"?' I shout over the opening bars of an Ibiza club filler.

My manager's ballooning. Way over two hundred pounds. And he's drinking again, wonder if his wife knows. 'We've got no power. The artist has no power any more.' He rubs his fingers together, indicating cash. 'It's a different market, son. They see "'orseman" as the first single, but not with that title – they worked out the heroin reference.'

'*First* single? "She Came and She Went" is gonna be the first single. I thought the record company agreed.'

'It was. They did. You know, it's this *new* guy. The new guy who's replaced Geoff. They're the New Guy. They have to differentiate themselves from the Old Guy.' Brunt leers at a passing arse.

'And he does that by getting me to change "Horseman"?'

'The minute he heard Faith singing on it, that was it. No-brainer.'

'Faith's coming back in to sing "She Came and She Went" tomorrow.'

'Yeah, that's a fucking score, how did you manage that?' I say nothing. 'Brilliant. Anyway, that'll be the second single.' He's hurt by my reaction. 'I don't know what you're complaining about, mate. You're going to have *two* fucking singles with an artiste *way* outside your league. This is it. This is what we've been waiting for. This is America.'

'*Way outside our league?*'

'Financially speaking. Which is all that matters nowadays.'

'All that matters.' I compose myself.

'Look, Jon. It's great. It was a great plan to bring Faith in. I was wrong, you were right. And I got it to work. I want this to work. But now you want me to change the whole . . . the whole reason why we wrote "Horseman".'

'And the version,' he says coolly.

'What? What about the version?'

'They want the *earlier* version. The pop one you sent to Faith's management.'

The room stops.

Behind Brunt, two fake-tanned burly chefs in white overalls and caps are threading chicken carcasses on to a long metal skewer. There's blood on their overalls. Electric filaments glow hot on the wall.

'You mean the shit one?' I find myself shouting. I lean across the table and say through gritted teeth, 'You mean *the early version that sounded shit*? The *shitting shit one*?'

One of the chefs takes a pallid carcass and forces it on to the skewer, while the other paints it in some brown goo with a shaving brush.

'They prefer it.' He takes a sip and looks for Nong.

'Faith doesn't sing on that version, she's on the new one,' I say triumphantly.

'They moved her vocals over. Technology's brilliant, innit?'

'*They* moved her vocals over? Who's *they*?'

'You shouldn't have recorded it! Once they 'eard it, it's out of my hands.'

'Who's this come from? Is this the new guy?'

'No, it's the radio plugger, Phil . . . Phil Monteri.' He tries to sit back but there's no back to sit back on, so he slumps forward. 'He 'eard the first pop version. Loves the song. "This is the single," he said. And that's it, argument over. These radio pluggers are gods now, so what he says goes.' He pinches his nose. 'Think I'm going down with something.'

It used to be record companies that chose singles. Now it's the radio pluggers, and I've met Phil Monteri – he's not the epitome of taste and style.

'What did *you* think of the new version?'

'*Personally?* I love it,' he says. 'But what do I know? I'm just an old man with dodgy knees. Monteri thinks it's depressing and the new guy agrees.'

I shout over the music. 'The earlier version sounded like . . . like a facsimile of how we used to sound. Jangly, brittle indie pop.'

'Exactly. That's why they like it.' He takes another glug of champagne. 'You're a victim of your own success, son.'

'We don't want to release a single that makes us sound like the old Fuckers—'

'You won't – not with Faith on it. And once her people have got hold of it . . . Apparently she's well excited, she wants to make it more funky with slap bass and everything.'

Fucking save me.

'So, you want a different lyric, sung on the early version?' He nods. 'Jesus, Jon . . .' I pause to stop my voice from cracking.

'Well, there's more, actually . . .' He looks down at the table, strategising. I brace myself.

'You know the end bit of the song . . .' He gets out his phone, prods it and reads,

She's just a miracle
Forged in a crucible
She's the one you cannot stop
She's gonna make it to the top.

'You mean the little tag we had at the end of the first shitty version, but dropped in the new one, because we thought it

251

was too SHITTY.' I'm shouting again. 'You mean *that* section?'

'Yeah . . . that section. It's perfect for Faith. That's the chorus. Phil's done an edit where he makes *that* bit the chorus – and it . . . it sounds like a single.'

Moustachioed chef drops a chicken on the floor. Bends behind the counter, picks it up, inspects it and glances around to see if anyone's seen him.

I can't breathe. I can't digest this. I want a drink. I want more than one. I shudder like a horse. Try another tack.

'I wrote "Horseman" about Al. You remember Alex?'

'Your best mate? From before the band?'

'Yeah. He ODed.' My legs are shaking. 'It was my fault. It killed him . . . didn't me.'

He reaches across the table and lays his hand on mine. 'I'm sorry. I'm so sorry, Seth.' He pats my wrist. 'Hardly the topic for a hit single, eh? But if you put the focus on the girl . . .'

I pull my hand away.

'No. That's not it. The song's about Alex and his daughter. It *isn't* a single.' I'm trying not to lose it, 'It's why I wrote the lyric. The only reason we didn't drop the song is because of the lyric.'

'Well, it's something else now, isn't it. Faith's management think it's about 'er dad. Brilliant. Her fans will lap it up. It's a done deal.'

Moustachioed chef is threading the sullied chicken back on to the skewer. Brunt taps the table and winces like he's eating lemons. 'You keep doing this, Seth.' He dips rugby player's fingers into a small olive bowl and teases a black olive out over the rim. 'You make these catchy pop songs . . . Damn,' he says as the olive slips between his fingers. 'And undermine them with a heavy lyric,' all eyes on the olive, 'undermine them with some . . . self-defeating lyric. You do realise you do this, don't you?' He nibbles the olive, avoiding the stone.

'You mean self-sabotage?' I say.

'Exactly! *Self-sabotage. You can't have self-expression and success. Doesn't work any more.* Unless you're as big as Beyonce, then you can do what the fuck you want'.

'So, you want me to rewrite a great lyric – and replace it with a shit one. Then we're going to put it out as a single – that will totally misrepresent this wonderful new album we've been creating.' I'm winded. Something has collapsed inside of me.

'You're being a diva, Seth. You've just gotta change some of the heroin references. It's a vehicle for Faith now. It will change everything. It will make you a millionaire, son. All of us. Isn't that what you want? Or would you prefer to be the indie loser —'

Nong dumps a plate of oysters between us and spins away.

Lee coached me to stay cool, knew this wasn't going to be a victory parade.

'Are the band in on this?' I blush at the realisation.

Brunt scratches the back of his head.

Fuck. I'm fucked. The band are in on this!

'So this is the deal with the Devil at the crossroads?'

'Thanks for the casting! The Devil . . .' He juts his chin forward and hisses at me, 'I'm the messenger! Yes, this is what your band want. This is what I want. This is what your record company wants. You know the record company? The ones that own the songs. The ones that pay for all this.' He gestures at the oysters and champagne. 'Listen, you ungrateful prick, you were this close –' he holds up a thumb and forefinger '– this close to getting dropped.' He wipes his mouth with the serviette. '*Now* you are on the verge of 'aving a worldie 'it single. *Two!* With a girl singer who the whole world's going bonkers for. Everything's great. The album's coming. We're filming the Brixton gig for Sky! All because of this association with Faith. *Everything you ever wanted.* Don't fuck it up, Seth Brakes. Don't fuck it up *again.* There's a million bands who'd die for this opportunity.'

The kid in me, that watched Nirvana, Chillies, Pixies, and thought, I can do that. I want to be that. Make great music, not give a fuck. Do what the fuck I want and be . . . valued – valued for expressing myself, sticking a finger up at this bullshit culture that has so little to offer. So little to offer any kid coming out of school looking for something to do that isn't just a pay cheque for a nine to five existence. Golden handcuffs, plastic handcuffs! Where your best hope . . . is a wage packet till death do us part. That kid in me, that thought he's found something true, something fun, something worth it. That kid *just died.* For here I am . . . whoring for success like all the other hucksters. I feel sick. What's the fucking point?

Brunt shucks an oyster. Sucks it down. I watch its progression down his throat.

'Nothing's easy for you, is it, Seth? All the bands which made me money, big money, have been easy as pie – and boring as Chelsea. It's you bloody artists who take up all my time – and make me fuck all. Well, we're gonna change that.'

'You fucking cunt. You agreed to this shit?' I'm standing over Lee, who's on the sofa, guitar in his lap. It's late. I've had a few, in a bar on the way back to the flat. He looks up at me calmly.

'It's one song, Seth.'

'It's not one fucking song. It's *the* song. It's *the* fucking song. It's the fucking song where we all came together to create . . . something, something magical.'

'Cool it, Seth, man.' Cream's restringing her bass. My mind clocks Lee's guitar and Cream's bass as potential weapons. I keep my eye on Lee.

'It was pure. If we let them do this—' I break off to prevent tears. I turn to Cream. 'Did you all agree to this, then?'

Cream looks at Lee.

'You fuckers. Why didn't you talk to me?' My anger's gutted by grief. I spin around to hide hot tears. *They all knew.* They let me walk into that meeting, *they all knew.*

'Look, mate,' Lee says, 'if this works, it will sell the album. It will sell the tour. It will break us. It's *one* song. It's what we have to do.'

I can't turn around.

'We didn't tell you, mate, because we knew you wouldn't agree. You wouldn't do what's necessary to be successful. You'd rather be an indie fail . . . an indie band than a . . . contender.'

'Tell me you think it's a good song.' I'm jabbing a finger in his face. 'Tell me with that shitty chorus on that shitty old . . . tell me—' I break off again, then I'm back in. 'It won't *mean* anything,' I scream at him. 'It doesn't come from *us*, it's not *real*. You're a fucking whore.'

He laughs at this. I grab a coffee mug up off the table and hurl it at the wall above his head. Shards of pottery spray out over him. Cream puts a hand on my shoulder. I twist away from it. '*You're fucking whores.*' Behind him I see Holly's legs coming down the stairs. I turn and bolt into the night.

Chapter 24

'What d'you fucking mean you don't like songs with "Romeo" in 'em? That's fucking bonkers.' Faith's blonde pigtails, shaped into a gravity-defying U, bounce as if curled around wire. They are curled around wire. She's wearing a white 1980s shoulder-padded shirt and a black and white plastic skirt that squeaks when she moves. From the sofa, Holly stares at her like a fish. Lee sits with his back to us, hunched over the mixing desk, pretending he's not listening. We've called a truce. We both want 'She Came and She Went' to work. I want it to be so good that they forget about 'Horseman'. Cousin Del is here, not as Kato this time, but filming us – filming Faith – for social media. It's for a new app called Instagram, that's going to be 'masssive'.

'That's the most rubbish thing I've heard. You don't like songs with "Romeo" in 'em,' she repeats.

'It's just . . . overused. I think we can do better. I've got these lines –'

I watch her pout get poutier.

She sings the line,

Men have no self-control, boy
Romeo set to explode.

She snaps her fingers and smiles. 'You worried they gonna think it's about you!' I look puzzled. 'You know . . . exploding prematurely.'

'No!'

'Cos, hey lover, I can speak to that lie –'

'It's not a great line,' I shut her up, checking Holly hasn't picked up on it. 'It doesn't work, it's a cliché.' I calm my approach. 'Look, the secret to writing is rewriting. I write tons of lyrics before I settle on one; can't you just have another go?'

Lee gives me a look.

Don't blow this.

Faith isn't taking well to lyric feedback, the filming isn't helping, and I'm hungover. We're in our living-room studio working on vocals for 'She Came and She Went'. Rupert is mixing the shit version of 'Horseman', with lyric adjustments, resung by Faith in her best *X Factor* fucking opera voice, in studio four. We've been arguing over the lyrics for ten minutes and I haven't even got to the line, *Barbie's fucking army*.

I promised Lee I'd make this work. For him and the band. But the lyrics – the ones she's written – I can't do it. I've got to make some adjustments, a few small adjustments.

The session had started out OK. I'd pre-warned Faith about Holly staying with me – I made up some story about her having a rough time at school.

'What was it, girlfriend? You getting bullied? They just jealous cos you're beautiful, girl. Sharp and beautiful. Great Mohawk.' She spiked up Holly's hair and launched into song:

Don't hate me cos I'm beautiful
Don't hate me cos I'm rich
Can't help it if I'm magical
Can't help you be a bitch.

Which I recognised from a YouTube clip as being one of her hits.

'There you go, girl, sing you that for free,' she said.

'What's that?' said Holly.

'That's from "Blaze" – that woz my first 'it in America.'

'Sorry,' said Holly, 'I don't know your music.'

Faith recoiled.

'OK,' she said. But the character that said 'OK' was not OK.

'Cut there, Del. Go get me a cappuccino, extra froth.'

Joe 90 enters with a flash drive and breaks up our lyric standoff.

'Got Rupert's mix for "Horseman" – he wants to know what you think.'

We sit and listen. Faith's moved to tears and our fight's forgotten. I'm crying for different reasons. Lee's watching my every move.

'That's fucking amazing,' Faith squeals. 'Love the new chorus. The whole thing – much more Lucky Fuckers – *fuck you all night* vibe.' She notices Holly, 'Sorry darling, me an' my potty mouth. Isn't that song great though!' She pats away tears with a tissue. 'He wrote it about me and my dad. My dad – died.'

Holly looks confused and says to me, 'I thought that was about Alex.'

'No, that's another song.' I cut in.

'You told me you wrote that for Mo?'

'No! That's *another song*. This is, this is about Faith's dad and . . . Faith.' I sound weird and awkward.

'Which one's about Al and Mo, then? You said you'd written one about—'

'It didn't make, it didn't make it . . . on the, on the record.'

Faith's looking at me so hard it hurts my face.

'I'm sure you—'

'*No, Holly!*' It's too strong. An awful silence follows.

'What song's that, then?' says Faith in a throaty whisper. She moves in on Holly.

'It was . . . it was just another song,' I intervene. 'Didn't make it on the record.'

Faith turns to Holly. 'Who's Mo? Alex's daughter?'

Holly nods.

Faith turns to me.

'Another song? About a daughter losing 'er dad. That's, that's incredibly . . . *two* songs about a daughter and 'er dad dying.' Her eye contact is ferocious. 'That's very . . . *feminist* of you, Seth. *Two* songs from a girl's view . . .'

I pull the sides of my cardigan together.

'Yeah, the first one wasn't working – I took the best from both and . . . kind of merged them, because I, I thought the same thing. Can't have two songs like that . . . on the same album.'

'Oh!' Holly's hand goes up to her mouth as she realises the shit she's got me into. Her reaction is more incriminating than her words.

'You fucking snake.'

Faith throws herself at me across the glass table. Mugs and glasses go flying. Holly screams and stands up on the sofa. I take my punishment and catch a few slaps. Lee and Joe 90 drag Faith away.

'Let go of me!' screams Faith and shakes them off. Cold coffee pools across the table on to my jeans. Her wig's askew, eyeliner smeared. She points a shaking finger at me.

'You fucking cunt. You *fucking cunt.*'

I can't look at her.

'Oh, I know who you are. So charming and . . .*fuck*, wondered why you called it "'orseman". I fell for that one, didn't I? You fucker.'

'Faith, it wasn't like that.'

"How can I get Faith to sing on our record?"' She imitates my voice. '"I know, tell her I've written a song about her dead dad."' She's pacing around, boiling up again. 'You're just another fucking man tryin' to get shit from me. "You should write your own lyrics, Faith. You've got a good ear, Faith,"' she mimics a whining me. I let out a nervous snort. She freezes.

'Bet you only said all that shit to get into my panties. *Fucking men.*'

Holly looks from me to Faith and back again.

'Fucking men.' She addresses Holly. 'Say anything to get a fuck.'

'Don't do this, Faith, it's not—'

She swivels to the kitchen cabinet.

'Oww, fancy a drink? I fucking do.'

'Faith, please.' I stand up.

She clops back into the kitchen, kicks off her black-and-white heels, lifts her tight squeaky plastic skirt to her thighs and with difficulty climbs on to the kitchen cabinet.

'Faith I didn't know your Dad had died . . . It was a mistake.'

We watch her standing precariously balanced, feet among dirty glasses and plates. She's almost being pushed over by the jutting wall cabinets. She kicks a plate that shatters on the floor. Her hand flops around the top of the cabinet reaching for the vodka.

'Fucking 'ere somewhere,' she says, straining to keep balanced, face squashed into a cupboard, arms above her head, her hand brings down clouds of dust as she searches blind.

'Faith – come down please.'

'Fucking alcoholics,' she coughs out dust, nearly falls. Lee's up and walks into the kitchen.

'It's further to your right,' he says. She doesn't hear him; her hand keeps flapping around over the wrong cabinet. He climbs up on to the marble top next to her, reaches up, pulls down the bottle, jumps back down.

'Is this what you're looking for?' he says. She goes silent. She's twisted up there in bad yoga.

'Can someone 'elp me down?'

Faith's gone. Holly's in my bedroom watching anime. It's just me and Lee.

'Don't you wanna drink? I thought you might need one after all that. I fucking do.'

He chucks me the vodka.

I catch it by the neck.

'Is it just booze?'

I nod yes.

'Can I believe you?'

I nod again.

'When did you start again?'

'Last gig of the tour.' I put the bottle down. 'Someone left me a present in my dressing room before the gig.'

He looks at me blankly. 'Someone left booze in your dressing room?'

'And coke. I think it was someone from the band.'

'Stanley?' he says.

I open my arms. 'Could have been Harry. I'm a red rag to a bull.'

'Fuck.' Then: 'So, you were drinking for the Trevor gig, the one where we improvised "Horseman"?' He's framed against the window, hands on hips.

'Yeah, the one good gig of the tour,' I say. 'If it's any consolation, I've not gone crazy with it, just a few drinks a day – till yesterday. It's been helping the writing.'

He gives me a sad look; it's harder to take than his anger.

'It's always helped with the writing – and the performing – just not so great when it comes to the living.'

He shakes his head. 'You know what you've just done don't you? There's no way Faith's gonna let us use her on that song, those songs. Fuck man, we were that close . . . again . . . and you had to go and fuck her!' He sits down heavily. 'Whatever you think of Brunt, that was a good plan, and it was going to plan . . .' He slumps forward, puts his head in his hands.

Light footsteps in the stairwell. Holly says, 'Mum's coming to get me.'

There's nothing I can do. She's better off with her mum than me.

'When?'

'Tomorrow.'

Holly disappears back up the stairs.

Lee sings under his breath.

Lucky Fuckers
Fuck you all night
Lucky Fuckers
Know how to fuck you up
Up right!

'Why do adults do shit things?' she says. 'I don't understand. Mum knows Dave's an arsehole. You know you shouldn't drink. Why'd you do this?'

We're waiting in the kitchen for Lizzie to arrive. Dave's Lizzie's new boyfriend, who lives in the shared house.

'Kids do shit things too – you just haven't had enough practice.'

'Am I going to end up like you and Mum?'

'No!'

'Grandma was a drunk, you are, Mum beats us . . . it's genetic, isn't it?'

'No, we're not victims to genes,' I say. 'People can have shit parents and react totally differently. You'll probably swing the other way in reaction.'

'Did you have sex with Faith?'

I say nothing.

'You did. How could you? What about Stella?'

'Relationships are . . . complicated.'

'Adults always say that.'

I need a drink. It's lunchtime. I need to get back to work. Anything but this.

'I wanted to live with you and Stella but . . . you're not real, are you?'

'We're real.' I say. 'It's just not like in films.'

The doorbell rings. It's Lizzie. She looks as fucked as we feel.

'Hi.'

'Hi.'

She sees Holly behind me.

'Come here, love.' She holds open her arms. Holly gets up slowly and walks into a hug. They stand there.

'Care to join us?' says Lizzie.

I do. We stand together.

'You're drinking again.' Lizzie says it with no edge, just a statement of fact.

'There's a lot to drink about.'

Lizzie drops down to Holly's height. 'I won't do it again. I promise, I won't do it ever again.'

'You can't say that. None of you can promise anything.'

She picks up her rucksack and leaves.

Chapter 25

One month later.

Camden bloody Market on a Saturday. I'm getting flashbacks, remembering when me and Al used to take acid, come laugh at the goths and shoplift the stalls. A tourist trap of cheap junk; a feeding frenzy where everyone's looking to get more for less. That's life isn't it?

Stella's arranged to meet me here – she has a surprise birthday present for me. She's running late. I'm wrapped up in scarf and hat, but few people bother me nowadays.

I'm not in a good place. I'm keeping the drinking under control, two shots a day. Stella doesn't know, and so, when she's in London, she insists on accompanying me to AA, encourages me to get up and talk about my sobriety – in front of the *whole fucking group*. Ex-addicts can smell bullshit a mile away.

She bought me a gold commitment coin.

To thine own self be true, it says. Which self are they referring to? I'm being pretty true to one of them.

Jada hasn't sussed me out. It's weird, I don't want to be busted – but when people I respect don't get it – I feel disillusioned, unseen.

I'm a great liar.

Talking of liars, I'm at our meeting point, a giant graffiti portrait of a puffy-faced Amy Winehouse. The poster girl of addicts.

Nobody stands between me and my Camden

is the quote on the picture. Something did.

God, she's only been gone a year. I recognise that vacant, sullen stare only too well from my world of empty ghosts.

Winehouse. If that was her name in a novel you wouldn't believe it. That rehab song – how many drunks and junkies have that as their theme tune? She made *not* seeking help so co-o-o-o-ol. When she wrote that song, may as well as ladled chum in the water. Tempting fate doesn't do it justice.

And now she's haloed in the dead popstars' club of instant martyrdom and sainthood.

I move away to allow some Japanese schoolgirls to take selfies.

'Seth?'

She's petite, cute, drowning in a pea-green parka, and she's looking at me as if I should know her.

A fan? Someone from the record company? A radio station? I keep my expression blank so as not to offend her. She looks familiar.

'You don't remember me,' she says in a northern accent.

Shit, have I slept with this girl? Scored drugs with her? No, she looks too . . . wholesome.

'It's OK, I wouldn't remember me either.' She smiles. 'You must meet hundreds of people. It's Jo, Jo Fleming, Christie's kid sister. From Harrogate.'

Relief.

'Jo.' I give her a hug. 'Look at you. I'm sorry.'

'I was thirteen.'

Christie was my first love at twenty. Jo this precocious, skinny teenager who would spring out of nowhere, like a ninja, just as we were getting it on. I thought she was fascinated by sex. Christie thought she had a crush on me.

'How's Christie?'

Her mouth opens in surprise. A shadow falls upon her. I know this is bad. I watch her search for words.

'Christie died last year.'

I feel like someone's kicked me in the chest. Jo and I stand still as stones in a river as people flow around us. I see Christie's open face, her smile, hear her laugh. *She can't be dead!*

She was my first girlfriend who really enjoyed sex – and it was catching. She made me feel good in bed, even though I knew it was her.

'I'm so sorry. Fuck.'

'Yeah, fuck.'

I'm about to ask her how, when I get a terrible premonition. Christie died of an overdose. I'm terrified that Christie died from smack – terrified because she first smoked it with me.

Jo reads my distress and holds me in a hug.

'I'm sorry. I shouldn't have told you like that.'

I can't speak.

'Hey!' Stella's voice breaks the spell. We pull apart.

Stella's looking at me suspiciously, waiting for an explanation. I'm lost in grief.

'Hey?' says Jo.

'That's my man you're hugging,' Stella says.

Jo smiles.

'He still is. I'm Jo. An old friend of his.' She reaches out her hand.

Stella folds her arms. 'That looked more than an old friends' hug,' she says.

'It was,' says Jo. She looks to me for help.

'Stop it, Stell; it wasn't what you think,' I say.

'What then?'

'Don't, Stell . . . Jo told me some really bad news. Her . . .' I can't finish my words. Stella misreads my guilt and a shock rolls over her, her suspicions confirmed.

'Fuck.' She puts her hands to her head, thinking, thinking.

She thinks Jo's someone I've fucked. I can see the dials of her mind turning. Hear the evidence mounting. I'm frozen by this, appalled, yet I deserve this. This is what it will be like. This is what it will be like if she finds out about Faith. It's a dress rehearsal. She's adding up the evidence. Calls not returned, my secret drinking. She's hearing the voices of her friends. *He's a rock star, for God's sake. What do you expect?* Her parents. I'm not a good bet, am I? Even if you love me, even if you adore me.

Someone said infidelity's just a matter of opportunity and rock stars, traditionally . . . She feels such a fool. Such a fool to have trusted me. She's about to burst into tears, sees me watching her, and her tears morph into anger; she's gonna kick off.

'My sister died,' I hear Jo say. 'My sister died in a hit-and-run. Seth went out with her years ago. I just told him my sister died.'

We're sitting on a wooden bench eating rubbery Chinese noodles, trying to get back to normal. But normal doesn't want us.

Stella: 'Why didn't you tell me?'

Me: 'I tried.'

'Not hard enough.'

'I was in shock. I'd just learnt Christie—'

'Oh my God, what I went through.'

'What you fucking went through? My ex has *died*!'

My noodles keep sliding off my chopsticks and splashing me.

'Sorry. But the way you were hugging.'

'Why do all your sorrys have a "but" after them? Why can't you just be sorry?'

'I'm sorry, but I got . . .' she catches herself and laughs, 'I got really jealous.'

'I noticed.'

'You would in my shoes.'

'I hope I'd wait for an explanation.'

'I'm sorry. It's hard. You're a singer with a record.' She laughs. 'Record.'

'In the past.'

'You said that about drinking.'

'It's kind of different, don't you think?'

'I hope so.'

Stella's phone trills. She looks at it.

'My parents.'

'Can't you block them, or get a new number?'

'Are you getting bored of me? It's endless complaints recently. Do you get what I've given up for you?'

She lets the phone ring out. Then it kicks back in again.

'I've gotta take this. My new agent.' She walks away to talk.

I hear the new song, 'Sucker', looping in my head.

Lying is how you still love me
Lying is how I love you
Lying is how you don't see me
But lying is all I can do

My lyrics are haunting me. I tried finding alternatives but they don't have the same power; at least I'm faithful to my muse.

Stella returns after a few minutes.

'I've got the job.'

'No! Solo?'

'Solo!'

'Brilliant, well done.'

This will be her first solo styling gig. We toast with Evian.

'Oh shit, it's time. Your present,' she says.

I hold out my hands.

'Not that kind of a present. I've booked you' she does a drum roll on the tabletop, '– *a clairvoyant reading.*'

'OK.'

A clairvoyant reading! Is this a present for me or her?

'Well, don't look too excited. She's meant to be great.'

'Oh. Really?'

'Peter swears by her.'

'I don't know . . .'

'Anyway, it's paid for. In there, five minutes.' She points at a building behind us. 'Come on, don't tell me you're not curious. You can ask about the album, us, the future . . . I could come with you if you want?'

It's for her!

'No. Fuck off. You can't give me a clairvoyant reading so you can sit in on it. If I'm going, I'll go on my own.'

I'm sitting in a hallway three floors up in one of the market buildings. Feels like I'm sitting outside the headmaster's office. There's a sign that reads, *Please Wait*. I've tried peeking in and listening by the door, but there are drapes on the window and all I hear is tinnitus.

It's quiet up here above the market. I'm glad for the space to get my shit together. Digest the turmoil, away from the constant deceit. Once you start lying there's no turning back. *I have to keep lying.* My relationship feels like a sham. Can't tell her I'm drinking. Can't tell her about Faith. Faith and her people have gone off the radar, I'm assuming it's over, scared she might go public about why. So far there's no hint of anything. I live in a state of fear that my house of cards is about to collapse; some part of me has pulled out already.

A few friends swear by clairvoyants, say it's better than therapy. So maybe this will help? Doubt it. I once had a reading on Brighton Pier. It was crap. Full of generalisations and adapting what was said to how I responded.

I hear a fire door swing open and shut, followed by the *tap-tap-tap* of a stick. This person's shoe squeaks, like treading on a rubber duck.

Tap-squeak, tap-squeak.

My senses prickle. The sound seems to go on way too long, like whoever's coming's got stuck in an Escher painting.

Tap-squeak, tap-squeak.

For God's sake, get your fucking shoe fixed.

The sound stops dead. I'm waiting for someone to turn the corner. There's a chilling silence that my attention pours into. I'm on my feet. Is this like the weird phone call?

'Hello,' I say.

The sound echoes.

This is crazy.

There's a laugh.

Around the corner comes a white stick, followed by its owner. She must be in her eighties, white hair tightly pulled back in a bun. She has one of the most radiant faces I've ever seen. Her smile's infectious.

'I'm sorry if I made you nervous,' she says.

'No.'

'I like to hear into where I'm going before I get there. It's amazing what you can pick up if you really listen.'

Her stick makes a crack as it hits the chair next to me. She aligns herself and drops into it, leans her stick against the wall. She undoes the top button of her thick black wool dress.

'It's far too hot to wear this today,' she says. 'What was I thinking?'

Spidery fingers touch her forehead and push back unruly wisps of hair.

'How do I look?' she says, turning her face towards me. 'Be my mirror, will you, my dear? Nothing too out of place?'

Her eyes look past me into some unknown landscape, but her face is so open and delightful, I'm disarmed. She's wearing too much talc, plastering the cracks of age.

'No, you look fine,' I say.

'I'm new to this. Macular degeneration. Only been fully

blind for a year now.' Her fingers brush imaginary lint off her dress. 'Are you waiting?'

'Yeah, I think she's overrun.'

'Oh, she always goes over. No sense of time that one.'

'That doesn't sound good for a clairvoyant.'

Her laugh is musical.

'No indeed, it doesn't. And you're here because . . .?' she asks.

'My girlfriend gifted me a session.'

'Hmm,' she says. 'May I take your hand? Since my eyes have gone my hands allow me to see.'

It's a surprisingly large, warm hand, quite masculine; makes me feel small. I'm thrown by this. I study her face with impunity but all I see is joy. I realise that I've never witnessed this so fully before in an adult, only children.

'I'm sorry about your mother,' she says. I sit up.

'I don't mean her dying, I mean – how she was.'

Her face doesn't change but the sensation in her hand has. The connection deepens with a tug. I start to pull away, she calmly places her other hand on my wrist to hold me there.

'Hmm,' she says, nodding her head, then she sighs as if in response to something heard.

'Mothers can really set the tone for a life. Fathers can ameliorate this . . . if they're present. His . . . leaving was very hard on you.'

I jerk my hand away. I'm fucking freaked out.

'I need your hand, my love.'

I want to run.

'You don't remember, do you?'

I'm trying to get myself together. She sits waiting, holding out a palm. I can't, can't believe this. *From my hand!*

One two three four

'I just say what the spirits tell me, dear. They want to help you. You can take or leave the advice; it's not *always* good, because they don't understand what it's like to be in a human body.' Her hand is waiting.

Fuck it.

I give her my hand. It locks in again like an octopus sucker. *Damn.*

'They didn't tell you . . . you were so young. And on your birthday . . .' I'm gutted. She pats my hand. 'We've gone ahead now – they're saying, "Go to the ball" . . . I'm seeing a big party . . . People dressed up.' Her free hand flaps around like she's conducting. 'It's going to be very revealing for you. Painful, though. The water bearer . . . though, in a way – they do you a favour.'

It's like she's watching a movie and relaying it to me.

'I don't understand?'

'I'm sorry, love, they show me what they show me – it's often . . . it can be a bit random because they have no sense of time. It should all make sense later.' She tilts her head up. 'Oh, you poor love . . . you and your sister, at her mercy. Your sister's older. Yes?'

I nod, then realise she can't see.

'Do you know that *her* mother was a drinker?' she says, then carries on before I can reply. 'No, you didn't. Her "sainted mother". Yes, a drinker. Very sly. A sweet drunk, though, not like her.' She pats my hand. Tears leak through my eyes.

'So,' she says, 'this is a ... hereditary thing you're struggling with. The two different ancestral lines of the father and mother. They could never ... harmonise the streams – you had no modelling, no modelling to make the two streams flow together – but you *have* to find a way.' She turns her face to me. 'I hope it's all right to say this? I know it's a bit strong.'

I wipe tears away with the back of my free hand.

'Ahh, you're in love,' she says, like she's opening a new chapter. 'Very delightful! Very outspoken. Oh yes, she'll tell you what's what.' She laughs at this, and through my tears so do I.

'This is your soulmate. I know you know that.' She pats my hand again. 'But we don't always end up with our soulmate. Sometimes the timing isn't right. Love her as best you can.'

I cry some more.

'You've been famous?'

'A little,' I say.

'Maybe enough. Hmm.' She cocks her head to one side. 'It's up to you.'

'I don't think that's true. We just blew our chance,' I say.

'I say what I see. You could have everything ... but there's a lot of pressure on you. Too much. You're in the cauldron. If it goes well, it will burn off the impurities. I can't see the end but they're showing me a rainbow, so I think there's hope. A rainbow and a star – "follow the star".' She stops dead, listening for

278

more. 'I know that sounds like nonsense, love, but that's all they're telling me. Sometimes they can be so – cryptic – as if they're playing with us.' She reaches out to feel the contours of my face.

'Try not to be so hard on yourself, love. You're doing your best. There aren't many others who wouldn't do the same as you – given the circumstances. It's only human. Trust yourself. Listen to your own words.' She then sings to me in a delicate feathery voice.

Live in awe, love your life
It's yours to live, regret, forgive
Make more mistakes, regret, forgive
Accept everything.

'That's one of my favourite artists. Up there with Barry Manilow.' She sits up and smooths down her dress. 'I know the singer. At the end of this, all of this, send your writings to him. He'll see you get them out.' I'm about to ask her what she means when she says, 'I hope that makes some sense, my dear. I hope that's OK.' She pats my hand. 'I'm sorry I can't give you more reassurance. *Accept everything*. Only a fool argues with reality.'

Chapter 26

Three months later.

Me, Lee and the minibar have been holed up in this Marriot for four days doing promotion for 'She Came and She Went.' The album title will direct fans to the first single and will 'look cool on a T-shirt', according to Brunt. Previously, charlie would get me through this bullshit.

We play the promotion game to give the album a shot. Last week we hand-signed 4,000 copies of CD special editions and vinyl. This encourages our 'fan base' to buy it in the first week of sales, which should crowbar it into the top 10. This is crucial for it to garner radio plays to create some form of momentum to get it beyond its five minutes of fame.

We love this album – *love it*. I've got the great version of 'Horsman' back on – cos without Faith the crap one was never going to be a single. I lost a band vote on the song 'Give It All a Name', the one I sang to Klaus and his gang, so that got dropped, which was gutting, *gutting,* but hey, that's band democracy, but overall the album's *wonderful*. Couldn't ask for more. Our best yet. Whether anyone's going to hear it or not . . .

And now we've got to sell the fucking thing. Hate this part of the job – makes me feel like a cream-pied porn star. If these journalists have heard it through once, it's a miracle. We're just one more album on an endless conveyor belt of product. The rumour of a Faith collaboration – which Faith's people have still weirdly not denied – and my racist accusations have brought in some decent long-lead press – the *Musical Imperative* is one of them.

The journalist from the *Imperative*, dressed in tweed, looks fresh off the university debating team. He has a clammy hand-shake and the skin of a man who's lived off crisps.

'So, how's the comeback coming along?'

This is the four-thousandth time we've been asked this ques-tion – our soundbites are well honed but my politician's patience has fucked off.

'Hardly a comeback, bro, last record was three years ago,' I say.

'The world spins ever onwards.' He adjusts his glasses to peer at his notes. 'Are you worried that your audience might have moved on – to younger bands? The Addickts, for—'

'There's room for more than one band,' I say.

'It shouldn't be about age – it should be about the music.' Lee steps in with a variation I've heard him use six times today. 'The wonderful thing about being in a band – it's not a competition. Addickts are a great band – but there's still room for the band that inspired them.'

'People see their platinum success as where you might have been if Seth hadn't . . .' He tapers off in the glare of my stare.

'People?' I say. 'Don't hide behind "people". Why is all music, *all* of it, now valued solely on its numerical and financial success? It didn't used to be like that in the 60s, 70s. The Velvets only sold – what? Twenty thousand copies in their day. I used to have faith that people would see through the fucking numbers . . .' I trail off.

The *Imperative* lifts his left ankle on to his right knee – there's dog shit smeared into the grid system of his posh shoes. 'How was the tour in Germany with them by the way?'

'Peachy.' I sip water.

'Great,' says Lee.

'The racism accusations . . .'

'Were bullshit.'

'That kind of shit sticks with you nowadays.'

'It does.' I laugh, looking at his shoe. 'You've seen the footage?' He nods. 'I was set up. *Fawlty Towers* doesn't translate well in Germany.'

'*Fawlty Towers is* racist.'

I look puzzled.

'Manuel, the dumb Spanish waiter, and the "don't mention the war" episode,' he says.

'Hmm. Times are a-changing. So you think I was racist?'

'The fucking of the Jews!'

'I was stating a fact – they got fucked! My girlfriend's a Jew!'

'That doesn't inoculate you.'

'We were pissing around, in private,' interjects Lee. 'I started that shit – not Seth.' Bertie Wooster makes a note. Feels like he's dishing out a sentence.

'He's English-Iranian. Does that give him a pass?' I say.

'No!' He continues to write.

'For me, racism's about intent rather than the words used,' I say. 'Something I learnt in therapy, at rehab. You can *say* reasonable things to someone, like in an argument with your girlfriend, you might *sound* reasonable, but if those words are in the mouth of your critic, or your killer, she'll react to that more than the actual words. Same goes for racism. What's the intent? We were two dickheads goofing around in private. There's no intent there.'

'And for me racism's in the eye of the person offended,' says Bertie.

'All the greatest art, all the greatest comedy, has usually had some offence to someone in it,' I say.

'For me it's more intent, but I get the other argument.' Says Lee. 'Seth can call me an Arab—'

'Arab,' I say.

'—and it's a term of affection,' he gives me a look, 'or a shit joke. But when I was called it at school, it was usually an invitation to fight.' He touches his broken nose.

'Tribalism, racism will be the end of us – let's move on from this,' I say.

Bertie looks to his notes. I'll give him his due, he's not skirting the difficult questions.

'You once said . . .' he reads me my quote: ' "*The X Factor* has destroyed a generation of talent." And now – if the rumour is true – you're working on a collaboration with Faith.'

'Well, let's see if the rumours are true, shall we?'

At least I dodged that bullet.

His leg is bouncing up and down on an imaginary bass drum. He *wants* this story. The *Imperative* wouldn't be bothering to interview us without Faith's celebrity attached.

'Do you still stand by that quote?'

'There are exceptions to every rule . . . but yes, I think those shows and the "winners" are all about fame, money and celebrity – nothing about art, self-expression. Faith might be the exception here.'

I put that last sentence in just in case she changes her mind.

He taps the screen of his iPhone to check the recorder's still on.

'So, how was rehab?'

'Peachy.'

'Did it work?' I can smell the dog shit on his shoes.

'Did it work? Did it work?' I spy with my little eye a plastic bin full of empty minibar bottles. I giggle. The *Imperative* looks unsettled.

'Are you sober?' he cuts through my giggles.

'Funny, you're the *first* journalist who's asked me that question.'

'Seriously?'

'No,' I answer, 'but most ask it in a more . . .' I look for the word, 'discreet way. They also save it till last in case I walk.'

Lee reaches across the table and points to the upside-down press release.

'It's here in the press statement. Seth's been sober for over a year . . .' I pick up the new press photo of the band. It's a generic shot of the six of us in a bar, *a bar, for fuck's sake*!

'So, it must be true if it's in the press release.' I lean towards him.

'It must indeed,' he says.

I allow my body to topple forward on to the coffee table with a bang. I'm on my knees, head on the cool glass. It shuts them both up.

'Is he all right?' the journalist asks Lee in a confidential tone.

'Yeah, he's just being a dick,' he says. 'Carry on.'

'Ask something about the songs?' I say, forehead down on the cool glass table.

I hear him shuffle through his questions.

'"Horseman" – what's that about?'

'Horses.' I don't look up. 'My past life.'

I look up at him. 'Ask a question about how we made the music.' He looks puzzled. 'In four days, no one, not one journo has asked us how we *made* the music. Go on, I dare you, *Musical Imperative*?'

'It's not what our readers want to know.'

'All these fucking "music" papers and no one, NO ONE,' I stub my finger on the table, 'asks a question about how the music's made.'

I sit back down. He riffles through his questions.

'Did Faith pull out of singing "Horseman"? That's the rumour.'

He saved *this* question for last.

Under the glare of my stare he says, 'Is it about you and Faith . . . taking . . . taking heroin?'

I laugh. 'You're full of shit, Sherlock.' I give him my biggest smile. 'Full of shit.'

Chapter 27

'When did you make *that*?'

I'm staring at an eight-foot sculpture of my head, mouth open in a scream. It looks like the rest of me is buried alive beneath the concrete floor.

'When you were in rehab.' Lee sips his Buck's Fizz.

'Looks like you didn't think I'd make it.'

'You haven't.'

He wanders off to the drinks table, picks up some flutes of wine and goes to receive hugs from friends arriving for his private viewing.

Stella steps from behind a white partition in the warehouse gallery. She looks amazing. Gorgeous. Her white three-piece suit matches her peroxide Mohawk, topped by a Westwood black hat with a hawk feather in the ribbon. 'Gifts' from solo styling gigs. She's blossoming with success.

'Damn you look good. Shame you're slumming it with me.'

'If you'd let me I'd dress you for free. The whole band. Then you wouldn't need Faith.'

'I want it to come from the music.'

'Bullshit. Look at Lee.' He's ponced up as usual. 'Every great musician has had to look good. It goes hand in hand.'

I try to think of an exception.

'The Pixies.'

'Would have been as big as Nirvana if they'd looked good.'

'Hmm.'

'The paparazzi are here.' She stares at the back of the floor sculpture.

'They don't come out for the Fuckers,' I say. 'So I don't know how he managed to get them here, for this?'

She walks round the sculptured head and stops in shock when she realises it's me.

'Holy shit! That's, erm, powerful. Wow!'

I'm hot with embarrassment. *He could have warned me.*

She takes it in. 'It's brilliant. There's more of your, er, inspiration round the back.' She indicates behind the screens. I walk off, stunned and apprehensive, into the small labyrinth that partitions the warehouse space.

The first area's full of paintings I recognise. Beautiful lurid flowers set against derelict industrial landscapes, the drab grey background highlighting the natural beauty and colour of the flowers. He gave me one of these when I got out of rehab. The patience needed to paint them blows my mind.

These paintings lead into another area of giant sculptured flowers, seven or eight foot high. The filament on the stamens is made of sweets. Some are Liquorice Allsorts, others hard-boiled bright-coloured ones glued together. Five of them surround a large Venus flytrap, lying horizontal, ugly and dangerous, teeth made of spiky metal, painted poison-frog green. I peer in. The teeth look like a salvaged bear trap, jaws open to reveal glistening vulva-pink lips. In the centre of the trap sits a miniature bottle of vodka and a used syringe. I'm hurt and blown away. I've never seen his sculptures before. Why'd he keep these from me? They're amazing.

'Not bad, huh?'

It's Stella, trying to contain her excitement.

'Got a surprise for you.' She beams.

From round the corner of a screen Holly and Joe launch themselves into my arms, followed by Lizzie.

'Hey!' I laugh. 'Little fuckers, good to see you.' I knuckle Joe's head. I give Holly a long hug.

'You good?' I search her face for the truth.

'If yer asking me about Mum, then yes.'

'Hey, brother.' Lizzie comes over and gives me a squeeze.

'Good to see you, sis.' She looks sad, older. 'A surprise, huh?'

'Lee invited us and we thought, why not? Catch you before you go on tour.'

'The head's amazing!' says Holly.

'He should have made a bigger one that you could climb inside. Then we could have all got inside Seth's head,' says Joe.

'You wouldn't want to go there,' I say.

'Yeah, you're on your own there, Joe,' says Lizzie.

'What? Now that he's drinking again?' says Holly.

'No he's not,' Stella says, but as she says it some part of a puzzle lands. 'Oh fuck.' She puts her hand to her mouth. 'Is that it? Is that why you've been so . . . off?'

We all go still.

'You all knew?' She looks at Lizzie, who closes her eyes. 'And you didn't tell me?' No one moves. 'You fuckers, the lot of you.' She walks off.

'I'm so sor—' says Holly.

'Why can't you keep your fucking mouth shut!' I snap. I go after Stella. Did she go deeper into the maze or back into the main room? I think she went deeper.

In the first boxed-in area is a skip. A bashed-up yellow skip piled high above the brim with empty booze bottles.

Fuck.

Empty bottles stuck together to form one enormous bottle, maybe ten foot tall. There seems to be a light pulsing red from within it. How did he find the time to create something of such intricacy? *Was my addiction his inspiration for everything here?*

It's like an artistic intervention?

At the base of the skip someone's left a glass of white. There's a faint outline of pink lipstick on the rim.

Is this part of the installation?

I stretch over the skip and toast the giant bottle with a clink.

'Lucky Fuckers' I knock it back.

I move on. Round the corner two half-finished glasses of white lie in the corner to the left of a painting.

Breadcrumbs in a Maze.

I drink and replace them. I step back to face the painting.

I'm face to face with the naked portrait of me. I haven't seen it finished. My body is photographically realistic but the face has been violently scratched out in a mesh of brown, red and blacks. That's new. It was perfect when I last saw it. *Did he do that in a moment of anger or was it an artistic choice?* Maybe to keep me anonymous? No, it's a statement. *I hate it.* It's a black mirror of me. He's caught something of my, of my essence – or lack of it.

I look around. I don't want anyone else to see this. *Is this how he sees me?* The thought eviscerates me. *Is this what I am?* I want to destroy it. I take a step towards the painting.

'What do you think?' It's Lee, with one arm round a tearful Stella; a weird sight, my best friend consoling my girlfriend.

'Why'd you fuck it up?'

'It felt . . . right.' He looks hurt. '*It's* not fucked up.'

I'm shaking.

'You don't like it,' he says.

'*No, I fucking hate it.*'

'How long have you been drinking?' says Stella. 'How long?'

'Not long.'

'None of you fucking told me.' She pulls away from Lee. 'I feel like such a fool.'

'It's just vodka—'

'*Just* vodka! Fuck me. So that's OK, then? No crack this time?'

'I needed it . . .'

'You needed it.' She moves in aggressively. 'What for, Seth?'

'Writing.' I bite my lip. 'Performing. Being . . . Seth Brakes. The other one.'

She lets out an angry roar.

'I wouldn't.' I say.

'Wouldn't what?'

'Stand by me.'

She gives a twisted laugh. Her blue eyeliner's run. She wipes her nose. I offer her a hanky. She snatches it from me then pushes me hard in the chest.

'Fuck you,' she says. I smile.

'I wish I could fucking leave you,' she snarls. 'I love you, you dick. All of you. I knew this would happen. *Knew it*. Still stuck around. Think I just want the white-bread Seth? God he can be boring. *I want all of you.*' She shows me her teeth. 'Fucking hell. *Fucking hell!*' She stamps her feet and snaps a heel.

'Fuck,' she says. Lee and I suppress laughter. She takes off both shoes and examines them. 'They're Prada.' She throws the broken heel at me. The action dislodges the feather in her hat.

'I'm falling apart,' she says.

'We all are.'

'Plucky Fuckers. Let me show you something.' Lee leads us into another space.

Ahead of us hangs a large horizontal painting, about five by nine. It's of Stella and me curled up on my sofa. We're bare chested, she lies on top of me. Our chests blend into each other, merge at the heart.

'Oh,' Stella gasps, 'that's beautiful.'

It is. The love between us in the picture is palpable, devastating.

Seeing us captured in this way, it's obvious that we're meant to be together, something I knew from day one, before I lost that. I didn't believe that I was allowed – allowed something *so good*. I believed I didn't *deserve* it.

She takes my hand.

She'll stand by me. Even as an alcoholic, she'll stand by me.

I didn't believe she would. I thought sobriety would be the limit of her love. *I'd set that limit, not her.* I find myself crying. I feel like a child.

We're standing before our future, a future I want.

'How have you managed to do all this work?' I turn to Lee.

'*It's not all mine!*' he laughs. 'There's three artists exhibiting here.'

'The skip?' I ask.

'Not mine,' he says.

'The Venus flytrap?'

'No!'

'Fucking hell.'

A couple in their eighties enter the space. She's strong and sturdy, he hunched up, frail. How come women weather life so much better than men? He leans heavily into her. They move like tortoises.

'Got to go,' Lee says to us.

'Are they important?' I say, thinking of the paparazzi outside.

'They may be buying this painting,' he says.

'I want to buy the fucking painting,' I say.

'You can't afford it.' He goes to greet them.

This is our painting.

After some minutes Lee leaves. The couple hobble over to stand beside us.

'It's so beautiful!' the woman proclaims.

We stand together, entranced.

'We were like that,' she says to us. '*Oh! It's you.* It's of you two.' She turns to the man and ups her volume. 'This is the couple, dear. The couple in the painting.' He looks at us with rheumy eyes. His gaunt face holds a grief that's hard to take. He looks as if something has exploded on the inside. A stroke? He has a tremor that makes him shimmer. There are flecks of dry spittle at the corner of his mouth. Some deep recognition sparks within him. He raises a shaking finger to point at me. I shudder. He shakes his head in disappointment.

'Oh, don't mind him,' says the woman, 'he's not all here.'

Stella's love stretches. She hasn't run.

We walk arm in arm back through the labyrinth. I feel liberated, released from something I didn't know had me. *Stella's love stretches. Stretches to the parts of me – that I don't love.* Is that how love works? Someone loves the parts of us that we can't love – *and that makes us whole? She wants all of me. What does that love look like? Feels so weird. Is this what hope feels like?*

We round a partition that opens up into the foyer. Holly skids to a stop before us. She's flushed and panicky. Behind her, through the entrance door to the street, cameras flash.

'Are you OK, Holly?' asks Stella.

Holly looks from her to me and back again. She looks down to think, lifts a hand, bites a knuckle, makes a great effort to control herself. Behind her, from the street, the sound of raised voices. Holly looks over her shoulder then back to us.

'Faith is here.' She struggles to keep her tone neutral. Behind her, Lee's guests step back from the entrance, all eyes on the doorway. 'I thought I'd better tell you.'

A chill sucks the life out of me.

'Why'd she come here?' Stella asks.

Not now. Not now, please.

Faith makes her entrance in a purple full-length figure-hugging dress, a queen's gold crown perched on a swimmer's black skull cap. White face, rouged lips that match a red cloak. She looks the fucking part. Everyone's gone quiet. I'm terrified, rooted to the spot.

If there's a fucking God, please don't do this.

Lee steps in front of her, offering a glass of wine.

'Hi Faith, so glad you could make it.' His tone suggests otherwise.

Faith brushes past him in a flurry of material. She stops before us, chin raised. She looks to Stella then back at me.

'Knew you'd be 'ere. I bought you a present.' She raises her arms, and folds of red silk hang like bat wings beneath them. In the palm of her outstretched hand is a green apple. 'But maybe it's for you.' She swivels her arm and offers the apple to Stella. Neither of us moves.

'No?' She swivels to the room. 'This fucker tried to con me into singing with him by sayin' he wrote a song about my dad dying.' She rotates back round to us, looks Stella in the eye, leans in and in a quieter voice says, 'And he fucked me.' The words land with the impact of a bullet. Stella grips my arm. Faith smiles. 'Catch.' She chucks the apple in the air, Stella catches it.

Faith sashays out the door. The room is hushed. We are underwater, no one's breathing. Stella stares at the apple.

Outside there's the flicker of camera flashes. The sound of breaking glass.

I'm packing for the tour. Packing and crying, raging and talking to myself like Norman Bates. Two days, Stella hasn't returned my calls and now I'm leaving to tour. I'm broken, how am I going to hold it together? I keep bursting into tears. Swinging between *I've lost her* and *She's better off without me*.

Who isn't?

My apartment was gutted of all her gear when I got back.

It takes four pills to get me to sleep at night. I know it's pathetic but it's better than the despair that's keeping me up. I'm circling a black hole, on each rotation I'm being pulled towards the event horizon. I used to drink to not feel, to not give a fuck. It's not working.

Chapter 28

Backstage our mobiles ping in unison. It's a group text from Monica. Oliver reads it out.

'Just to let you guys know, the mid-week chart positions are: single's at 33 – Faith's announcement gave it some uplift on streaming but like the rest of the world, Radio 1 and 2 want interviews with Seth, for his side of the story. Until then it's B listed. We are negotiating with them now.

'The album is faring better – midweek at 7. This is great if we can keep it in the top 10. So far it's been generated by fans buying it early but Adele – midweek 13 – and, God bless 'em, The Addickts 14 – are likely to come back strong in the second half of the week.'

The fucking Addickts! Their album's been in the charts for months, it's like a bloody yo-yo.

'Give us one week, you bastards,' I say in an Irish accent. Oliver stops reading and gives me a look.

'Did I say that out loud? Sorry,' I say to the room. This is becoming a thing.

Dan files his nails for the gig. He doesn't look well.

I chug back my Perrier but I'm staring at the Ghost Vodka bottle on the drinks table. On the label is a shadowy figure outlined against the frosted glass. A trapped genie in a bottle? I should let the poor thing out.

Oliver continues to read.

'*The* Sun *interview and the* Mail *would really help, Seth!! But it needs to be today.*'

I've told management I won't talk to those rags, especially a Murdoch one. Including it in a band text is their way of pressurising me. I won't do *any* interviews right now as all they want to do is talk about Faith.'

Brunt's furious. 'You fucked it up with Faith you prick, the least you can do is milk the fallout, give the single a chance.'

Don't want Stella to read anything. Door closed if she does.

I walk over to the bottle, pick it up. All eyes are on me. I stare at the genie.

'Free the little fella.'

I unscrew the top and stand back, expecting a spirit to fly out. 'This one's empty.' I pour myself a shot. I turn to the room. 'Anyone fancy?' I enquire.

They're stone-faced.

'No, well, don't mind if I do.'

'It's midday. Steady on there, Seth,' says Oliver.

'Don't you be worrying about me now, Ol.' I imitate his accent. 'I'll be just fine.'

Dan's staring at me, lips pursed in disapproval.

'What? Lee didn't tell you? Na zdorovie.' I knock it back then slope off, bottle in hand.

Back in my bleak little dressing room – strip lights, no window, the smell of some cancerous disinfectant mixed with indie-band BO – I check emails and texts, hoping . . .

I know she won't – she shouldn't.

I know I shouldn't look – but I can't not. Story of my life – I can't not.

Monica has sent me an email compilation of album and single reviews and Facebook fan responses. The fans get it. Pages of positive comments. How they never thought we'd top the first album, how happy they are to see us back, so much goodwill. Even with the limited airplay the gigs are selling. London's sold out.

The press and online reviews? Not too bad, mostly a six or seven out of ten; reluctant praise. The *Guardian*, God bless 'em, gave us eight:

If this were a new band, or a young band, journalists would be hyping them to the hills. But it's The Lucky Fuckers' comeback album so . . .

I stop reading at the words 'comeback album'. I can see the bit about Faith in the next paragraph.

Some interviews are included in Monica's compilation. The article from the *Musical Imperative* has the headline 'Seth Broken!' and a picture of me looking fucked. The biggest photo in the article is one of Faith outside Lee's exhibition and a caption quote from her saying, 'Seth Brakes tried to con me into rescuing their careers with a collaboration. Told me he'd written a song about my dad dyin'. A dirty, low-down trick. And the song was shit. I ask my fans to blacklist The Lucky Fuckers. Don't buy 'em, don't stream 'em.'

It's a message she's reinforced on Instagram and the sheep follow. The other caption quote has me slagging off *The X Factor*. They miss out the bit where I said Faith was an exception; making it sound like I'm slagging off Faith.

There's a brief reference to the German TV debacle. Apparently Lee and I have 'an older generation's attitude to racism'. There's none of our nuanced and highly intelligent thoughts on the matter – we're just racist.

Of course there's little mention of music in the *Musical Imperative*. Like the rest, it focuses on speculation about what happened with Faith to piss her off. There are quotes from 'friends close to the artist' story-lining her as the snow-white victim and me as the evil villain. The journalist spied the bin full of minibar bottles and makes a strong case for me being back on the booze.

'No shit, Sherlock.'

Thank God no mention of us having sex.

I guess she didn't want that known.

I've watched the video footage on YouTube over and over again – the moment when Faith threw the apple to Stella. You can't hear Faith's words, thank God, but you see the impact on Stella as she crumbles like a tower.

I don't want to brag or anything, but it needs saying, again. I'm a brilliant performer loaded. Whatever else happens, shit-faced onstage, I am king. I'm the poster boy for booze and coke.

Did I say coke?

Well, I'm just having a line before I go on, nothing radical. The coke adds the *je-ne-sais-quoi* bit. The not-giving-a-fuck bit. I'm a life hacker in a lab, looking for the sweet spot between Iggy and Perry Farrell. My generation are so fucking lame. Too ambitious for fame to make a statement.

Now I'm singing them live, the new lyrics hit me in surprising ways. Some only make sense now.

We gamble love will last – the bookies laugh
If love's a crime
Ending it is murder.
If love's a crime
Betraying it is murder
Love's a shrine
Murder. Murder. Murder.

Feels like I'm singing for my life.

Lee's been keeping out of my way since the exhibition.

'You even turned my exhibition into being all about you, you selfish cunt.'

'Hey, look on the bright side; she brought the pap with her.'

'Everything you touch turns to shit.'

We haven't spoken since.

He turns up on time to soundcheck, then disappears till gig time.

He's playing with an added fire. It drives me on. It drives the band on. All the songs have an angularity to them, a sharper edge than the recordings. I've started to dance again. I find my body throwing shapes, shaking, spasming. Sometimes I'm so lost in the dance I miss my cue, and the band have to improvise. I forget lines – I make shit up. I get in the audience, get in people's faces. Our fans don't give a shit about the pronouncements of an X factor pop star. The new songs go down as well as the old. It's a live event, not some safe, pre-programmed light entertainment. It's what it should be.

Our swagger's back.

Brunt looks like he's about to give a military briefing. The Fuckers are draped nonchalantly around the room, pretending to be casual yet waiting for a dressing-down.

We're backstage in Brighton. Tomorrow's our day off in London before our big Brixton show. Listen closely and you'll hear a drum roll.

'Hey, Jon, you made it out of London,' I say on entering the dressing room. I move to hug him but he shuffles papers. I pull up a chair. He waits for me to settle.

'The single's at twenty-three, the album's thirteen.' Shit, I'd completely forgotten, chart day.

I can't work out the maths but the room's funereal.

'Bingo?' They glower at me. Tough audience this. 'Well, at least the single went top thirty.' I look up and stretch my arms above my head. 'Thanks, Faith,' I shout up to the ceiling.

Their ire amps up. 'Don't shoot the messenger.' I put my hands up. 'Oh, I guess that's you, Jon. Don't shoot the . . . guy who fucked it all up.' Still don't get a laugh. 'Fuck it. It's just a fucking number. The gigs are going great.'

'Who pays for this, you prick?' Brunt snaps. 'You can't help yourself, can you?' He looks as the group. 'What happened with Faith, Seth?' He waits. 'I already know. Their manager told me. You fucked her.'

The band are shocked. Lee and Joe 90 must have kept it quiet. I shrug.

'Yeah, although technically speaking, she fucked me. What? You said keep her sweet.'

'You told her you wrote the song for her dead dad?'

'That was a misunderstanding . . .'

'*You fucking shit. You selfish little shit,*' he barks. Then turns to the rest. 'I did my best, guys. I really believed in you.' Then his voice goes cold and final. 'Universe will drop you on these numbers. You won't get a crack at any other market; they'll take their lead from here. I'm sorry to be the bearer of bad news but there it is. After this tour we'll re-look at our future together.'

That's a gut punch.

'You mean you and us? Aww, come on, Jon. We've made a *great* album, the gigs are great. We should be celebrating, not freaking out about sales.' My voice is cracking. '*Don't go.* You're

302

the force that holds us together. Without you, we'd go flying off into the void.' *How much did I drink this morning?*

'You drinking again, Seth?'

'Is it obvious?'

He gives me a withering look.

He turns to the room.

'Sorry guys, I tried.'

'You wanted more drama, you hated it when I was sober,' I shout back at Stanley. '*Edge walkers fall over the edge.* That's what they do! You're like the husband who wants his wife to be a whore in the kitchen and a domestic goddess in the bedroom . . . the other way round.' Lee and Dan are not making eye contact with me. 'Sulky twats.' I turn my back to walk away. Stanley jumps me, raining fists on my shoulders.

'Hey. HEY!' Lee steps in and grabs him. 'Knock it off, will you?' He locks his arms round Stanley and hauls him back.

'*We fucking waited for you,*' shouts a red-faced Stan. 'All of us. *Years, years of our fucking lives, wasted.*' He's nearly crying, hating being this emotional. So am I. 'We're not twenty any more, Seth. What are we gonna do now, work in Tesco's?' He bares his teeth and punches the air. 'We were so close . . . Why do you think we waited?'

'Lack of initiative?'

'Because we're fucking good.' Lee keeps adjusting his body to block Stanley from getting closer. 'Any talentless shit can be famous, with a bit of self-belief . . . and promotion . . . and good looks.' I can't help but laugh. 'We're a good fucking band and you, you twat, are a great frontman. And he's . . .' he points at Lee, 'an amazing guitarist. That's why we waited. This doesn't come round often. I'm actually in a band whose music *I love*. Music I believe in. Do you know how rare that is? I know so many great musicians, in *shit* bands, and they know it, *they know it!* They're just whoring. *Great musicians.* And we are lucky enough to be in a great one.' I look around the group; they don't seem to be disagreeing with him. I look at Cream. I look at Dan, Lee.

It hurts.

My cue for coke.

I'm strumming some chords and singing a new song alone on the top-deck lounge. I've had this song haunting me for days. Two songs, actually. This one's a love song – to Stella. A song to get her back – a spell. It's so simple and romantic, I'm embarrassed by it. It's not a Fuckers kind of song. It's called 'I Do'. Won't play it to the band. There won't be a band to play it to. The second song is really sparse, almost country. It's called 'Happy'. It's about seeing Stella with someone good for her and hoping she's happy. Or maybe it's the other way round; lyrics are never cut and dried.

I put the guitar down and pick up the whisky. Cars drift past on the motorway. I watch their tail lights disappear into the darkness.

Do they exist when they go out of sight?

As a kid, I remember sitting in the back of the car looking out the window and believing that what I was seeing, the passing cars, the countryside, was just CGI. None of it felt real. Now I hear some scientists are saying there's evidence that we live in a simulation.

What's the computer game I'm in? *Dysfunctional Families*? Why did I get dealt *this* hand, *this* family, these addictions?

Never fitted in. Always felt like an actor with amnesia. Did I create my addictions?

It's easy for happy rich people to talk about 'creating your own reality', less so when you're at the bottom of the pile.

Buddha was a rich prince slumming it – he could always go back to Daddy if it failed.

I tried meditation, just seemed like too much hard work to get nowhere fast. I guess I'm a twentieth-century consumer, a line of coke, a spliff, Stoli, all easier than trying to shut the fucking mind up.

I've fucked the band up. Again. Me again. How do I break this cycle? I'm on uppers by day, pills by night. Stella's gone. This couldn't have gone better if I'd tried. Casualties everywhere. What's the fucking point.

'Interrupting anything?' Lee stands in the doorway.

'Self-pity.'

He's holding a glass of red in one hand, a near empty bottle in the other. The bus goes over a bump and he spills some on his hand.

'Shit.' He licks it off, half stumbles into the room and sits down beside me.

'You talking to me again then?' I say.

We sit in silence, swaying to the movement of the bus.

'I talked to her.'

The hairs rise on the back of my neck.

'She's done, Seth.'

I'm not breathing.

'Did you talk on the phone?'

He nods.

'She's back in Paris?' He nods again. 'She won't answer me. Could you ask her to call—?'

'No, I can't.'

'Thought you said she was good for me?'

'She is. You're not, you're not good for her.'

'Fuck off, love doesn't work like that.'

'Oh yeah it does. There's a price that comes with trying to save a selfish cunt like you.'

Roadworks ahead. Orange and white cones corral us into one lane and we slow down.

'You aren't in any . . . space . . . for someone like her.' He takes a gulp of wine. 'You're on a different . . . trajectory.'

'*You don't—*'

'*I fucking do. She doesn't want to talk to you, she's saying no.*' He sits back.

The sound of air brakes and the bus lurches to an emergency stop nearly tumbling over an orange beetle beneath us. We catch ourselves. Lee puts his hands out to steady bottle and glass. We rock back into place. Half a mile ahead there's flashing orange and white lights.

'How is she?' I ask.

'Trying to forget.'

Fuck, my heart hurts. Like, physically hurts.

I look up at the *No Smoking* sign and feel in a pocket for my packet. I offer one to Lee. He lights us both up. 'She's making contact with her family. I think there's some communication . . .'

'They're cunts.'

If she returns to them she'll be lost to me.

He finishes his glass, pours himself another.

'Well, she *has* a family,' I say.

'Everyone has their shit, white boy. It's not all about you. *Everyone* has their shit. My life wasn't exactly a bed of roses. As a kid, I thought Paki was my middle name. Cream! You think you've got problems. Her family tried an "honour killing" last week.'

'What!'

'Yeah man. Organised a birthday party for her brother. She was lucky to get out alive. One of her sisters tipped her off and now she's in the shit.'

'Fuck.'

'To family.' He raises his glass. He shudders, belches. '*You* can't understand that about Stella. You *thought* you broke from your family by rejecting them – but you haven't stopped running since.'

A jack-knifed lorry blocks the middle and fast lanes. Red and orange lights flash around its backside. On the hard shoulder a white car is crushed as if a giant's trodden on its roof. Lee and I lean forward, nose to glass.

'Fuck,' he says. 'No one walked away from that.'

The whole scene is strobed by out-of-phase lights. Someone is being lifted onto a stretcher into an ambulance. A man sits at the kerb, head in his hands, sobbing, a policeman stands awkwardly behind him.

'So, what do I do, Lee?'

He takes his time.

'You'll do what you do, Seth. You'll play the part you were made for.' He clears his throat, finishes his wine. 'I don't know. It's your story. How do you want it to end? At the moment, you seem hell-bent on following your path to its . . . *creative* conclusion. You've tried LA – AA,' he corrects himself with a laugh. 'Why not fuck off to South America and work with one of those shamans and their drugs – ayahuasca. Is that how they say it? A mate of mine did it, scared the *bejesus* out of him, but it got him off heroin.'

We slide past the scene. A cop squats at the crushed car's side, shining a hand torch through a jagged window, talking to someone.

'Shit, there's someone still in there.' We pass the wreck. 'They'll need a can opener.'

'It's too late for that,' he says. We sit back.

'You're too fucked for a relationship. Apart from with me.

I'm here for the ride, I figure; if you can't beat them . . .' He lifts the bottle, finds it's empty, sighs, looks at me. 'Do you know I sold most of my artwork? Good money, too.'

'Brilliant. Mazel tov. Molotov.' I toast him. 'You going to jump ship on me, then? Become a real artist?'

'I *am* a real artist.' He looks me flush in the face. 'Whether it's here, with you, or on my own. But I won't babysit any more. I'll see the tour through, but after that,' he slumps back in his seat, 'all bets are off . . .'

'*A real artist* – you sold us out, mate. "Horseman" . . .'

'You're like a child. All art's a compromise with money. Always has been. Always will be. We've made a great record. Be proud of it for the rest of my life. *A great one*. But without Faith, who's gonna hear it?'

Chapter 29

I wake mid-afternoon in a London hotel room I have no memory of getting into. The sleeping pills make me feel like shit. My body aches. My brain's wrapped in cling film, can't think straight. And then all the reasons why I might not want to think straight come pouring in.

I make a strong coffee. It doesn't cut it. My mind plays piñata with my soul. It rotates between losses – Stella, Brunt, The Fuc£ers and Lee. A movable feast of loss.

Time for a line.

After a healthy line I feel a bit more positive. Well, I'm aware I'm towing a storm cloud behind me, but I'm looking ahead – instead of back.

Day off today and I'm going to a party!

Me and Lee have been invited to The Addickts' after-show.

Fuck yes. Just what I need.

Bling Records are throwing an 'End of the world' party for the band to celebrate 160 gigs in 190 days.

160! I couldn't hack it, but I'm jealous as fuck.

Bling's owner's the billionaire Mick Garrity; an A-list

crowd's guaranteed as is a level of decadence that the man's famous for.

Pick-up's after The Addickts' show, entrance only for the bearer of the invite, rules about no filming, etc., etc. The invitation's topped off with the lame *Matrix* quote about choosing the blue or red pill.

Bring it on.

Lee and I catch the end of the gig and are hustled into crowded limos that take us to Garrity's Palatial Hotel overlooking Richmond Park. Pretty boys and girls drink champagne from the bottle and snort lines of coke off the plush interior, giggling and screaming with delight as the vehicle takes corners. They don't share.

In the gravel driveway we're greeted by security guards in formal black suits, wearing carnival butterfly face masks.

We line up at tables where our names are ticked off a list, then we sign non-disclosure forms, *then* pass through metal detectors.

Our phones are taken from us. Three Gen Z girls in front of us kick off like rednecks being asked to give up their guns.

Lee and I are escorted by a drag queen in an upside-down ice-cream-cone-shaped dress. She looks like an art nouveau chess piece.

'Follow me, ladies.'

'She looks like an art nouveau chess piece,' Lee mutters.

We enter a high-ceilinged ballroom filled with racks of high-quality fancy-dress costumes. There's a babble of excited voices as people try on outfits. I recognise a rising star in the Tory party just before he puts on his Spider-Man mask. *Hope Faith isn't here.* We pass rows of Halloween outfits, action heroes and Venetian ball capes and masks.

'Flown in at great expense,' says our guide.

We stop at a rack.

She pulls us out highwayman outfits. They're natty but a bit obvious compared to the rapper slipping into Tutankhamun's regalia and someone prancing around in a Lion King outfit further up the aisle. We get boots, scalloped hats, waistcoats, frilly shirts and pistols.

'Adam Ant,' says Lee.

'This is how you normally dress.'

She gives me a simple black eye mask but Lee gets a white full-face mask with a lascivious smile and black outlined eyes.

'Looks great, but I can't breathe in here.'

We step out the elevator, first floor. Ahead of us is a large lady rammed into a leather bra and panties, whip in hand, stalking the hallway. She opens a door and tendrils of baby-blue smoke snake out.

'I'm coming,' she says in a playful voice and closes the door behind her. Smoke wafts and curls across the plush carpet before dissolving into nothingness. We're instantly adrenalised.

'I thought these kinds of parties became extinct in the eighties.' Lee lifts his mask to speak.

'Mick Garrity's old school.'

'I smell lust.'

He's right. There's an odour of excitement, fear and pheromones.

'Welcome to the Twilight Zone. Shall we . . . er . . . follow the rabbit?' I nod at the door the dominatrix went through.

'*Not* my first choice.' He adjusts the strap at the back of his head. Muffled beats overlap from all directions.

'Where to, then, my fine sir?' I strike a pose and offer him my arm.

'You're a cunt, you know?' He steps in close and adjusts the collar of my shirt. 'But you're my cunt.'

Feels like the good old days. Me and Lee, on the town, buzzed up, looking for adventure.

I'm just going to enjoy myself. Fuck Stella. She's gone. Nothing I can do about it.

Along the corridor grim aristocratic portraits frown down on us.

Ahead of us elevator doors ding open, disgorging a group of ladies in full-on French royal outfits, replete with powdered wigs and wedding-cake dresses.

Damn the tyranny of beauty!

Marie Antoinette's white-green dress is so wide she has to navigate it through the door sideways, as if parking a boat. It's gorgeous and a cut above everything I've seen so far. She lowers her ivory stick mask and hoicks up the dress. There's an intricate wooden cone frame beneath the material. She straightens the white wig that sits on her head like a dollop of ice cream. She looks straight at us, eyes the relative simplicity of our gear, and says in a Southern belle accent: 'I'm beginning to regret my sartorial choices.'

It's Cat Ripley, the latest next big thing from Hollywood. An ex-Disney child actor run riot across the pages of celebrity scandal mags after playing years of too-good-to-be-true girls in ponytails. I remember an hilarious interview where she out-flirted Craig Ferguson, gave him a lap dance. She's in her late twenties, with a face you could gaze at for ever.

She turns back to her gang.

'1515?' she queries.

'1515,' is the authoritative response from an imposing wizard who shepherds the group out the lift. His purple gown is luminous with photographically rich images of planets, constellations, black holes.

'Looks like the quality of the outfit denotes rank,' I whisper to Lee.

'This way.' The wizard points his white staff forward and walks on.

'They look like they know where they're going.'

We trail them at a polite distance while they trundle down the hall. Ripley's running her fingers across the embossed wallpaper. She stops.

'Oh look,' she says, peering in closer. The group cluster round.

'No shit!' says one of her ladies-in-waiting. 'They're fucking!'

Lee and I turn to our section of wall. Among fractal patterns in the indented wallpaper there is, indeed, much fucking going on.

'There's a woman with a horse here!' Lee traces the outline with his forefinger.

Techno booms from a room ahead. We turn in unison as the door opens. A distraught woman in blazing red, face flared to match her dress, careens towards us on six-inch heels. We part to let her through.

'It's a fucking orgy back there,' she throws over her shoulder.

The door closes behind her; the music dulls to a muffle.

The group from Versailles turn wide eyed to the wizard. He manages a crocodile smile. 'It's an option,' he says in a cool Scottish brogue.

Ripley pushes her way through the group in a flurry of outrage.

'Garrity, have you flown me and my friends in for a fucking orgy? Really!'

'It's like Burning Man; you get whatever you're looking for.'

Her nostrils flare like a colt's. He continues smoothly. 'An orgy is one option – but all the rooms are different.'

'You fuck. You didn't think to tell me?'

'You said you wanted to ditch the Disney image.' He shifts the staff towards his midline as she thrusts her face up to his.

'Ditch it, not sodomise it!' she spits. 'That doesn't mean I want to get fucked by you and your vampires.'

'Well, you can leave if you want.'

There is a l-o-o-ong pause while a truckload of feelings pass across her face. She snorts out a breath, takes a step back, her eyes ping-pong from Garrity to the women and back again. They wait patiently for her to conclude a position on this.

She turns back to him.

315

'And room 1515?' she asks.

'It's neutral. Orientation for A-listers,' he adds and, on this thought, he turns around as if seeing us for the first time. Relieved at the diversion, he steps forward. 'Mr Brakes?' He formally shakes my hand. 'And you must be—'

'This is Lee,' I cut in.

'Some party you have going on here.'

Cat Ripley steps in.

'You . . . you're that singer?' She attempts to peer through our masks. Her blushing makes her more stunning. 'The Lucky Fuckers?'

'Only in name, ma'am.' I remove my mask and hat and take a bow. 'Seth Brakes, my lady.' I straighten up and push my fringe back.

'Lucky Fuckers, fuck you all night, Lucky Fuckers . . .'

'Yes, that's us.'

Why does everyone only know that *song?*

'Fucking love you. *Love you.*' She stubs her forefinger to my chest.

A warm feeling spreads over me.

'The feeling is mutual, ma'am – loved that witches movie.'

'You can call me Ripley.' Her Texan drawl goes steely. 'Did you know this was an orgy?'

'No idea.' I raise my palms. She stares blankly at me. *Stoned?* 'Hand on heart.'

She bites her bottom lip, sucks it then lets it go with a *swick* sound. She weighs me up, and then Lee.

'You're sober now, aren't you? You did rehab?'

'Yeah,' I say, on instinct. *She must be a proper fan to know that. Though clearly not the latest instalment with Faith.*

She makes up her mind and says, in a perfect queenly English accent, 'Will you promise to protect me and my ladies if anything untoward goes on this evening?'

'On my honour, my lady,' I say and hold another deep bow. She looks at Lee, who jerks to life and follows my lead.

'He's not got a pass to room 1515.' Says Garrity.

'He has now.'

She takes my arm, turns and raises a white-gloved fist in the air.

'Onwards, then.'

We follow as one.

In the short walk to room 1515 our group has unified with an unspoken camaraderie. Garrity's banished from the kingdom. Stella's banished to the back of my mind.

She finished with me! I repeat like a mantra.

When I hit bottom, I'll return to AA, go back on the choker; may as well enjoy my freedom now.

Ripley leads the way. I think she was voted sexiest woman of the year in the trash mags. She's glorious, intoxicating, Hollywood. I keep stealing glances, not quite believing she's on my arm. Is this how a bee feels when confronted with the beauty and scent of a flower? Damn.

She halts before the double doors of room 1515. She gives me an are-you-ready-for-this look. She inspects the ladies of Versailles, a sergeant reviewing the troops. I adjust my mask. My palms are clammy, heart's racing. Feels like we're about to go onstage. She raises her wand mask to cover her eyes, nods to me, and I throw open the double doors.

I'm relieved, and disappointed, that there doesn't seem to be any fucking going on in room 1515. Opulent, baroque, sexy, yes, but no orgy. The room is all crimson, scarlet and gold, with ornate painted Japanese arches.

Blooms of colour and historical incongruencies assault the senses. Samurais sprawl on Regency velvet sofas getting it on with cowboys. A couple of male cancan dancers are snogging twin sister Wonder Women. Batman and Robin boogie with a troop of suffragettes to an orchestral dance remix of an Addickts song. Most people are standing round awkwardly, chatting at the bar. Same old, same old.

On our entrance the fifty or so revellers turn their gaze upon us. Ripley and Garrity are spotted, and the world tilts in our direction. I've got vertigo, touched by the grace of second-hand fame. There *are* celebrities here, some look familiar, but none are more famous than these two.

Ripley takes my arm again, the group clumps together, we glide into the room.

'Look up,' she whispers.

Suspended above our heads are five gold birdcages. Caged

couples in thongs and masks simulate sex. Limber, oiled bodies move lazily in semi-choreographed movements. A masked redhead, shoulder-length hair cascading down like fire, sits in the nearest cage. Her legs spread, dangle down through the bars. Ruby satin panties contour her labia. She gives off a do-you-dare look.

Garrity pushes through the pack and assumes leadership. We clop behind him across a parquet floor. He stops under a glass chandelier.

'The bar is that way.' He looks at Ripley. 'Are you really going to do this? I flew you here by private jet.' By way of an answer she tightens her grip on my arm. I draw myself up to my full height.

'Make yourself at home,' he says to me, in a flat, dangerous voice.

I quail inside but my face mask deflects his voodoo. *Fuck you.*

Garrity spins round to face the rest of the group.

'I'll be announcing the game in ten minutes.' He turns and stalks off to the bar.

'The Game?' I ask Ripley.

'No fucking idea.' She shrugs. 'He's playing games with *me*, bringing me to a fucking orgy without telling. "I flew you here." Motherfucker.' I nod in outrage. 'My agent would kill me. It's a fine line between having a wild reputation and being seen as a whore! Something you men never have to bother about.' She grips her mask-on-a-stick. 'Wonder who's here?' She scans the room. 'This fucking mask's useless. He wanted me to be recognised!' She turns to her ladies-in-waiting.

'Juliet, would you mind swapping masks with me?' She offers an apologetic smile.

'Sure, Rip.' Juliet lifts her mask delicately over her coned wig. She hands it to her mistress.

Ripley swaps masks, turns to me.

'How does it look?'

'Who are you?'

'Felt so naked in that.'

Juliet looks glumly at the wand.

'Come on, let's sit.' Ripley wheels me towards a sofa then stops. 'I can't even sit down in this fucking dress. I'm keeping it, though, that will teach him.' Her dress is handmade in some Parisian fashion house for the price of my mortgage. Stella would know where. She'd love this room . . . I stop my train of thought.

'You could squat on that bar stool.' She gives it a withering glance, steps in close and whispers in my ear.

'Marie Antoinette's dresses were made so wide that her lovers could hide under them and pleasure her in court gatherings. Just imagine, she would cuckold her husband while standing next to him.' Her tongue glides around the contours of her full red lips while she sways her dress, brushing my legs. 'She'd be, ahh,' she whimpers, 'talking to him, ahhh, about affairs of state, whilst, ahhh, harbouring some fine young stable boy beneath the umbrella of her skirts.'

Holy Fuck.

I look around to see if Lee's witnessing this but he's laughing with the handmaids.

'Did I actually make Seth Brakes blush?' She runs the edge of her fan down the side of my jaw. 'That wild man still in there somewhere? Hope you haven't gone all boring and straight on me. That would make for a dull evening.' She turns and floats off to her entourage at the bar.

Someone taps me on the shoulder. I jump. Harry Addickt as Santa Claus stands before me, an open bottle of Perrier in his hand.

'Santa brought you a present.' He hands me the green bottle. 'Glad you made it, bro. You're in the premier league now.' He cracks a huge smile under his white beard.

Huh, he still thinks I'm sober.

'Thanks.' It's chill to the touch. 'Wild fucking party. Well done on the single – and the tour – and the album.' My list droops at the end. 'Don't suppose you've got any ch—'

'Cheers.' He raises his champagne flute. We clink and drink.

'You're thirsty.' He laughs.

'It's hot in this gear. Haven't got any charlie, have you?'

'Nah, mate.' He scans the room hungrily. 'Left it in my jeans. You don't need it, though.' He pats me on the back.

From a small stage a man in butler's livery bangs a gong. From behind him a buff, bare-chested male in an oversized papier mâché rabbit's head pushes a trolley into place.

Three battered Victorian top hats lie upturned on the trolley.

The music subsides, the butler and rabbit boy step back as Garrity steps forward.

'Gather round, gather round, you magical creatures of excellence. I have a game for you.' The group take a while to hush. He stares a laughing cowboy into silence.

321

'*Life* is a game for you, you Sun Kings and Queens. You who have fulfilled your dreams and become those whom ordinary mortals dream of becoming.'

He raises his staff; the lights dim except for a spotlight shining down on him. The astrological images on his cloak turn 3D.

'*Three hats.*' He touches each top hat in turn with his palm, a priest blessing his altar boys. 'Three hats of adventure. Each hat contains a room number where other guests – extras to you, ordinary punters – are already playing.'

That would have been us if we hadn't bumped into Garrity at the lift. I deflate a little as I remember my place in the celebrity food chain.

'So – you come up here, you put your hand in the hat and you pull out a room number – you go to that room, where all manner of adventures await.' His palm hovers over a hat. 'This first hat is for an *innocent* game, something fun, magical even.' He shifts his weight.

'Hat number *two.*' He places a hand on the middle hat. 'A bit more risky.' He gives us a serpentine smile. 'More *fun*. It could go either way.'

He scans the room to check we get his meaning. 'You can leave the room at any time,' he reassures a blushing Wonder Woman.

'Hat *three.*'

He whispers. The group lean in. An adrenalin switch flicks on, breathing stops like a clock.

'Well – hat *three* is what you'd expect.'

He holds Ripley's gaze.

'More risk. More adventure. *Might* . . .' He looks lazily around, enjoying our heightened attention. *Oh, he's good.* Garrity isn't handsome, but he's sexy. Sexy because he's dangerous. You can see he's done what most only fantasise about. The media hate him with a blatant prurient jealousy. He's good copy when headlines are thin.

'Room three *might*,' he continues, 'take you outside your *normal* . . . boundaries.' He strokes his beard.

'But who of you here is normal? Who among you would want to be *normal*?' He looks like he's smelt a turd. 'Who of you got here by staying within societal boundaries?' A cowboy whoops and slaps his chaps in a fast drum roll. People jump followed by a ripple of soft laughter. The wizard pounds his staff.

'And if you are someone who plays it *safe* . . .'

He picks people out with his stare.

'If you are someone who lives within the straitjacket of normality, who lives life according to an echo of hand-me-down religious morality, aren't you *bored*?' He raises his staff to indicate the golden cages above us.

'Don't you long to taste some more exotic fruits in the garden? Don't you have questions about yourself? And if not, why not?'

There's a rising hunger in the room.

'*The unexamined life is not worth living.* I advise you to take at least two room numbers. Maybe one room number from each hat. Maybe *start* safe.' His hand hovers over the first hat.

'Then decide if you want to keep going.'

Will Ripley go for this?

'The masks give you anonymity. The non-disclosure agreements permission. *Permission*. Permission to act on your fantasies *without* repercussions. Permission *not* to be – yourself. That fucking *boring* self that you show to the world. That self, hemmed in by the need for likes and Facebook followers.'

He pauses and makes eye contact with three YouTubers that even I recognise.

I can handle this but I need a line now.

'No pressure, then.'

There's laughter.

His voice drops into a matter-of-fact tone. 'You have ten minutes to think about it and then I will invite you, one by one, to come up here and . . . show us what you're made of. This is a great opportunity, my friends. How often in your life will something as *insane* as this happen? *Don't* have regrets tomorrow based upon yer timidity.'

He holds up his staff, the music and lights come back on. A wave of excited conversation escalates round the room.

Two white feathers sway down from a cage. One lands in Lee's hair. I pick it off and twiddle it between finger and thumb.

He takes it from me, straightens out the vanes, slugs back his cocktail.

'Get me one of those, will you?'

'Get your own. I'm not enabling. Anyway, Ripley thinks you're sober, that's why she trusts you.'

'Fuck.' I look at my Perrier and finish it off.

'What d'you think?' Lee asks.

'I think he's a cunt.'

The bar's packed.

I reach down to a table brimming with glasses, pluck out a half-full shot glass and knock it back. Whisky burns my throat. I follow it with a revoltingly sweet discarded cocktail.

'Garrity wouldn't let any press in here; it's got to be airtight. And there's the masks . . .' Lee's thinking aloud.

Behind him, Queen Ripley is circled by her handmaids, discussing their choices behind fluttering fans.

'Stop drooling. You're an open book. Even in a mask.' He takes off his hat and mask and waits for me to do the same.

'I'm a free man, done with being a fucking monk,' I say. 'That, that other guy. Fuck, he was boring. What's wrong with pleasure, for fuck's sake? Or fucking, for fuck's sake? Don't tell me you're gonna walk from this?'

'You think!' He gives a snort. 'I'm not going to be the guy, you know, the guy who left this soon-to-be-legendary party. I don't want to be *that* guy.'

'So, we're in?'

'We're in.'

Ripley glances over at me, puffs out her cheeks and pulls a mad face. She gets the smile she was looking for.

'What happens on tour stays on tour,' Lee says.

'Planet of no ripple – I'm with Ripley for fuck's sake. How did *that* happen? Its not a coincidence that we're here for the maddest party on the planet . . .'

'Don't fucking say it's fate! We get to choose, Seth. Just because it's right in front of us doesn't mean we have to take it.'

He drops the feather; it continues its arching journey. 'The universe could be playing all kinds of tricks on us.'

'That's a pretty paranoid view of the universe.' I lean in. 'If you had one of the most sought-after women in the world suggesting you slide under her dress, you tell me you'd walk away from it?'

'Doesn't happen to me that often.'

'Nor me.'

'Yeah, right. Seems to be happening a lot recently. Brunt would be over the moon. Might make up for Faith.'

'Fuck, it might!'

'That's a point.'

'This is fucking *rad*.' Harry Addickt's white beard has gone, his hood's up. '*Garrity*, man . . . Did he say if we could pick all three choices from one 'at?'

'I'm sure you can do whatever you want, Harry,' says Lee.

'Where can I score some coke, Harry?' I ask.

He stands back, takes me in. 'You won't need it.'

'What the fuck, man?' An angry voice turns us around.

Phil Addickt stands there dressed as a jockey, in a bright billowy red shirt, hat and britches. A large pantomime horse, attached to his waist.

'Was this your fucking idea?' he spits. 'I come to an orgy on a horse. A fuckin' jockey!'

The three of us crack up.

Phil throws a punch at Harry, but his swing is restricted by the horse. Harry grabs him by the collar.

'Listen, shit head. Don't fucking try it on here or I'll fuckin' kill ya.' He bares his teeth. 'You *and* yer fuckin' 'orse.' Phil goes limp in his hands.

'That's better.' Harry lets him drop. 'Now go play with the other boys.' Phil doesn't move. 'If it's an orgy, dickhead, you won't be wearing any costume.'

Phil leaves.

'Midget,' says Harry.

Ripley drifts into view, fluttering her fan.

'Do you, sir, intend to keep to your pledge to guard me against any villain that might impugn upon my honour?' It takes a second for me to interpret.

'I do, my lady.'

She turns to Lee, 'And you, sir, will you do the same for my ladies-in-waiting?'

'Aye, milady.'

We bow, she curtseys, snaps the fan shut, pirouettes and glides away.

'You're in there, la, she's boss,' says Harry. 'Garrity flew her in for this . . . Watch yer back. Fuck that, all's fair in love and war, eh!' He squeezes my shoulder and sniffs.

Dong dong dong dong. The music and lights dip down. The spotlight's back on Garrity.

'Time's up. Come and make choices.'

We all play statues. The longer we wait the more the tension builds.

'Fuck this,' says Harry, and steps forward to the podium. A few people cheer. He puts his hand into hat number three and brings out three numbers. There's laughter in the room.

'What?' he says. 'Is that not OK?'

'It's OK for you, Harry, it's your party,' says Garrity. 'Just one from each hat for the rest of you.'

Two samurai follow Harry. The next ten are all men. I'm going to wait for Ripley to show her hand.

C3PO's sex is indeterminate under the full clanking outfit. I think it's some comedian. *Poor fucker, he has to wear that to an orgy. We got off lightly.* He takes a number from the third hat, turns to the room and says in character, 'R2D2 and I have an agreement.' The room erupts.

A knight in full amour clanks up to the hats. He turns to C3PO's retreating figure. 'I'm right behind you, metal man.'

'Not too close, I hope.' Responds R2.

Ripley is the first woman to approach the hats, her entourage close behind. She takes a number from the first hat, one from the second, pauses to look at Garrity, then one from the third.

Oh shit, she's trying to make him jealous.

The tension lifts, her group follow her lead.

Lee joins the queue. I snatch more dregs of drinks and follow him. We both take one number from each hat then return to the ladies.

'We won't get to the third number.' Ripley whispers to me. 'Just wanted to fuck with Garrity.'

'I guessed.' *Damn.*

We watch the final guests filter through. A few have left.

Phil Addickt is the last in line. He whips his horse's flanks with a riding crop. The beast rears and whinnies.

Chapter 30

Lee, me, the court of Versailles, Phil Addickt, Gay Batman and Robin stand before room 220. We pooled our choices together from hat number 1 and Ripley, eyes closed, chose the room. Start safe.

It's a long and winding hotel and someone has fucked with the numbering so it took for ever to get here.

I couldn't find any coke but from the way Ripley's sniffing, she did. I'm feeling a bit spaced out, sloppy; everything's vaguely ridiculous. Batman has a washing label hanging out the back of his top: cold wash, do not tumble dry. I giggle.

The door to 220's amazing. An antique Indian wooden affair with distressed hand-painted panels. Shiva sits at the top of one panel, and Durga, his beloved, atop the other. There are painted panels of elephants, tigers, rural scenes of rivers. From inside the room I hear the muffled sound of Underworld's 'Rez'.

Ripley's leadership of this group is unquestioned. 'So, let's see what Garrity's idea of an "innocent game" looks like.' She clicks her fingers. It takes me a moment to realise that's my cue. I pull my gaze away from the wallpaper where an octopus is having sex with four people and step through the group to take her arm. She feels warm. We push open the door into another world.

It takes a moment for my eyes to adjust to the dark. Thirty or

330

so people in costumes are dancing. It's a large empty cream-walled room with a sad mirrorball turning slowly on its axis. There is a haze of dry ice. It's lame. We look at each other, confused. A doorman steps forward and asks us to enter and close the door.

'May as well,' says Ripley.

Our party rivers into the room. A few dancers look up to watch, but most seem lost in their own worlds. Captain America's on uppers; he's doing a crazily energetic dance wielding his shield too close to two sumo wrestlers whose brown-skinned heads contrast with the dull pallor of their fat suits. Two glorious angels dance sexily with a red devil. The devil keeps whipping them with his tail. He spooks me out. The Joker spies Batman in our group, rushes over, grabs his gloved hand and says, 'Come dance with me.'

'Batman! Don't leave me,' shouts Robin. Batman's absorbed into the dancers.

The door's closed behind us.

I'm light-headed, dreamy, disorientated. The fusion of realities is getting to me.

I dance around Ripley, the bulk of her dress restricts her movement.

We dance as a relief from the tension of this whole crazy situation. We dance in character. We dance. *God, I love this song.* The trippy keyboard lines seem to be coming from all around the room. The sound system's incredible. Everyone's dancing, smiling. Two ninjas are running at the walls, doing flips, dodging in and out of dancers. The handmaiden, Juliet, dances with Lee. He's buzzing. I throw off my hat and mask. I help Ripley raise her mask to sit on her wig. It looks funny. We dance around each other, giggling like kids. I bounce off the springy frame of her dress, again and again. I feel incredible Ecstatic. I don't need an orgy. This is a blast. My body is moving faster than I can think, moving around her, beside her, against her.

This is the first time I've felt good since Stella left. Shut up. Don't curse it.

Dry ice pours into the room from vents around us.

'I'm invisible,' sings the singer over and over in an autotuned metallic voice. The music hovers in suspense.

'I'm invisible,' we shout back.

Ripley grabs her dress frame and herds me backwards, bumps me up against the wall, grabs me by the wrists, leans in and kisses me on the mouth. She tastes of cherries, and of a sweet, shaped like a fish, that I remember from childhood. I'm lost in the memory of its taste.

'Holy shit.' She pulls back and releases my hands. I hear whoops and applause from around the room.

I open my eyes. There's so much dry ice in the room that I can only see the dancers closest to us. We watch in wonder as the world dissolves into clouds. All I can see is her face, less than a foot in front of me. We are disappearing. Disappearing into the mist.

She grabs my head.

'Go under me,' she says urgently. *What's she saying?* She reads my confusion. 'Under my dress.'

She grabs my wrist and yanks me down. I crouch. She lifts the frame of her dress over me.

It's pitch black, the music's muffled. The scent of her. *Does she want me to just hide here?*

Through the dress, she pulls the back of my head toward her hips.

OK!

I kneel, take my gloves off and grip her thighs from behind. In the dark, my mouth finds the front of her knickers. Feels like silk. I blow hot breath on to them, running up and down the crease with my nose. She opens her legs wider. I pull her pants to one side. She's clean shaved. I bury my tongue inside her, slide up lips that fall open like ripe fruit. I feel her slump against the wall. She tastes like white wine. I slide her pants down to her ankles, she lifts a foot, I slide them over a heel. I rub my tongue up and down over the top of her.

I can feel how each micro-movement affects her, seems to last for ever. Electricity from her body pulses into mine. It's like I'm merging into her experience. I pull back in shock. I can see nothing. I'm panting in this womb space, it's hot and claustrophobic. I panic and lift the frame of her dress. It's still a total white-out out there. She taps the top of my head.

Don't panic now, not now, not now. Breathe.

She taps me again. I take deep breaths and dive back under. I'm in the ocean. I gather myself and lean in. I use my fingers to spread her open and lick upwards, slowly, rough-tongued. She rocks backwards. She staggers and I shiver. My body ripples with the pulse. A shock of pleasure. I see sparkles of light. *It's as if I'm on the receiving end of this.*

Two hands on the back of my head pull me into her. I do it again, and again and again, lost in the sensation as she thrusts her hips into me. I'm sucking and licking, fingers inside, moving urgently. Her legs buckle.

I hear a faint knocking sound.

It repeats over and over, getting louder.

Bang, bang, bang.

The sound from my dream. I panic. I have to get out.

Focus on the pleasure. Focus on the pleasure.

I try to keep going but dry retch.

Two hands on the back of my head again, rubbing my mouth where she wants me, my tongue where she wants me. I'm freaking out, sweating, *can't breathe.*

Bang. Bang. Bang.

Her hands.

I thrust harder, deeper, faster.

I have to end this.

Her movements are becoming erratic, frantic. She jerks hard into my face. I hold her up, as she spasms into me, I see—

I see—

I see the twin-tub washing machine. The lid's open. Mum's lined the metal tub with sweaters. She's going to lower me into it, me as a toddler. I'm struggling, kicking, screaming. She's so strong. I can't fight her. She drops me in and closes the lid on a sweater, so it's ajar, so I can breathe. I cry and scream but no one comes. No one comes. Lizzie's locked in her bedroom.

Mum's gone to the pub. No one comes.

It's deep, it's dark. I can't get out. The lid's open but the room door's closed. It's pitch black.

I puke with terror.

No one comes.

Not till she comes back pissed.

When I shit myself, she leaves me in here overnight.

I'd forgotten.

But I knew.

I'd forgotten.

I remember.

Ripley comes and my energy roars up

to meet her,

up and out,

       like the

like the birds escaping

    out of my body

   up and out   out of my mouth

I throw up

   bitter bile

all over her thighs

down her legs

all over myself

as my body

convulses and spasms

convulses and spasms,

she steps off me

the dark bell of her dress

     like a passing ship in fog

        leaving me gasping

a mewling baby born shipwrecked into the room

now clear of clouds,

     full of staring revellers

frozen in poses

hands to mouth

     grouped round

like shocked statues . . .

'Seth! What the fuck, man?' Lee shouts over the din.

He's miles away.

I'm down a well.

'Are you OK?'

Not OK.

I'm foetal on the floor. The pistol in my belt sticks into my ribs, it's a hold-up, I can't move.

I'm pinned like a Victorian butterfly specimen.

The highwayman's cloak is a heavy, hot shroud, wet with

vomit on thick black felt. There's a damp warmth going cold around my crotch.

What's happening to me?

I'm unravelling.

My gold clasp has a leather loop around its neck, making the cloak throttle tight. I tried to undo it before this, this paralysis came on, but my fingers were as clumsy as twigs. *Try not to panic, breathe.*

At least I'm out of the washing machine.

Can't stop the images.

    They're switched On;

                and the Off is

broken. I've lost my leash,

my thoughts keep   b u tt e r fly in g

FOCUS ON THE ROOM!

Lee is squatting over me like a toad, a disgusted look frozen on his face. A lazy tongue flicks out and licks his eyeball.

IT'S NO BETTER OUT HERE!

Glitter sparkles twinkle in his hair like stars, stars hanging in the vast firmament, and suddenly I'm out there, in the expanse of space, the infinite void. The distance between them is immense,

I M M E N S E

The space is,
it just *is*.
The world is
s   p   a   c   e
It's cold, impersonal. I am so insignificant.
I'm ashamed at my own self-importance.

I see everything through my own lens and my lens is full
of shame.

Full shame.

A bead of sweat bubbles on Lee's forehead. My vision details colour in the bubble, metallic blues and coppers, the
kind you find on a dragonfly.

Dragonfly's eye

The blurred swirl of the costumed partygoers suspended in
motion, staring. Colours intensifying like a Polaroid burning in
a fire.

*I used to love the smell of Polaroids, the chemical smell, Dad holding
it to the heat of his hairy tummy, then showing us the image appear
out of nothing, out of a grey-white void.*

Wires sprout from Lee's nose. Is he an android?

He looks funny, arms puffed up and gathered at the elbow
like those cheap Chinese streamers that hung across our living
room at Christmas. They start out flat and you open each one
out three hundred and sixty degrees, so they hang off string.
Red lanterns were my favourite. Dad got them for us.

Dad. I never think of Dad. Ever.

My vision is `kaleidoscopic`, three-sixty, one-eighty. I don't know.

'One hundred and eighty!' shouts the darts match umpire, echoed by my dad and me, mimicking his sing-song voice of success, after the third dart thuds into the board, bunching tight to the preceding two, squeezing into that tiny metal segment of the treble twenty.

Can't seem to focus.

'Hocus Pocus', that yodelling prog-rock song from the 1970s that the whole family used to sing along to as he ascends the scale in a falsetto to that ridiculous note only I could reach.

Can't turn off the tap.

Where are these memories coming from? The before-Dad memories. Happy-family memories.

Did I suppress happy memories?

My vision's like the mirrorball, streams

of light coming down like snow, flakes

of light glinted off the masked revellers, catching sequins,

spangles, jewels. The court of Versailles

have become transparent beings of light,

multi-dimensional

escaped from their deck of cards.

Mirror, mirror on the wall. Mirrorball. Is this how a fly sees?

Flyball, e y e b a l l . *Allllll information coming in at once. No. Not like a fly*
Like a baby
Undifferentiated
Everything

all

at   *once*
ALLTIMEATONCE

Babies outside the tyranny of the clock
In space – they come from
S P   AC   E
then they fall to earth and get stuck in the mud with the rest
of us.

s t u c k   i n   t h e   m u d

We are taught to see the world our parents see. We
are taught to see the world our parents see. And my
great-great-grandparents long before me.

Wish I had my notebook. Never remember that.

Masked revelers stare down at me, frozen

in a Velázquez painting whose colours have r

u

n

Tears? Can't feel them. Know they're there.

Ripley looks like a figurine on top of a wedding cake.

A frown welded to her forehead. Her face

shimmers

v i b r a t e s

and I swear it's FAITH

FAITH *and then* RIPLEY *again.*

FAITH *and then* RIPLEY

R a i t h F r i p l e y

Aaaaaaahhhhhhhh

What's happening to me?

A handmaid's on her knees wiping Fripley's leg. She rearrang-
es the dress. The crinoline bustles

and ruffs of her bell-shaped costume cascade

like a waterfall.

Waterfall . . .

. . . cascade like a waterfall.

w
    a
       t
         e
           r
             f
               a
                 l
                   l
                     .
                      .
                       .

There's a constant rainbow at Niagara Falls.

Just hanging there, from the spray — an endless rainbow, even at night.

Lunar

r   a   i   n   b   o   w   s

from 750,000 gallons
of water a second.

I'd forgotten this family holiday! What's it doing here?

'One person a week attempts suicide here,' says our tour guide in the blue kagoul.

'Maybe they're all trying to get to the end of the rainbow,' Dad shouts

over the roar of water.

'Twenty-five-thousand-dollar fine if you survive,' replies the guide, wiping spray from his eyes.

'What a culture that fines you for trying to commit suicide. That's enough to make anyone commit suicide. If you survive, they should pay you twenty-five. Get you back on your feet.' He strokes his beard. 'Hope the pot of gold's worth more than twenty-five K. What a way to go!'

He marvels up at the falls, opening his arms to the sky, unlit pipe in hand, painting the clouds.

'Don't you think, son? If you're going to go . . .'

Yeah, Dad.

Over the edge of
Niagara

F
A
L
L
s

Better than hanging by a belt strap off the back of a door.

It's my birthday
It's the worst day
I won't remember
Nor will you

The lyric falls into place.

My seventh birthday.
I keep pushing and pushing the door,
thumping on it, screaming
for him to
open it
but he's too heavy,
hanging on the other side.
I know he's there.
I know something's wrong.
I'm too small
to push open the door.
Too small to push open the door.
The knowing but not knowing.

The guilt,
  the hot, hot shame
that I couldn't save him,
       that it was my fault,
that he just disappeared,

POOF

just like that.

                              He was ahead of his time.

Everything comes in waves.

Hanging off the back of the door, even.

Like suicide bombers or plagues

or accusing women of witchcraft.

It takes off like a pop song and then

POOF

Gone.
No More

  How do you break a cycle?

  Will I wake up one day and not
  want

  a drink? A line? Oblivion?

When will I be NORMAL?

That's a chorus.

This is exhausting, isn't it, Dad? Endless.

E
N
D
L
E

S

S

I can feel that thought echo
                    echo
        echo

in the empty space of my body

R   I   P   P   L   E

                    through my **dark matter**

the

emptiness

            of

                    me

A   HALL   OF   MIRRORS   IS   MY   MIND

A grotesque fairground.

Dad ahead of me

on the dolled-up merry-go-round horse

turns round laughing, laughing way too hard,

shouts back at me, 'Hold on, son,'

while I cling on to my horse's neck.

Up and down,

round and round,

soundtracked by that

creepy Wurlitzer organ

```
'Daa, da-da-da-daaaaaaa.
Da-da-da da-da-da da-da-daaa daaa . . .'
```
I'm holding on, Dad, I'm holding on.

Dad puts 20p in the slot machine

and the clown in the glass box starts to LAUGH

and LAUGH and **LAUGH**, *lips rouged, his jaw clacks up
and down while his body jerks and collapses –*

That's entertainment.

Never trust a clown.

Lee's torso moves like the clown in the glass box.

His lips are podgy pink caterpillars with

sunburnt hammered metal patches.

`The plump caterpillars are wRiGgliNg`

F O C U S

'Seth.' He's cradling my head in his lap. 'Harry slipped acid in your drink. Do you understand? He spiked your drink.'

He's wiping my face. I can see his actions but I can't feel them.

An old woman's face looms into focus over Lee's shoulder. Grey Brillo-pad hair, sad eyes, the smell of talcum powder and Elnett hairspray. She takes me in. She's shakes her head with an unspeakable grief.

There's a piece of shrapnel in my heart. Its ice cold.

Can hardly breathe it's so painful – hear this sound coming out of me –

animal grunts, sobbing

'Daddy's dead', over and over,

'Daddy's dead.'

Chapter 31

Click, click, click.

I'm in bits.

Lee's got me back to a hotel room. I'm cleaned up, in a tracksuit, not mine. Shivering under a duvet, shivering and sweating.

In bits.

Feel like I'm trapped in a Bacon painting.

Ha-ha-ha.

Just saw an image of a big slice of fried bacon –

Not a painting of bacon. Francis Bacon, the artist. You know the one –

their heads a blur, like in that movie, *Jacob's Ladder*.

I can't stop giggling. Giggles are like fizzy bubbles.

I keep yawning to regulate pressure.

Got the bends. Must've been

some mighty motherfucking dose of acid.

Phil Addickt told Lee.

'You're thirsty!' said Harry.

Have you ever watched your mind break down?

Mine ran on into a jagged chasm

I can't climb out of.

Dad's suicide?

I knew it. Somewhere.

I knew it, just never talked about it.

Feels like a fresh flesh wound.

Flesh wound.

Fresh womb.

Scab ripped off.

Like it happened yesterday.

We never talked about it in our family.

It was as if he just left one day and never returned.

Which he did.

I have no memories of the funeral, no nothing.

No idea if I went.

A scab ripped off.

Rip-off.

I can feel everything – all the pain.

Can't clamp it down with –

you know,

with something.

Not acid.

– oh, God –

everything's cut loose

gravity's mangled. Hate this shit.

People meet   GOD   on acid!

How's that?

What's the dose to meet God?

Lee says I didn't reach escape velocity, played pinball in my mind.

Everything's all at once –

now.   Now!

Now?

It's only now.

Ha-ha-ha.

You can't capture a now.

Fizzy bubbles

keep floating up—

I want to go home.

Where is that?

People keep putting their fat heads into the room.

Cream, Oliver. Fat balloon heads on string.

    They come in and laugh.

Think I'm jabbering.

Dan sat with me.

He talked. Talked a time.

Dan talked! I must be hallucinating!

Talked and wept.

Said he's got prostate cancer. Is that real?

Gibbering.

Gibbon baboon.

Gibbonous moon.

Click, click, click.

Mum put me in the washing machine

So she could go on the razz.

What was she thinking? What was she drinking? What was
she washing? *Remember that,*

Mum put me in the washing machine

When she was drinking.

What was she thinking?

What was she drinking?

Claustrophobe.

Kept the lid ajar.

A jar. Ha.

When is a door a jar?

When is a jar a pint?

When will this fucking STOP!

I'm exhausted by my brain.

Is everybody's brain like this?

Lee's been on Google looking for something to bring me down.

On Google, ha-ha-ha.

Making me, making me coffee.

Not making me coffee, making me *a* coffee.

Ha-ha-ha. Everything's punny.

Am I making sense? I'm making sense.

Lee put on swirly-whirly music to calm me down

but there's all this weird stuff in the swirly-whirly

he doesn't hear.

He's showed me some of his new art.

It's moving and nobody's eyes are straight.

Is that me or his new style?

I look like that in the mirror, cubist.

Mirror man doesn't look like me.

He's an imposter.

Or is that me who's the imposter?

Mirror man does look fucked like me.

Shit must be going down in his world too.

Looks lost, miserable.

Put him down like a dawg.

It's in the eyes. Lee got that right.

He showed me a picture of Stella.

Not a good idea. I lost it.

He tried calling her for me.

She's not there.

What have I done?

Stella, my love,

                my star—

Weeping.

Click, click, click.

Daylight outside. Mum sits in the corner of the hotel room, knitting. She's been there for a while. If I don't look at her maybe she'll go away. If I look then she'll know. I know she's there.

She'll know

I know,

she's there.

Lee crashed. I've escaped. Mum isn't following. Going to get a train to Stella. Paris. *'Follow the star.'*

I know it's important, but I keep forgetting.

'Follow the star.'

Stella = star. *Dummy.*

Got to get myself together.

Got a bag together. That was an achievement!

St Pancras station. Tall, arched, glassy. Was there really a St Pancras? What did he do to get a station named after him? Patron saint of transport. He must've died for his faith. Isn't that the only qualification for being a saint?

St Pancreas. St Colon, St Gallbladder.

Lots of people going to work. Echoey voices. I still feel strange, buzzy on my left side, feel lopsided. Could tip over.

Look confident.

Look like them. The normals. They know what they're doing, where they're going. They have purpose. Porpoise. Pretend to be one of them.

I weave confidently through the station

concourse, with my porpoise pod, dragging my dog behind me.

Ha-ha

Keep thinking my bag's a dog. It bashes into my ankles. Design fault. Probably me. Design fault.

Nearly bump into a man with a briefcase – do that you-go-this-way I-go-that-way dance. He smiles. I'm sweating.

Gotta get to Stell.

I stand before an automated ticket machine. Fuck. Fuck. How does this work? London to France. She's in France.

There's so many people. All going somewhere. All thinking, furrowed brows. Not here really. All in their heads.

Crooked noses, bulgy noses. Earlobes!

Earlobes are ridiculous. What are they for?

What am I doing?

Stella, yes.

Stella.

I can't work this machine.

'Don't panic.' Did I say that out loud? That makes me panic. Saying 'Don't panic' makes you panic.

Can feel it rising in my guts, past my solar plexus into my heart, flapping like a bell-jarred butterfly.

I'm going to scream.

I'm trying to stop my body, my face from giving me away. My face is twitching.

This molten scream is going to break the banks and pour round my flood walls, rising to my throat, to my tongue curled up in the roof of my mouth.

This is the Norwegian scream.

The man-on-a-bridge, hands-to-his-face, landscape-curdling scream.

My jaw's clenched tight, straining, straining to keep it in.

I see a toilet sign!

Head to it, find a cubicle.

Get your shit together, Brakes.

As I approach the toilets, I see the spokes of the metal rotating barriers.

50p to pee.

50p to pee!

Do I have it?

Without slowing, I thrust my free hand into my jean pockets. My fingertips touch coins, but the pocket's too tight. I can't tell how much is in there. Damn skinny jeans! I hop to a stop ten feet from the barriers. My fingertips scrape coins up against my thigh and out.

Fuck, fuck, 25p.

In jagged movements I turn to my roll-on dog bag, squat and

open the zip pocket, looking for my wallet. The bag's guts are crammed to bursting with pens, wrappers, gum, pills in a variety of bottle sizes, some keys I thought I lost a year ago. My iPhone clatters on to the marble concourse, followed by a cascade of receipts.

I'm on hands and knees now, scrabbling around

panhandler in a stream.

The screen's cracked. Again!

Fuck, fuck, fuck. There's no wallet in the case.

'Where's my wallet?'

Did I say that out loud? Fuck.

I'm stuffing receipts back into the bag's compartments as two pairs of feet come to a stop by my case. Sensible shoes, two brown, two black. Polished.

Cops?

Mum?

I'm scared to look up.

I look up.

A beaming round woman in her forties wearing a too-bright floral dress is staring down at me. She's escaped from a Beryl Cook painting, the flowers on her dress sway in the breeze. Red, orange, purple. Her hand clasps a boy's hand. He's in grey school uniform, cap and shorts, grippy grey socks pulled up to the knees.

'Excuse me. Are you that singer?' she says, steely behind her best Sunday-tea-and-cakes smile.

No, no, no, not now.

My hands carry on working the zip of my bag, but I can't take my eyes away from that smile.

I look at the boy. Maybe eleven. Pale white skin, with a flush of hot embarrassment taking the shape of Australia on his cheek. The boy senses my attention on his blush and Australia spreads and swells into Africa.

Africa!

I can't pull my eyes away.

What's next?

'Excuse me,' she says, more bite. 'You are. William here is a big fan of your music. Can we have a selfie?'

She answers her own question, produces a phone and pokes at its buttons with stubby fingers. William's blush goes off the map.

'Shigleshliglight,' he says in some unknown dialect lost to man. He tugs her arm.

'Dishmiel istak,' she answers, then turns to me. 'The camera's on here somewhere,' she gurgles, '. . . ah, yes. Here it is.'

I break my gaze from the boy and look down at my bag. Receipts are caught in the zipper. The boy's left shoelace is knotted tight and hangs long and frayed around his shiny black shoes. There's a nasal tannoy announcement in some Chinese dialect. *What was I looking for?* How does this boy know The Lucky Fuckers?

I can feel my face distort into a Maori war mask.

I stand and scream.

I scream in the woman's face. One loud singer's breath of a scream. The woman's arms jerk up to protect her face.

Everyone around us stops dead.

The sound dies away. I look around at everyone staring at me.

'AHHHHHH!' I scream at them.

'AHHHHHH!' to the old man with a stick in a tweed suit.

'AHHHHHH!' to the three gum-chewing Japanese schoolgirls.

I grab the handle of my bag and run. I run through the station, legs banging into bag. I run as fast as my skinny jeans allow.

Chapter 32

Click, click, click.

It's the afternoon of the Brixton gig. I'm still frayed. My electrics are sparking. I'm not back in my body. I've called off sick from soundcheck.

Soundcheck.

The guys can check without me. I've got to get some sleep. I haven't slept *at all*! My body is prickling with needles. Knitting needles.

What's she knitting?

She's got to be in my mind, right?

Click, click, click.

Should I talk to her?

When I close my eyes I alternate between the

Mum-used-to-put-me-in-the-washing-machine-when-she-went-out-on-the-piss memory

and the

me-pushing-against-the-door-with-dead-Dad-hanging-on-the-other-side one.

Alternating current.

I'm still there, there's no time between that little boy and this fucked-up man. They've merged.

I can feel the desperation of trying to get out of the twin tub, trying to get through the door. Pushing. Knowing, but not *knowing*, what's on the other side.

How can you know and not know?

'That's magic!' Bicameral mind?

Click, click, click.

Pushing, pushing the door . . . screaming, tears, Mum pulling me away, but it's a different Mum to the hag I remember.

This is the pre-Dad-suicide Mum. Pre-alcoholic Mum.

My mum.

Before she curdled and whey'd.

The one who also died that day.

I'm crying as much for the loss of her, as him.

I don't know.

Just crying.

He made a choice, the fucker. To leave us, to devastate us. Weak motherfucker.

It fucked Mum. It fucked me. It fucked Lizzie.

I keep swinging from rage to grief and back again.

Click, click, click.

'WILL YOU STOP FUCKING KNITTING!'

I shout in her face.

She does. She's wearing the lilac shirt and pleated skirt we buried her in. On her lap is a purple scarf that hangs down to the floor. She looks surprised to be acknowledged.

Fuck! Now she knows I can see her. Don't look in her eyes. I daren't lock eyes.

I look in the full-length mirror to the side of her. She's not in it. I look like shit, fucked. I'm fucking exhausted. I've got to sleep. How many sleeping pills have I taken? Nothing works. Nothing puts me down.

I'm groggy, staggering around, desperate to black out. I take out the bottle. I need sleep before the gig. Then I'll be fine.

Well, not fine, *not ever fine*.

I take three pills to be careful, just three. No, four. Four to be sure. I see her stand up from the chair. I knock the pills back with water – yeah, water, I finished the minibar hours ago. How many pills have I taken now? That should do it, that should knock me out.

Oliver's bass drum is fucking loud. And irregular. I turn and scowl at him. He laughs and his head tips back into the face of the fairground clown, laughing, laughing hysterically. Fuck, I'm onstage. We're in the gig.

How did I get here?

The bass drum drowns out the Wurlitzer organ.

Bang, bang, bang.

Shit mix, all I can hear is the bass drum.

Bang, bang, bang.

It's not the gig, it's the door.

Someone's pounding on my door and shouting my name. It's a long way back from the dream into this body, into this hotel room.

'Seth! Open the door.' It's a man's voice. It's Josh's voice. My body feels like it's someone else's. I'm not home. I have to tell it to sit up. I sit on the side of the bed.

I'm parched. Desert.

Bang bang bang.

Each thump of the door reverberates sand.

'All right. All right.'

Check to see if Mum's here; she's not.

I drag the door open. Josh bursts in.

'Where the fuck have you been?' He drinks me in. 'Oh fuck.' He takes my arm and whirls me round to the bathroom. 'You're on in an hour and a half.'

'I need to sleep.'

He swishes back the shower curtain and turns on the tap. The jets set off a dull roar.

'My head hurts.'

In one quick movement, he lifts off my T-shirt and takes me by the elbow.

'Get in.'

In seconds I'm shouting, bollock naked, being held under a stream of freezing-cold water.

I'm in the back of the car watching London streets glide by, listening to Iggy Pop's 'The Passenger' on earbuds.

I am the passenger
And I ride and I ride
I ride through the city's backside.

I feel like shit. Hollow, shattered, numb from the pills. I want to sleep for a thousand years. How the fuck am I going to do a gig in this state?

I recognise the street we're on as we pass two curry houses. I know this place.

I know this place!

'Stop the car!' I shout.

'No, continue.' Josh overrides my order.

The driver slows.

'I'm gonna be sick. *I'm gonna be sick.* You don't want it all over your Merc, do you?' I start to gag. He pulls over. I get out, turn back to Josh, 'Wait here. Won't be long.' I stagger off down the street to the Asian corner shop. I take a left, then another left. I stand in front of a yellow door. I look up into the opaque eye of the security camera, give it a goofy grin and press the doorbell in a Beethoven sequence.

Da-da-da daaar, da-da-da daaar.

After a long time and no response I look back up at the camera, look at an imaginary watch on my wrist, tap it.

Josh is loping towards me down the street.

The door unlocks automatically. I push my way through and haul myself up the stairs. At the top of the stairs, arms folded, stands Pitbull.

I feel better already.

The Merc pulls up at the stage door in Brixton.

I heard once that the human body has the energy potential of eight atomic bombs. Well, it feels like a countdown's started on one of them.

Pitbull gave me some rapture to get me through the night.

'Don't mix it with anything.'

'It's one of your mixes!'

'Yeah, don't mix it with anything else.'

Didn't tell him about the sleeping pills.

He said it would take an hour to come on, yet I can feel it start to devour my heartbreak, my fractures.

My rupture is raptured.

My fracture's ruptured.

I feel kingly, imperious.

The only fear I have is how long will it last? That's always the fear with feeling this good.

How long will it last?

He says he's given me enough powder for eight hits, but you know Pitbull. Cheap shit. So I took half of it.

'Fifteen minutes to show time,' shouts Josh at my back as I sprint up the stairs to my dressing room.

'Seth, where the fuck have you been?' I keep walking past Brunt.

'No time, got a show to do.' I wave a hand in the air without looking back.

I find the door to my dressing room, throw it open.

Lee's sitting there on the sofa holding Stella's hand. She's crying. They look up. They drop hands.

'What the fuck.'

My imperious mind zooms back in to close-up. The blood drains from me. They're flushed. They look guilty as hell.

I squeeze my brain to think. Think back, back to any moments where they have shown affection for each other. They must read me, cos Lee says, 'No, no!' He stands. 'She's come to see you.'

'Really?' I say.

Stella rises.

'Yes, Seth.' Doe eyes wide and honest.

'Oh, you're good, you're very good.' I point a shaky finger at her.

'Seth.' Lee steps forward.

I put up both my hands and take a step back.

'So, this is it?'

'No! Lee was consoling me. He told me you're in trouble.'

I'm grinding my jaw again; I must stop that. The window behind them's painted shut. A siren wails in the distance. I take a breath and realise it's the first in a while.

'Don't do this, mate,' says Lee. 'Your mind's out of whack.'

It is. It's a gyroscope.

'You asked me to contact her,' he continues. 'I did.'

'So, what's this, then?' I say.

They look at each other.

'An intervention,' Lee says. 'Lizzie's coming too . . . but she's stuck in traffic.'

'An intervention?'

Stella steps in close.

'You've got to stop being in a fucking band! You're going to kill yourself – again! You don't have the temperament for this . . .'

'I have the *exact* temperament to be in a band,' I laugh.

There's that scent again, cardamom, sweet corn. Home. As near a home as I've ever had.

It's a trick.

'You can't do this, Seth.' She looks like she hasn't slept. Oh, no, that's me.

'It's not good for you. You just can't say no,' she says.

'No. There. Did it.'

I'm overwhelmed by her energy field, it's so, so pitying.

'So you came here to stop me being a singer?' I walk past her, go pick up a bottle of water and gulp a mouthful. I'm parched, I drink the whole bottle, chuck it into a metal bin and unscrew another one.

'You can't do this mate. You need help.' says Lee. 'We're back where we started. Look at you.' I glance at the mirror.

There he is, the madman. I try to adjust his hair.

'Not too bad if you ask me, could look worse.' There's this quivery thing going on with my voice. 'My drink was spiked, my band's fucked, my woman left me.'

'You fucked Faith. You fucker,' says Stella.

'You could be fucking my best friend.'

'Oh, fuck off! Don't you dare make it about you.' Stella whacks me in the chest with conviction.

She loves me.

'Don't you dare play victim with me. Lee persuaded me to come back to try and help . . .'

'A pity mission.'

'I'm fucking pregnant!' she shouts.

I exhale.

'Are you sure?'

'Course I'm fucking sure.'

'And it's . . .?'

'Don't you fucking dare.'

'Holy shit.'

There's a knock at the door.

'Why aren't you dressed?' says Josh. 'You two, out now.'

'He's not in any state to go on stage,' says Stella.

'Well, I was . . . Now, not so much. Afterwards. We'll talk afterwards. I've got to do this gig. I've got to do this one,' I say.

She looks to Lee, who nods. 'All right. I'll come here after, but don't . . .'

'You want to have the child?'

She looks away.

'Afterwards . . . we'll talk afterwards.'

She's at the door when I remember.

'Stella!' I take her hand and place in her palm the rainbow eraser and the toy soldier. She looks at them in confusion then nearly drops them as understanding kicks in.

'Oh shit.' She shakes her head. 'So you did see!'

'I did see.' I coil her fingers around them. 'Take them.'

'They're yours, not mine. They're not for me.' She hands them back. 'They're your proof.'

I've locked the door. I'm staring at the red plastic pillbox Pitbull gave me. I place the toy soldier on one side and the rainbow eraser on the other. Hope versus shame. With hope comes dread. Dread at the work involved to stay straight. Dread at the fear of failure, again.

'Afterwards,' she said.

375

Fucking hell, she's up for an afterwards?

Pregnant!

I could be a Dad.

I could be Dad.

The word 'Dad' induces heartburn. I could puke.

Stella and a kid, a package deal.

And what? *I walk away from this?* I feel more me now than I did straight. Straight Seth's a dog on a choker, boring exhausting, would never hold.

OK. Enough!

I place the eraser on its side. A corner is softened from use. The rainbow's faded with age. But it feels hopeful. Impossible really. It's a fucking joke.

A rainbow rubber and a toy soldier – my proof of the existence of God? Ha-ha. Fucking joke. That there's a meaning to life?

No tablets from Mount Sinai for Seth Brakes. No being struck by lightning and hearing the voice of God.

A rubber and a soldier.

Pretty weird, though. I did see it. It means . . . something.

Taking my father's hand through the ceiling.

I shake my head. *Can't focus on this now.*

Do the gig. Do your shit.

If I'm quitting, this will be my last hurrah. Make it a good one. London, the press are here.

I want the state I was in before, before that, that scene with Stella. I want a rewind. I want to feel that power again before I go onstage.

I open the pillbox and tip the powder around, so it gathers at one end. How much have I had? This can't have been eight hits. Four at most, maybe three.

I halve the powder and shuffle it into parallel lines using my credit card. I stop.

A kid.

No.

Yes.

In the corridor the band is waiting.

'Olly!' I hug him.

He stiffens.

'Creeeeam.' She looks resplendent in a white dress and veil. 'You look like a Christmas fairy, you fucking hero, you look gorgeous.' She hugs me back.

Dan looks panic-stricken. I grab him anyway. 'I'm so sorry, man.' I whisper in his ear.

I approach Stanley with a smile. He takes a step back. I put my hands on his shoulders.

'Stanley, mate, I know, I know, we've been through some shit, but I have to say, you are the dog's bollocks. The dog's bollocks.' I give him a hug.

I turn to the group. 'All of you. I love you all. I think you're brilliant, I haven't said this enough. I'm the lucky fucker to be in the band with you all. Thank you for sticking with me. Please forgive me. If this is it, let's leave them a night to remember.'

I move to Lee and fiddle with his Edwardian high collar, stand back and take in his black dinner tails.

'Come on, Seth. Get through this.' He tries to read me.

I lean in and kiss him on the cheek.

'Love you.'

'OK, children, it's time,' says Josh.

We turn and follow him.

Afterwards, she's up for an afterwards!

Iggy gets louder as we approach the stage doors.

Josh holds them open. I switch on my belt pack. The music pops into life.

Here comes Johnny Yen again.
With the liquor and drugs
And a flesh machine
He's gonna do another striptease.

A dance mix of 'Lust for Life'.

I can *smell* the audience.

Beer, sweat, perfume, pheromones.

They sway to the beat like strands of seaweed in a swell. Fists in the air. London, up for a Saturday night .

A cameraman's circling us. Shit, yeah, forgot that, *we're filming this!*

The music snakes into my body, coils up my spine. I'm shuffling side to side like Tyson. Feels so good to move. I yawn as the drug escalates. I yawn to acclimatise; a free diver.

Here I am. *Here I am.*

This is my domain. The cameras, the crowd. Power surges through me. *My super power.*

I'm worth a million in prizes
With my torture film

I love this song. *I love this song.* I can feel myself being taken over, taken over, plugged into the mains.

That drum pattern.

I'm Baloo seduced by King Louie's beat.

'Three more minutes,' shouts Josh. 'Three more minutes.'

My body's electric, snapping, jerking past Josh. Circling, spinning past the band as they brace themselves to go on.

Three minutes. *Fuck that!*

I spin past Lee with a fag in his mouth. Make eye contact, dancing in his face. He drops the fag in realisation. I'm past Bones at the mixing desk. Onto the stage. Into the lights. Legs pumping. Arms punching. The crowd roars. I pull gargoyle faces, arms snapping over my head.

I know he's gonna do another striptease . . .

Two men climb over the crash barriers, taking the security by surprise. The larger of the two gets to the lip of the stage but is smashed in the flanks by the shoulder of a bouncer. He face-plants with a thud on the floor, a fine spray of blood fountains from his mouth.

The skinnier one benefits from the diversion, leaps for the stage and makes it past the hands flailing for his legs. I'm straight to him, pull him to his feet. We're dancing, don't miss a beat, dancing with him, at him, chest to chest. Arms slashing, jack-knifing around each other.

I've got a lust for life
I've got a lust for life

I grab him by his leather jacket and shake him as we spin. He's skinnier than me! All angles and intensity, an Egon Schiele. Black floppy fringe whipping my face. He has me by my white shirt. It rips, buttons fly. We are locked and spinning, locked and spinning, stepping on cables, avoiding effects pedals gaffer-taped to the stage. Our roadies scramble to clear space around us, moving mic stands and guitars. Nothing matters, except me and him, me and Egon, locked and spinning, holding on for dear life, building a fire.

I've got a lust for life.
Lust for life.
Lust for life.

Spinning round, faster and faster, his face mad with laughter.

I mirror him.

We are one, shadow puppets. We will fall apart at any moment. We will fall apart. Centrifugal force.

Another wild boy's made it to the stage, bare-chested, balanced on a monitor speaker, screaming at the audience, 'Come on!'

I've got a lust for life.
Lust for life.
Lust for life.

I feel it coming. Egon feels it too, an agreement between us. As he spins me, I use his force to propel me.

Out.

Out over the monitors, which my feet run up for leverage, up and out I fly over the heads of the security in the pit. I arch over them in s l o w   m o t i o n

Over the crash barriers, flung into the audience, who raise their arms, hands, to catch me, to break my fall.

A mother catching her baby.

There's a

pause

as I land, face down, held on a wheat field of raised arms.

It's silent and still as I hang over their heads, rippling in the
breeze.
None of us can quite believe I'm here.
Then the song kicks back in with a roar
and they throw me around
a rag doll,
polystyrene   in choppy waves –
thrown up, over, tumbling.

The crowd
beneath me

roiling to the beat, churning me over
and over in their   spin cycle. I'm screaming,

screaming –
not from fear.
Not from fear.

From pleasure –   screaming
to be part of this, this – this mass,

this connected mass.

So alive.

I'm so alive.

I'm   So   Fucking   Alive.

Someone has me by the ankles,

     I'm scraped back

across the top of the crowd.

don't want to go!   I'm trying   to hold on

to hands,   to shirts.

I want to be one out here –

but I'm tractor-beamed back to the barriers.

Two security guards   have caught a fish –

they drag me   over the railings, my head

whacks the metal bar.

I see sparks,

everything's dark.

Shut your eyes.

Go on, shut your eyes a second.

There's space inside. It's familiar, right? It has a quality to it that's familiar.

A size, shape, a sound even – even if you can't define it exactly. We take it for granted. It has a you-ness to it. *It's your energy.* Your awareness with the lights out.

I'm not crazy. You do get this, don't you?

When you close your eyes to sleep at night but you can't. You lie there listening to your thoughts. But what we miss – what we miss is that we hear our thoughts within a space and that space has a quality.

That's me!

That's you.

Connected.

Not the thoughts, the space, dummy.

WE ARE NOT WHO WE THINK WE ARE!

This   v a s t

space

is
    who
        we
            are

I open my eyes. I'm back in the room.

Left slumped on the lip of the stage.

I see Lee over my shoulder.

The band are here!

Early Man places a mic in my hand and the band kick off into 'Luc£y Fuc£ers'.

Shitbull, you didn't cut this shit!

To my left the speaker stacks beanstalk invitingly up to the dress circle. Stella will be up there. Guests get the seats.

Follow the star.

As the band loop round the intro I stagger to the speakers. I can climb the metal handholds on the speaker bins. I need both hands. I try to push the mic into my pocket. Skinny jeans, no luck. I try wedging it into my belt. It lands with an amplified THUNK.

I pick it up. The mesh is dented. People are laughing.

I put the mic into my mouth cock-tip first, clamping it in my teeth.

Applause.

I climb the stacks. Each step upwards raises a roar as the audience anticipate my route. The third tier of speakers wobbles as I lug myself up to the top. My last shirt button falls into the pit, past the upturned gawking faces of security. A grey-bearded bouncer shouts into a wireless mic, rushes to a fire exit.

I'm twenty feet up, but the top of the balcony's a further six or so and there's a gap of a few feet between the stack and the wall.

I can do this.

Two men lean over from a private box. A chunky bloke with thinning hair screams, 'Come on, come on.'

He waves, gesturing me to make the jump. The boom camera on a crane swings up towards me. I look down. Lee's staring up at me like he's moongazing.

Where am I?

There's a bare-breasted statue carved into the column holding up the balcony ahead of me. She's carved in alabaster. There's chips and cracks in her façade. Her arms twist up and above her head to take the weight of the dress circle. Her eyes roll up in ecstasy. Across the front row I meet the gaze of a child. He stares at me in wonder. His father slips his arm over the boy's shoulder, holding him fast.

From the box the man folds his body over the red velvet lip and reaches down to me. On his forearm's a tattoo of an octopus.

It's all falling into place.

I look into his face. He's solid, made of oak. I interlace my fingers in his and swing across the gap. I turn my face sideways as I slam into the statue.

The mic thuds loud, jars my teeth. Rough hands hook under my armpits and hoick me up, over the lip, into the box.

Two girls help me to my feet, hug me, skunking me with perfume. A brunette with a beehive stands back, staring at me. She points a ringed finger at her mouth. I peer into her mouth. Her tongue flops around like a fish in grease, a silver scale catches the light. It's a stud. She points furiously at my mouth, mouthing words I can't hear over the music. I lick my lips, it's wet. It's blood, tastes metallic. Men pull me up to the front of the box.

Oh shit. I'm doing a gig!

A roar greets my appearance. *We're playing a song!*

I sing down the mic and a thousand voices join me, including the bear with his arm around me.

Lucky Fuckers
Fuck you all night
Lucky Fuckers
Know how to fuck you up right!

What a buzz! All these people joining me in a song, a song I wrote. Everyone's standing, fist-pumping, into it.

The red velvet safety rail snakes from our box across the front of the circle, all the way to the other side. I place my foot on it. The bear takes my free hand and I lift myself up to balance on the lip.

I should be singing.

I've gone blank on the verse, so I sing

Lucky Fuckers
Fuck you all night
Lucky Fuckers
Know how to fuck you up right!

That wasn't in the right place in the song, but who cares? The crowd shout 'up right', then repeat it like an echo, 'up right'. It's brilliant. I start to walk the red-velvet river. Bear lets go of my hand and I flap my arms to keep balance.

People at the back push forward to get to me. People on the front row are shitting themselves they'll knock me over the edge. Arms winged open, they push back on those pushing in. I'm wobbling again.

Fuck, this rail's narrow.

My arms swing wildly. A hand grabs my hand and stills me.

How does the fucking verse go? Fuck knows.

Lucky Fuckers
Fuck you all night
Lucky Fuckers
Know how to fuck you up right!

'Up right' echo the crowd.

This time the band change chords with me. I look down. Stanley's laughing manically with Olly. Dan and Cream are frozen in concern. Lee's gaze blazes at me like he's doing telepathy or something. I give him a smile; God, I love him. I love him. I love them all. They gave it another go. With me! I walk on. I feel like Jesus. Everyone's coming to greet me with love. A new hand takes over from the old. I'm passed hand to hand, walking a tightrope of the balcony lip.

They're looking after me.

I well up.

Where's Stella? Hope she's getting this. A new hand jerks me, nearly loses me. The room trembles.

Wobbly dancing on a clifftop thirty feet up.

'*Wobbly dancing on a clifftop thirty feet up*,' I sing into the mic.

'*Will you catch me, will you catch me, will you catch me, if I jump?*' I sing to those below.

This is fucking brilliant.

'*Wobbly dancing on a clifftop thirty feet up.*

'*Will you catch me, will you catch me, will you catch me, if I drop?*'

They sing back the echo, 'if I drop.'

People are laughing.

It's a fucking riot.

I feign to jump and the audience below raise their arms. They would, too.

A strong grip on my shirt tries to yank me off the ledge. It's Greybeard, the bouncer from the pit. He's in the second row reaching over. I try to shake him off but he's got my sleeve. Then my wrist. He's shouting furiously at me.

Fuck you.

I arch my body in a bow, out over the edge, to give me purchase against his pull. I'm dragging him forward over the wood-backed seats. Two men grab him, anchor him.

Arched over the drop, I look up.

Michelangelo's creation is painted on the cupola of the auditorium – God reaching out, about to give life to Adam.

Discordant chords bring the song to a train-wreck halt.
Everything freezes.

Behind Greybeard is my mum. She's looking at me with an
expression I've not seen for . . . I don't know how long. It looks
like love. A lot like love. A sad love.

On the other side of Greybeard is Stella, wide eyed, hands
cupped to her face in terror. I see all that she is, all that she will
become. It's a kaleidoscope of Stella. She's amazing! I can see
she has new life in her. *See it*. Our life. Our child.

She glows with a biblical light that streams out of her.

A wave of love blasts through me like an underwater explo-
sion. My body spasms, I gasp.

My cells explode inside out with a deep *whuuuup* sound that
realigns everything, my DNA, my RNA, obliterated, the letters
scattered, the double-helix ladders snapping, unthreading.

All that is Seth Brakes . . . breaks!

Let it go.

Let it all go.

And I do.

My wrist slips the guard's grip.

Looking up at God,

Michelangelo's God,

God's reaching out.

God's reaching out to man.

But Adam

looks fucked, wasted.

He's had enough.

Chapter 33

The man in the white bathrobe, lying on the white lounger, on the white sundeck, adjusts his sunglasses with the two fingers on his right hand that aren't encased in the plaster cast. The Californian sun, reflecting off the deck, is blinding even at 5.45 p.m. With his left hand he picks up his Marlboros and flips the top open. He cranes his neck and plucks out a cigarette between sunburnt lips. He puts the packet down and picks up his lighter.

'Huhhumm,' fake-coughs a fake blonde, ten feet behind him. Emily? A CEO of some bank, someone from his therapy group. She's reading a magazine on her lounger. She doesn't look up.

He reaches for his crutch, slides his elbow into the half-tube, and, with some effort, raises himself upright. He slips his feet into flip-flops to protect them from the heat of the deck. He stands swaying, light-headed, then shuffles across the deck to the smoking area overlooking the vast ocean a hundred feet below. From the fence a complaining gull launches itself to glide on an upswell. It watches him with impassive orange eyes. When it determines he isn't budging it wheels away and floats down, down the cliff to land on a craggy island splattered with bird shit. The sea swells in lazy rhythm, causing white spume to fizz up over rocks, hinting at the power beneath.

He fumbles for his lighter, flicks some fire. It's immediately extinguished by the breeze. He turns his body to shield the flame and after the fourth attempt manages to transfer flame to cigarette. He glances over his shoulder. No guard trails him today. He must be out of the high-risk category, although with his injuries he'd be hard pushed to climb the fence. A clinic on a clifftop is tempting fate, even with the safety netting system. He had to sign a phone-book-thick legal waiver on the way in.

TV Footage of his fall from grace made recuperation in Britain impossible. They flew him to the States. He hasn't been allowed to see the footage, no phone, computer, TV even, but his infamy seems to have followed him across the Atlantic, as even here in Malibu he seems to be a somebody.

First-class flight and a Malibu rehab. He couldn't work out where the money had come from, but he wasn't complaining.

He feels more pain today. They were lowering the dosage of oxycodone to prevent addiction. He faked some of the pain, to buy himself time, but he knows the day is approaching when they'll cut him off.

Must be six soon.

'Telephone call for Mr Brakes.'

On cue.

Today's reward – a first phone call.

A black man walks towards him, mobile in hand. Even beneath a baggy white shirt the man's physique is apparent. Seth tries to straighten his own body, a shooting pain down his left leg makes him think better of it.

'Fucking Malibu, even you guards look like film stars.'

'I am an actor,' he laughs. 'Keeping you from jumping and whooping your ass at Texas Hold 'Em's just a hobby.'

'Have I seen you in anything?'

'Maybe as a pimp, dealer or gang banger, that's all they cast us as round here.'

'Thanks, Christopher. We on tonight?'

'Seven. Sign your phone back in when you're finished with it.'

He reads the name on the screen. His heart drops.

'Jon Brunt.' Seth turns to face the ocean. 'Give me a minute.'

Seth clumsily checks for messages.

None from her. Tonnes from Lee.

He scrolls through the missed calls.

She called. She called three times!

He slumps on the fence. Tears leak out the side of his eyes.

A coal black seal surfaces and hangs stationary as a wave passes through.

One two three four

He wipes tears away with the back of his hand.

'Jon.'

'How you doing, Seth?'

'This *is* heaven, isn't it? I could stay here for ever, Jon.'

'Yeah, hasn't changed much since I was there. Don't get too used to it. How are you doing? I mean physically, can you walk and stuff?'

'Getting there. The cast comes off in a few days.'

'Neck brace?'

'Gone.'

The density of the ocean calms him.

'How are the people I landed on?'

'Oh, they'll be fine . . . the last one came home yesterday. Don't worry about them; Universe will take care of that. Their legal department's on it.'

'I didn't mean that . . .'

I could have killed someone.

He takes a final drag of his cigarette and heels it into the deck.

'Would you be ready for some . . . for some interviews?' Embarrassed by the question, Brunt ploughs ahead. 'I mean, I know it's soon, way too soon. It's just with the album at number one in the UK and top twenty on *Billboard*, there are some great offers here for TV, *major* players. The footage . . . of you falling. It's beyond fucking viral. It went round the world like a tidal wave.'

Seth squints at the sea line looking for the seal. When no response comes, Brunt continues, 'I mean, you're in LA, you wouldn't have to travel or anything. The Leno show approached us, Ellen, . . . people are interested, this is, this is happening now.' Brunt pauses, trying to read the reaction at the end of the line. 'Faith . . . Faith's people called. She's getting blamed for this. Pilloried. They'd like to . . . they'd like to . . . release the other version of "Horseman" to show there's no . . .'

The phone slips from Seth's grip, he leans forward to watch it clatter, once, twice off rocks and be consumed by the ocean.

They should make those things waterproof.

A row of pelicans flies low to the waves, necks kinked, chests puffed forward, almost cartoon. The one up front creates a slip-stream for those behind. When the frontrunner flaps a wing, the one behind follows and it ripples down the line. Musical notation, if he could work out the tune. Up ahead, a commotion of gulls and a pod of dolphins circle a frothy surface.

The pelicans break formation and bat their wings to gain height. The lead pelican halts its ascent, freezes in mid-air, then plunges beak first into the ocean like a javelin. Moments later it emerges to bob on the waves. The pelican tips its head back. Its body jerks and spasms, jerks and spasms, as it attempts to swallow what it has caught.

Thanks

I blame Jack and Josh Grapes. Their wonderful writing classes gave me the crazy notion that I could write a novel.

Who's next in the mitochondrial network that got me here?

I have spent over forty years singing and songwriting with this incredible band James. The inspiration is still there! I am constantly turned on by these magnificent musicians. Thank God you decided to steal my drink that night, Jim. It has been my life's pleasure to create with all of you. If you've seen us play live, you know how lucky I am. Jim Glennie, Saul Davies, Mark Hunter, Dave Baynton-Power, Andy Diagram, Adrian Oxaal, Chloe Alper, Deborah Knox-Hewson and of course Larry Gott. Paul Gilbertson, Gavan Whelan, Ron Yeadon, Michael Kulas, Jenny Glennie and Martine McDonagh.

I would like to thank here the incredible crew we have worked with over the years: tour managers, lighting men, onstage/ offstage sound, keyboard/guitar/drum techs – whose individual names would fill pages. It takes particular people to work with James, to work with our unpredictability, our spontaneity, to catch us when we fly, to catch me when I stage dive, to support us on our crazy journey. Particular thanks to our long haulers – Geof, Dick, Nigel, Early Man, James, Nick, Alex and our wizard Aled Ifan.

Our fantastic engineers and producers, the ever present Brian Eno, Max, Charlie, Lee, Jacknife and Leo.

My amazing body techs who have looked after me at all hours, with so much love, to keep me on the road: Juliet Vinçon and Lucy Trend.

This book has been described as a love letter, or a therapy session, with James, Kate Shela and Lee Baker. Love you all.

Bonnie Soloman for the years we read our embryo novels to each other.

Andreas Campomar for his patience – I read him the whole damn thing. Along with Josh Grapes, he taught me how to edit.

My beloved manager of thirty-three years, Peter Rudge, and the all-seeing Neil Hughes and Charlotte Malecki for stepping in to take the reins.

Our legendary team of Simon Moran, Colin Young, John Giddings, Charly Bedel-Smith and Kirk Sommer. Thank You.

All my early beta readers who gave great feedback: K8, Lee, Ian Gittens, Graham McPhail, Peter Rudge, Greg Saunders, James Rickman, Erika Rosenast, Chris Atkins, Ross Katz, David Donnelly, Dave Brown, Carla Stang, Penny and Mandy Booth and any who I've forgotten or who didn't give me feedback.

Paul Bessenbacher for the songs that accompany this book. Bernie Chadwick, Dan Leavers and Chloe Alper for playing on them. Leo Abrahams for production +.

My amazing boys Ben and Luka.

Saville and Sheila Shela my much-loved in-laws.

My Parents, without whom I wouldn't be in this mess.

Carrie Dinow and Jonathan Nadlman for endless love.

Holly Blood for her guidance and everyone else at Little, Brown.

Matthew Hamilton for opening the door.

Thank you Muses, love you forever.

Niamh Dowling, Kate Maravan, Gordon Strachan, Meredith

Plant, Gene Bua, Larry Novick, Roger Tempest, Paris Ackrill and my global dancing tribe.

Jeremy Bates my sixth form English teacher – the reward for winning his essay competition was to see Monty Python live at the Leeds Grand Theatre.

Roger Parks – the school church organist who Ralph persuaded to take us to see Iggy Pop when we were sixteen.

Inspirations:
Doris Lessing, Cormac McCarthy, Robert Anton Wilson, Brian Eno, Gabrielle Roth, Patti Smith, David Mitchell, Iggy Pop, Nina Simone, Leeds United, Leonard Cohen, Regina Spektor, Seafood, Barcelona, Lou Reed, Nick Cave, Avril Dorney, Yorkshire, Big Sur, Martin Amis, DV8, Ronnie Burkett, Daniel Day Lewis, David Hockney, Brando, Messi, Egon Schiele, Lenny Kaye, Bill Hicks, Tony Wilson, Van Gogh, Esther Perel, Jon Stewart, Craig Ferguson, Entheogens, Burning Man, Buffy the Vampire Slayer, The O.A, Cloud Atlas, Shikasta, William Llerena and Nila, Kukicha tea, Bruce Springsteen, Flea, Bruce Lee, the Memphis Grizzlies, One Hundred Years of Solitude and

on and on.